KT-169-527

The Darkness Around Her

NEIL WHITE

ZAFFRE

First published in Great Britain in 2018 by

ZAFFRE PUBLISHING
80–81 Wimpole St, London W1G 9RE
www.zaffrebooks.co.uk

A CIP catalogue record for this book is
available from the British Library.

ISBN: 978–1–78576–460–8

Also available as an ebook

3 5 7 9 10 8 6 4 2

Typeset by IDSUK (Data Connection) Ltd
Printed and bound in Great Britain by Clays Ltd, Elcograf S.p.A

Zaffre Publishing is an imprint of Bonnier Zaffre,
part of Bonnier Books UK
www.bonnierzaffre.co.uk
www.bonnierbooks.co.uk

One

Lizzie marched along the unlit towpath. She was angry, hurt. She wiped tears from her eyes and the warm blood that streamed from her swollen nose smeared across her hand and coated her lip.

The town was quieter now; the New Year fireworks had finished and people were starting to queue for taxis home. Not Lizzie though. She'd bolted for the darkness, just to get away, too ashamed to head into the bright lights. The canal, brought in on an aqueduct, curved high above the town, clinging to the steep side of one of the many hills that surrounded Highford, before it disappeared into the valley on the other side and made its way across the Pennines.

The glow of the town-centre streetlights didn't make it this far. The water was black and still, catching only the gleam of the moon. Canal barges were moored in the distance. The smell of their wood smoke in the air told her they were occupied, and another one cruised towards her, its headlight just like a torch beam, but too far away to illuminate her path.

She was alone in the dark.

Then she heard a noise.

She stopped, looked back, strained to hear it again, needing the reassurance that it was just rubbish, like the rustle of a plastic bag blown against a fence. It was more than that though, more like the crunch of footsteps on gravel. She peered into the darkness, a tingle of fear making her senses keen. Only shadows and silence greeted her.

Lizzie turned around, panic rising, looking for a way off the towpath, but she knew it was pointless. High fences that protected the scrapyard and small workshops that lined the canal kept her from a quick exit, razor wire in rolls across the top. She couldn't go back, she knew that. He'd be waiting for her. She was there because of him.

She quickened her step. Her heels rang loudly on the cobbles, the sound skimming across the water and echoing from the wall on the other side. Dread tightened her chest, made her breath come faster.

All she had to do was keep going. There was a low bridge ahead that would take her to an estate on the other side, built on a hill that rose steeply. She could aim for that and find a way home.

She cursed him. It had been just another stupid argument.

He'd started it, as always, too much booze fuelling his jealousy, the beast that was always lurking. He'd accused her of looking at someone else. The idiot just didn't get it. He was pushing her to leave, with his snide remarks, the put-downs, saying how she'd let herself go, but then accused her of tarting herself up for other men whenever she made an effort. Didn't he get the irony?

She went to wipe more tears from her cheek but stopped herself. Let them fall.

It had been good once. Beautiful Liam. Kind Liam. The flowers. The messages. The lies.

There'd been punches before tonight, digs into her back that made her cough in pain, leaving bruises only he saw. There'd been the late-night beatings, of course, blurred by alcohol, where she'd called the police but had backed down by the time they arrived, somehow persuaded that he'd change, that the good times made up for the bad.

This time had been different, because it had been in public, outside the pub, people seeing her go down, the stars blurring into white streaks as she went backwards, ending with a thump on the ground of the car park. Another night out ending in pain.

No more. She'd had enough. This time she wasn't going back.

All she could think of was to get away, to keep running. Customers from the pub had blocked his way as she pushed herself up from the ground, but that wouldn't last. No one could take him on; he was too big, too angry, his shoulders hunched, his body tensed, fists clenched, his shouts loud. She'd fled to the sanctuary of the towpath, hoping he wouldn't see where she'd gone.

There was a dark shape ahead, making her slow down, but it resolved into a bench as she got closer. There'd been no more noises. It had been her imagination.

She stopped to sit down. She needed to calm herself and work out what to do. She couldn't go back to his place, but she had clothes there, and jewellery. He had photographs of her, intimate ones. He'd use them against her.

That shouldn't matter. Leaving didn't have to be harder than staying. Get her stuff. Go. Stay out of town.

The streets on the other side of the low bridge weren't far away, lining the higher slope on the other side, the town centre just a swirl of orange lights below. The streets meant safety, but she needed to steady her nerves, to work out her next move. It got dark ahead before it got brighter and there was something about the shadows ahead that made her nervous.

She took a cigarette from her packet, and was about to light it, when there was another noise. A bottle kicked over, rolling along the towpath.

He was following her. He'd seen where she'd gone, would know that she either had to keep going into the darkness or turn back towards him. He'd said too many times that he'd never let her leave him. He was waiting for her in the solid blackness of the towpath, she knew it.

She put her cigarette away, left the bench, increasing her pace as she went, not caring now that the click of her heels echoed like loud cracks along the path. She looked over her shoulder as she ran, straining to see who was there.

The bridge was getting closer. Shadows underneath.

She looked back again. There was movement on the towpath behind her, a dark mass flitting across.

The bridge was just twenty metres away. She was almost at the steps.

She took off her shoes, holding them in her hands like weapons, the heels long and pointed. 'Leave me alone,' she shouted, just to attract attention, her eyes going to the windows of the houses opposite, trying to make someone open a curtain or turn on a security light.

There was no response.

The steps were just there. The sharp stones between the cobbles made her wince, slowed her down, but once on the bridge she could run, make it to the tarmac on the other side. To the streetlights. To where people would see her.

Someone stepped in front of her. She let out a scream, but he rushed her, one hand going to her throat, choking it quiet, his other hand pulling her back by the hair.

She gasped and searched for air, but there was none to be had. She flailed her arms, heard him cry out as a heel dug into his head, and for a moment she thought she was able to fight him off, but she was thrown off-balance.

He pushed her towards the water. Her arms thrashed at him, but she dropped the shoes. Her bag fell off her shoulder and became tangled round her legs. Her feet couldn't get a grip as she tried to push back, the stones tearing at the soles of her feet. He was too strong.

He kept on pushing her until one of her feet was in the air, the ground no longer there, and then she started to fall backwards.

The splash of the freezing water made her gasp in shock, but it was drowned out as the dirty water filled her mouth. She spluttered, fought to keep her head above the water. Her feet scrambled for something to push against, but the canal was too deep.

She floundered up, her head above the surface, and coughed out the water, dirty and acrid, her hair plastered across her face. She snatched a gulp of air before he pushed her down again, holding her this time, pulling her body against the wall of the canal and her head under the surface

She pushed against the stones but she couldn't fight him, the water providing too much resistance. Her mouth was clamped shut. Images flashed into her head. Her mother, raising her on her own, tough but loving. Liam, those early days, tender and doting. The later months. Bullying, spiteful, drunken.

If he would only let her up, she'd try harder. She'd understand him better.

Her arms splashed in the water, tried to reach for his head, but he was using the strength in his arms to hold her under the surface.

Her lungs ached, her lips pressed together. She was tired, cold, couldn't struggle any more.

Just hold on. She needed to breathe, but she had to fight it. Why didn't he let her go? He loved her.

No more struggles. Her strength had gone. Her chest was willing her to take a breath, her brain telling her she needed the oxygen even though she knew what would happen when she opened her mouth.

She gave in.

The water rushed in, cold and dirty. She coughed, her lungs fighting, but there was just more water.

Then there was darkness.

FOUR MONTHS LATER

Two

Dan Grant set down the expert witness report he was reading and massaged his temples.

He lived in one of eleven apartments squeezed into the stone frame of an old wharf building at the end of a cobbled yard. Highford had been built on cotton, a small northern town hidden in a valley, with the skyline once dominated by mills and high chimneys that belched out smoke so thick that the streets became lost in the gloom. Soot coated the lines of terraced houses, the town laid out in tight grids. The cotton industry had died in the eighties and, as the smog cleared, the remains lay scattered across the valley floor as vast empty stone blocks, the windows broken, rough grass sprouting between the cobbles.

Some of the wharf buildings had been resurrected as office spaces; the canals that once fed them, no longer clogged by the queues of barges that had sailed from Liverpool, were now home to canal cruisers and wildlife. Others, like the apartment block Dan lived in, had been converted into modern living spaces, with the old wooden canopy that had once provided shelter for the cotton bales as they were winched inside now broken up by steel balconies.

Dan's apartment gave him a view along the water and a base in the town he'd grown up in. It usually felt like a sanctuary from his work pressures, but the following day he'd be defending a client in a murder trial and his home had turned into an extension of his office, every surface covered in papers as he reviewed all the evidence he had, obsessed over every detail, worried that he'd missed something crucial. It was only mid-morning and his head felt already clogged by facts.

He went to the window, knowing the view would relax him. The water glistened, the hills in the distance brightening as late spring brought fresh life to the countryside.

His mind went back to a freezing night in January, to the phone call that had started it all.

'Dan Grant,' he'd said, tucking the phone into his shoulder and picking up a bottle of wine.

'This is Highford custody office. We've got someone here who wants someone from Molloys. We called Mr Molloy but he said he's been on the whiskey and I should call you.'

Dan paused with the corkscrew. 'Just a phone call or an interview?'

'Interview. Peter Box.'

He sighed and put the bottle down with a clink. As a defence lawyer, he was used to the clock meaning little, because crime doesn't happen only during office hours. He answered the phone every time though. If it rang, someone needed him.

'He's been arrested for murder,' the sergeant continued.

That got his attention. A murder case trumped everything. He put the wine back in the fridge and headed out into the night.

DI Murdoch was waiting for him, pacing by the automatic doors, despite the cold winter wind, her police ID swinging from a purple lanyard, her shirt creased, although in Murdoch's case that was probably more to do with lack of an iron than long hours at a desk. She was part of the Major Incident Team, a small unit that investigated serious cases all over Lancashire, using local officers for the mundane tasks.

Dan liked Murdoch, but it was a feeling borne out of respect rather than affection. She was tough and tenacious, and honest. He suspected her integrity had stopped her being promoted beyond inspector; from Dan's experience, the higher up the ladder he looked, the less he could trust those looking down. He trusted a grafter like Murdoch, though, because she'd always listened to him. A detective who can change direction is one who'll usually end up in the right place.

Murdoch seemed impatient. He hadn't seen Tracy Murdoch for a few months. Her hair was long and dark, but unnaturally so, with an inky tint to it, and her skin showed the ravages of chain-smoking, with lines around her mouth that aged her much more than her fifty years.

Dan followed, acting weary, but he was alert, looking out for any hints that he was not getting the full picture. Whatever Murdoch told him would shape Dan's advice to his client, and he ran through the options in his head.

If the case against him was solid, Dan might tell his client to stay silent. Admitting a serious offence never improves a client's situation and it buys time to think of an excuse. The same went for a weak case, because Dan couldn't allow his client to fill in the gaps for the police. It was those cases in the middle that were the hardest, where his client had a story to tell that he'd need to repeat later, and Dan had to judge whether he should tell it straightaway. A misreading of the case might send him the wrong way, and in a murder case, the stakes were even higher.

'What have you got?' Dan said, as they approached a solid wooden door that led them to the custody suite.

'You know it's a murder?'

'So I was told.'

'You heard about the woman found by the canal on New Year's Day? Elizabeth Barnsley? Attacked and drowned.'

Dan had seen the news reports and remembered the name, Lizzie to her friends. He felt a twinge of guilt, because when he'd seen them he'd thought the same as every criminal defence lawyer thought when they heard of a murder: he'd hoped he'd get the case.

'Why do you think Peter Box did it?'

'Ah, the evidence.' She opened the door into the custody suite. 'Simple. When Lizzie was fighting for her life, she must have used her shoe to defend herself with, because her stiletto heel had blood on it. Peter Box's blood.' She held out her hand. 'After you.'

Dan grimaced at the glare of light. The custody suite used to be dank and dark, with an old wooden desk, high and scarred, opposite a holding cell and by large steel doors, through which the prisoners were brought from the police cars and vans that parked just outside. A gloomy corridor beyond led to a set of stairs that rose into one of the courtrooms in the next building. A recent revamp had made everything brighter and shinier, but the process was still the same: prisoners came in through the large steel doors from the back of a van, usually kicking and screaming; they were catalogued, stamped, and taken into the court the following morning, and the court would send them somewhere else, either back out onto the streets, or into a van with tiny dark windows for a trip along the motorway to the nearest prison. For many, it was a regular occurrence. They might call it a 'custody suite' but it was merely the first stop in a small factory that processed raw material to be repackaged further down the line, a little more dented, and a lot more broken.

'Any more evidence? Doesn't sound like much on its own.' Dan was trying to sound unimpressed, knowing that what lay ahead was a series of interviews meant to wear the suspect down, but a DNA link to the victim was a good start for the police. If Murdoch was hoping to rattle him though, she'd better not keep him up too late. Tiredness increased his desire for the fight.

'He sought hospital treatment for a wound to his temple. That's how we traced him, asking around the hospitals, because we knew from the blood on the heel that Lizzie had hit someone hard. And in case you're wondering about the wound, it's the same shape as Lizzie's heel.'

They had arrived at another wooden door, which led to the 'bubble', a small enclosure where lawyers were expected to make notes with their knees pressed up against a narrow desk, leaning in towards the tiny holes in the glass screen through which their clients could give instructions.

'I hope you're not planning on hanging around to accidentally overhear,' Dan said. 'I'll be wanting the custody footage if I hear anyone outside.'

'Don't be a prick, Dan.'

'Ditto.' And he went inside, closing the door behind him.

Sounds echoed in the bubble. The rustle of his papers. The shuffle of his shoes. The tap of his pen on the desk. The footsteps along the corridor on the other side of the bubble and then the rattle of keys.

He closed his eyes for a moment and breathed deeply through his nose. Dan had been a defence lawyer for ten years and the nerves around murder cases had long since gone, but that didn't mean he could relax: whatever advice Dan gave now would affect what happened once the case started going through the courts. Cases were often won and lost in these weary visits to the police station, advice doled out after a long day in the office, the eye on the clock more than on the evidence presented by the police.

Dan opened his eyes as he heard a lock turn. A civilian guard appeared in the far doorway, a chain hanging from her belt, and ushered Peter Box in. She locked the door behind him, leaving them alone together.

It was hard to reconcile Peter with the image of a murderer, someone who would brutally attack a woman on a dark towpath. He was scrawny, an oversized blue paper suit hanging from him, his own clothes seized for forensic examination. The neck gaped wide, his shoulders thin. He rustled as he moved. His eyes were wide and scared.

'Sit down, Peter.'

He looked at Dan for a few seconds before he shook his head. 'No, I'll stay standing.'

'Why?'

He stepped closer to the glass. 'If I sit down, I'll relax and slip up. No, I've got to stay alert. That's why you're here, to protect me, to stop them from getting inside here.' He jabbed the side of his head, close to where some of his hair had been shaved away, revealing a small horseshoe of stiches.

There it was, the anger. Was that fury the last thing Lizzie Barnsley had seen?

Dan closed his folder and leaned back in his chair. Peter was framed against the light in the ceiling, a bright panel, so that he appeared almost in silhouette, dark and glowering, his hair high and lit up like a halo.

'Tell me your side of it,' Dan said. When Peter stayed silent, he held out his hands. 'I'm not writing anything down and if you decide you want to tell me a different version later, we can pretend we've never had this conversation.'

'You can't do that.'

'Who's going to know? But if I'm staying up late for this, you've got to make it good.'

Peter shook his head and wagged his finger. 'I knew you'd do this. It's a trick to get me talking.'

'If you don't talk to me, I can't give you proper advice.'

'I'm not saying anything to you, to them, to anyone.'

'So why the hell am I here?'

'To protect me, to be my shield. Otherwise,' he paused and closed his eyes and clenched his fist before continuing, 'they'll do anything to get me talking. I'm not doing that. Not ever.'

Dan looked down and thought of the evening he'd planned for himself: a bottle of wine and a film. 'How did you get your injury?' He pointed towards Peter's head.

'I don't have to tell you. Nor them. They've got to prove everything, right?'

Dan shrugged his agreement. 'But if you don't explain away the obvious, like how your DNA ended up on Lizzie's shoe and how your head looks like it once had a stiletto heel stuck into it, you'll be found guilty.' Dan watched him for a few seconds. 'Is there an explanation?'

Peter leaned forward, his hands on the small desk in front of the screen between them, his mouth so close to the glass that he misted it up. 'I'm not talking. Your job is to keep it that way. No tricks. No stunts. Just silence.'

'What about some neutral questions, just for my sake?'

Peter thought about that before he nodded. 'Try me.'

'Do you know the part of the canal where Lizzie was murdered?'

Peter was about to say something when he stopped himself. 'Very clever.'

'I don't understand.'

'They haven't told me where she was murdered, so how can I know whether I go there?'

Dan sighed. 'I'm not your enemy here. Whatever you tell me today stays between us. That's how it works, the client-lawyer privilege.'

Peter considered that and sat down. He softened, and for a moment he looked scared, as if he'd just realised what lay ahead. 'I go there sometimes, mostly at night. I like the darkness. It protects me. You can't know if you've never truly felt the darkness around you, but the sound is clearer, every footstep, every drone of a car, every bit of birdsong.' He raised an eyebrow. 'That surprised you, didn't it, that birds sing at night too? But they do. I hear them, sharp calls from the trees.'

'Why the canal though?'

'It's where the true darkness is. Don't you know that? Go there during the day and what can you hear? Not much, that's what. Then go later, past midnight, and listen again. To the ripples against the banks, where the water settles against the grass growing along the side, or the way it reacts against the moon shining across the surface, pulling the water towards it. You won't be able to tell that, but I can, because I'm attuned to it. I've been in the darkness all my life.'

Dan had tried to remember all that Peter was saying, because he'd known he'd need to recount it later, to look for some clue as to what was driving him.

'Did you know Lizzie? Were you meeting her there?'

'No, I don't know her. I saw her name in the papers, that's all.'

'Were you there on the night she died?'

He sat back in his chair and looked towards the ceiling. 'I can't talk about that. Not ever. Just get me out of here. I can't go to prison. It wouldn't be right, or fair.'

Dan let out a long breath. This was the worst part of the job, knowing something and trying to keep it from the police, but it was what he'd signed up for. He was a defence lawyer. He believed in the justice system, that everyone deserved a fair trial, because it was about fairness. Sometimes though, when his career choice helped to keep murderers or rapists or child molesters on the streets, things didn't seem quite so noble. If Peter Box had murdered Lizzie Barnsley, and it was due to a compulsion he couldn't control, any success Dan had defending him would always be clouded by the knowledge that he could kill again.

Sometimes, that weighed heavily.

'You've got the right to silence,' Dan said. 'Let the police do their job and see if they can prove it against you. If you won't talk to anyone, that's the best we can do.'

'Don't let me talk. That's all I ask.' Peter turned to bang on the door.

'Last chance to talk to me before the interviews start.'

'I'm ready.'

He banged again until the same civilian guard appeared.

Peter bolted through the door and screeched when he got into the corridor, like the sound of a wounded and cornered animal. Someone else thumped on a cell door and shouted.

*

That had been four months ago. Peter had maintained his silence, even during Dan's visits to the prison, which meant that it was up to Dan to find a defence.

He'd scoured his medical records, hoping to find a history of mental illness, an abnormality that could account for a random attack on an innocent stranger. It wouldn't secure his release, but it could replace murder with manslaughter and get him transferred to a hospital rather than a prison.

The only entries he'd found were some periods of anxiety years before, and they were wide apart. The first one was around fifteen years ago, and then a few years later.

For reasons Dan couldn't fathom, Peter Box wanted to go into his trial in the hope that saying nothing would save him. Dan knew that wouldn't work, because jurors like to have a reason to free a murder suspect, and Peter wasn't giving them one.

Dan was jolted from his thoughts by the sound of his door buzzer. He wasn't expecting a visitor and he didn't want any distractions. When he went to the security panel, he saw it was his boss, Pat Molloy.

Dan frowned. He loved to spend time with Pat, he had been Dan's boss and friend and mentor since the beginning of his career, but this visit was unusual. Pat had never been to his apartment. Dan had been to Pat's home often enough, a large old redbrick, ivy on the walls, in a small village nestled in a steep valley a few miles from Highford. Pat had never been the sort of person to hang around other peoples' houses though. He was the genial host, never the happy visitor.

Something wasn't right.

Three

Jayne Brett sat in her old Fiat Punto. Pale blue, with a passenger door that was dented from a crash a long time ago and a passenger window that didn't shut properly.

She was in a car park of a small supermarket. She'd been there for two hours and the rear seat was already covered in drinks cans and wrappers from a fast-food breakfast. She was too tired to laugh at her situation, the so-called glamour of the private investigator. It wasn't how she'd imagined it would be when she first started out. It had been Dan Grant's idea: stick around Highford and he'd feed her work, he'd said.

Yeah, he'd tried his best, but he couldn't manufacture investigations for her. He'd given her work but it was often too far apart, and his scraps didn't pay the rent. She'd touted herself around the other local law firms and it had led to work like this, spying on cheating spouses. It made a change from serving court summonses or injunctions to angry recipients, but she was becoming aware that she shouldn't have drunk so much coffee. Her bladder was full but there was nowhere for her to go discreetly. There was a take-away cup somewhere; she might have to use that and tip it out of the window.

Jayne was helping a law firm in a divorce case, looking for evidence of the husband's adultery, which the wife had started to suspect at the appearance of the usual unsubtle signs: sharper clothes, too much aftershave, an attempt to dye his hair. It was up to Jayne to complete the picture. She was intruding on someone else's life but she had her own problems: she had no money left on her electricity card and her rent was two weeks overdue.

Jayne had been following the husband for a week, and the most useful information she'd gathered was that he didn't like to go home and spent long hours walking in the park instead, staring straight ahead or gazing into the flowerbeds. Whatever else was going on in his private life, he wasn't a happy man.

Then it came. Last night he was supposed to be travelling to a work conference, an overnight trip. Jayne had expected to merely follow him to a railway station, but instead he'd left his car in the supermarket car park and rushed into an apartment building opposite.

Jayne had got some pictures of him entering the building, but it was dark and she couldn't risk her flash going off. She could have waited all night, but the thought of sitting in her car as the husband got warm and cosy on the other side of the bedroom curtains hadn't appealed to her. She'd got up early and waited instead, except she had to keep on wiping her windscreen as she misted it up with her breath.

The early start was killing her, especially on a Sunday. The effects of the night before clung on to her though. She'd gone out for a drink after her brief vigil, just a few drinks at one of the pubs in town, sitting in a corner and watching the locals get more drunk as they danced and sang to the efforts of an eighties cover band. There were a few of her conquests among them, men who'd filled a need, some of whom she remembered, although she'd never sought a second date.

She sat up when the door of the apartment building opened and he emerged, checking around first. He was wearing different clothes and carrying a small bag. Jayne raised her camera and got some shots.

A woman emerged behind him, her dark hair tousled from bed, and they kissed, passionately and at length. She was wearing a silk dressing gown and his hand went behind her, to pull her close.

More clicks of the camera.

Jayne checked the images on the display screen. She had enough now. It was time to pass on the bad news. Or good news, depending on how it was received.

As she drove away, she checked her petrol gauge. Nearly empty. She hoped the firm would pay for her work promptly, because she was down to the dregs in her account and it was looking like food or petrol were her only choices.

Jayne sighed. Her life needed to amount to more than this. In her mid-twenties, she shouldn't be scruffing around a small northern town. It had been partly her choice and partly circumstances, but she was starting to feel restless. She had once expected more from her life.

Her thoughts turned to Dan, as they often did.

He'd been there for her when she was at her worst point, so it was natural that her thoughts drifted to him when she was alone. She'd been a client once, accused of murdering a violent boyfriend. Somehow, they struck up a bond, but she wondered whether she should sever it. She was a different person now. Whatever had gone before was just that: gone.

She thought of Dan too often, when she felt aimless, or lonely, her flat cold and empty, her bed only ever filled with fleeting encounters, just flurries of limbs and false affection.

It wasn't the brevity she minded, she had needs to fulfil as much as the men who passed through, but sometimes she missed having a companion. Someone to trust.

All that lay ahead for now was the report she had to write. The suspicious wife would want something to confront her wandering husband with when he returned home with tales of his non-trip out of town.

As she made her way home, she wished she had enough fuel to just drive and keep going. After all, what would she be leaving behind? A small apartment. Debts. A business that just about kept her afloat. She could drive over the hill and find a new life. Somewhere brighter, with more hope. Highford seemed to be strangling her somehow, the hills that surrounded it like a barrier. It kept the wider world from coming in, so that the residents knew only each other and too many had no thoughts of ever leaving.

She turned down the hill to begin her journey across town.

Jayne knew she wouldn't leave. Not yet anyway. The insularity of the town was her protection, her sanctuary.

Damn you, Dan Grant.

Four

Dan pressed the buzzer and waited by the door for Pat Molloy to come up. He hadn't seen his boss for a couple of weeks – he'd been caught up in his own cases and Pat had been working from home a lot more.

When the lift door opened, Pat stepped out slowly, coughing, a large brown envelope in his hand. He looked round, as if he wasn't sure where to go, before he spotted Dan in his doorway. Outlined against the lights further along the corridor, Pat looked bent with age, his walk more of a shuffle.

'This is a rare treat,' Dan said, although there was no levity in his voice, shocked by the change in his boss.

He realised how little he'd seen of Pat recently. They'd both been busy, and whenever they came across each other, Pat was in a suit. On a Sunday morning, Pat was more casual, in corduroys and a cashmere v-neck, and his frame seemed more fragile.

'Daniel, we need to talk.'

Dan showed Pat into the living room, still littered with papers from Peter Box's case.

As he took them in, Pat said, 'Are you all ready for tomorrow?'

'As much as I'll ever be.'

'You're not worried? Your first solo murder trial?'

Dan gave a small laugh. He didn't need to be reminded of that.

He was a solicitor, normally found in the Magistrates Court, but he'd acquired the qualification to conduct trials in the Crown Court, once the sole preserve of barristers, the wig-and-gown brigade. It wasn't Dan's first murder trial, but it was the first without a Queen's Counsel to handle the serious stuff. Peter had wanted Dan to do it alone, one of the few things he was specific about.

Dan tried to dismiss the pressure he felt. 'What have you always said, that a murder is just an assault with one less witness? I've never forgotten it.'

'This is different, though.'

'Why's that?'

'I'll come to that in a bit. There's something else I've got to mention first.' Pat looked down, and for the first time Dan could remember, he looked sad. No, more than that; he looked miserable.

'Pat? You all right?'

Pat didn't respond straightaway. Instead, he looked towards the window and took some deep breaths.

Eventually, he turned back towards Dan. Gone was the usual gleam in his eye, the twinkle of mischief. In its place was a greyness. There were dark shadows under his eyes and his silver hair was dishevelled.

'There's only one way to say this, so I'm going to spit it out,' he said. 'I've got cancer.'

The shock hit Dan like a punch in the gut. He sat down, open-mouthed.

He'd worked for Pat his entire career. When he was still a young trainee, Pat had knocked the edges off his idealism, teaching him the realities of being a criminal lawyer, and all with a touch of panache. Once he qualified, Pat taught him his best tricks, the wise words of a seasoned professional. Pat had been more than a boss. He'd been his mentor, his teacher, a splash of colour in an increasingly drab world, with his exaggerated mannerisms and his attempts to play at being the small-town eccentric, in red braces and bright ties, his fedora keeping his head warm in winter. Dan knew it was fake, just a way of attracting attention to get the clients, or a way of distracting the local magistrates from the cold realities of the evidence, but after a while everyone becomes the person they pretended to be.

There was none of that extravagance now. Pat's pallor was grey, his eyes heavy. Dan cursed himself for not noticing that perhaps his suits hung a little looser than normal, or that his shirt collars gaped too much.

Dan swallowed before he spoke. 'How bad?'

'Can it ever be good?' He shrugged. 'I don't know. I've not been good for a while. You've heard me wheezing and getting out of breath.'

'That might be just you getting old. Come on, Pat, it can't be cancer.'

'They've done all the tests. It's lung cancer.'

Dan put his head back and blew out. Pat meant so much to him.

'I know what you're thinking,' Pat said. 'How long? They think they've caught it early but that depends on how fast it spreads. It's all those years locked in small rooms with clients smoking like it was about to be taken away from them. An occupational hazard.'

'Jeez, Pat, I don't know what to say. You need to look after yourself, fight this thing. You know I'll cover for you if you need to take time off or . . . whatever.'

Pat smiled, but it was thin and watery. 'It's not just that. It's Eileen.'

'What do you mean?'

Pat leaned forward. 'She says I should retire now, that I've got just the one shot at life and, if what I have left isn't long, I shouldn't be spending it at the office. I should be at home with my family. And she's right.'

'What are you going to do?'

Pat chuckled, despite himself, although it quickly broke into a cough. 'For once in my life, I'm going to do as I'm told. I'm going to go home and fight this.'

'I don't know what to say.'

'You don't have to say anything. My retirement was always going to happen. I've just been forced into a decision a bit earlier than I'd planned. You can ask me the question, though, because it doesn't have to be only about me.'

'What question?'

'When do I go?' Pat held up his hand as Dan started to object. 'It's only natural that you'll worry about your job.'

Dan looked out of the window as he tried to process everything he was being told. He had a murder trial starting the following day, his first one on his own. Now, his future seemed suddenly uncertain.

'The end of the month is the answer.'

That made Dan turn round. 'So soon?'

'I don't know how long I've got left. I'm going to write to my clients, perhaps have a party or two, say goodbye to a few special people, and then I close the doors.'

'And that's it?'

Pat smiled. It was weary but there was some sparkle to his eyes for the first time. 'There is another way.'

'Which is?'

'Molloys could be yours.'

'*What?* Me, buy the firm? I can't afford it, for a start.'

'I don't mean the building. I own that; it's my pension and my children's inheritance. If I close the firm, I'll sell the place. But you could carry it on. Just pay me rent, and when I'm gone, pay it to Eileen. The rest of the firm is free of charge.'

'How do you mean, free of charge?' Dan scratched his head. 'This is all going too fast.'

'Think about it, Daniel. What do I actually own? Some good-will from some of Highford's criminals? That's not the same as a proper client list. I've got no repeat contract work or a cabinet full of civil claims waiting to be cashed in. No, we've got the regu-lar churn of criminals, most cases wrapped up and billed within a few months. There's no value in that, because the punters swap and change depending on how they're feeling and who's avail-able when they make the call, or how their last attempt to avoid jail went.' He held out his hands. 'No, you've earned the firm. If you want it, I've got just one condition.'

'Which is what?'

'You keep the name of the firm as it is. If I'm going to die' – and he held up his hand – 'I'll die, I know that, because we all do, but if I die soon I want to leave a legacy, and my name on the window is just that.' He looked down for a moment. 'It's not much, I know, some gold-edged lettering on a window in a small grey town, but it's all I've got.'

'How can I think about that right now?'

'You'll need to see the books.'

'Pat, stop it.'

'I'm serious. Do you think I'd joke about this?'

'It's a big decision.'

Pat winked, some colour coming back into his cheeks. 'Your sentiment didn't last long.' He put the envelope he'd been carrying on the table. 'I've printed these off for you already. The balance sheets for the last ten years, and the profit and loss accounts. You can see how it grows and shrinks, perhaps even work out how to run the firm more cheaply.'

Dan stared at it. 'Are you sure about this? Just handing it over, you mean?'

'I'm not being that generous. If you don't want it, you'll leave and get a job somewhere else. Who'll carry it on then? I'll just end up closing the door and that will be it, my name scraped from the window and you'll be after a redundancy payment. You'll have earned it too. I'll sell the building and live off the proceeds, but I want more than that.'

Dan picked up the envelope. 'Why today, though? I've got a murder trial starting tomorrow, and now you throw this at me.'

'I've had a long weekend with Eileen, and I made her some promises. This was going to come, cancer or no cancer. It's just been brought forward.'

Dan stared at the envelope for a few seconds before saying, 'When do you need an answer?'

'By the end of the week.'

'So soon?'

'I'm going at the end of the month. I need to know whether I'm putting a FOR SALE sign outside.' He smiled, more warmth there now. 'Have a bottle of wine tonight. Think about it.'

'I might do now. I didn't want to go into court tomorrow stinking of booze, I've got the judge on my back as it is, but then you hit me with this.'

'Ah yes, the hopeless cause. How's it going?'

'It's a strange one. He won't talk to me. He stayed silent during the police interviews and won't talk about the case with me. All I can do is attack the prosecution case.'

'Have you got anything to go at?'

Dan lifted the report that he'd been reading earlier. 'The lab used for the DNA result got in trouble last year. A couple of employees were manipulating blood tests. They were caught and went to prison, so I've got an expert to describe how easy it is for DNA samples to become contaminated, talking about that lab in particular. He even found a couple of errors with the paperwork.'

'That's something then.'

'But not enough. We needed to get our own testing done. Because if Peter Box is innocent, if that blood on her shoe isn't his, the prosecution case crumbles.'

'Have you done that?'

'Peter won't co-operate. He's a man saying nothing, with an injury to his head that looks pretty heel-shaped. The jurors will want more than that to find him not guilty.'

'You can only advise, Daniel, not lead. How are you finding it, doing it all on your own?'

'Challenging, but good to be in charge, to do it all my way.'

Pat pointed at the envelope. 'There's your answer. If you want to keep it that way, make my place yours. I'm not just here about the firm, though.'

'Go on.' Dan's voice was filled with caution.

'There is one stain on my career, which is another reason why I came today. I'm sorry about this, and I wasn't going to tell you, but it's about your trial.'

'Peter Box?'

'Yes.' Pat leaned forward. 'Do you remember Sean Martin?'

'*The* Sean Martin? How could I forget?'

'There is something about that case I haven't told you, not told anyone, but I want you to know. This could be a long story. It might be early, but I'll need a drink for this.'

Five

He watched the entrance to the cobbled yard from his car on the other side of the road. It wasn't the first time he'd been there. He'd followed Dan Grant home from his office one night, two cars behind, just to know where he lived. It's always good to know these things. He hadn't got any closer to him though.

He put his head back and closed his eyes. It was becoming too much. There'd been too many deaths. They weighed too heavily, a line stretching back through the years, those missed by the police, written off as suicides or accidents or unexplained missing persons. That had to stop. They had to recognise it. They had to recognise him.

The faces of the dead flashed through his mind, snapping him alert. They did that sometimes. They came to him in his sleep, or when he relaxed for a moment, as if forgetting wasn't allowed.

He rubbed his chest. It hurt whenever they jumped back into his head like that. Too much pressure, but he couldn't act. Not yet. There was someone in there with Grant. An old man, worn down and grey.

Instead, he kept his focus on the view ahead, towards the stone buildings of the town centre. It was quiet, the Sunday trade confined to the out-of-town retail parks. It made him conspicuous. Perhaps he wanted that, to be noticed.

All he could do was wait.

*

Dan was confused. 'Sean Martin? I don't understand.'

The Sean Martin case had been Pat's biggest victory, the one that got him a speech on the court steps that was played out on every national news bulletin, his story dominating double-page spreads.

The case had caught the media's attention quickly.

Sean Martin's fourteen-year-old stepdaughter, Rosie Smith, had been stabbed to death with a thin sharp instrument as she'd been walking along the canal towpath to meet Sean.

He'd arranged to meet her off the bus after she'd spent the day at a friend's house, except that they lived on the other side of the town to the one-way system that the bus was funnelled along. He'd told her to get off the bus and walk the hundred metres along the canal, where he would be waiting for her. When she didn't arrive, he went looking for her, finding her on the towpath, blood pooling around her.

He'd rushed to her and held her close, listened out for her breathing as he lifted her from the ground, his hands and clothes covered in her blood as he searched for any sign that she was still alive.

Suspicion hadn't fallen on Sean Martin straightaway, but when the police started to delve into Rosie's life, they were disturbed by some of the messages that passed between Rosie and her stepfather. It was the early days of social media, still used mainly by young people, but Sean Martin was quick to get on it as well. It seemed as if whenever Rosie posted a picture of herself in a pose that was a young teenager's attempt to look sexy, Sean Martin posted a comment that appeared to cross the line. Rosie might have wanted her classmates to say that she looked hot, but perhaps not her stepfather.

It was the blood mist that changed everything.

A blood-spatter expert had examined his clothes. There were the expected contact stains, from where Sean had held her after he found her, but there were other blood stains, microscopic spots of blood on his fleece jacket and his shirt collar, invisible to the naked eye. The expert said that these had come from the mist of blood created during the attacker's frenzy, as her murderer leaned over her to strike the fatal blows to her chest. They made Sean the killer.

'I don't understand,' Dan said. 'Sean Martin was your biggest success.'

'Let me talk about your client first. Peter Box. Has he mentioned Sean Martin at all?'

'No. Why should he?'

'Because when Sean was awaiting trial, Peter Box came to my office and tried to claim responsibility for Rosie's murder.'

Dan stood up, his arms splayed out, his mouth open in shock.

'What the hell, Pat? Why are you telling me now, the night before the trial?'

'Think about Sean Martin.' He stopped to cough. 'What do we know about him? He was acquitted in the end, innocent in the eyes of the law after his retrial. If I'd told you, how would it have helped Peter Box for you to think he'd killed before?'

'I was a trainee when I sat through Sean's first trial, and it was what, twelve years ago now? I don't remember the possibility of another suspect ever being mentioned.'

'I went to see Sean without you, because I thought I was breaking great news by telling him there was someone else the police could focus on. It didn't go as I expected.'

'Why? What did he say?'

'He told me to ignore it. As simple as that. Said Box was probably some fantasist, and that if there was any evidence linking anyone else, they'd have found it. He said it would make him look desperate.'

'So that was that?'

'I pressed him on it, don't worry, and I ran it past the QC to see what he thought, and he agreed that it was too risky. We didn't know enough about Box, and you know the rule: never ask a question to which you don't already know the answer. What if we asked the police about him and there was a history of false confessions? How desperate would that make Sean look? It was Sean who gave the most noble answer, that he knew what it was like to be wrongly accused of a crime, and that his conscience wouldn't allow him to let it happen to someone else.'

Dan sat down. 'But why are you telling me now? I can't use it, because it doesn't matter what people think of him, his retrial turned him into an innocent man wrongly accused, haunted by the memory of holding Rosie as she died, while the killer is still out there roaming the canals. They'll look at Peter Box and wonder whether Sean Martin had been right all along, that he *was* innocent, and that now, after all this time, they have a chance to nail her killer.'

'I can't die with this case hanging over me.'

Dan looked down for a moment. 'I'm truly sorry you are ill, and I can't stand the thought of you dying, because you've been my boss, my hero, but I'm the wrong person to grant you redemption. Take this the right way, Pat, because you've done so much for me, but if the stain is that you stayed silent about Peter Box and he's murdered someone else, you've come to the wrong person. I'm not conspiring to get Peter Box locked up. I'm here to defend him.'

Pat shook his head. 'Peter Box isn't the stain. Think back to Sean Martin. He'd been the victim of a police force determined to convict someone for Rosie's murder, a prosecution that had latched onto minor pieces of evidence and exaggerated them. But when I'd given him someone to blame he'd turned away from that path: a man of principle, stronger than I could ever have been. You remember how he stuck by me even though we lost his first trial? I fought for him, Dan. I believed in him.'

'I remember. I was proud of you.'

'The police had fastened onto any old morsel: like the fact that no one else knew that he'd made the arrangement with Rosie, and that he went out too early to meet her, or that her phone disappeared, as if there was something to hide on it.'

'I remember the innuendo about their relationship, the press calling it "complex".' Dan made the sign of inverted commas with his fingers. 'There was no actual evidence that Sean had any sexual interest in Rosie but they repeated the whispers anyway, suggesting that she was about to make accusations against him, so he had to silence her. But you fought hard, Pat. His conviction is no stain. You got it overturned.'

Pat reached out and grabbed Dan by the forearm. 'You misunderstand me. Getting nearer to death has allowed me to reassess it all. I took his conviction badly because he was so reviled in the press, and I got some backlash for that in Highford. It felt like I'd failed him. He wrote to me all the time, and he had supporters and campaigners, and I was determined to get him out, to rescue him. I was able to find my own expert to say that Rosie could have been breathing as he held her, because looking dead isn't the same as being dead. The poor girl might have covered him in the blood mist as she took her last breaths. Or it could have been expelled when he lifted her. It was enough, just enough. He got his retrial and doubt was found, because it *was* possible that the blood mist got there while he held her during the last moments of her life, rather than while he leaned over her as he killed her.'

'And Sean hasn't been bitter about it,' Dan said. 'He's put his experience to good use and become the go-to man when they start talking about miscarriages of justice. That's down to you, Pat.'

'Yes. He's advised ministers. He's a real star.' There was no pleasure in Pat's voice. 'That's why he's my stain. Sean Martin, not Peter Box.'

'Sorry, Pat, but you've lost me.'

'Do you remember the night of his release? The party we held?'

'How could I forget? Most times, we help guilty people to walk away from their crimes. For a change, we'd done good. It's not often we can say that.'

'All of Sean's supporters were so happy. It was a grand old night. Until later.' Pat let out a long breath that turned into a coughing fit, grimacing until it subsided. 'Do you know what he said to me that ruined it?'

Dan drummed his fingers on the table. 'Do I want to hear this?'

'You *need* to hear it.' There was some of the old fire in Pat's eyes now. 'It was almost the end of the evening and everyone was a bit drunk, but not Sean. I realised then that he hadn't been drinking too much, but I put it down to the fact that he'd spent his time talking and perhaps felt bewildered after six years in prison. I was wrong. He was staying in control, that's all, because he doesn't like to lose control. He pointed towards his supporters, all wearing the same black T-shirts. Do you remember them, with that giant yellow ribbon logo, twirled into the initials SM? He leaned over to me and said, "What's funny is that they never found the murder weapon."'

Pat held out his hands. 'What could I do but agree? But he didn't stop there. He wagged his finger at me and whispered, "Because I hid it well."'

Dan's eyes widened. 'He said that?'

'Oh, he did, all right. He said something else, too: "By the western corner, just under the surface, below the mason's mark – an itch you can't scratch." I thought I'd heard him wrong, or perhaps it was a joke, but when l looked at him he nodded and winked and said, "But you can't tell anyone because you're my lawyer. I just thought you might like to know."'

'What the hell did you say?'

'I asked him whether he'd killed her. I told him that new forensic evidence could mean a new trial, that *not guilty* in a murder case doesn't mean he's off the hook for ever.'

'And?'

'He just laughed and said nobody was going to find it. And if the police ever came after him again, he'd know who'd tipped them off, because I was the only person he'd told.'

Dan sat back, perplexed. 'Why did he tell you that?'

'To taunt me, because I'd been so pleased with myself, and he wanted to puncture me. He enjoys cruelty, and it worked. It felt like the air had been sucked out of me.'

'He might have been just winding you up.'

'He wasn't. I saw it in his eyes right then. But he knew I'd think it was a sick joke so he sealed the deal. He smiled at me, mocking me, and said, "That dirty little slut would have given me away, and I couldn't allow that." And then he left me to circle the room, talk to his supporters, knowing that I was bound to keep my silence.'

Dan shook his head. 'I don't believe it. Sean Martin was guilty after all?'

'The one part of my career I wish I could rewrite, to walk away from him when he was first convicted. That's why he didn't want us to look into Peter Box, because he would have been discounted easily. It wasn't Peter, but Sean all along.'

'And you've kept this quiet since then?'

'Client privilege, you know how it is. And what could I do? I couldn't bring Rosie back and it would have ruined my reputation. I'd have been the lawyer who'd freed a murderer. It's a poor excuse, I know, because I could have made an anonymous call. If he had complained about breach of privilege, he'd have to admit that what he'd told me turned out to be true, but I'd have been disciplined for betraying a client. Cowardly, I know, but I can't change the past.'

'But now things are different?'

'I want this removed from my conscience.'

'How does this involve me?'

'Peter Box.'

Dan stood up and went to the window, tried to conceal his frustration. 'I'm not using my case to ease your conscience, Pat. I just can't.'

'Don't you see? Peter Box came to see me and tried to confess in Sean Martin's case. Either Sean Martin killed Rosie or he didn't, but my gut tells me that he did, which makes Peter flaky. It might explain why he's keeping quiet, because he has a habit of incriminating himself for things he didn't do. If nothing else, it will explain his silence.'

'It won't explain the DNA, and if I introduce a murder he tried to claim responsibility for, where a man has been cleared, the jury will think Peter killed Rosie too.'

Pat stayed silent, to let the obvious sink in.

It dawned on Dan slowly. 'You want me to go after Sean Martin.'

Pat nodded. 'Find out why Peter came to see me all those years ago. What's the connection with Sean Martin? You already have an expert to discredit the DNA lab. All you need to do is explain Peter Box's silence, and you do that by showing that he's falsely claimed to be a killer in the past.'

'And I do that by proving that Sean Martin killed Rosie?'

'Exactly. If you can prove that Sean Martin killed Rosie, you can show why he stayed silent.'

'How do I do this?'

'We find the murder weapon, first of all, and do more digging on Sean Martin.'

'The trial is tomorrow. I've no time.'

'And neither have I, but I want to do it, and it's relevant to Peter's case. But I have a warning for you.'

'Which is what?'

'Sean delighted in the cruelty of the things he said. Remember, too, why he killed Rosie: to keep her quiet. If you go down this path, you are in danger. Me too, because he will know where the information has come from, but it's the right thing to do. Not just for me, or for Lizzie Barnsley, but for Rosie too.

Let me go to my grave knowing that I've scrubbed away this stain.'

Dan couldn't think of a good reason to say no. But he knew something else too: Peter Box's trial had just got a hell of a lot more complicated.

Six

Jayne put the camera to one side and stared out of the window as she waited for the kettle to boil.

Her apartment was on the top floor of a crumbling Victorian terrace on one of the steep roads into Highford town centre, the hallway muggy with cannabis and the air often heavy with the thump-thump of music from the other flats. Small steps led to a long hallway, with a bedroom off it, the bathroom on the other side, a kitchen and living room at the end. It gave her great views over Highford but, more importantly, it was somewhere she could hide.

She'd escaped there a few years earlier after Dan had helped secure her acquittal. As great as it was to be free, memories of it made her shudder and came back to her in her quieter moments.

She'd killed a man. An abusive man, Jimmy. Their relationship had started with professions of love, but it only ended when she stuck a knife into his leg and severed his femoral artery. He bled out on the kitchen floor to the sound of her screams.

She hadn't meant to do it, but Jimmy had been too close, the knife in her hand when he attacked her. She remembered his spittle landing on her face as he snarled out another threat. She wasn't a killer, but in her darker moments of reflection, she still wondered whether she'd merely snapped, lashed out when he'd hurt her once again.

She'd come to Highford to escape from Jimmy's family, to start a new life, with a new name and a new job as a private investigator, but her life had changed since then.

She'd gone back home a few months earlier and it had worked out. Jimmy's family hadn't attacked her, even though she'd made her presence obvious, and it felt like all the stress of the previous years had melted away. She didn't need to be in Highford anymore. She had her business, and a few friends that she kept at a distance. Only Dan Grant and Pat Molloy knew about her past, so her friends didn't feel real. She used to have friends in her hometown, but Jimmy had made her give them up.

Dan had saved her. She could never forget that.

The kettle clicked off. Empty takeaway cartons littered the surfaces and there were three empty wine bottles, cheap stuff from the local supermarket multibuy.

She turned away. She'd deal with the mess later.

This was it then, her Sunday. She checked her pockets. A fiver, some change, and an empty fridge.

She went into the bedroom. If she was going to go hungry, she needed the time to go quickly. Sleep might do it, the early start catching up with her, and at least it would save on the heating bills.

She sprawled on her bed with her laptop to browse some newspaper sites, but there wasn't much going on. She noticed a thriller she'd bought in a charity shop lying half-finished, the pages open. That might pass the afternoon, losing herself in someone else's story for a few hours.

She reached for it and started to read. After a couple of pages, she remembered why she'd put it down as she re-read the same paragraph three times.

She was rescued by the buzz of her phone in her pocket. It was Dan.

She sat up as she answered. 'Hey. What's this for, on a Sunday?'

'Do you want some work?'

'I always want work, you know that.'

'Can you come now? This is urgent.'

'Have you got food?'

'Always.'

'Okay, see you soon.' And she clicked off. She gave a small punch in the air. Somehow, she felt like she was always able to avoid absolute rock bottom.

Seven

He couldn't put it off any longer. The old man had gone and, as far as he knew, Dan Grant was alone. He checked in his rear-view mirror, and then ahead. No one was watching him. He was just an anonymous man on a quiet street.

As he stepped out of his car, he pulled his coat tighter. The morning was fresh and he felt the cold more than he used to. He reached down into the side compartment for his baseball cap, old and green and faded, to hide his unkempt hair.

Now was the time. The trial started the next day. He couldn't leave it much longer. He'd left it too long already.

He crossed the road and walked into the cobbled car park, the entrance to Dan's building in the furthest corner. It was one of Highford's grander apartment blocks, the old wharf character maintained, the millstone clean and brightened by steel balconies.

He hesitated. Was this the right time? He should wait, pick his moment. How would he get into the building? Did he expect Dan to buzz him in? He thought about the old cliché of pressing every button until he got someone lazy enough to unlock the door without asking questions, but he wasn't sure he could do that.

There was a rumble of tyres behind him. An old blue Fiat, a young woman driving.

He turned away and made as if to tie his shoelace before he cursed himself. If it was an attempt to be inconspicuous, all he'd done was to make himself look suspicious. He kept his face out of view as she drove past, and once she stopped, he walked back out of the car park, stopping to peer round the wall at her.

She was slim and pretty and didn't live there, because she pressed a button rather than using a key. Dan's girlfriend? Could be, although there were other apartments in the building.

He walked towards her, hoping to sneak in behind her, but the door buzzed before he could get there. He cursed. He'd been too hesitant and he was running out of time.

He went back to his car. He was prepared to wait.

*

Dan left his door ajar and went back into his living room. Jayne knew the way in.

His mind was whirring as he slumped onto the sofa. Pat's visit had left behind a mix of adrenaline and despair.

Jayne bounded in, grinning. 'I thought you'd forgotten about me.'

She lifted his mood straightaway. Her energy, her brightness, despite the darkness that he knew wasn't far beneath. 'How could I forget you?'

She sat down on the chair opposite. 'You promised food.'

'Are you not eating again?'

'It requires money and you've stopped sending me work, which means the cupboards are bare.'

'I'm sorry about that. We'll eat soon, but we've got work to do before that, if you want it.'

'Paid work?'

'Of course, but it isn't going to be easy.'

'It's always like that with you. What is it?'

'You heard of Sean Martin?'

She pulled a face and shook her head. 'Puff Daddy?'

Dan laughed, despite the sadness he felt about Pat. 'That's Sean Combs. No, Sean Martin was convicted of murdering his stepdaughter but was freed on appeal.'

Jayne thought for a moment, taking off her coat and throwing it over the back of the sofa. 'Oh, him. He's from round here, isn't he?'

'Yes, from Highford. Pat Molloy represented him. The murder took place on the canal towpath.'

'I don't remember the original trial but I remember him being cleared. My opinion? Guilty.'

'The jury said he wasn't when he had his retrial.'

'How is Pat? I saw him walking around the town centre a couple of weeks ago and he didn't look so good. I say walking, but it was much slower than that. It looked like some of his spark had gone.'

'He's not good.' Dan sighed. 'Damn, he's worse than that. I'm sorry to have to be the one to tell you this, but he's got cancer and he doesn't think he's got long.'

Jayne's hand went to her mouth and her eyes moistened. 'Not Pat. That's not fair. They've got it wrong, they must have.'

'I wish they had but Pat seems pretty clear.'

'And how are you? I know how much he means to you.'

'I'm all mixed up. He's taught me so much. He's the lawyer I wanted to be when I started out. And now this.' He shook his head. 'I can't imagine him not being here.'

'I'm sorry, Dan.'

'He wants me to take over the business at the end of the month, you've seen how he's fading, so I've got that on top of everything else, but it just seems unreal.'

Dan stopped talking as emotion choked him. He swallowed it back before continuing, 'It's not just about him being my boss though. I remember when my mum died, and my dad was all over the place, too much so to be there for me. Pat was, though; he knew how to say the right things.'

Jayne came over to him and put her arms round him. 'I'm sorry,' she said again, and kissed him on the cheek.

For a moment, he closed his eyes and let her aroma envelope him, her skin warm and soft against his. For a moment, her fingers were in his hair, her breath hot on his neck, her body pressed against his as she hugged him.

'Thank you,' he said, pulling away awkwardly, his voice thick. 'We should talk about Sean Martin, though.'

Her hand went to his cheek. 'Back to business then,' she said, and sat away from him. After a few seconds Jayne broke the silence. 'Everyone thinks he did it. I know he's in the press a lot, a spokesman for dodgy convictions or something, but everyone looks at him and thinks he did it, because if not him, who else?'

'It sounds like you'll be just the right fit for this, then,' and he pointed at the papers strewn across the table. 'That trial starts tomorrow; Peter Box. You might remember it. A murder in the early hours of New Year's Day, just after the midnight fireworks. Lizzie Barnsley is the name of the victim, and Pat has this idea that it might help my client if I can prove that Sean Martin murdered his stepdaughter, Rosie Smith.'

She gasped in shock. 'Why are you doing that? You defend people, not the other way around.' She stood up and walked over, leafing through the papers and then recoiling when she saw the crime scene photographs. 'This looks grizzly. Is it a good case against him?'

'Very good. He left his blood on one of her shoes.'

'What does he say about that?'

'Nothing, and that's the problem. He won't talk about what happened.'

'How are you supposed to defend him, then?'

'That's just what I told him. All I can do is undermine the prosecution case.'

'And set free a guilty man if you win.'

'That's my job.'

'I know, the lawyer's cop out, that it's about the evidence, blah blah.' She held up her hand. 'And before you say it, I know the system worked for me, but I don't attack people on towpaths.'

'We don't pick and choose when it fits.'

Jayne gave a mock salute. 'Understood. I'll do what I can and let justice prevail.'

'I appreciate the dramatic flourish but I need results, and fast.'

'But what has Sean Martin got to do with this case? Apart from the canal, what's the link?'

'Peter Box tried to claim responsibility for Rosie's murder when Sean Martin was awaiting trial.'

'What? The case where Sean Martin ended up being innocent?'

Dan nodded. 'That's right, except that he isn't.'

'Who isn't what?'

'Sean Martin *isn't* innocent.'

'Hang on, you made me sound wrong when I said that.'

'Your opinion is based on what? Media reports? Mine is on more than that: he told Pat Molloy he'd done it.'

'No way.'

'After Pat got him acquitted, Sean told him that he'd hidden the murder weapon.'

'Shit, Dan, this is *huge*. Imagine what the newspapers would make of it.'

'I can't think about that. I've got to get through the Peter Box trial and somehow make this Sean Martin angle work, because there isn't much else going for him. It might explain his silence but that is all, but that's how these cases work sometimes. Attack each part of the prosecution case until it all crumbles, but it won't work at all if I can't prove Sean Martin's guilt.'

'Because the jury will think Peter Box killed Rosie too, and then he has no chance.'

'That's pretty much it.'

'Didn't Peter's confession come out in the Sean Martin trial?'

'Sean didn't want to use it. He said it was probably just some fantasy and didn't want to look desperate by throwing all the blame Peter's way. He didn't want an innocent man to take the blame.'

'What a hero. What are you going to do, then?' And then she started to nod as it dawned on her. 'You're going to suggest that Sean Martin killed Lizzie Barnsley too, but you've got to prove he killed his stepdaughter to make it credible.'

'That's too far, but if I'm honest, I don't really know what to do. This grand idea arose today and the damn trial starts tomorrow.'

'Why are you being so timid? After all, if you're going to accuse Sean Martin of Rosie's murder, why not go all the way and accuse him of killing Lizzie too? If the jurors hate him enough for getting away with murdering his stepdaughter, they might be prepared to think he killed Lizzie too.'

'You've got ambition, but there's no link between Lizzie's murder and Sean Martin.'

'There is: Peter Box. Sean Martin was accused of killing some-one, and he more or less told Pat that he was guilty. Peter told Pat that he was the guilty one. Well, they can't both be guilty. Or can they? And if they are linked somehow to the murder of Sean Martin's stepdaughter, they might be linked to Lizzie's murder.'

Dan frowned as he thought about that. 'I see where you're coming from but it's a real stretch. I don't even know if Sean Martin was ever a suspect in Lizzie's case or if he's got an alibi.'

'Start there, then.'

Dan thought about that, and his smile grew. 'You're good at this. I'll speak to him. If nothing else, it might spook him, and we might see what he does. I worked on his case when I was a trainee, so he'll remember me enough to talk to. I'll find out where he was on New Year's Eve too, the night that Lizzie died. That part should be easy, because everyone remembers where they spent New Year's Eve. We can check it out.'

'How will you get him to answer your questions? He's not just going to confess to you that he killed his stepdaughter and tell you where he hid the murder weapon.'

'By pretending I'm not asking them, of course. I'll knock on his front door for a friendly chat about Pat. If he offers a drink, I'm accepting.'

'Why?'

'It will buy me fifteen minutes, maybe more.' Dan paused. 'You've changed. We've had this conversation before, about how I can't go about ruining people's lives, throwing around wild accusations, just to get an acquittal.'

'If he murdered his stepdaughter, he's got this coming to him. But if you're rattling his cage, you can't spend your time watch-ing him. What's important is how he reacts, not what he says to you, so you need someone he doesn't know.' She grinned. 'That's me.'

'I knew you were the right fit.'

'We'll drive up in separate cars. You speak to him, and I'll hang around. Something else first, though.'

'What's that?'

'You promised food.'

'I know just the place. Come on.'

As they stood up, Jayne said, 'Didn't he kill his stepdaughter to stop her from accusing him of abusing her?'

'That was the subtle inference, the press hinting at it, although it was never said out loud during the trial.'

'If that's the case, what theory can we give about why he'd kill Lizzie Barnsley? That's like a random attack, not a secret he's trying to cover up.'

'Yes, a good point.'

'And what's the big deal with Sean Martin for Peter Box? Why would he get involved?'

'I'm hoping he'll tell me in the morning.'

'Unless he was telling the truth, of course, which means that not only will you free a killer, you'll also ruin the reputation of a man trying to rebuild his life.'

Dan pulled on his lip. Now that she'd said it, he realised she was right.

'The law is a dirty place sometimes. Come on, you said you wanted food. We'll stop on the way, but I need to decide about Sean Martin.'

Eight

Dan stopped in a lay-by close to the village where Sean Martin lived, on one of the roads that cut through the hills. Jayne pulled in just behind him.

As she joined him in his car, he pointed to the snack van sitting at the end of the lay-by. 'You said you were hungry.'

Jayne squinted towards it. 'If I'm honest, I expected a little more.'

'If I call it al fresco, will that make it better? Come on.'

They were soon tucking into bacon sandwiches, sitting on a bench in silence. A low cloud blotted out the sun, but it was a typical Sunday in the countryside, the roads quiet, a group of ramblers heading towards a footpath into some woods further along, the peace disturbed only by the hum of the occasional passing car.

'Okay,' said Jayne eventually. 'This was a good idea.' She screwed up the paper wrapping and shoved it into her coat pocket. 'You ready for your visit to Sean Martin's house?'

Dan chewed as he thought about it. 'Yes. And then we need to find out more about him.'

'What about searching for the murder weapon?'

'We don't know where it is. He told Pat that it was by the western corner of something, just under the surface, below a mason's mark?'

'A what?'

'It's what stonemasons used to mark houses with back in the old days, like a personal signature, but he didn't say where that was, and he's hardly going to tell me. If we're doing this, we need to find a smarter way to go about it.'

'You're right, I'm sorry. Like you, I'm just trying to think it through.'

'Ideas are good, except time isn't on our side.'

'Who's the senior officer?'

Dan gave her a wry smile. 'You'll like this.'

'Let me guess: Tracy Murdoch.'

'One and the same.'

Dan and Jayne had become involved in a murder case the year before where Tracy Murdoch was the senior officer. She'd been an ally at times, but she fought hard as well, and Dan knew that she'd be thorough in investigating any last-minute madcap theories from him.

'What about going back to Murdoch with what you've been told? I bet the police don't think Sean Martin is innocent.'

'She isn't going to dig around an old case just because of what Sean once said to his solicitor. It doesn't matter what they think; it will have gone down as a loss and they'll have moved on.'

'What are you going to do as I watch Sean?'

'I'll go see an ex-copper about Sean's case. You can always count on a retired copper when it comes to talking about the job because they all miss it, and he'll have time.'

'You know who to see?'

'I called Pat while you were queuing for the sarnies. He gave me a name and a phone number. I get the impression that Pat has been setting this up for me, knowing that I'll go looking.'

She stood up. 'Come on then. Like you say, time is limited.'

It wasn't a long drive. Dan parked outside Sean Martin's cottage. Jayne was parked just out of sight, around the corner, and she would pull up closer to his cottage once Dan was back in his car, to watch what happened after he left.

As he stepped outside, he fastened his jacket. The wind blew harsh and cold now that they were out of the shelter of the valley. Highford was spread out in the distance, bordered by tall barren hills and brown heather rather than by the brightness of grass and trees.

Sean Martin lived in a double-fronted stone house opposite a granite cross that marked the centre of the village of Cranston, with an old white pub next to it. From the cars lined up outside, the Sunday lunch trade was going well.

The bright red cottage door was ringed with roses. Dan rapped the brass knocker and stood back. He waited a few seconds and then rapped again before there were footsteps on the other side.

A woman opened the door. Tall and athletic, her hair long and dark over sharp cheekbones and deep green eyes. 'Yes?' Her tone was flustered, her cheeks flushed.

'Hello, can I speak to Sean?'

'Who are you?'

'I'm Dan Grant. I work for Pat Molloy.'

She pursed her lips at that before turning back into the house and bellowing up the stairs, 'Sean, someone for you.'

She went back into the house. 'You might as well come in,' she said, indicating with a flick of her hand which room he should wait in. 'I'll put the kettle on. Coffee?'

He went into a dark room that was made no brighter by the glow of a standard lamp in one corner, nor by the light from the windows, even though it was the middle of the day. There were country paintings on the wall; a fox hunt, some trees. It wasn't those that grabbed the attention, however; it was the filing cabinets along one wall and the framed newspaper clippings: miscarriages of justice overturned, Sean the spokesman in each one.

There were footsteps on the stairs and then Sean Martin appeared in the doorway.

He was bigger than Dan remembered. He was in his mid-forties now, his hair greying but still full and long for his age. His stomach pushed against the buttons of his checked shirt.

Dan went towards him and held his hand out. 'Hi, you might remember me. I'm Dan Grant from Molloys.'

'Oh, hi,' Sean said and shook the proffered hand, although it took a few seconds for recognition to filter in. 'You were helping out the barrister during the trial.'

'I was. I was just a young trainee back then. Twelve years ago now. I've never forgotten the trial, even though there have been so many since. I was a bit skinnier then, a little fresher-faced, but I've stayed with Pat. He did a good job for you.' Dan smiled. 'I feel like I'm meeting a celebrity.'

'Oh, hardly,' Sean said. 'Please, sit down.'

Dan looked around.

'Here, let me.' Sean moved some papers that had been piled on top of two swivel chairs onto the floor. 'Can I get you a drink?'

'The woman who let me in is making me one.' Dan settled into one chair. 'Sorry, I don't know her name.'

'That's Trudy, my wife.' Sean leaned against a filing cabinet. 'Things have changed since I got out. What can I do for you?'

'It's about Pat Molloy.'

His eyes narrowed just for a moment, but then he smiled, like he'd flicked a switch. 'Yes, Pat. A good man. I owe him so much. How is he?'

Trudy brought in a tray with two mugs on it. Dan thanked her as he took one. Sean received his in silence.

Dan sipped from his mug but leaned forward, his expression darker. He lowered his tone and said, 'That's why I'm here. He's got cancer and the prognosis isn't good.'

'I'm so sorry to hear that.' Sean's face showed concern.

'I'm thinking of doing something for him, like a party or a tribute, but I don't know what. I thought you might want to be involved, because of your profile and what Pat did for you. And you've put it to good use.' Dan gestured towards the cabinets.

'Pat taught me the value of fighting for the right causes. I owe him my freedom, so I try to pay it forward in other ways. He is responsible for every one of these successes, indirectly.'

'There you have it. That's the speech.' Dan raised his mug in salute. 'Do you think you'd say a few words? I'm sure it would mean a lot to him. He wants to go out with a real bang and, well, you were pretty much his biggest bang of all.'

'I bet he does.' Sean took another sip, his gaze never leaving Dan. 'Yes, I'd love to say a few words for him. I don't mean to be indelicate, but how long has he got? I've got a lot of events on at the moment and for the foreseeable future, with my book having just come out.'

'Book?'

'My autobiography. I didn't want to be accused of cashing in on Rosie's murder, but I've got bills to pay, just like everyone else.'

'I'll look out for it. As for Pat, they're saying a few months, maybe. Perhaps not even that. He's been getting bad for a while. At first, I thought he was just getting old. Like forgetting things. He remembers his old cases, can reminisce all day, and lawyers love to trade war stories, but the more recent stuff?' Dan shook his head. 'It's like it never happened. Take New Year's Eve. We were talking about it last week, and he couldn't remember where he spent the New Year. I mean, everyone remembers that, don't they? I know I can. Watching Jools Holland with a bottle of wine, like most years. Not very exciting, I know, but I still remember it. I'm sure you do too. And, you're a writer now, and you writers must get invited to lots of parties?'

'It's not the life you think, but yes, I remember it. I spent New Year's eve here, with Trudy. After prison, there is more pleasure in the simple things.'

'You see how easy it is, but Pat couldn't even think of that.'

'I've had the prison experience though, and it makes you appreciate the people who are actually important. Family, friends, loved ones.'

'Any room for lawyers on that list?'

'I regard Pat as a friend, even if I don't pop by the office. He was my lawyer, but he went further than that.'

Dan pointed to the walls again. 'How's the organisation going? What's it called again?'

'Innocent Out. It's going well, getting more volunteers all the time. Mostly from the university, students motivated by justice. Most people get jaded when their studies end, or become distracted by a career, family, money. Get them when they're young, however, and they see the cases for what they are, a stench, and they're prepared to fight for them. Justice is important.'

'That's Pat's greatest attribute. He's never stopped believing in justice, about doing what was right, whatever the cost.'

Sean nodded, although his eyes had narrowed again. He straightened himself. 'Thank you for stopping by. I'm sorry we can't talk for longer, but you caught me by surprise. Is that all?'

'No, you've helped. Thank you. Pat will be so touched that you'll speak up.'

Dan went towards the door. They shook hands again, Dan watching him more closely this time.

Dan didn't look back as he got into his car. He drove down the hill and stopped behind Jayne.

She wound down her window as he walked to her car. 'How was it?'

'Weird. It felt like we were circling each other. Let's see how he reacts now, because if he's suspicious of me, he'll behave differently. We don't have the luxury of time, so if he's going to give himself away, he needs to get a move on.' He paused for a moment, and added, 'You know, it's strange. When I shook his hand at the beginning, his hand was dry and firm, a good robust handshake. But at the end? He seemed quite different. He realised that I knew something. I could see it in his posture, his eyes, his expression. He was more cautious and defensive.

I really thought I'd rattled him, but his handshake ...' He stopped and looked thoughtful.

'What about his handshake?'

'It was just the same. Dry and firm. If he suspected I know something, he didn't panic.' He grimaced. 'That worries me.'

*

Trudy appeared behind Sean as he watched Dan Grant walk down the street. His jaw was clenched, his shoulders tense, standing in the gloom of the room so that he couldn't be seen if Grant looked back.

'What did he want?'

Sean didn't move for a few seconds, until he took a deep breath and looked towards her. 'It's nothing to worry about.'

'I need to know it all. That's the deal with us. I need to know that we're okay.'

Sean rubbed his eyes. 'Trudy, it's fine. It was about Pat Molloy, that's all. He's ill, has cancer, and the firm wants to throw him a tribute or dinner, and as I'm his most notorious client, I get the privilege of giving a speech.'

'And it takes a personal visit to do that? He could have phoned you, or written to you. Instead, he's come all the way out here.' She shook her head. 'There's something you're not telling me.'

He grabbed her by the chin and glared into her eyes. 'I've told you everything.'

She waited for the rise of his temper to pass, because that's how it came, in a snap.

He pushed her away so that she stumbled into a chair. He went into the kitchen as she swallowed her anger, tears prickling her eyes.

'Don't walk away,' she shouted after him. She listened as the fridge opened, followed by the familiar clink of a beer bottle.

She closed her eyes and pinched her nose. The air became heavy.

It was starting again.

Nine

Jayne drove up the hill to park closer to Sean Martin's house.

The cottage was nicer than she anticipated. She hadn't been expecting him to be doing quite so well, living in a home that struck her as being very desirable.

There was no movement in the house for a few minutes. She had her phone to her ear, to make it look as if she'd pulled over to take a call, but her eyes were fixed on the house. Then the front door opened and a man came out.

She recognised him immediately. It always gave a strange jolt to see someone familiar from the news; they never looked quite how she expected, usually smaller or older. In Sean Martin's case, he looked bigger.

Jayne's memories of the newspaper articles and television coverage were of a man seemingly bewildered, shrunken. She had a vague recollection of Pat Molloy on the court steps, speaking into the microphones, with Dictaphones thrust in front of him, thanking the jurors for their courage. Sean had stepped forward and spoken with less certainty, his voice breaking with emotion, his eyes flitting from reporter to reporter as he pleaded for the real killer to be found. The Sean Martin she was watching climb into a black Hyundai was very different. He was bolder, larger, as if he'd rediscovered himself.

She threw her phone on to the passenger seat as the Hyundai pulled out of its parking space, but waited until it was some distance away before starting her engine. She didn't want him to realise he was being followed.

He took the road to Highford, **driving** right past her. She turned her car around and went after him.

His progress was steady as he cruised through the hedge-lined country roads, getting lower in the valley, a canal glinting below and getting closer, open fields on either side broken by the occasional wood. If he'd spotted Jayne following him, it wasn't making him speed up.

Just before they reached the edge of Highford, the terraced streets visible, he turned into a garden centre car park and drove up to a large gate at the opposite end of the car park. Jayne followed him but parked amongst the cars belonging to customers. She watched as Sean entered a code into a keypad by the gate, which made it swing open, and in he went.

She'd driven past the garden centre before but had never been in as she didn't have a garden. She made a note of the time and took some pictures, before climbing out and pretending to browse the outdoor plants by the entrance doors. There were racks of bedding plants further away, and she was able to conceal herself behind one and peer beyond the gate Sean's car had gone through.

The gate seemed to be an entrance to some sort of compound separated from the garden centre car park by a high chain-link fence. She could make out small structures on the other side of the fence, like brightly painted sheds, green and red, blue and yellow, with writing on some. It was when she saw the gleam of water that she realised what she was looking at. Canal boats. It was a marina for narrowboats.

Sean sauntered along the dock, his head visible over the top of the cabins lined up in rows, until he disappeared out of sight.

She stayed where she was until the gentle putter of a diesel engine broke the peace. Sean was visible again, standing high as a boat moved away from the dock.

Jayne moved away from the rack. Sean had managed to evade her this time. There'd be other times, though, she'd make sure of that.

Ten

Dan pushed on the shop door. A small bell tinkled as it swung open. His nose twitched at the unmistakable smell of dust and old paper. It mingled with the aroma of pipe tobacco, warm and comforting somehow, like going back in time. Books were piled high on shelves, divided into genres but crammed in untidily, the edges loose and ragged. There were only two aisles and he had to shuffle along them sideways.

Dan was in a second-hand bookshop in Melbrook, a village a few miles from Highford. It had once been just a cluster of cottages by a bend in a river, part of a floodplain away from the hills, but new developments had attracted lawyers and accountants and those who wanted country living with all the mod cons.

The shop was at the end of a row, the interior dark, book covers in the window faded by the sun. The only other shop open was a convenience store further along, the sign bright, out of place amongst the grey slate roofs. The others were all in darkness, remnants of small village life from decades gone by and now part of the lifestyle craved for by the newly arrived professionals; a butcher, a bakery, a greengrocer, mostly organic.

He didn't spot the proprietor until a small cloud of tobacco smoke appeared in the air.

Dan peered around the end of the row of shelves. In the back corner of the shop, a man was sitting in a threadbare old armchair, stuffing leaking from one of the arms, the other worn out to a shine and coffee-stained. His grey beard was stained brown under his nose, his hair unkempt.

'Bob Marshall? Former Detective Chief Inspector Marshall?'

The man smiled, his eyes warm behind thick lenses, his teeth clenched around the stem of a black pipe.

'That's me.'

Dan produced a business card and handed it over. 'I want to talk to you about the Sean Martin case.'

Bob Marshall's eyes narrowed. 'Molloys. That was his defence firm. If this is about compensation, I'm not interested.'

'It's not about compensation.'

'And I don't call it that, the Sean Martin case, because it makes it about him. As far as I'm concerned, it's the Rosie Smith case.' He gestured with his pipe towards a curtain hiding an alcove. 'There's a stool through there. Bring it over and sit down.'

'Not the usual kind of retirement for a senior detective,' Dan said, as he sat. The kitchen stool was much higher than the armchair, so he found himself looking down at the older man.

'I like to think that I wasn't the usual kind of detective.' He looked around his shop. 'I ran this place when I was in the job. I've always loved books. Back then, it was a fun little sideline, and I sold new books, too, but the supermarkets killed that. My wife helped out when I was on duty, but, well . . .' His eyes clouded. 'She's gone now.'

'I'm sorry to hear that.'

He shrugged. 'It's all right. She was sleeping with some sales rep. I caught them one day, right behind that curtain. In fact, it might have even been over that stool.'

Dan fought the urge to stand. 'I thought you meant she was dead.'

He chuckled. 'No. She's living in our old house. I live in the flat above the shop now, and spend my days down here, reading, running my own little bookshop, just like I always wanted.'

'Do you sell much? I can't imagine there's much passing trade.'

'I do it for the company. People call in, and I get some collectors dropping by, looking for first editions and rarities.' He took a long pull on his pipe and, through the smoke, said, 'But you're not here about my marriage or business. Sean Martin is your reason. Why is that?'

'I've got a murder trial starting tomorrow and Sean Martin's name has cropped up. I'm just checking it out, but it's hard, because he's innocent as far as the rest of the world is concerned. Except, you know more than the rest of the world.'

'Too much, perhaps.'

'I'm still curious.'

'That's not enough. Tell me about your murder case and why it's connected to Sean Martin.'

'Peter Box,' Dan said. 'Accused of murdering Lizzie Barnsley by the canal in Highford in the early hours of New Year's Day. His DNA has been found on the heel of her shoe.'

'And how does he explain that?'

'He doesn't. He's opted for silence, even with me.'

'Are you all right to tell me this? I thought you lawyers got all protective about what your client tells you.'

'I don't think it counts when he hasn't said anything.'

'What's the link with Sean Martin?'

'I can't tell you that. I've come across some information about Peter in connection with Sean's case, but I won't go any further with it if Sean Martin is innocent. I don't want my client implicated in Rosie's murder.'

Bob looked surprised. 'You think Peter Box might have killed Rosie?'

'Do you?'

'No, I don't,' Bob said. 'I know who killed Rosie.'

'Sean Martin?'

'Bullseye.'

'You get my point, then. So, what makes you think Sean murdered her?'

He scowled. 'It's what I know that's important, not what I think, and what I know is that Sean Martin killed his step-daughter.'

'He was cleared, though.'

'Since when did an acquittal mean innocence?' Bob waved Dan's card. 'Your firm blew a lot of smoke, but I saw it in his eyes. It's always in the eyes. When he appeared distressed, it was faked, never any tears. You can always spot them in the press conferences because the relatives who are innocent do their best to get through them. They don't always manage it, but they try their hardest because it's all about getting the information out there. It's a plea for help and they know they have to do it clearly.'

'And the guilty ones?'

'They cry and wail and contort, because the whole performance is about convincing everyone they're innocent. Sean Martin was the same. He clutched a handkerchief and pretended to sob, completely overdid it. He made himself out to be the victim, not Rosie. You watch that press conference again and it was Rosie's mother who was the strong one, speaking slowly, her voice breaking. Sean was the one who couldn't cope. He was different afterwards, though, once the cameras had stopped.'

'At the retrial, there was an expert witness, however, who put a different slant on the evidence about the blood mist.'

'You know as well as I do that you can get an expert to say what you want if you look hard enough for the right expert. Charlatans, the lot of them. All your guy said was that the blood mist *could* have been from her final breaths when Sean Martin held her, but that doesn't mean it *wasn't* mist caused by the murder itself. They're all just possibilities, opinions, so it all comes down to what you think about Sean Martin, and I know how I feel.'

'Any suspicions about the murder weapon? Where it might be?'

Bob shook his head. 'Whatever he used, it's long gone. That's my fault for not keeping him at the scene, but he wasn't a suspect at first. He was found cradling her, so how were we to know it was all an act? Whatever he had, he disposed of it.'

'That's why I'm here.'

Bob sat forward. 'What's going on?'

'What would you do if you could locate the murder weapon?'

'What?'

'You heard.'

'How?'

'Someone has given me a hint as to its whereabouts.'

'Who?'

'I can't tell you.'

Bob's eyes were animated, no longer the genial bookshop owner. 'You've got to do something about this.'

'I'm trying, but my trial starts tomorrow and I can't spend my days with a spade, looking for whatever Sean Martin hid all those years ago.'

'What do you want me to do?'

'Help me out. Do you have any idea where the murder weapon might be?'

Bob shook his head. 'Nothing. If I'd had one, I'd have looked.'

'What about a mason's mark?'

'I'm sorry, nothing at all. Have you spoken to his wife?'

'I've just been to his house. She didn't seem pleased to see me.'

'No, I mean Rosie's mother, Karen. She left him after he was convicted. She's still convinced he killed her daughter. She's never spoken publicly about any of it, not since the press conference, but she might help you out. They were together at the time.'

'Why would she do that?'

'Because she hates him for taking her daughter away.' He reached for a scrap of paper and wrote down an address. 'She comes to see me sometimes, and we talk over a coffee. A word to the wise though: don't go yourself. She knows that Sean's lawyers conned the court to get him free. It doesn't matter how you dress it up; for her, you're part of the problem.'

Dan took the paper. 'And does the name Peter Box mean anything? Did he ever come up in the investigation?'

'Never heard the name before.' Bob sat forward in his chair. 'If you find anything, tell me. I've waited too long to see him pay; Karen too. Justice is more than just a verdict.'

Eleven

Jayne was still in her car near to the garden centre when Dan called her.

'How is it going?'

She looked at the half-full car park. 'He's gone for a sail in a bloody narrowboat.'

'A pleasure cruise?'

'Looks like he owns one. He keeps it in a marina by a garden centre.'

'Leave him sailing, then. Can you speak to Rosie's mother instead? She's called Karen.' He reeled off an address. 'Just keep quiet about where you're from. She blames Pat, and me indirectly, I suppose, for Sean getting out.'

'What am I trying to find out?'

'Follow your instincts. She won't know where the weapon is hidden, or else she'd have spoken out, but she knows Sean Martin. What he does, where he goes.'

'Will do. And what about you?'

'I'll go back to my trial preparation. We'll talk later.' And he rang off.

*

It wasn't a long journey to Karen Smith's home, a small detached house at the end of a cul-de-sac on the edge of Highford. It was unassuming, shadowed by trees and hemmed in by the buildings and cars around it, almost as if the place had been chosen as a hideaway.

Jayne was nervous; she knew there was grief here and she was about to trample all over it. Sean appeared to have done quite well out of killing Rosie, whereas all Karen Smith had left was a hole in her life.

The door opened before she reached it. A woman stood in the doorway, her hair cut into a grey bob, her arms folded.

'Karen Smith?'

'Are you the press? I know Sean has got a book out, but if you're here about him, and a glory piece, I'm not interested.'

'No, it's not that. I'm a private investigator, working for a client who's trying to prove that Sean murdered your daughter.'

She put her head back in surprise. 'That's quite an opening. Who's the client?'

'I can't tell you, I'm sorry. I've been sworn to secrecy.'

Jayne felt bad about the slight bend in the truth, but Karen thought for a moment before stepping aside. 'You'd better come in.'

Jayne went along a hallway lined by wooden flooring and into a living room with sagging sofas, candle jars dotted around the room, their sides blackened and the walls bearing dark streaks from their smoke. Framed photos adorned the walls, all showing a girl growing up, from baby to teenager. They were starting to fade, which made them more poignant somehow, a future snatched away.

As they sat down, Karen said, 'Why should I trust you? I'm pretty washed out of trust, you see. I trusted Sean and he took away the most precious thing I had. His whole life was a sham: his time with me; how he was with Rosie. One big lie.'

'Why was it a lie?'

'He was playing at happy families, except none of it was true. Have you seen who he's with now? You must have read the press stuff, all about lovely Trudy, the childhood sweetheart who never lost faith in him. Except that she never stopped being there, throughout our marriage. You remember what Princess Diana said about her marriage, that there was always a third person there? That's how it was with us.'

'He was seeing Trudy when you were married?'

'He didn't have to be running around with Trudy for her to be there, because she was always in here.' She slapped her chest with her hand. 'The love he couldn't walk away from.' She screwed up her face. 'Don't make me laugh. She was never there during his trials, but she popped up as soon as he was freed, thinking there was money to be made. Who cares about me though?'

'What makes you think he still loved her?'

'Come on, I know you're young, but you know how it is with old sweethearts. When you talk about them with your current partner, you slate them, because you want your new man to think that there's nothing to worry about. And you're supposed to be able to make little digs about your partner's ex, because that's just how it is.' She snorted a laugh. 'I couldn't do that with Trudy. God, no. Not ever. If I ever said anything against her, he'd defend her, couldn't stop himself. It always felt like he really wanted to be with her but couldn't, for whatever reason. That he was somehow stuck with me.'

'Were they having an affair?'

'I don't know. Why does it matter now?'

'Because the whole point of the case was that he murdered Rosie to cover something up. What do you think it was?'

'All I know is that I'm the one who bears the guilt that I didn't watch him enough. I should have realised what was going on. I mean, why did he pick me? Look at me compared to Trudy. You don't have to be polite. I'm frumpy, plump and quiet, a single mother. Was that the reason? That it was never about me but about Rosie? I've lost more hours of sleep than I can count going over it all in my head. Were there nights when he wasn't in my bed because he'd crept into her bedroom? Do you know how it feels to think that and then realise that I could have stopped it, but I was blinded by love?'

'And you had no suspicions?'

'I'd have stopped him if I had. He deceived me. I shouldn't say this to you, because you've got so much of your life ahead, but men are just pigs. That's how it feels. My first husband walked out on me not long after Rosie was born, preferred other beds to mine. Then Sean came along, and look what he did.'

Jayne winced. 'I wish I could offer some comfort, but my past isn't so great.'

'My mum used to say, "Don't hang around waiting for a good one, because there aren't enough of them to go round." She was wrong. Don't grab the first one that comes along. Look how it ended for me.'

'Why do you think he killed Rosie?'

Her eyes narrowed. 'Why do you think he did? Because that's why you're here. You said you're trying to prove that he did it, so what's your theory?'

'I haven't got one. I'm just digging around for now.'

'But why?'

Jayne paused as she worked out what to say. 'I'm working for a defence firm, and we think there might be a link with our case and Rosie's murder.'

'What kind of link?'

Jayne knew the answer was that she had no idea, but she wasn't prepared to admit that to the person most affected by Sean's case. 'I'd love to tell you but there's the client confidentiality thing.'

'Promise me one thing though: that you're not working for him. For Sean.'

'I can promise you that much.'

Karen sat back. 'That will have to do, then. I know nothing can bring Rosie back, but I'll help no one who wants to help him. He killed her. I knew it as soon as the police accused him, that it all made sense, just from how he was. I've never doubted that.'

'What stands out the most?'

'His coldness,' she said, nodding. 'He's dead inside.'

'Was someone called Lizzie Barnsley one of Rosie's friends? Perhaps your daughter might have known her from school? She'd have been about twelve when Rosie died, so they wouldn't have been in the same class, but –'

'It doesn't sound familiar, but I can check her stuff. Hang on.'

Karen left the room and returned shortly afterwards, holding a large black photograph album, the sort that you add pages to, a relic from the days before digital cameras.

She put it down on the table at the other end of the room. As Jayne walked over, Karen turned the first page.

'That's Rosie as a baby,' and there was a picture of Karen looking much fresher and younger, beaming from a hospital bed.

Karen clenched her jaw and turned instead to the pages at the back. 'I'm sorry, you haven't come here for my nostalgia.'

Jayne reached out to put her hand on Karen's wrist. 'I'd love to spend a day with you, I owe you that much at least, but I'm pushed for time today.'

Karen started flicking back through the pages, each shiny with a cellophane cover. 'These are what I saved after she died. Not the cuttings about her murder but the tributes from her friends.'

The pages were filled with small notes and clippings, some photographs. Karen leaned closer, trying to read what was on the pages. 'I can't see the name Lizzie anywhere and I don't remember hearing it. I'm sorry.'

'No need to apologise, and I'm sorry for taking up your time.'

'It's never a waste of time to think about Rosie. But who is this Lizzie?'

Jayne's mind raced, not wanting to reveal her link to Molloys. 'Oh, just a name that was mentioned in relation to Sean. One more thing: was there ever anywhere special that Sean used to like to go?'

'He spent a lot of time on his boat. Too much time, as if he used it to get away from us. I hardly ever went on it because he said it was his retreat. You know how men like to have their own special place, like a shed. The boat was his and he didn't like me on it. He used to live on it before he met me, although he spent most of his time at Trudy's house. I know they've got a fancy place in the countryside now but, back then, she lived in a small house near that mosque you can see from just about everywhere.' She scowled. 'Yeah, they've done all right out of Rosie's murder.'

'He never talked about a certain place, then?'

'Thinking back, he didn't say much to me at all.'

'What about a mason's mark? Have you ever heard him use that phrase?'

Karen shook her head. 'Never.'

Jayne was about to leave when she glanced back at the photograph album and she spotted a newspaper clipping. 'What's that?'

Karen passed the book over.

In the black-and-white picture, six teenage girls were sitting in a circle on a patch of grass, each holding a candle. It was a vigil, their faces lit by the small flickering flames. Their names were underneath.

'Are these Rosie's friends?'

'Yes. They were so good to me, so strong. It was such a comfort to know that there were so many people who'd loved her.'

Jayne jotted down their names and thanked Karen again for her time.

Just before she left, Karen scribbled her number on the back of an envelope. 'If you hear anything that proves Sean killed my girl, let me know.'

Jayne made the promise, and she felt she was making some progress as she left the house.

For now though, it was time to report back.

Twelve

Jayne was looking in the fridge for wine as Dan put the takeaway cartons on the kitchen surface. She smiled when she saw a bottle of white on its side at the bottom.

'You always get the good stuff,' she said, pulling it out.

'Not too much of that. I've got a murder trial starting tomorrow, remember.'

'Yeah, and we've got to update each other. What do you suit-and-tie types call it? Debrief.'

He laughed. 'What about my trial preparation?'

'Come on, I know you. And what is there to prepare anyway? You told me the defence case was all about pulling apart the prosecution case. If you don't know the holes by now, you never will.'

'And what progress are we discussing? I've found out that the cop who arrested him thinks Sean's guilty. How far does that get me?'

'Don't forget Rosie's mother. She's convinced, and I've got details of Rosie's friends too. They might tell me something useful.' Jayne lifted out the bottle. 'Shall I pour?'

He was about to object, but when she raised her eyebrows, he said, 'Okay, get it open.'

Jayne collected a couple of glasses as Dan spooned the food onto plates.

As they ate, Jayne asked, 'Is there any CCTV in Lizzie's case?'

'Quite a bit, but it's just cameras sweeping the town centre and dotted along the canal. I asked for the hour leading up to when Lizzie left the pub and the hour after.'

'I thought the prosecution didn't have to hand over the stuff they aren't using unless it undermines their case.'

'Yes, usually, but I persuaded a judge to order the prosecution to hand it over. The CCTV might show other witnesses, for example, and there's no more reliable eyewitness than a camera.'

'And you've watched it?'

'I have, and it never gets interesting. Six cameras, two hours from each. I did a camera a day, just to stay fresh.'

'Perhaps we should look again, now that Sean Martin has come into the picture?'

'I don't understand.'

'There's a link between Sean Martin and Peter Box. According to everyone, Sean Martin killed Rosie by the same canal.'

'According to everyone except a jury of twelve people who heard all the evidence.'

Jayne stopped eating for a moment. 'Are you telling me that juries never acquit people who really did it?'

When he didn't respond straightaway, Jayne added, 'And you can include me in that answer if you like.'

'You know I don't think you're a killer. The jury got it right.' He shrugged. 'But yeah, I get your point. The jury will find it easy in this case though. After all, how did Peter's blood end up on her heel?'

'Maybe he was trying to save her from Sean Martin and got caught up in the fight, and now he's scared? Scared of Sean? Scared of people not believing him, because it sounds far-fetched?'

'There's your problem: it *is* far-fetched, and I can't invent a scenario. It's got to come from Peter, and right now he's not telling me anything.'

'Shouldn't we still look though? You've always banged on about the burden of proof, that it's about creating doubt. You don't have to prove that Sean Martin killed Lizzie Barnsley, or why he would have done. If you can prove that he did kill his stepdaughter and that it's possible he killed Lizzie, you'll have something.'

He shook his head. 'I see where you're coming from, but it's a waste of time. We're doing this to explain Peter's silence, nothing more.'

'I can watch the CCTV, if you want. You can do whatever you need to do.'

Dan sighed. 'Okay, if it makes you feel better.' He pointed with his fork to a brown envelope on a cushion next to the papers he'd been going through earlier that day. 'The discs are in there.'

Jayne skimmed through the discs and loaded the first one into the DVD player. They settled on the sofa, silent as they finished their food, both staring at the screen.

She glanced across at Dan as he watched it, his eyes fixed on the footage, just a grainy image of a badly lit empty street. The camera turned regularly to one of the four static positions, every fifteen seconds, and occasionally the operator would spot something and the camera would zoom in: a small crowd of people outside a taxi office or a group crossing the road in fancy dress. The camera would always linger on groups of young women dressed in clothes that were unfeasibly skimpy for a cold night in December.

Despite the mundane footage, Dan's gaze was intense, always looking out for a detail he might have missed.

As they finished their food, their plates on the floor, Jayne said, 'You're right, it's dull, but you've got to remember that I spend my time hanging around outside peoples' houses, waiting to photograph cheating spouses.'

'We've many hours to watch before we finish.'

'Yeah, but here it's warm, with toilet facilities, so I'll get comfortable.' She swung her legs onto the sofa and laid them across Dan's lap. He raised his glass before they both turned back to the television.

Jayne suppressed a smile. It felt good to share an evening with someone, even though it made her feel needy. She'd promised herself that she would never rely on a man again, but that didn't mean she couldn't enjoy the warmth of another human being.

They'd been watching for around thirty minutes, Dan's arms across her legs, when he said, 'You seen anything yet?'

She shook her head. 'I'm worried that it might catch me stumbling along the street.'

'A wild night?'

'Just another one that I can't remember.'

He tipped his glass towards the screen. 'This is the bit you need to watch.'

'Why, what is it?'

'Just watch.'

The camera did its usual pan and settled on the bright lights of a pub car park, the cobbles gleaming. A figure tottered into the car park, walking quickly on high heels. Someone confronted her, a man, his body tensed. The camera zoomed in closer, the operator spotting the danger. They argued, both waving their arms.

Jayne gasped as the man lashed out with his fist.

The woman went to the ground, her handbag spewing cigarettes and tissues onto the cobbles. Some people intervened, pushing the man back. The woman picked herself up, her heels wobbling, before she shouted at him, her finger pointed.

He started towards her again, but the group of people moved to block his way. The woman turned and rushed out of the car park, wiping her nose, her hair dishevelled. Someone made as if to go after her but was called back to the group.

'That's Lizzie Barnsley,' Dan said. 'Her boyfriend is the bully. The police have this part as an exhibit, with Lizzie highlighted.'

Jayne sat up, swinging her legs off Dan, the warmth of the evening disappearing fast. This was a murder victim living out her last moments. Jayne was transfixed as Lizzie headed away from the bright lights, towards a street leading to the darkness of the canal towpath.

The man was being pushed back, his arms out and by his side, his anger obvious. Some of the women in the car park were shouting at him, jabbing their fingers, before being pulled back by some of the men in the crowd. After a few minutes, the darkness acquired a strobe effect as a police vehicle pulled into the car park, lights flashing. Two officers got out of the car and went over to him.

'There's his alibi,' Dan said. 'The boyfriend never left the car park and was taken away by the police. The camera stayed focused on him, and I understand why, but it meant that Lizzie was allowed to disappear into the darkness.'

NEIL WHITE | 84

Jayne stared at the screen. It was a terrible reminder that her evening was about more than food and wine. 'We might still see something though. Perhaps a particular vehicle circling. We know what we're looking for now, because we know Sean's car. A black Hyundai Tucson. I've got the reg number in my notebook.'

'And there's plenty more hours to look at.'

They both settled down to watch another hour of footage, Jayne's attention focused on the screen, always watching out for headlights, but her mind went back to Sean Martin's car on the drive. The black car. The number plate. The memory niggled her but she couldn't work out why.

Twenty minutes later, it came to her. The date. The car had been a new one. That's what had struck her, how Sean Martin was doing well for himself, a brand-new car outside that desirable cottage. But it was April. The plates last changed in March. The murder was during the opening minutes of the New Year. Whatever he had been driving when Lizzie died had been replaced.

'Hey, Dan.'

No answer.

She looked across. He was slumped to one side, his eyes closed, his breathing regular and deep. He looked cute, different from the man he tried to be in the courtroom. He seemed softer, more vulnerable somehow. She thought about waking him, but that could end up with her going home, and she didn't feel ready for her own cold bedroom and worn-out duvet.

She tiptoed out to fetch a blanket from the cupboard by his bedroom; she'd spent a few nights under it herself when working on other cases. She turned off the television and smiled to herself as she put the blanket over him.

His bedroom was just along the hallway. If he wasn't sleeping in there, it was a shame to waste it.

She closed the door and slipped under the covers once she'd stripped down to her T-shirt and knickers. His pillows smelled of him; the light musk of aftershave mixed with whatever fabric conditioner he used, and a soft scent that was just Dan.

She pulled the thick duvet around herself. It felt good to be working again.

*

Trudy raised the wine glass to her lips. It was cold, the liquid faint yellow in the light that strained from the bulb over the back door. The bottle was nearly empty, and she was already feeling the sway that told her she was drunk. That's how she preferred to end her evening sometimes. To blot things out.

She was sitting in a garden chair, a blanket around her shoulders, her feet propped up on a log. The hills behind their cottage were in darkness, just the edges in silhouette against the starry sky, a half-moon casting very little glow.

Sean had gone to bed, the steady stream of beer he'd put away during the evening sending him to sleep early. She preferred to drink in solitude, so that she could be away from his self-pity, his finger pointing and ranting. Booze didn't suit him, and he always looked back when he had too much. Their lost years, he called them.

She didn't go along with those thoughts. The years spent inside were his. She didn't have to count her own years alongside them. She'd lived those her own way, waiting outside while the world turned against him, but still her life had carried on.

She raised her glass to the stars. Leave the self-pity to him; she'd learned how to rise above that. She preferred the gentle glow of the booze and the uncertainty of where it would take her. Sometimes it was to laughter, thinking back on happier times, or at least her version of them. Other times, it was to darker memories, but she tried to shut those away.

The visitor earlier that day had unsettled her. Dan Grant. He'd come to her house, and that was the problem. Her eyes narrowed as the glass went to her mouth.

They'd built a life in the hills. No one was taking that away.

She huddled under the blanket a little more. Her mood was taking her back. She didn't want that. She knew where it led and what it meant, but at times it was hard to stop.

A smell could do it. Stale cigarettes and booze, or a certain hairspray.

She snapped her eyes open. She was letting herself sink. She didn't want that.

She threw the wine on the grass and tipped out the rest of the bottle. It was time to end the day.

She slammed the door as she went inside, the blanket left behind.

Thirteen

Jayne opened her eyes slowly. In the fog of her first thoughts, everything was unfamiliar. The pillow too soft, the bedding too heavy. There was someone else in the room with her, treading quietly.

She lifted her head and groaned. It was too early, the sunlight bright against the thin curtains. A mug of tea was placed next to her. As she looked up, one eye closed, her hair ragged across her face, she saw that Dan was in his suit already, with a bright white shirt and sober blue tie behind the black waistcoat, his hair still wet from the shower.

'Come on, we've got a full day ahead,' he said.

'What time is it?'

'Nearly eight. I'm heading out soon.'

'Okay, okay, I'm moving.' She swung her legs out of the bed, grabbing her tea from the side as she went towards the living room. 'Before you say it, I know I've looked better.'

She sat on the sofa and curled her legs up, cradling the mug in her hands. 'What's the plan?'

Dan went behind the kitchen counter. 'I go to court and start the murder trial.'

'Have you got enough?'

'As much as I'm ever going to have.'

'I'll speak to the other girls in that photograph, Rosie's old friends.'

Dan nodded. 'Good idea,' and then he smiled, but his eyes were filled with sadness. 'I'm doing this for Pat more than my client. If you dig around, I can at least tell him that we tried.'

'Both victims were killed near the same place just over twelve years apart, and in both cases there is a link to Peter Box. It's not a waste of time. I'll find out what car Sean Martin was driving on New Year's Eve.' Before Dan could reply, she added, 'The one he's got now is brand new, maybe only a month old. I realised that last night, but you'd dozed off by then.'

'So, we *were* wasting our time watching the footage?'

'I've got an idea about that. Let me do some digging before I say more.'

'Yeah, well, sorry about falling asleep. Yesterday was a long day.'

'Did you sleep in here last night?'

'No. I woke up around two and climbed in with you. Hope that was okay.'

'I didn't even notice.'

'You were too far gone.' He grabbed a jacket that was draped over a chair and collected a couple of folders that were on the table before picking up a key from the sideboard and lobbing it over. 'Lock up when you're done.'

'I might have a bath. Your place is warmer than mine.'

'Help yourself. But remember we've work to do.'

'Okay, Mr Serious. Let a girl wake up first.'

He went to the door, turning around as he opened it to say, 'Did you know that you snore?'

'No, get lost, I don't.'

'Only softly, but it was cute. Like a nasal whistle,' and he laughed.

She threw a cushion at him. 'Go to court.'

He shut the door before it landed, leaving her grinning after him.

Fourteen

Dan was walking towards the courthouse when he saw him.

The man was fifty metres away from the courthouse entrance, standing in a doorway, but Dan knew straightaway he was waiting for him. His gaze was direct, but he turned away as soon as Dan looked over.

He was in his sixties, Dan guessed, tall, dressed in a dirty black mac, the collar up even though the breeze was warm, his hair hidden under a tatty green baseball cap, his jeans clean and black, matching his V-neck jumper.

Dan clenched his jaw. There were always threats in his job. He helped bad people get away with bad things. It gave him friends in some of the darker corners of Highford, but it made him enemies too.

But this wasn't Highford. The Crown Court was in Langton, the city at the other end of a short motorway, a different environment to the daily grime of his local court. The city was the big noise, where barristers' chambers clustered around a Victorian park, grand high buildings with pillars by the doorway, and the courthouse was a large, stone monument in the city centre that overlooked an open and bustling square.

Murder cases always brought the biggest threats and, because this was the first day, Dan was alert. It could be a relative of the victim, or even of the defendant, or just a member of the public with an unhealthy interest in local justice. When someone dies, the hurt festers, and Dan knew that at times it became hard to control.

Still, the man hadn't looked back again. His hands were in his pockets, his head down. Perhaps Dan had read him wrong.

He trotted up the steps to the courthouse door and sought the sanctuary of the dark interior. Once he was inside, he glanced back, the city centre shops visible through the glass doors, framed by the security barrier. The man was still there. He'd moved to the front of the courthouse, and it was obvious that Dan was his focus.

If the man came inside, he'd speak to the security guards, just ask them to keep an eye on him. It was unlikely any weapon could be smuggled in, but Dan had represented people who made creative uses of everyday objects, like keys, and someone determined to get him would succeed.

Dan headed towards the robing room, accessible through a green door at the end of a long corridor lined with black-and-white tiles, part-worn by the nervous footsteps of the accused through the decades. The courtrooms on either side had seen all the county's tragedies, with murderers sent to the gallows from them, and Dan could sense the weight of history whenever he entered.

He passed a group of people on the way. Stern-faced, mouths etched in fine lines, tattoos running on to the backs of their hands from underneath their shirts, stretched tightly across their forearms. Large rings dominated their fingers, thick gold chains across broad tanned chests visible through the open shirt buttons. Lizzie's friends and family. In the centre of the group were her parents, their washed-out complexions betrayed the devastation of the previous few months. They'd been at every pretrial hearing, silently supporting each other. He admired their dignity. He knew they didn't admire him.

As he passed them, Dan gave a small nod, just a gesture of politeness to say that they weren't the enemy. The father went as if to move towards him, his lips pursed, but a hand on his arm stopped him.

One of the court ushers looked as if she was about to say hello but Dan kept on walking. With the victim's family so close by, cheery pleasantries weren't appropriate. Soon, he was in the hush of the robing room, where thick carpets dulled the noise and the air was heavy with expensive perfume.

There were a few barristers in there, emptying leather bags and thumping thick legal texts onto the tables. Some were in front of the mirrors, fixing their stiff white collars.

Someone guffawed from the other side of the room. 'Here he is, the latest star.'

Dan wasn't amused. It was a jibe, a lot of the older ones resenting his presence on an important case. Barristers had run a closed shop for a long time, with solicitors not allowed to appear in the higher courts. That had changed more than twenty years ago, but only recent funding cutbacks had made a real difference, and old prejudices died hard.

'If you're good enough, you're old enough,' Dan said, although he knew it was just a boast to make himself feel better.

'A murder though. You've hit the big time.' A smirk. 'Or perhaps you'll find out the opposite.'

Dan found a quiet corner and ignored the snipe. They came often, and he'd trained himself to ignore them. Dan's background was humbler than most of the barristers he came across, who bragged of their good education in their exaggerated vowels.

Dan had been raised on a Highford estate, his father spending his spare hours fighting trade union battles, drilling into him that life was all about class war.

Dan hadn't taken on his father's views – some people just got better starts than others – but that didn't stop him bristling whenever some of the country set tried to put him in his place.

The barrister was right, though: this case was different from the rest, because it was a murder case and he was defending it on his own, for the first time. In most murder cases, if Dan was part of the team in court, he was junior to a Queen's Counsel, fielding the routine questions. This time, he had a client who had insisted on Dan doing it alone.

It might work for him. The case was a good one, and if it looked like he was hiding behind an expensive legal team, even if it had been thrown together using government handouts, the jurors would take an instant to convict him. If Dan defended him alone, however, the jurors might see someone corralled through the system and feel sorry for him.

Provided they were prepared to look past his silence, of course. Virtually no one gets to stay silent when facing a murder allegation and keep their freedom.

Dan delved into his bag for his collar before sitting back, rolling the stiff piece of white cloth in his fingers.

He was taking a risk and he needed it to pay off. His client had made his will clear. It was one of the few times Peter had said anything. He'd jabbed at the table in the prison interview room and told Dan that he had to conduct the trial. No help. No Queen's Counsel. That wasn't how Dan did it normally, but margins were tough in criminal law and that forced people into difficult choices. There was no reason why Dan couldn't do the trial alone, although he knew the judge would give him a hard time. Judges liked fresh meat, and a solicitor-advocate conducting a murder trial would be just that. The Law Society might have its say too. His client was allowed to make bad choices. Dan wasn't. If he lost the case through inexperience, he could be struck off, but he couldn't afford to turn away a murder case just because of stage fright.

He got to his feet and removed his normal shirt collar, held in place by a brass stud at the back and buttons at the front. He fastened the stiffened wing collar in its place, the tabs hanging from it, just two white cloth strips. He straightened his black waistcoat and took a deep breath, before slipping on his gown. He felt like he had when he first started out, a mixture of nerves and energy. Once the case started, it would be different, because the case was only ever going one way, and that was forward. It was this part, the anticipation, that made him crawl with nerves and question whether it was all worth it. The late nights, the worry, the way his life often felt like it was only ever about others, not him.

He couldn't think like that now. He had to do his job. He had to trust his own abilities.

Dan collected his bag and left the robing room, preferring the echoes of the corridor to the sideways glances in there. He knew the chatter would turn to him, as they questioned his arrogance. Let them talk. The only way to shut them up was to win the case.

Next door to the robing room was the entrance to the cells. He keyed in the combination for the locked door and made his way down the stairs, past the grubby tiles, until he reached the window at the bottom.

Dan paused and closed his eyes. The whole case had been building up to this moment. The first day of the trial. His mouth felt dry and he had to take a few gulps of air to suppress the slight rise of panic. Be professional. He couldn't show whatever nerves he felt.

He pressed the buzzer and waited.

A face appeared at the window. 'Morning, Mr Grant.' It was one of the security guards, whose job it was to ferry the prisoners to and from prison, making sure they weren't let out in error. 'You've got Mr Box, haven't you?'

'That's right. How is he this morning?'

'Calm.'

The door buzzed as Dan opened it. He made his way to a small kiosk and waited for Peter Box to appear on the other side of the glass screen.

They didn't have to wait long.

Peter slouched as he came through the door, slumping onto the seat on the other side of the screen. His left eye bore the marks of a fading bruise.

Dan pointed. 'What happened?'

'A friend of Lizzie's boyfriend was remanded last week. He couldn't resist when he saw me.' He gave a rueful smile. 'I've got dressed up for court, though,' and he tugged at his tie, making the knot smaller. 'What happens now?'

'You could cut out this charade where you hope that staying silent will make the case go away.'

'So you keep saying, but I'm not going to prison for the rest of my life. Your job is to get me out.'

'Based on what you tell me, but you're not telling me anything. You're making it hard for yourself.'

Peter scowled and folded his arms, a posture he'd adopted through most of Dan's conversations with him, if they could be called that.

Dan lowered his voice. 'This is your last chance, Peter. The trial is here now, today. If you just want to shorten your prison stay, manslaughter is the way, but you've got to talk to me.'

'Right to silence, I've told you. And I'm not staying in prison.'

'You'll stay in prison for longer if you don't talk.'

'You make it sound like I don't have a chance. Why should I trust you?'

'Because the judge won't let you change lawyers today. You chose me, didn't want anyone else.'

Peter slammed his fist on the desk. 'Because if there's a QC here, I'd get the same as I get from you. More jabber, more pressure. I'm not talking.' He closed his eyes and took some deep breaths. When he opened them again, he said, 'Just get me out. I can't stay in prison. People spit in my food and bang on my cell door, telling me how they're going to get me.'

Dan stayed silent, hoping that Peter was about to have a change of heart, but Peter didn't seem interested in talking. He thought about what Pat had told him about Peter trying to confess to Rosie's murder all those years ago and decided to confront him.

'You're not talking about Lizzie's murder, but you were happy to talk about Rosie Smith?'

Peter looked up, his eyes clearer now, his gaze more intense. 'What do you mean?'

'Rosie Smith, a fourteen-year-old girl murdered on a canal bank twelve years ago. Sean Martin stood trial for the murder of

Rosie Smith, and you went to see my boss about that and tried to confess to it, but you weren't believed.'

'Twelve years ago, whatever, it's a long time.' His voice was quieter.

'It is, but it makes me wonder why you'd do that? And Rosie was murdered along the same stretch of canal?'

'Was she? I can't remember.'

'Can't, or won't?'

Peter folded his arms and scowled.

Dan let him stay like that, hoping that Peter would blurt an answer out, give him something he could work with, but he kept his silence.

'You say that you can't stand it in prison because of the threats,' Dan said, 'but that won't stop once you're out. The press will write up the case, how you got off on some technicality, because that's all I've got to work with, just some hope that a witness reveals an error in the paperwork that I can blow up to be something important. Everyone who meets you will know what you did, except you'll be on your own out there. No guards to protect you when you walk out of a pub, snarling men watching you go.'

'Stop it!' Peter clamped his hands over his ears.

'What was it about Rosie Smith? What did you do?'

No response.

'What do you know?'

Peter stood up, knocking his chair back, and banged on the door. When it wasn't answered straightaway, he thumped it.

As the door opened, Peter took one last look back at Dan before rushing through.

Dan closed his legal pad. As he looked at the closed door, he knew one thing: Peter was holding back, but about what? If he'd murdered Rosie, Dan owed it to Pat to show that Sean Martin's taunt at the party was just talk, a sick joke, nothing more, except that he could only show that by revealing his own client as a murderer. Whatever loyalty he owed to Pat, his job was to protect Peter.

There was another thought too that he wouldn't allow to take proper form, because it was in the background of everything a criminal lawyer did, that acknowledged truth smuggled behind every comment about professional duty, and that was the fact that Peter was most likely Lizzie Barnsley's murderer. If Peter really had killed her, a random victim in the dark, and he was acquitted, then he'd do it again, because it was possible he'd murdered Rosie too.

Dan didn't know how he would deal with that.

Fifteen

Jayne looked up at the building that housed Chase Walker, the law firm that had engaged her to spy on the cheating spouse. She was wearing jeans and pumps, her green army-style jacket showing its age with frayed cuffs and collar. She almost laughed at the contrast. There were men and women buzzing around the entrance to the office in pressed suits and shiny shoes. Her job gave her freedom but didn't do a lot for her self-esteem.

She'd stopped by her flat to get a change of clothes after her bath at Dan's, her skin smelling of his foam bath and the freshness of his towels. She had to finish the job for this client before she could start properly on Dan's.

The building was grit-blasted stone, cleaned up once the mills had stopped belching smoke over the town, the firm's name displayed on a large sign. It stood opposite a small park enclosed by black railings. This was what passed for Highford's professional quarter, populated by dental surgeries and accountancy firms, with the law firms alongside, but not many did criminal law. They didn't want thieves and drugs dealers, or worse, sharing the reception with company directors and farmers.

She went inside and into the reception area, bright from the sun streaming in through large windows, the ceilings high and the internal walls replaced by glass partitions, every part of the layout designed to look minimalist and modern. She could see right through to the Mercedes and BMWs in the car park at the rear. She guessed that the parking spaces by the building were reserved for the people whose cars made the firm look good, the high-earning partners and solicitors. All the junior lawyers and support staff were probably forced to pay for parking further off in some urine-soaked piece of concrete in the town centre.

The receptionist looked up as Jayne got closer. Her bright smile was fixed in place but had none of the deference she might have shown had Jayne walked in wearing a business suit.

'I'm here to see Anna Ellis,' she said. 'I'm Jayne Brett.'

'Take a seat please,' she said, before she whispered into a phone, and then, 'She'll be down in a minute.'

Jayne sat back and stared out of the window until the loud click of heels on the stairs announced Anna's arrival. She strode across the reception area with that mix of grace and arrogance that was present in many of the lawyers Jayne met.

Jayne stood. 'I don't know how happy your client will be, but I got some pictures of him leaving an apartment block, and a quick kiss from the woman waving him off.'

'Let me look,' Anna said, snapping her fingers as she held out her hand.

Jayne handed over the envelope. As Anna flicked through the pictures, Jayne pulled a folded piece of paper from her inside jacket pocket. 'I've got my invoice too.'

'Hand it to her.' Anna waved a hand towards the receptionist and set off up the stairs again. She hadn't said thank you.

Jayne rolled her eyes, but the receptionist wasn't prepared to show any solidarity. She snatched the invoice and said, 'Thank you,' before going back to whatever had occupied her before Jayne had walked into the office.

Jayne bit back an acerbic comment. They were her customers, after all.

In the legal world, Dan's office was a long way from Chase Walker. At times, it seemed even further from her own world, but at least Dan's cases generated something interesting, rather than grubbing around in the debris of a broken marriage.

She checked her watch. Just before ten. Now, it was time for some real work.

*

As Dan emerged onto the court corridor, the usher approached him. 'Mr Grant, the judge wants to see you.'

'Open court?'

'Chambers.'

Dan took a deep breath. He guessed what this was about.

The Honourable Mr Justice Standage was a High Court judge drafted in from London because of a local shortage. He'd called Dan the week before, to check that he was ready. Dan had assured him that he was. The judge had done the same with the prosecution, but it wasn't routine, and seemed to be just part of the judge's picky ways.

With those preliminaries out of the way, there could be only one other question: why was Dan defending his client alone, without a team?

Dan followed the usher into the courtroom. There was no one else there. Just three rows of wooden desks with rigid wooden benches, in front of a raised dock protected by glass. Behind that were seats for the general public, so that the defendant sat like a specimen in a glass tank. The walls were lined with paintings of past judges, and the sunlight was blocked out by long green curtains.

It was like entering a church; it seemed appropriate to whisper.

Dan pointed to the space behind the judge's bench. 'Is it just me in there?'

'The prosecutor as well.'

The usher went up the few steps to the space behind the judge's bench and Dan followed her. She pushed one of the wooden panels that lined the wall, which was in fact a door. They walked through and immediately the reverence of the courtroom was replaced by the absolute hush of the judges' corridor. The corridor was lined with thick carpets that deadened all noise. The doors on this corridor led to small, plush judges' chambers.

The usher knocked on the first door and waited until she heard a deep rumble: 'Come in.' She opened the door and went inside. Dan followed.

The room was dim, the sunlight straining to get through frosted windows, there as a security measure. There was a bookcase along one wall and a large desk in the middle of the room, with a burgundy leather inlay.

The prosecutor, Francesca McIntyre, was sitting in a chair opposite a man pale and creased by too much time spent indoors. Judge Standage.

Dan hadn't come across him before, although his demeanour hinted that he regarded his trip up north as slumming it. He was wearing his court robes, red and black silk, although his horsehair wig was on the desk. He looked like a man who moved slowly but Dan had been caught out by that before. He'd once taken a trip to the Court of Appeal and watched in astonishment as three old judges had almost dozed off as the barristers spoke, but then ripped into them with questions that showed that they knew every fact in the case. The judgment had already been made, but they had enjoyed toying with the junior counsel like a cat playing with a mouse before the kill.

Francesca looked up and smiled politely, but there was a slight twinkle to her eye that told Dan that she had been exchanging pleasantries with the judge before he arrived, and regarded herself as one-nil up.

Francesca was shrewd and confident and knew how to play the game. Always honest, like all good prosecutors are, because the bad ones get found out early on in their careers, she knew how to make the small plays. She was diminutive and understated in appearance, her hair pulled back into a black clasp, not too much make-up, but once in court she was bold and aggressive. Alongside her, Dan looked like exactly what he was: younger and less experienced.

The judge pointed at a chair. 'Sit down, Mr Grant.'

Dan nodded and gave a small bow before sitting down. He crossed one leg over the other and placed his bag next to his chair as he waited for the grilling. Always wait for the judge to speak.

The judge looked up. 'You're doing this alone, I understand.'

'I am, My Lord.' Dan's voice contained no apology and he ticked a mental box. A High Court judge is always 'My Lord', not 'Your Honour'. That was reserved for the everyday judges.

'First murder trial without Queen's Counsel?'

'It is.'

'Should it be?'

'It's how my client wants it.'

'I thought it was for you to assess if you have the required competence, not your client.'

'It is, and I have assessed. If my client wanted Queen's Counsel, I would have sought one. He didn't, and I know the case. I was there at the beginning and I'm competent enough to be there at the end.'

The judge put his fingers together. 'Your client stayed silent in his interview.'

'He did.'

'On your advice?'

'I'm not at liberty to disclose my advice. I'm sure Your Lordship understands that.'

'Don't play games, Mr Grant.'

'I understand, but I'm not prepared to disclose whatever my client has said to me in the presence of the prosecutor.'

'I'm trying to manage the case, not tease out evidence.'

'Teased or not, if it is evidence, I'll disclose it when the time comes to disclose it.'

There was a glimmer of a smile, but Dan knew that there was no warmth in it. 'Does your client agree with your assessment of your own competence?'

'He does.'

'Mr Grant, for your sake, I hope you're right, because if I see a man out of his depth, I cannot guarantee that I will throw out a lifebelt.'

Dan didn't respond, but he knew the judge would test his ability during the trial, and that he had better stand up to scrutiny.

The judge turned to the prosecutor. 'Are we ready to go, Ms McIntyre?'

'The prosecution is ready.'

'Mr Grant?'

He nodded. 'I'm ready to start.'

'Good. I don't want any delays or tricks. This is a simple case.'

'I agree, My Lord,' Dan said. 'There is only circumstantial evidence tying my client to the murder.'

'Save your cutting asides for the jury, Mr Grant. We don't argue the case in here.' He waved his hand to indicate that the meeting was finished.

As they both walked along the corridor back to the courtroom, Francesca said, 'Why do you do it, Dan?'

'Do what?'

'Look for a fight in everything.'

'The judge, you mean?' He smiled. 'I get it from my father, I suppose.'

'Do you know the real skill of being a prosecutor?'

'Enlighten me.'

'Spotting the cases we can win and the ones we can't, and only fighting the winners. It's not how you fight, but which fight you choose. You'd do well to remember that.' And with that, she set off ahead, down the steps and into the well of the court.

The courtroom was no longer empty. There were people in the public gallery, reporters and members of Lizzie Barnsley's family.

Just then someone else came in and made his way to the furthest corner of the courtroom. It was the man who'd been watching Dan outside. His baseball cap was in his hand, his hair matted and unkempt. As he sat down, he stared straight at Dan, his jaw clenched.

Dan switched his gaze to the front, his mind working fast.

He pulled out his phone, already set to silent so as not to disturb the court, and sent Jayne a message, his fingers working quickly. As he did, there was a knock on the door and everyone rose to their feet as the judge made his theatrical entrance, shuffling towards his chair.

He was able to put his phone away before the judge looked around the courtroom, delaying the moment when everyone could join him in taking a seat.

Dan hoped she got the message. Jayne had enquiries of her own to make, but if there was someone in court who could present a danger, he wanted to know what the danger was, and why.

Sixteen

The Hyundai showroom was a bright glass box on an out-of-town business complex. Jayne parked in the customer car park and wandered over, her hands in her jacket pockets. If Sean Martin had a new car, he must have traded in the old one. She'd a vague idea of how to get the information she wanted, but she knew she'd be mainly making it up as she went along.

There were three men visible through the glass, all dressed the same: black trousers, white shirts and corporate ties, black fleeces keeping them warm whenever the large doors opened.

She knew she didn't look like the normal kind of customer and wondered whether they'd just shoo her away, but as she went inside two of the men exchanged glances and did a quick rock-paper-scissor routine. The rock beat the scissors and walked over, a broad grin on his face.

'Good morning,' he said, clapping his hands in the cheery way of seasoned salesmen. 'What are you looking for? New or used?'

She tilted her head and smiled, making him blush. 'My daddy is getting sick of me driving that old tin box around,' and she gestured towards her car. 'He's paying, so impress me.'

'New it is, then.' He grinned as he glanced over her shoulder to her car. 'It looks like it's been a loyal friend for a long time, but we all have to move on. What kind of car are you looking for?'

'What would suit me?'

'Sporty, most definitely.'

'Sporty is small. I'm thinking of something a little bigger. Not a four-by-four, but similar.'

'I've got just the car.' He walked over to a large black car parked on the bright tiles in the middle of the showroom, Jayne following. It was the same as Sean Martin's car, a hatchback, but bigger than the usual five-door. Jayne imagined it parked on the driveway of a modern estate, all red brick and shiny double glazing, rather than bouncing along a farm track. 'These are very popular.' He opened the door. 'Get in, see how it fits.'

Jayne clambered in, the salesman leaning on the roof, looking in. His cologne was too strong.

'What do you think?'

For a moment, Jayne got a snapshot of the lives other people led, where they could look for new cars and think about buying them and where life wasn't a daily struggle to pay the bills.

'I like it,' she said, and ran her hands round the leather steering wheel, cool under her fingers.

'If you like it, this could be yours. We can always find a way to make you afford it. Or rather, Daddy.'

'Don't you worry about Daddy. And I know someone who's got one. He's just bought it, and says he likes it. That's why I came, but I didn't know the model name, just how it looked. It's so different from what he had before.'

'These are big sellers.'

'Sean Martin, he's the guy. You might have sold it to him?'

The salesman frowned. 'The one who went to prison for killing his stepdaughter?'

'That's him, although he didn't do it. We all know that now. I wouldn't be friends with him if he had.'

'I didn't sell him the car. It was my boss, I think.'

'He thought the same as me, though, that what he said he liked about it was the contrast with his old car. I just can't remember what he had before. Weird that, how you forget something you've seen so many times.'

The salesman stepped back. 'What's going on?'

'What do you mean?'

'Sean Martin went through the manager because he wanted privacy, because of his public profile. Me, I don't care about stuff like that – he's buying a car, that's all – but it was a big deal to him and the customer is always right. Now you turn up, and within a couple of minutes you're trying to find out what car he used to drive, when you'd know that if you were his friend, because you'd just ask him.'

Jayne sighed. 'Okay, I'm not buying a car, but this is the chance for you to help out your manager. I'm a private investigator and I'm working on a murder case.' She dug out a business card from her jacket and handed it over.

He glanced at it before making as if to put it in his shirt pocket. 'No, you don't,' she said, and snatched it back from him. 'I don't make enough money to give those away. The car he was driving earlier this year might be crucial. I need the make, model and colour, that's all, and you either tell me or I get a witness summons to make your manager turn up at court and hand over the information. He can do it from the witness box and lose a whole day when he could be selling cars, or you could get it now and I'll be gone.'

He looked around the showroom, his arm still on the roof. 'Wait here.'

The salesman walked over to an office visible through a window. Jayne stepped out of the car as a door opened and an older man, sandy-haired and with his stomach hanging over his belt, a keychain dangling from it, headed towards her. When he got close, he said, 'Tell me again what you want.' He planted his feet apart and folded his arms, pushing his stomach out even more.

'I'm guessing you know, if you're adopting that tone. What car did Sean Martin trade in for his brand-new Hyundai?'

'We don't give out customer information to someone who just wanders in like you did, waving around a reusable business card.'

'You're wasting your own time, because the court will make you hand it over. As I'm going to get it anyway, you might as well tell me.'

The manager pursed his lips. 'If you could get it through official means, you'd have written to us or sorted out the court summons already. Instead, you come here, all tits and teeth, trying to flirt your way to it. You'll have to do better than that. Now leave.'

'And that's your last word?'

He pointed towards her car. 'Go.'

She shrugged and said, 'Fine,' and turned to go. She tried to look nonchalant as she made her way back across the car park, but she was angry. It hadn't gone as she'd hoped and all she'd done was to make her intentions obvious.

As she got back into her car, she saw that all the salesmen were standing by the windows in the same pose, feet apart, arms folded, glaring at her. Her phone buzzed.

She pulled her phone from her pocket. A message from Dan.

The message was simple. *Man watching Box trial watching me. I need to know who he is. Don't let on or speak to me but who is he?*

She started her engine. Her plans for the day had just changed. She smiled. She was starting to feel alive again.

*

Trudy Martin was in her garden when the phone rang.

The morning had been quiet. The first good spring burst of grass had arrived, so she'd mowed the lawn and was tending to the flowerbeds. The cherry tree was starting to show its pink blossoms, just a few weeks until when they'd be scattered all over the garden by one of the cruel breezes that drove across the hillside.

Sean wasn't answering it, so she put down her small garden fork and went inside, taking off her gardening gloves as she walked towards the phone.

It was the showroom that had sold Sean his new car.

She put her hand over the mouthpiece and shouted, 'Sean?'

'Yeah?'

'The phone.'

There was a short delay and then there was the steady clump of his footsteps as he came down the stairs.

'Who is it?'

'The car showroom.'

She passed him the phone and went to go back outside, picking up her gardening gloves.

He held up his hand, making her stop.

She put her gloves back down and waited.

He thanked whoever had called and put the phone down. He took a deep breath.

'What is it?'

'Someone's been asking about me, wanted to know what car I was driving before I bought the new one.'

'Who?'

'A young woman. Jayne Brett was her name. One of the salesmen remembered it from her card.'

'Why did she want to know what car you'd been driving?'

'It's to do with a court case this week. A murder case.'

'What did the showroom say?'

'They told her to go away.'

She put her gloves on and went back outside, sliding the door closed and letting the hush of the outdoors take over. The tranquillity was gone. She stabbed the ground with the fork, leaning down to yank out the weeds, her jaw set.

The door opened behind her, followed by the soft clumps on the lawn as Sean made his way over. She didn't look round.

'It'll be okay,' he said.

'How do you know? Dan Grant was here yesterday, and this woman today asking about you. Why? And what was all that bullshit from Dan about Pat Molloy?'

'The man at the showroom said that he could be summoned by the court to say what car I was driving before my new one.'

Trudy stabbed her fork into the ground. 'Why, though? I don't get it. Is there something you're not telling me?'

'You trust me, don't you?' He was behind her, and there was a tremble of anger in his voice.

'Of course I do. I just worry about you. About us. The rumours never stop. We'll never get away from this.'

He took her hand. 'No one will split us up again, I promise.'

'How can you be so sure?'

He stepped closer. 'Because I won't let them.'

He went back into the house as she dug at the soil again. Eventually, she threw her gloves and fork down and followed Sean into the house, although she didn't speak to him. Instead, she headed for a shower, to wash away the garden grime.

Once inside the bathroom, she closed her eyes and put her head back against the door. She wanted it all to end, but still people kept on digging. Why can't they leave him alone? The court cleared him. That should be enough.

Don't make him angry. Don't let them get too close. She swallowed back tears as she thought of his anger. She couldn't stand that.

Seventeen

The prosecutor rose to begin her opening address to the jury.

The atmosphere in the courtroom was tense. Lizzie's friends and family filled one side of the public gallery. Liam, the boyfriend, was sitting further along, apart from them. That space said what everyone thought, that he'd caused it, that if he hadn't been such a petty and jealous thug she wouldn't have run off into the night, towards her death. Liam didn't see it that way, his glare alternating between Dan and Peter Box.

Dan looked away. He expected that. Instead, he tried to focus on what lay ahead, the words of the judge stamped hard onto his memory. He couldn't mess this up. The judge had warned him that he was being watched, ready to report him if he turned out to be not good enough.

As Francesca turned to the jurors, Dan closed his eyes for a moment, just to get some focus. He tried to shut out the atmosphere and tension in the courtroom, so that all he heard were the soft creaks of the carpet under Francesca's feet along with the occasional rustle of clothes as people settled down in the public gallery. Concentrate on the evidence. Let the facts speak for themselves.

He opened his eyes and turned to look back towards the dock. Peter Box was sitting up, rigid in his posture, staring at the prosecutor, his head cocked to listen to what was about to be said.

Francesca held out her papers, but they were more of a prop than an aide. Her speech would come from years of experience. Like Dan, Francesca used a laptop in court, all the police statements and exhibits on it, but would use a paper bundle when on her feet. Holding out a witness statement was more dramatic than scrolling with a mouse.

'Members of the jury,' she said. Her tone was slow and rich. The jurors craned forward. 'I'm going to take you back to just after midnight, the early hours of New Year's Day in the town of Highford. Once the fireworks had died down, Elizabeth Barnsley was assaulted by her boyfriend in the car park of a local pub. She was Lizzie to her friends, and over the course of the next few days, you'll hear details about her life. Some of it happy, some of it not so. You'll hear details about her death too. Violent and brutal and senseless.'

Murmurs from the gallery accompanied her words.

The judge looked up from the notes he was making and leaned forward. 'A reminder to the members of the public in the gallery that you are here because you have an interest in this case and because it is your right. It is not unqualified, however, because the bargain you make with the court is that you remain quiet and do not disturb the proceedings.'

He let his words linger for a few seconds before he nodded at the prosecutor to continue.

Francesca turned back to the jurors.

Dan stared at his notepad as she spoke. He knew what Francesca was going to say because the opening address had been sent to him two weeks earlier, part of the pre-trial protocol.

Francesca moved on. 'Unbeknownst to Lizzie, in her desire to escape the violence of one man, her search for a place of supposed safety led her into the path of another violent man: Peter Box, hiding in the darkness. Her friends sought to stop her from being followed, but it meant that she was alone, and it was in that solitude that Peter Box attacked her. He fought with her and forced her into the water on that freezing night.'

One of the jurors swallowed and the look of intrigue had been replaced by something much darker: sorrow for the ending of a young life, anger directed at the man sitting in the dock, and fear at what they were about to be confronted with.

'Members of the jury, Peter Box held her under the water until she drowned.'

Francesca looked each juror in the eye to let that fact sink in before continuing.

'The prosecution has to prove the case against Peter Box beyond any reasonable doubt, so that you are sure of his guilt.' Her voice softened. 'It is a high burden, and in this case the evidence is circumstantial.' She smiled. 'Do not be fooled by that word. No one saw Peter Box murder Lizzie Barnsley. Instead, you will look to the circumstances of the case and you will be drawn to one unavoidable conclusion: that Peter Box murdered Lizzie Barnsley. You will hear from witnesses who watched her break away from her violent boyfriend. You will hear how no one from that public house followed her, and how her boyfriend was prevented from going after her. You'll hear from forensic specialists who will explain how she was assaulted and held under water, from the marks on her neck and body, and then on her legs and feet as she struggled against the canal bank. And most importantly of all, you'll hear from the Crime Scene Investigator who discovered Lizzie's shoe with blood on its stiletto heel, and from the nurse who tended to a wound on Peter Box's head. The blood on her shoe, members of the jury, belonged to Peter Box.'

Francesca softened her tone even more, so that the jurors leaned forward, drawn in by her address. 'Ladies and gentlemen of the jury, Peter Box murdered Lizzie Barnsley. When you've heard all the evidence, you will be sure that this is the truth. The only truth. Nothing but the truth.'

As she moved on to calling the first witness – one of the men who'd been drinking at the Wharf pub that night – Dan made a tick on his notepad. It had been a strong opening statement. Not so detailed that the jury would spot her case going wrong if a witness didn't give evidence as well as she hoped, but with enough detail to let them know what the case was about.

Dan looked back to the public gallery, gazing beyond Peter towards the seats along the back row, to the man who'd been watching him outside the court that morning. Whoever the stranger was, he wasn't concentrating on Francesca. Instead, he was staring at Dan and then back at Peter, his brow furrowed, his finger tapping his lip.

Dan picked up his phone, which he'd secreted under some papers. As everyone waited for the usher to come back from the witness room with the first witness, Dan scrolled through his messages. No response yet from Jayne.

He checked quickly that the judge wasn't watching him and then sent another message before he put his phone back under his papers.

He sat back as the usher returned with the witness. All he could do was put aside whatever thoughts he had about the danger sitting in the gallery. He had a murder case to deal with and his focus had to be on that.

As the witness stepped into the box, he lifted his papers to check again for the small flashing light that would tell him he had a message. There was none.

He was frowning as the witness took the oath.

Eighteen

Trudy was outside Pat Molloy's office, pacing, trying to work out what to say. Her reflection in the window didn't reveal her anger. She looked the same as ever. Dark hair, her eyes softened by round glasses, a scarf around her neck. Inside, however, she was furious at the sudden flurry of interest in Sean. Her fortunes were too wrapped up in his, and if there was trouble coming her way, she wanted to know what it was.

As she walked in, the crisp spring air was replaced by smothering warmth, spewed out by the central heating. The receptionist looked up and gave her a quick appraisal in the process.

'Is Pat Molloy in? I'm Trudy Martin, Sean Martin's wife.'

The receptionist looked surprised. 'Yes, of course. Please wait there,' she said, and made a quick call to Pat as Trudy looked out of the window, not sitting down.

'How is Sean?' When Trudy turned back to her, she said, 'I'm Margaret. I was here during Sean's trial, and I remember the party when they released him, but I don't think we met then.'

'Sean is fine, thank you. I came along afterwards really. We knew each other years ago, and when I contacted him to congratulate him, well, things rekindled.'

Before Margaret could reply, a door burst open and Pat Molloy was standing there. 'My dear Trudy. I've heard all about you.' The bounce in his voice didn't match the grey in his skin and the bones in his shoulders, visible through his shirt. 'What can I do for you?'

'I need to ask you some questions. It won't take a minute. It's to do with Sean.'

'Of course, come through.'

Trudy followed him through a room used for interviewing clients and into a grotty office behind, the Venetian blinds pulled down and a desk piled high with files. Her nose twitched from the dust. As Pat opened the blinds, it swirled in the light.

She took off her scarf and coat, her blouse unbuttoned far enough to keep Pat interested. Sean had told her before that he had a reputation for being a flirt.

'Take a seat,' he said, and moved some legal textbooks from a chair. 'I don't normally see clients in here but, well, you're different.'

'I'm not a client, for a start.'

'Well, yes, absolutely, and I hope it stays that way.' His weak smile was broken by a cough.

'You don't look well, Mr Molloy.'

'Just getting old. But you didn't come here to ask about my health.'

'No, that's true. It's about Mr Grant. He's your employee, right, not a partner?'

'Dan? He's been with me since he started. He's a good man. He helped with Sean's case.' He steepled his fingers under his nose and his gaze grew sharper. 'What's wrong?'

'He came to see Sean yesterday, and today an investigator has been asking questions about Sean. Jayne Brett? Does she work for you?'

Pat waved his hand. 'Oh, I might be his boss, but I leave it to Dan who he uses for investigations. I trust him.'

'But you can see how it would bother me, right?'

'I don't understand.'

'Dan was at our house yesterday, and this morning Jayne Brett went to the showroom where Sean bought his car, asking questions about it. I don't understand why she'd do that, but she said the questions are connected to a murder case. Is it Sean's case? Why is she interested in Sean's case?'

Pat's eyes narrowed. 'Dan has a murder case starting this week. It might be connected with that. Someone called Peter Box.'

Trudy blinked and sat back. 'But I don't understand why. Peter Box has no connection with me, or Sean.' She tilted her head. 'Has Peter Box said his case is connected to Sean?'

'Why would he?'

'I don't know, but Dan and this Jayne are digging around Sean, and I want to know why.'

Pat leaned forward, hands gripping the arms on his chair. His eyes grew hard and he spoke in a tone that belied his frail appearance. 'Dan is a damn good lawyer and whatever he does, it's because it's the right thing to do. I wish I could say the same about my career, but I can live with my mistakes. Can Sean?'

'I don't understand what you mean?'

'Ask him.'

'I don't need to ask him. Sean was cleared.'

'Because of an expert *I* found.'

'And he's done so much good since then. You helped to make his life matter. There'll be talk of honours soon; especially now he's got his book out. He's campaigned, helped people escape injustice.'

'So have I, all of my career, but I can't think of many people who I thought were completely innocent.'

Trudy pursed her lips. 'What are you trying to say?'

Pat coughed, his hand going to his mouth, his cheeks turning red once more. 'Just ask him.'

Trudy stood up and grabbed her coat and scarf.

'You be careful what you do, Mr Molloy,' she said, her cheeks flushed with anger. 'Sean is innocent.'

'What could I possibly do? Reveal his secrets?'

'I thought a client's secrets died with you.'

'They do, but then again, they can't touch me when I'm gone.'

Trudy slammed the door behind her.

She didn't speak to Margaret on the way out. She marched out on to the street, her jaw clenched, tears in her eyes, but they were tears of rage, not distress.

As the cold air hit her, she stopped. She closed her eyes and tried to regain her poise. Anger was destructive, she knew that. She had to stay calm and work out what to do.

As she opened her eyes, she looked back towards the office. Pat Molloy was watching her.

Nineteen

Jayne was sitting on a bench near the war memorial when the court broke for lunch. It gave her a good view of the entrance.

She'd decided not to sit in the courtroom, because whoever she was supposed to be following would recognise her if she had to go after them. Despite what the movies showed, public galleries in courts were mostly empty. Murder cases brought more of a crowd, bereaved relatives and their supporters, but even in those cases the seats were rarely full.

There was a street market in full flow just down the road, and for a few moments she'd been enjoying the bustle of the city, so different from Highford where the town centre was just a tunnel for the wild Pennine winds and everyone looked pinched and red-faced. It told her that her feelings were right, that Highford had served its purpose and it was time to leave. Her life had held more promise when she was a young psychology student, before Jimmy took away her confidence and she took away his life.

She was wearing a baseball cap, with her long hair pulled into a ponytail and hidden underneath. There was enough sunshine to justify sunglasses and it was warm enough that she could wear a white T-shirt without feeling cold. Her black jacket was in a small rucksack, so that she'd be able to instantly make herself look different if she thought she'd been spotted.

Some people spilled out of the court building. A small group in tight shirts and gold jewellery dug into their pockets for cigarettes, but no one like the man described in Dan's second message. *He's tall and scruffy, old, all in black, green baseball cap.*

Perhaps Dan had got it wrong and it was just some local obsessed with court cases? There were people like that, who saw court as local entertainment, and what could be better than a murder?

She waited for another fifteen minutes, her phone in her hand, making it look as if she was checking for messages, but her eyes never left the front door.

As she held her phone, the light started to flash. There was a notification on her Facebook account.

It was an account she used purely for business. There were no pictures of her, just periodic announcements to keep her page in peoples' timelines. It didn't have many followers, but it was another way of spreading the word and for prospective clients to contact her. It was dormant most days, apart from people asking her what it was like to be a private investigator.

Her page had a new *like*. She clicked on it, wondering whether it was more work, or perhaps one of her old conquests wanting to hook up again.

When she saw who it was from, her hand trembled.

She'd had this great plan at the car showroom, but she'd been clumsy and given herself away. And here it was, the proof.

Her new *like*? Her new follower?

Sean Martin.

She cursed, angry with herself, but as she looked up from her phone, she saw her target. A man dressed all in black leaving the courthouse, scruffy and furtive as he looked up and down the street, his hands in his coat pocket. Dan was right, there was something shifty about him.

He made swiftly for the street market. She pushed the thought of Sean Martin away and followed the man, hanging back, wary of being seen. He weaved through the stalls, past racks of cheap clothing and boxes of knock-off microwaves, not stopping to look. He seemed to know where he was headed.

There was a small side street next to the market and he ducked into it. Jayne shot after him, worried that she'd lost him. Perhaps he'd seen her and run away.

As she reached the alley, she looked along, breathless, but he was there, in a doorway, his phone in his hand, dialling a number. He paced as he waited for an answer. Jayne backed away towards a stall filled with second-hand books and DVDs and pretended to browse. Whoever he called must have answered, because he was talking quickly, his face animated.

The stallholder came over and was about to start his patter when the man hung up and walked out of the alley. Jayne held up her hand in apology and followed again. He was walking quickly, straight back to the courthouse.

As he rushed back inside, past the small group of smokers by the front door, Jayne pulled out her phone to message Dan.

The man had left the building just to make a phone call, but he'd gone somewhere quiet, where he could be certain no one was listening.

Dan was correct. Something wasn't right.

Twenty

The afternoon passed with no real surprises from the witnesses for the prosecution. Just before four thirty, the judge rose from his seat and gave his final bow of the day, aped by the lawyers, the tension in the courtroom released as he shuffled through the small door and into the corridor behind. The jurors were released for the night, all sent home with a warning not to look at any news about the case or discuss it with anyone. Some would comply, acknowledging the solemnity of their oath, whereas others were bound to spend the evening messaging friends.

Peter Box was taken to the cells below the court, waiting for his transfer into a secure van, then on to the prison just further along the ring road.

As they gathered their papers and put away their laptops, Dan looked over to Francesca and rolled his eyes. 'It's going to be a long week.'

'For you, perhaps. For me?' She smiled. 'It seems pretty straightforward. See you in the morning, Mr Grant.'

She paused on her way out to exchange pleasantries with another prosecutor who was coming into the courtroom. It was Zoe Slater. Dan had come up against her many times and their scores were pretty even. She appeared in the Crown Court occasionally, but Zoe spent more time in the office, doing all the background work on cases, other lawyers doing the trial work. It had been Zoe's name on all the correspondence related to the case.

Zoe carried on into the well of the courtroom. 'Hi, Dan, how's your first solo murder case going?'

'I might as well cut my teeth on a no-hoper. No one will be surprised if he's convicted. What are you doing here?'

'Just checking my case has got off the ground.'

'Francesca is doing a good job.'

'She always does. You could make it easier for yourself, though, and get him to plead guilty.'

'How do you know I haven't tried?'

'What's his defence?'

'I'm making you prove it. I'm still allowed to do that.'

'Is he going to give evidence?'

'Perhaps. We'll decide that when the time comes.'

Zoe chuckled. 'He's going to need to come up with something good.' Before Dan could say anything, she held up her hand. 'I know all about the burden of proof, that any doubt goes in your favour, but do you really think a jury will let him walk out if they think there's a good chance that he's done it? No matter what direction they get from the judge, they're human beings who will be scared about freeing a murderer.' She folded her arms and leaned back against the desk. 'Can I tell you about my experience though?'

'Please do.'

'I've been a prosecutor for fifteen years, and you know me well enough to realise that I don't back away from tough decisions. And do you know what the toughest decisions of all are?'

'I'm intrigued.' Dan didn't hide his sarcasm.

'Those cases where I think the suspect has done it, but I can't see that piece of evidence that will put him away. I have to look police officers in the eye and tell them that all their work has been in vain because, in my opinion, and that's all it is, an opinion, we can't prove it. And I watch someone who has committed a heinous act walk free, ready to do it again. It's much easier to just go along with the police and rubber stamp a charge, get them before the court and let the jury decide, but that isn't how I do it.'

'What's your point, apart from fluffing yourself up?'

'That this isn't one of those cases. I have never prosecuted anyone I believed was innocent. That's a luxury you don't have, Dan, because you know most of your acquittals involve people who've done it but squirm through a gap in the evidence.'

'Usually because you didn't collect the evidence you needed. There's no guilt trip coming my way, and now you're getting twitchy, because this case hasn't got any stronger since you started it, and yet here you are, waiting for the speech on the court steps.'

'That doesn't mean I think he didn't do it,' she said, irritation in her voice. 'When I look at this case, at your client, I've no qualms about seeing him locked up for life. None at all.'

Dan shrugged. 'All you've got is his blood on a shoe. If there's an explanation for that, he walks free, and you know it.'

'It's not as simple as that.'

'Isn't it? If the DNA evidence doesn't get used, you've no case.'

'And why shouldn't it?'

'The lab you used, Meladox, is dodgy. Two people went to prison for doctoring test results, prosecuted by your office. How will that look?'

'That wasn't about DNA and you know it. That was about alcohol and drug levels in blood.'

'A dirty lab is a dirty lab. Once the jury hears that, they might start questioning what they hear.'

Zoe pushed herself away from the desk. 'I hope you can sleep well, because you know you're blowing smoke, nothing more.' She smiled without warmth. 'Have fun, Dan.'

'Has he ever been suspected of murder before?'

Zoe stopped. 'Sorry, what?'

'Like I said. You've got access to all the secret stuff. Has Peter Box ever been suspected of anything before?'

'Tell me which case and I'll look into it.'

It was Dan's turn for the cold smile. 'Do you know what the hardest part of this job is? Doing it mostly alone. You have a whole police squad looking into your leads. For now, I'll keep what I know to myself.'

Zoe turned to go, much quicker than before, the urgency in her stride telling him that her day wasn't over yet.

Dan sighed, weariness taking him over after a tiring day. Trials were like that, having to keep the mind focused every single minute of the day, always looking out for that wrong word, that slip-up he might be able to use in the case. So far, however, the prosecution case had gone well. All he had was a gut feeling that something was amiss, and he hadn't worked out how to make the jurors feel it too.

In most trials, there was a tipping point. It could be an unexpected comment from a witness, or a flaky witness who turned out to be strong and confident. Or it could go the other way, when the high point of the prosecution case turned out to be vague and inconsistent. The sands shifted and the jury shifted with them.

In Peter Box's case, Dan didn't know what the tipping point would be. The prosecution had already hit its high point with the revelation that Peter's blood was on Lizzie's shoe. That point would be repeated throughout the trial. But strong cases can only get weaker. That was Dan's main hope.

The court usher picked up some loose papers from the desk, screwing them into a ball. 'You've got a tough one this week, Mr Grant.'

'If they get this far, they're never easy.'

'You'll try your hardest, and that's all that matters.'

'Yes, I suppose so.'

Dan picked up his bag and went back out into the court corridor. It was deserted, theatre over for the day, only his own footsteps for company.

The exit was one way, the street visible outside, with the robing room the other. He didn't want the lawyerly bonhomie. He took off his tabs and gown and put them in his bag, before unfastening the first button of his shirt. Hoisting his bag over his shoulder, he headed for the exit.

The day had turned fresher, the warmth in the spring air disappearing after its false start at lunchtime. Dan checked up and down the street, looking for the tall man, but the street was quiet. There were late-afternoon shoppers and office workers making their way home, but no one loitering.

He pulled his phone from his pocket. It was blinking a blue light. A message. It was from Jayne. *I'm following. Will report back.*

Progress. Jayne would find out what he needed to know. He was used to threats, which came with the territory of dealing with crimes. It was the unknown he didn't like.

He rummaged in his pocket for his car keys and headed for the car park.

Twenty-one

Jayne had almost missed him.

She'd been distracted by a young mother grappling with bags of shopping, a pram, and two small children, when she spotted movement at the edge of her vision.

When he came outside, he didn't look around or give any sign that he'd noticed her. Instead, he headed towards the bus station, his hands jammed in his pockets, his pace quick. Provided she hung back, all she had to do was get on the same bus.

He trudged across the bus station forecourt, green and blue buses lined up in front of stands highlighted by large red numbers.

Jayne kept the same pace but always with a few people between them, so that it looked like she was just another weary passenger. She'd have to ask for a ticket to wherever the end stop was and then come back to collect her car, but at least it would get her somewhere.

But he wasn't getting on a bus. Instead, he turned towards a stairwell dominated by the stainless-steel doors of a lift. He was heading to the car park above.

For a moment, she panicked. Her car wasn't parked too far away but he'd be on the road before she had a chance to catch up. Still, she might be able to get his registration number and work out who he was from that.

He pressed the lift button and looked around as he waited.

She fought the urge to duck into a hiding spot, because it would make her more conspicuous. Instead, she stared straight ahead, past the lift entrance, as if she were merely looking for a bus somewhere further along.

She could feel him watching her, but he must have been satisfied as she walked on past, her gaze never switching back to him, because she heard the doors open, followed by the echo of his feet as he went inside. She knew she couldn't get into the lift with him; it would make her too memorable. She stopped to check out a bus timetable, running a finger down a column of numbers, until she heard the lift doors close and the whirr of the mechanism taking him upwards. She bolted back into the tiled entrance and watched the numbers light up.

The numbers stopped rising at four.

Her footsteps rang loud as she raced up the concrete stairwell. She tried not to breathe in the acrid stench, but by the time she reached the fourth floor, she was panting hard, bending over to regain her breath before she pushed open the door to the car park.

Although they weren't on the roof, the walls of the car park were open, and the light and steady breeze from the outside world blinded her for a moment after the dark stillness of the stairwell. A stream of cars was leaving, the engine noises loud as their tyres squealed down the ramps. As her eyes adjusted to the light, she looked along the row of cars and saw him.

He was by the edge, looking out over the bus station below and talking to someone. A woman with dark skin and a close-cropped afro.

Jayne skipped up the nearest ramp to the mezzanine level. She crept between the cars closest to the pair and peered down at them through the gap between the floors.

The woman was much younger than he was, late twenties at the most, smartly dressed in a dark trouser suit and white blouse, but looked as if she was trying to keep herself hidden. He leaned in as he spoke to her, his eyes darting around, whereas she was looking over the wall towards an ugly office block, so that it was hard to get a full view of her face.

Jayne took her camera from her pocket and snapped a few pictures as they got into separate cars. The man was driving a silver Fiesta, average and forgettable, so she made sure she got a shot of his registration number.

As the squeal of their tyres was lost in the general noise of the car park, Jayne checked the pictures on her camera. She had them.

She ran for the stairwell, bolted down the stairs and rushed through the bus station towards her own car, parked a few hundred metres away in an outdoor car park. She looked over her shoulder as she ran and saw the silver Fiesta pull out of the multi-storey and take the road towards the motorway. Her chest was pounding as she reached her car, her hair sticking to her forehead with perspiration. The Fiat started on the second turn of the key and then, with the exhaust rattling as if it was barely attached, she swung it out into the rush-hour traffic.

She peered ahead, trying to see the Fiesta in one of the queues making stop-start progress towards the motorway and a couple of miles of traffic lights and out-of-town shopping parks. She was despairing of seeing his car again when she thought she spotted him on the long climb to the motorway, driving below the speed limit, steady and careful in the left lane.

Jayne took up a position behind him, far enough back so as not to raise suspicion.

The miles passed and not even the faster motorway traffic made the Fiesta speed up. The grey city blight gave way to open fields grazed by cattle, stone villages dotting the distant hilltops.

They drove fifteen miles before he turned off the motorway and headed towards Whitton, one of the small places that lie along the canal but were now connected to the rest of the county by the motorway, another valley town dominated by lines of old grey terraces and a high brick viaduct. Jayne was able to keep the car in sight but dropped back behind another commuter until the Fiesta turned into a small estate of new-build houses, all open lawns and curved cul-de-sacs.

He turned into a driveway, but Jayne drove on to a turning point. She turned round in time to see the man unlock the door and disappear inside.

She pulled out her notepad and started to jot down all that she'd seen. The car. The address.

She checked the photographs on the back of her camera and scribbled in her notebook.

The knock on the window made her yelp.

The man was glaring through the glass. She thought about driving off but realised that would look worse. Her heart was pounding as she lowered the window.

'I think you need to come inside.' His voice was quiet, filled with the tiredness of a long day.

'Do I?'

He nodded and opened her door. 'You do.'

Twenty-two

Trudy closed the door softly, so that Sean wouldn't know she was back. She needed time on her own. She'd spent the day driving through the hills around Highford, working out what to do next. She hadn't found any answers.

She hung her scarf and coat over the end of the bannister rail and looked around the hallway. It was quiet, their haven in the hills. A grandfather clock ticked, an affectation Sean had picked up from an antique shop, trying to finish off the cottage vibe. The floor still had the original black-and-white tiles from when the house was first built, preserved by years of carpets and brought back to life by polish.

There was a box of books on a chair in the hallway, delivered by Sean's publisher, the contractual freebies of his autobiography. She picked one up to flick through. It was his big attempt to rehabilitate himself. He'd been cleared but too many people were cynical, not always prepared to see him as innocent, and the book advance would see them through the next couple of years, with public appearances filling the calendar.

The cover showed him outside the Crown Court, his cheeks red from tears of outrage, standing in front of a microphone as he readied himself to give the speech that he hoped would change the public perception of him. Before the retrial, he'd been the sick child-abuser who'd preyed on his stepdaughter, every mother's fear about their new boyfriend.

The retrial had changed that for many people, and Sean had given a tearful speech about how he'd been mistreated by the system, how it had closed its mind to anyone else but him and, as a consequence, the real killer was going unpunished. He'd vowed to continue the fight; not just to clear his name, but to find the real person who ended the life of the girl he'd loved as if she'd been his own child, who'd breathed her last breath in his arms as he held her, unable to save her.

There were two sections of photographs, dark patches in the pristine white edges.

She went to the first section.

It started with shots of Sean as a younger man, unaware of the infamy that would come his way, and then some with Rosie on a family holiday. Sean, the perfect stepfather, sitting behind her on a merry-go-round, both grinning happily, his arms around her. In another, they were relaxing with Rosie's mother, Karen, on a picnic blanket, the grass of the canal bank behind them.

She knew the rest of the pictures; she'd helped Sean compile them but it was different seeing them between the pages. It made the story seem more real.

She put the book back in the box. Not everyone would believe it, of course. They got regular hate mail, particularly by email, but they'd learned long ago to ignore it. It was part of the price for his past.

There was a noise towards the back of the house. She went into the kitchen. Wooden cupboards and unvarnished furniture. Eggs in a wire basket. Lavender in a stone vase. Pithy slogans on battered metal signs adorned the walls.

Sean was taking off his boots, grunting with exertion as he threw them on to some newspaper put there for that purpose.

'You been out?' she said.

'Just checking the boat.'

'Why?'

'Too many vandals around here.'

She went to the window and looked out over the lawn, just for the distraction. The boat was their escape. It was complete solitude once they were away from the town. Even when gliding through, they felt apart from it, only ever in transit. Waking up to breakfast at a small country pub or enjoying a glass of wine with ducks and swans for company, damp grass trailing on the water, was idyllic.

'Is it all right?'

'Yes, fine. I'd have gone out in it later but I've got something on tonight.'

'Have you?'

'Just an author event at a library.'

'Ah yes, your adoring public need to hear you speak.'

'No, I need to sell some books. Sitting on local justice committees doesn't put food on the table.' He straightened, once the boots were off. 'Where did you go?'

'I went to see Pat Molloy.'

He unwrapped his scarf and threw it over the back of a chair. 'Why?'

'Why do you think? His underling came to see us yesterday and seemed pretty intent on making us feel awkward. I wanted to know what was going on. Pat Molloy was your lawyer. His job was to protect you, so why was Dan Grant here?'

'And?'

'Pat was just as hostile.'

'How?'

'It was as if he disliked you.' She shook her head. 'No, it was more than dislike. He kept on telling me to ask you, as if he knew you had some secret.'

Sean went to the sink and poured himself a glass of water.

'Sean, please don't turn away from me.'

'I'm getting a drink.'

'You're avoiding me.'

'What do you want me to say?'

'Tell me what Pat meant.'

'Why is it important?'

'It's important to me, you know that. He didn't look well. Coughing. Grey. Does he know something about you?'

'It's fine, relax.'

'I don't believe you.'

Sean didn't move for a few seconds. He gripped the glass tighter and Trudy braced herself, expecting him to throw it, but instead he put it down and turned around. He pulled her in close, his hand round her throat. 'Don't worry about Pat Molloy.'

She closed her eyes and tried not to think about what he could do. 'How do you know?'

'I just do. He doesn't matter. He was my lawyer, nothing more.'

She nodded that she understood and he released his grip. She rubbed her neck as she said, 'I worry, that's all.'

'You worry too much. We'll survive. We always do.'

He pulled her in close again and held her, but she couldn't relax. The darkness was always close by.

Twenty-three

Dan strode through the care home, wanting to get to his father's room as quickly as possible. He hated visiting the place. The residents were nice enough, and he knew that everyone there had a story to tell, but the care home's quiet atmosphere amplified how far his father had fallen.

Dan's father had been a servant to the trade-union movement, spending late nights in the family kitchen planning campaigns, his evenings lost to secret meetings in smoky pub back rooms. Dan had grown up with talk of revolution, of strikes and protests, tales of battles in the Yorkshire coalfields and poll tax protests in the capital, hearing his father's anger in the crash of his fist against the kitchen table.

That fervour had become spent as his father got older, the trade union battles lost one by one, until all he had left were memories of defeats and frustration at a changing world.

A stroke had weakened him, withered his left arm and confined him to a wheelchair, the man who'd once seemed so fearsome, now broken. A shadow of his former self.

The corridor was long and dark and too warm, the aromas of the meal that had just been served filling the building, steamed vegetables and meat, the peace broken by the clatter of someone clearing away plates.

An old woman was sitting at the end of the corridor, staring out of a window. She turned towards Dan but didn't respond to his greeting as she turned back to the view.

His father was in room twelve. He knocked. The television was on too loud so he knocked again, not wanting to scare him. The television went quiet and a familiar gruff voice shouted, 'What?'

Dan sighed and went inside.

His father was sitting in a wheelchair, a glass in his hand half-filled with cider, the squashed plastic bottle on a bookcase.

Dan raised the bag he'd brought with him. Four more bottles of cider.

'Put them over there.' His father gestured with his glass towards a cupboard in a part of his room designated as a kitchen, although it amounted to nothing more than a microwave and a kettle, a small fridge on top. He spilled cider on to his shirt.

Dan put the bottles away and sat down. 'How are you?'

'I'm stuck in here. What do you think? Do you want a drink?'

'I'm driving.'

'Got your eye on some of the posh stuff, more like.'

'Good wine doesn't give you hangovers.'

'I didn't know it was medicinal.'

Dan smiled. His father infuriated him with his bloody-mindedness, but he knew he'd inherited many of his traits. Stubbornness for one, and a willingness to fight.

His father took a drink and said, 'What can I do for you?'

'I was passing.'

'You don't just pass. You call in when you want help, especially when you bring cider.'

'Can't a son seek guidance from his father?'

'I knew there was something. Go on, what is it?' He raised his glass. 'I guess you've paid the admission fee.'

'Pat Molloy's packing up at the end of the month.'

His father raised an eyebrow. 'Is he now? Why's that?'

'He's ill. Cancer.'

His father looked towards the window, with a view to a small patch of grass and a fence. 'Cancer's a bitch.'

Dan had lost his mother to cancer, and he'd seen her decline taking its toll on his father.

He turned back to Dan. 'The town will be missing a good man. He's served us well.'

'Yeah, he's hinted before that you used to send work to him.'

'It was rough back in the eighties. Everyone was against us. The courts. The police. If someone local got into trouble, we sent them to Pat. He didn't always charge. With Pat, it never seemed like it was about the money.'

'Pat is one of a kind. And it changes things for me too.'

'I don't understand.'

'Pat's retiring because of his illness, which will leave me without a job if the firm closes. That was always your focus when a mill went to the wall, wasn't it? The jobs.'

His father blushed. 'Some fancy lawyer isn't the same as someone on the bottom rung losing their only hope for a good job.'

'Not even when it's your son?'

'We move in different worlds and you've sold out. What do you expect me to say? What's next? The Freemasons?'

'My job is the same as Pat Molloy's but I don't get the same pat on the back?'

'Pat is different, because he had the upbringing to do something much better with his life, but he chose us.'

Dan sighed. He didn't want to get into an argument. 'Perhaps I just wanted to say hello.'

'Some time with your old pa?' He pointed towards the bottle on the bookcase. 'Pass me that and I'll give you all the attention you need.'

Dan stood up and went for the door. 'Get it yourself. And for your information, I'm thinking of taking over. How will you like that? The son of Highford's biggest peoples' champion becoming a boss?'

His father didn't respond at first. Dan went for the door, but just as he was about to go through, his father said, 'You've earned it.'

Dan stopped and looked back into the room.

His father smiled. 'It's a different world today, and you've somehow got to make your own way in it. Just promise me one thing, though.'

'What?'

'Treat your staff well. Don't chase every penny. Look after your people. That's all we were trying to do.'

Dan sighed. 'I don't know what I'm going to do yet, but if it happens, I will, don't worry.'

His father raised his glass. 'Don't slam the door as you go.' There was a glint in his eye.

Dan laughed and shook his head. His father did that to him. Whatever words he used to lash out, he always ended with something softer, revealing the father he could be.

Once Dan got outside, he had a view of the town and for the first time in his life he knew he could end up being tied to it. He'd have a business, a stake in the place beyond a family history, all so permanent. He wasn't sure how he felt about that.

His apartment wasn't far, down a long hill and over an old stone bridge. As Dan pulled into the yard, the cobbles rattling his wheels, his phone beeped to tell him that he had a message. He parked in his space and read.

It was from Jayne. It didn't say much. *I followed him. You need to come here. Urgent.* She included an address a few miles away.

He thought about the bottle of wine he'd picked up at the same time as his father's cider but realised it would have to wait.

He keyed the address into his satnav, backed his car out, and headed for the motorway.

Twenty-four

Sean had been getting ready for a while. Shower, hair-dryer. Trudy sat in the dark living room as the sun got lower, thinking back through the years about all they'd been through together.

Just over twenty years since they first met. Those times felt so innocent as she thought back, neither knowing what lay ahead. They'd been young and full of hope; the world had seemed so exciting. Now that they were both in their forties, everything felt a little more jaded, even though they still had each other.

There were the times apart, of course, and those memories hurt: his life with Karen and then the years he was locked away. She'd felt that hurt every day.

She was jarred from her thoughts by the thump of his feet as he came down the stairs. He was humming to himself, clean clothes on, hair swept back. He was wearing the shirt she'd bought him. Normally, she liked how it looked on him, hiding his growing stomach if he left it untucked, but today he was strutting like a peacock as he stopped in front of the hallway mirror. The smell of cologne drifted towards her.

'Who are you getting dressed up for?'

'I've got to look nice if I'm talking in public.' He flicked his hair as he said it.

'What, for some old dears who've little else to do for the evening but listen to you talk about yourself?'

She saw the flash of temper in the clench of his jaw, but he turned it into an unconvincing smile. 'We need the sales, and the exposure and the goodwill.'

'I'm sure they'll all think you're wonderful.'

'We've got to pay the bills.'

'And tonight you'll make a million?' She regretted it as soon as she said it, but he didn't respond.

He grabbed his car keys.

Just as the door was about to slam, she shouted, 'Your books!'

There was a pause before he came back into the living room. She pointed to the box in the corner of the room. 'You'll need your books, won't you?'

'Of course. Yes, thank you.' A flicker of a smile. 'I'm new to this author game.'

He collected the box and left the house. She didn't move as the engine started and he pulled away, the sound slowly fading, leaving her with just the steady clunk of the grandfather clock.

*

Dan's satnav alerted him that he'd arrived as he turned into an estate of new houses, all the windows bright and clean, the doors white PVC. He'd driven faster than he should have done, growing worried about Jayne's mysterious text the more he thought about it.

He scanned the street, but it was as ordinary as any he'd ever seen. The evening was drawing in, the sun fading to a burnt red in the distance, and lamps and flickering televisions lit the windows.

A door opened, casting a faint light over grey tarmac. The man in the doorway was backlit, his face in shadow. Dan recognised the frame, though. It was the man who'd been at the court earlier in the day.

Dan looked around himself as he approached the house, cautious in case it was a trap. The man didn't move or speak until Dan reached the door, when he stepped aside and said, 'You'd better come in.'

'Where's Jayne?' Dan said, not moving.

'Upstairs.'

'What –?'

Jayne's voice filtered down from above. 'Dan, come up.'

'Jayne? You all right?'

'Just come in, Dan.'

The man gestured again for Dan to go in, which he did, and looked up the stairs. Jayne was peering over the landing rail, a line of wooden spindles painted white, her long dark hair hanging down.

He looked back at the man, who pointed towards her. 'Go on up.'

Dan did as he was told, Jayne watching him all the way.

When he got to the landing, he said, 'What's going on?'

She went towards a room at the back of the house. 'You've got to see this.'

The man shouted up the stairs, 'Do you want a drink, Mr Grant? Coffee?'

Dan was confused but said, 'Yes, coffee with milk would be great.'

The room he followed Jayne into was a small study, with a desk and computer against one wall and a bookcase filled with black files on the other. Maps, photographs and scraps of paper were taped over the walls, hints of green paint showing through whatever small gaps there were, so that the whole room looked like a giant scrapbook. When he looked closer, he realised there was more order to it than a scrapbook. Dates typed on sheets of paper went around the walls at the top, with the cuttings and other papers arranged in columns underneath.

'What the hell is this?' Dan said.

'Peter Box's defence.'

Before Jayne could explain, the man came in with a tray containing three mugs of coffee and a small plate of biscuits.

'I don't have much in. I wasn't expecting visitors.'

'My fault,' Jayne said, sitting down on the computer chair. 'I'm not as good at subterfuge as I thought.'

Dan took the mug he was offered and put it on the desk. 'I don't know when you two became best buddies, but someone needs to tell me what's going on here.'

'I'm Bill Maude,' the man said, picking up a framed photograph from the desk and handing it to Dan. His eyes clouded. 'This is my son, Tom. He was murdered three years ago.'

A man in his early twenties stared out from the frame, a selfie taken high on a hill, his grin bright and wide, his dark hair cropped short. There were traces of Bill in him, but now Dan looked up he could see that Bill looked worn out, his pale skin marked by the broken veins in his cheeks.

'He took that picture a week before he was killed,' Bill said.

'I'm sorry to hear that, but what –?' A thought occurred to Dan. 'If you're interested in me because I represented his killer, I'm sorry, but that's what I do for a living.' Dan handed the photograph back to Bill, who put it back on the desk, turning it so that it was in the same position as before.

'No one has represented his killer,' Bill said, his eyes staying on the picture. 'Whoever killed Tom hasn't been caught, and he's not alone. Look around.' He turned in a circle as he gestured towards the walls. 'In the last twenty years, over a hundred people have been killed or have gone missing around the northern canals, all unsolved. Or so the police say.' He wagged his finger. 'There's a serial killer on the waterways and no one seems to care.'

'Are you serious?'

'My son was murdered. I don't joke about that.'

'All right, I'm sorry, but why does this involve me?'

'Because there is one case where the killer has been found. That's your man. Peter Box.'

Dan rubbed his eyes. He was too tired for this. 'Are you saying my client is a serial killer?'

'Possibly, unless he's innocent, of course. That's why I was there today, to hear the evidence, to find out what it was about, to see whether Peter Box is in fact the killer. If he is, he might also be the man who murdered my son, because he's killed someone by a canal. But the police won't go looking unless they see a link.'

Dan's mind flashed to Pat's revelation that Peter had confessed to Rosie Smith's murder that also happened by a canal. 'And how do you feel now, after hearing what the case is about?'

'There isn't any direct evidence. All I heard from the prosecutor was about blood on a shoe, but what if they've got it wrong?'

'That's the defence case, in a nutshell.'

'And if they have got it wrong, the real killer is free to do it again. And all of this carries on. More murders. More unexplained disappearances.'

'What do you think, Dan?' Jayne said.

Dan turned slowly as he took in again the displays around the walls. 'It's the second day of the trial tomorrow, and you want me to start uncovering a whole series of attacks that no one believes are linked, in the hope that the jury thinks that it might be all true? I mean, come on, over a hundred?'

'That's my fault, I'm sorry. I should have come to you before today, but I was scared about what you might say. I was even outside your apartment yesterday, but I lost my nerve.'

'How do you know where I live?'

'I followed you from your office.' He held his hands up. 'I know how it looks but I was desperate. No one takes me seriously.'

Dan considered Bill Maude for a few seconds and then looked around the walls again. He shook his head. 'I'm sorry but it's not going to happen. Peter Box is on trial because there is physical evidence against him. If the jury start wondering if there's a serial killer out there, they'll look at the dock and come to one conclusion: that it's him.'

Jayne held her hand out. 'Don't you think you should at least hear what Bill has got to say?'

Dan picked up his mug and leaned against the door. 'All right. I started this, I suppose, and I trust your instincts, Jayne, but it's been a long day.' He took a sip. 'Bill, tell me about your son. He looks like he was a good man.'

'He was. I was very proud of him. He'd just finished an English degree at Leeds. He wanted to go into teaching and was a real outdoors type. Walking, climbing. Caving and potholing were next on his list, but he never got the chance. He went out for a drink in Manchester and missed the last train.'

'Who did he go for a drink with?'

'Just friends from university. They'd promised each other that they'd stay in touch, and this was the first reunion. They'd chosen Manchester because it was an easy train ride for some, but Tom hung on too late. He knew Manchester, so he reckoned he could walk part of the way. He texted me, told me he was walking home but could I collect him. I told him to wait where he was but he said he'd already set off, to get away from the city centre to make it easy for me, but I don't get how he could have got lost and ended up where he did. His phone must have run out of battery, or else he was attacked before he had a chance to answer, because that was the last time I heard from him. They never found his phone.'

'Where was he found?'

Bill went to a large map on a wall and jabbed at it with his finger. 'By the Bridgewater Canal, close to Castlefield.'

Dan stared at the map. Castlefield was practically central Manchester, and not on the way out towards rural Highford. He could see the need in Bill's eyes and forced himself to ask the obvious question, though he could already guess the answer. 'What was the cause of death?'

'The post-mortem said drowning. But how could he drown like that unless he was held underwater? Young, fit men don't just fall into canals and drown.'

'Any other injuries?'

'His cheekbone was fractured, with tiny shards of stone in the cut. The coroner said it was accidental, that he tripped and hit his head on the canal bank and fell in.'

'Perhaps he did.'

Bill went to the wall furthest from the window. 'Like he did?' He pointed to a newspaper clipping showing a young man in a graduation gown. 'And him?' He pointed at another. 'Do you know how many people have died in the canals around Manchester in just the last seven years? Sixty-one, that's how many. Can you believe that?'

'It sounds a lot, but if that was unusual, the police would be doing more.'

'So you'd think, but they've just written them all off as accidental drownings. But that number? Too high, so I expanded my research and I looked beyond Manchester, and went back further, to twenty years ago.'

'Why twenty?'

'Because 1998 was the year the Internet really took off, so the newspapers started to get websites, which gave me somewhere to search. The thing with canals is that people travel on them, so if someone wants to remain undetected, they keep moving. That's why I looked further afield.'

'Is that figure high though? Over a hundred in twenty years means just five a year as an average, and there are a lot of canals.'

Bill wagged his finger. 'You were surprised at the figure, and these are only the ones I've discovered so far. I've only just started to look beyond Manchester, so there'll be more, you can trust me on that.' He pointed at a clipping further along. 'Take her, for example, Tammy Riches. She was walking her dog along the canal in Todmorden but never made it home. Just like your case, Lizzie Barnsley.'

'Sexually assaulted?'

'Yes. She was found in the bushes near some canal locks.'

'How can it be the same person, then?'

'I don't understand.'

'Yes, you do,' Dan said. 'If this was the work of a serial attacker, there'd be a pattern, specific traits, you know, a clear motive. This is all too random. Lizzie Barnsley wasn't sexually assaulted.'

Bill shook his head. He sounded impatient when he said, 'You've got to look at the numbers. Why can't anyone else see it? I thought you'd be different, but you're just like the police, talking about patterns and behaviour. I'm not saying they're all by the same person, but isn't a high number a pattern too?'

Dan sighed. He could see that Bill was trapped in grief and had no desire to trample over it. He looked around the clippings again. 'Tell me how some of the men died?'

'What, the Manchester ones? A lot of those were men.'

'No, the ones nearer here.'

Bill pointed to some photographs further along. 'These two were slashed and dumped. These other two' – he tapped the pictures as he spoke – 'were beaten to a pulp, and the last one was drowned but found on the canal bank, not in the water.'

'And the women?'

'Like Tammy, four were sexually assaulted or raped, and another one was strangled. Then there was Rosie Smith and Lizzie Barnsley.'

Dan exchanged glances with Jayne and said, 'Rosie Smith?'

'Yes. Sean Martin went to prison but got out on appeal.'

'Yes, I know it all right,' Dan said, not wanting to give anything away, 'but it's too random.'

'But don't you see how it's too much of a coincidence, all these people found by or in the canals?'

'Canal towpaths are dark and quiet at night. Just the right kind of place for someone to be killed. The numbers sound high, but they're over twenty years.'

'There've been other people who've disappeared too, on top of the ones I've mentioned. What about them?'

'How many?'

'Just in Lancashire? Seventeen people in the last twenty years who've left their houses and never returned, and who all either lived by the canals or were heading that way. Men *and* women. It's getting worse too. Eight in the last five years compared to the nine before then. The killer is gathering pace.'

'*If* there is a killer. People run away and start new lives for many reasons.'

'I thought you at least might listen, since it might help your client.'

'How can it help Peter Box? If I turn up with your cuttings, I'll be laughed out of the courtroom.' Bill looked hurt, so Dan softened his tone and said, 'What happened to your son is awful, but I just can't see any connection to my case.'

Jayne stood up. 'I'm sorry, Bill. I did say that what you've got might not be enough.'

'But there's something here, right?'

'It's not about whether or not I believe you,' Dan said. 'It's whether I can use it in *this* case, whether it will help Peter Box. Right now, it's too late to gamble on this. It will make me look desperate.'

'At least look.' Bill reached for a folder in a corner. 'It's all in here, just for times like this, when people take an interest. If I keep on pushing, eventually someone will prove that I'm right.'

He held it out to Dan, who took it and looked inside. It was crammed with printed copies of the cuttings that lined the walls, along with typed notes. Bill's dossier.

Dan handed it back, despite the desperate plea in Bill's eyes. 'I'm sorry, I just don't think I can help.'

'I'm not crazy. I know that people don't believe me, but it doesn't make me wrong.'

'Have you spoken to the police in my case?'

'Of course I have. They were nice to me but fobbed me off with some young detective. She's polite, but she talks to me to keep me out of the way, that's all.'

'Is it the woman you met earlier today in the car park?' Jayne said, and she pulled her camera from her pocket. She scrolled through the screen until she found a picture. 'Her?'

Bill looked at the screen. 'Yes, that's her, but I wasn't meeting her. We just happened to be parked in the same place.'

'Really?'

He blushed. 'All right, I'd been looking out for her and had parked in the same place deliberately. She was angry, thought I was stalking her. I just wanted to know whether she had changed her mind.'

'Show me.' Dan held out his hand for the camera.

The screen showed a woman in a suit, talking to Bill, but she was too far away on the small screen for him to make out who she was.

'Can I zoom in on this?'

Jayne took it back from him and pressed a button until it made the woman's face fill the screen. When he took hold of it again, his eyes widened in surprise. 'This is her?'

Bill looked at the screen and then nodded.

'You know her?' Jayne asked, taking the camera back.

'Amy Hunter,' Dan said. 'DC Hunter. She was in on Peter's interview. I don't know why she was at court though.'

'Hand-holding the witnesses,' Bill said. 'Is she in trouble for speaking to me?'

'I don't know, but I'm going to find out why no one has mentioned another line of inquiry.'

'You are interested then?'

Dan looked to Jayne and then back to Bill. He sighed. 'Jayne, can you find out as much as you can about this? We'll talk later.'

With that, Dan went downstairs to leave, the hallway filled with Bill's excited chatter as he took Jayne through some more details.

Although Dan's focus was on his case, he hoped he wasn't about to disappoint a grieving father.

Twenty-five

Dan checked his watch. DC Hunter had been keeping him waiting for too long.

He'd found her number from when Peter was still locked up at the police station. At the time they'd exchanged numbers so that he could be available for the next interview as soon as they were ready for him.

When he had called her he'd mentioned Bill's name so that she knew why he was ringing. She'd told him to come to the station, but ever since then he'd been left in the reception area, pacing before the glossy crime-prevention posters.

The door opened. It wasn't DC Hunter but Murdoch, a scowl on her face.

'What's going on, Dan?'

'Where's DC Hunter?'

'You've got me.'

'I'm just discovering things I haven't been told.'

'Bill Maude?'

'You know it is. I told your DC that, but I'm suspecting there's more to this if you've been sent to speak to me.'

She was silent for a few seconds before saying, 'Come through.'

He followed her into the long corridor that ran behind the reception, towards the squad rooms and canteen, a labyrinth of corridors built in the days before architects decided that natural light was a good thing. Yellowing strip lights illuminated the station and the doorframes were all dark wood, making everywhere look old and jaded.

Murdoch turned and put her hands on her hips. 'I didn't want this conversation in public, because I don't know who's going to walk in.'

'I don't keep secrets if they help my client.'

'Nothing helps your client. His blood is on her shoe. He won't put forward a defence.'

'I know, that's what the trial is all about, but let's pretend for a moment you're wrong. Bill Maude came to see you with his theories about a serial killer along the canals. What did you do about it?'

'Come on, Dan, do you really think there's anything in what he's saying? He was talking about a hundred deaths over twenty years. It's the desperate plea of a grieving father who can't accept his son was taken by an accident. How did you find out about him?'

'Bill was lurking around the court and I didn't know whether he was a threat. He seemed too interested in me, watching me. I asked Jayne, my investigator, to find out who he was. She was successful, so here I am.'

'You're not telling me you believe him?'

'I'm investigating it. Did you?'

'Seriously?'

'Deadly.'

Murdoch sighed. 'None of it seemed relevant. The man is obsessed. Surely you saw that?'

'Why didn't you disclose this though?'

'You think it's disclosable? If he has any credibility, it's as an informant, and we never disclose those details. We don't list every wild claim we hear.'

'When did he get in touch with you?'

'After we charged Peter Box. He thought it might be part of a series, kept calling the squad. I sent Hunter to warn him off.'

'And see whether there was anything in it?'

'A little bit of that, but she wasn't convinced. Said he was just some grieving old guy.'

Dan smiled. 'That's fine. It's the answer I wanted.'

'What do you mean?'

'Nothing.' He went to the door. 'Can you let me out?'

Murdoch pressed a black fob against a metal plate on the wall. The door buzzed. Dan opened it, but before he could let it close Murdoch held it.

'Tell me what you mean?'

'I'll see you in court tomorrow.'

'You can't do this, Dan.'

'Tomorrow,' and with that he headed out of the station, knowing that Murdoch was watching him all the way.

The answers he'd been given were exactly what he expected, but if there was anything to what Bill Maude was saying, he'd just fired the first shot.

Twenty-six

Pat Molloy grimaced and shifted in his chair.

He'd been home for an hour and had spent it with a whiskey, reading Sean Martin's book. Not to see how he described the case, but looking for some clues to add to what Sean had told him all those years ago. He'd stayed up late reading it the night before, but the visit from Trudy had hardened his resolve.

His large house was shielded from the countryside by high brick walls. He and his wife, Eileen, had bought it years before, when there was still money to be made in criminal law, aided by an inheritance from his father.

A few years ago, Pat thought the wall gave him privacy, so that neighbours and passers-by couldn't see in. Now, he'd changed his mind. His life was ending, he knew that, and he wanted to see the hills beyond and the passing traffic, the dog walkers and the ramblers. He wanted to see *life*. Instead, all he had were the small fruit trees that broke the monotony of the lawn and a solid line of brickwork.

He put his head back and closed his eyes. It had been a long day. He'd taken a walk to the courthouse, just to see some old faces, but it had all seemed so jaded. The ones who had been there for years looked worn out, and the younger ones seemed disinterested. He thought he missed it, but really it just reminded him how he should have left it all behind a few years earlier. When it came to the final moments, none of it mattered.

The ones who knew him tried to hide their shock at his appearance but didn't do a good job of it. That wasn't how he wanted to be remembered, as a tired and ill old man. He wanted to scream at them that they'd all end up like this too, that life shouldn't be all about chasing the money, but he knew no one would listen. He'd have ignored the warning when he was younger too.

Eileen came into the room. 'Do you want some supper?'

He opened his eyes and gazed at her, and not for the first time marvelled at his good fortune. They'd made a good team and had enjoyed some special times. He hadn't always treated her well, but she'd stayed with him, certain that they were better together than apart, and for that he was grateful.

'I'm all right with this for now.' He raised the glass.

'You need to eat. You've got a fight ahead of you.'

He shook his head. 'I'm not up for a fight, my dear.'

She folded her arms and glared at him. 'I expect better from you, not to just give up.'

'Just let me sort out my affairs and then I'll focus on me. Dan is thinking about my offer.'

'Do you think he'll accept?'

'I don't know if he wants to be a boss. He could join one of those big firms and be part of a team, but I hope not. It makes me sound vain, but that firm and my name on that window is my legacy.'

She kissed him on his forehead. 'And us, and our children.' She looked down at the book. 'So, what's all this reading? You need to rest up.'

'Just a book by an old client.' He showed her the cover of Sean Martin's book.

'Oh, *that* man. I never liked him.'

He took a drink as he flicked through the photo section. 'Nor me.' Something caught his attention, and he stopped, lost in the book.

Eileen stood and considered him for a few seconds, but it was clear his attention was gone. 'I'm going to have a bath.'

'Very good, my dear,' Pat muttered as she left the room. He stared at the picture and tried to work out what it was about it that had made him pause. He closed his eyes again and rubbed his chest. It was almost as if he could feel the cancer growing inside him, devouring his organs, taking him over. He felt robbed, cheated. He'd been looking forward to his retirement and then bang, it was all taken away.

Forty years earlier, he'd been a young articled clerk, fresh from university, following in his own father's footsteps. It had been his vocation, but he had taken a different route to his father. Not for Pat the grind of commercial law, his father's career spent drawing up contracts and taking debtors to court. Pat had been attracted to criminal law because of the excitement, back when justice was often meted out by the police in the back alleys, neither side interested in a court hearing.

Then there was the day-to-day stress. The judges who wanted to embarrass him. The clients who wanted to hit him because they didn't like his advice. The tedium of form-filling. The stale stench of clients who came into the office from a dirty home. The despair in the eyes of people whose lives had turned out wretched and had realised that it was never going to get any better.

Those times seemed distant but, in some ways, it felt like they'd only just happened. Life was simpler back then. No Internet. No smartphones. No micromanagement. The job was conducted by notes written on scraps of paper and in rooms heavy with cigarette smoke, with police officers who relied on trickery and deceit, and often brutality.

In some ways, things were better now. In others, they weren't. However they compared, he'd lived through all of it, and those years had enriched his life.

Then he remembered Sean Martin. The shock of his words at the party. The whole room had seemed to retreat, his mind focused on what Sean had said and the sadistic gleam in his eyes. It hadn't been enough that he'd got out; he'd wanted Pat to know that he'd cheated everyone.

Perhaps it had been a drunken joke?

He took another sip. He didn't believe that. Not for a moment.

Pat couldn't work out why that case in particular still bothered him so much. He'd freed more bad people than he could count. Not just killers, but robbers and rapists and child molesters, and he'd never given it a second thought. He had just been doing his job. Perhaps it was because the evidence had been the problem in those cases, so that it was the fault of the police that the cases weren't strong enough. In Sean's case, the evidence had been fine. Pat had just found an expert who was able to throw in some doubt, and he'd searched so hard because he'd been convinced of Sean's innocence.

Because Sean had made him believe in his innocence.

Sean Martin was the shadow on his career. He needed to know whether he was right, or whether it was just a drunken joke; Sean enjoying the look in Pat's eye, stupid from the relief of being out of prison. If he was innocent, prison might have done strange things to him.

Pat looked again at the book, and suddenly the clue was clear to him. Sean Martin hadn't been able to stop himself; he must have enjoyed the thought that the answer was right there in the book for everyone to see but no one else would ever spot it. It was the same arrogance that had allowed Sean to admit to Pat where he'd hidden the murder weapon.

And that arrogance would be his downfall. The book might be Sean's own little private joke, but for Pat it was the final section of the picture Sean had painted for him at the appeal party.

Pat put his glass down and creaked to his feet, coughing as he did. He shuffled to the hallway and grabbed his coat from the hook by the door.

'I'm just going out,' he shouted up the stairs, hoping to be heard over the sound of running bath taps.

There was no answer.

He was pleased about that. He knew Eileen would disapprove.

The cold night hit him hard, making him cough again, but he needed internal peace more than he wanted a warm night.

He knew exactly where he was going.

Twenty-seven

Jayne knocked on the door and stood back. The sound of a television came from inside. The house was part of a long terrace with no front gardens, just a line of stones broken by doorways and windows, like regular patterns, so that the noises from indoors were hard to conceal.

It was one last stop, back on the trail of Sean Martin before she went to Dan's apartment. She guessed that Dan had been humouring Bill when he told her to find out more, but she had Bill's folder in the boot of her car. She wasn't giving up yet.

A young woman wearing a supermarket uniform answered. When she saw Jayne, the woman sighed and said, 'Whatever you're selling, I'm not buying.'

'Victoria Mason?' Jayne handed over her business card. 'I want to talk to you about Rosie Smith.'

The woman frowned. 'How do you know where I live?'

'I'm an investigator. It's what I do.'

Victoria stared at the card. 'You'd better come in, then.' She stepped aside to let Jayne in, who took the business card back from her and walked straight into the front room. There was barely a hallway. She knew this kind of terrace well enough: there was always just a room at the front, and a kitchen at the back.

As Jayne took the seat she was offered, she didn't want to admit that her detecting skills had been much less spectacular than she'd made out. A quick Internet search had revealed a court appearance the year before, for benefit fraud after Victoria had failed to disclose that her boyfriend was living with her, and with it came an address.

Victoria sat opposite, perched on the edge of her cushion. 'What do you want to know?'

'You were friends with Rosie Smith at the time she was killed. Rosie's mother showed me a newspaper article from then.'

'I was. We were close. A group of us used to hang around together, outside the local shop.' She smiled. 'It's funny, because I see other girls doing the same now and it seems so childish, but we thought we were so grown up. You must know what that's like. You look about my age. Twenty-four?'

'Twenty-five.'

'And how did you get to be a private investigator when I ended up working in the same local shop I used to hang around?'

It wasn't the right time for the real story. 'It's not as glamorous as it sounds. Tell me about Rosie.'

'What do you want to know? She was a sweet girl. She could be a bit naughty sometimes, but there was no spite in what she did. We all do stupid stuff at that age. I think about her a lot. Sometimes, when I do something new, I think how Rosie never got to do it.'

'How did she get on with her stepfather?'

'Oh, him. Okay, I think. He used to collect her from school sometimes and he was a bit creepy, but Rosie seemed okay about him.'

'How do you mean, creepy?'

'He was one of those older guys who still want to be cool and pretend to know about young people's stuff, but to us he was

Rosie's stepdad. He wasn't that old really, but it was still a bit weird, you know, like your teacher trying to be your friend or something.'

'What did you think when he was charged with her murder?'

She scowled. 'Amazed. Couldn't believe it. Like, I met the guy and he could do that? Didn't seem right.'

'Did you believe he was guilty?'

'The police said he was.'

'What about now?'

'I see Rosie's mum sometimes and I know what she thinks. She knew him better than I did.'

'Why did you think he would have done it?'

'Same as most people thought, that he'd killed her to silence her because he was abusing her. What else could it be? That's what the papers hinted at, even if it was never printed. Just because Rosie never said it, doesn't mean it didn't happen.'

'Rosie never told you anything about Sean that would justify him needing to silence her?'

'No, and Rosie seemed all right with him. She moaned about him being a bit strict, because he wasn't her real dad, but that's it.'

'Have you heard of Lizzie Barnsley?'

Victoria thought hard. 'No, I don't know her. Is this to do with Rosie's murder?'

'Lizzie was murdered on New Year's Day, just after midnight. I'm working for the law firm that represents the man accused of her murder.'

'Hang on, is that the murder on the canal?'

'That's her.'

'Yeah, I know who you mean. When I saw the picture in the paper, I thought she looked familiar. It's a small town, and you recognise people. What has it got to do with Rosie though?'

'Perhaps the same person was responsible for both murders?'

'Oh, I get you.' Victoria thought about that as she pulled a cigarette from her pocket. She lit it and took a long drag, watching Jayne through the smoke. 'Are you saying your client might have killed Rosie?'

'No, exactly the opposite, but the two might be connected. Is the name Peter Box familiar?'

She shook her head. 'Never heard of him.'

'Not even back then?'

'Nope.' Another long pull on the cigarette. 'I've just answered your questions. Now you can answer mine: this name you mentioned, Peter Box, did he kill Lizzie? Or Rosie?'

'I don't know.' Jayne held out her hands. 'I'm being honest because I really just don't know.'

'That will have to do, I suppose.'

Jayne dug out her business card from her pocket again and handed it back. 'Keep it this time. If you hear of anything, let me know.'

Victoria took it from her and tapped it against her knuckles. 'Will do.'

As Jayne left, she looked back at the house. She hadn't made any progress, except to learn that there was no link between Lizzie and Rosie. That meant that any link had to be between Peter and Sean. She just didn't know whether there was enough time to find it.

Twenty-eight

Dan was lying back, trying to make the stresses of the day disappear when the door buzzer sounded. He groaned as he shuffled over to the security monitor. When he saw it was Jayne, he jabbed at the button to unlock the entrance door.

By the time she bounded in, closing the door with a clatter and sitting down on the sofa, he'd gone to the fridge and pulled out the wine bottle he'd opened not long before. She was carrying a bag, which she dumped on the floor, along with her coat. 'You're working me hard today. On the way back from Bill's house I went to see Victoria Mason, one of Rosie's friends, to find out more about her and Sean.'

'And?'

'She said he was just a normal guy. A little embarrassing as a stepdad, tried a bit too hard to be cool, but nothing suspicious about him.'

'And Sean Martin still gets away with that act.'

'Does that matter?'

'It matters to Pat, so yes, it does.'

'He knows we're watching him.' She raised her phone. 'He *liked* my Facebook page. You said you wanted to see how he reacted. You've got your answer.'

'How do you feel about that?'

'What, having a killer following me, and making sure I know it? Oh, just fantastic.'

'I'm sorry. I can keep you out of it.'

'No way. Not after speaking to Bill.'

'I wish you hadn't.'

'What do you mean? Am I getting too expensive?'

'No. It's because the trial has started and I don't want a distraction.'

'It was your idea to follow him. Anyway, it was interesting.'

'When I'm in the middle of a murder trial –' He realised he was repeating the same old complaint. 'I'll rephrase that. When I'm in the middle of the first murder trial I'm doing on my own, I could do without something extra.'

'Ignore it then.'

'I wish I could, but I've been to see Murdoch about it.'

'Why? You dismissed it all at Bill's house.'

'I didn't want to give him any false hope, but in trials I can't rule anything out. All I wanted was the information that the police had been given another line of enquiry and didn't pursue it. Whether there's any truth in it doesn't really matter. It adds weight to the defence that they fixated on Peter and relied on bodged forensics.'

'How long have they known?'

'Right back to the beginning. They just ignored it.'

'You'll be glad I brought this with me then,' she said as she reached into the bag to pull out the folder from Bill's house. 'We could go through it together.'

Dan groaned and then laughed. 'Why did I get you involved in this?'

'Just ignore it then. We can watch television, if that's what you want. Pretend you've never seen Bill's clippings, and when you see him at court, tell him you've decided not to use it but wish him all the best.' She went over to the coffee table and put the folder there, patting it with her hand. 'There, just pretend you can't see it.'

Dan rolled his eyes and sighed. 'I said *the truth* of it is irrelevant, but you're going to make me do this.'

Jayne smiled. 'You've got to know the truth, whether you use it or not, and I spent a long time with Bill. I think he might actually have something.'

'Really?'

She pulled a face. 'Well, I'm a sucker for the conspiracy programmes and murder mystery stuff.'

'What has he got, apart from big numbers?'

'I wonder whether there might be a different pattern to how he sees it. For Bill, there are three types of victims. First, there are those who died by being pushed into the canal . . .'

Dan raised an eyebrow. 'Or fallen in, drunk.'

'It's Bill's theory, not mine.'

'Sorry, go on.'

'The majority of the deaths are clustered around Manchester city centre, mostly around Canal Street.'

'Close to the nightlife.'

'Exactly. Taking a short cut in the dark when they weren't at their sharpest, most likely. Same as Tom, I suppose. He ended up in the Bridgewater Canal, and Bill thinks it's foul play. Perhaps he was mugged or attacked or got into a fight, but maybe he just stepped off the edge and cracked his head on the way down, like the police thought. He's only managed to get the big numbers by casting the net wider.' Jayne took the elastic band from the bundle with a twang and lifted some papers before putting them to one side. 'But the further away he's moved from Manchester, the more he's included those who were attacked or murdered around the canals, and then those who went missing.'

'What's your theory?'

'Bill has concentrated on how close they were to the canals, but in every programme I've ever watched, they say focus on the victim or how they died, not where they are found. We should filter them differently. Sex attacks. Gang fights or muggings. Women who have gone missing who are similar in profile to Lizzie.'

'I see where you're coming from,' Dan said, flicking through Bill's folder with more interest. 'They've got to be relevant to Lizzie. We'd have to show a theme, a pattern, not just throw random numbers at the jury. But how strict do we make it? Lizzie Barnsley was found by a dog walker and she'd been killed only a few hours earlier, but there was no sexual assault.'

'Men who attack women always have a sexual motive, even if it is power rather than sex.'

'Let's do our own list then and see if we can spot patterns Bill hasn't. He's too close to it. List women who were attacked or killed, whether or not there was an obvious sexual motive. And then the people who drowned in the canal where it could be accidental, so we can discard those. Get rid of the male victims too. And then a list of the missing women.'

They went through Bill's folder, checking with each other about each case, moving papers around as they decided which category to put them into.

'We don't have to be precise, remember,' Dan said. 'We're not trying to catch a killer. We're trying to throw some doubt around, that's all, and this will just let the jurors play at being detectives. They won't have time to scrutinise the list.'

'Perhaps Bill was right, then. Just go for the big figure and ignore the detail.'

'No, stick with this for now, we're doing okay.' He stood back. 'What have we got?'

The papers were arranged in columns, covering the living-room floor.

Jayne went to the fridge. 'My glass is empty.' She poured herself a drink and refilled Dan's glass. 'This list here.' She pointed to the column nearest to the kitchen. 'This is our key list: women between twenty and forty. Some were attacked and murdered. Some were sexually assaulted and survived. Twenty in total. Twenty-two, if we include Rosie and Lizzie. Rosie is younger than the other women, but she's connected to Peter and Sean.'

'That's a lot.'

'It is. Eight fatalities. Twelve reported sex attacks, over twenty years.'

'And limited to the ones Bill has discovered.'

'Exactly. Now, of the seventeen women who've disappeared, twelve are women between twenty and forty.'

'Why under forty? Why are you drawing the line there?'

'I thought if the victim profile was important, age might be too. Lizzie was in her mid-twenties. We've got to make the jury think the victims are similar.'

Dan shook his head and looked at the pile. 'Across the north, and over the course of twenty years, it's too random. No chance the judge will let them in.'

'Can he do that?'

'If he thinks I'm just fishing for a connection and that there's no real link to the case, he can rule it out. More prejudicial than probative and all that.'

'But how can it be prejudicial if it helps Peter?'

'Prejudice cuts both ways. For the prosecution, too, which is why I can't start spouting random stuff.'

'But we've got a good number, and Bill might be right, that it's all about the number. And we haven't been too random. We've discarded men and those who might have drowned by falling in.'

'Twenty years,' Dan repeated. 'Are the figures that out of line? I'm trying to think of what I'd do if I were a sexual predator. I'd hang around parks and canals. They're quiet, often leading to fields, which provide a good escape route.'

'What you're saying is that these kinds of attacks are more likely in places like canals?'

'Exactly. Which means that the judge is more likely to say that they have no relevance and exclude them.' Dan furrowed his brow. 'There is one category though: the missing ones.'

'But what have they got to do with Peter Box? Lizzie wasn't missing.'

'An abduction gone wrong, possibly?'

Jayne swirled her drink in her glass. 'I see what you mean. If a murderer was patrolling the canals, they wouldn't get away with it for so long if the bodies were found easily, because there'd be forensic evidence or eye-witnesses eventually.'

'Exactly. If we mention survivors, those people might have given descriptions that show they can't be the same person. The same where a body was found, as there might be forensic results that show they were killed by different people. Bill was relying on newspaper clippings, not evidence. But missing persons? No bodies means no forensics, and if we want to put doubt into the minds of the jurors, we should make them think someone is getting away with murder. We do that by looking at those who went missing. Lizzie was killed by the canal, but was that because she fought?' He frowned. 'But there is one problem.'

'Which is?'

'You've just made my night a lot longer.' He raised his glass. 'We need more of this.'

Twenty-nine

Pat almost didn't see the gateway.

He'd been driving along a country lane bordered by hawthorn hedges when he saw the gap. He swerved to a stop and switched off his lights, but not before they illuminated the building squatting on the other side of the field. For a moment it was dark. Then headlights from a car passing on the motorway above swept the area.

He was in the countryside a few miles outside Highford, the rural quiet broken only by the slow click of his engine as it cooled and the smooth hum of traffic. The nearest village was a couple of miles away.

As he stared ahead, the half-moon came out from behind a cloud and gave him a clearer view of the field he would have to cross. It was damp and rutted, large tufts of grass hiding whatever would make a mess of his shoes.

His breath misted before him as he put on coat, scarf and gloves. He felt the cold more than he used to, as if his whole being was becoming thinner.

His feet crunched on gravel. He opened the boot to take out the spade that he'd picked up from the garage before he'd left the house.

Pat pushed the metal gate, and it creaked open on rusted hinges. He trudged across the field, the grass trailing against his trousers.

There was a canal on the other side of the field, a long slow curve as it made its way through the sheep farms that occupied the land between Highford and Whitton. The field rose steadily, so that his breath became laboured as he walked, his hand clutching his chest. The air he sucked in chilled him, but he could see what he was aiming for: a small stone structure, a ruined cottage, its outline visible against the distant sweep of headlights. The orange glow of the next village along was in the distance, but it served merely to highlight how isolated he was. The motorway blocked the view ahead and behind him was just a line of dark hills.

He gasped as he pushed on and the field got more uneven as he got closer to the water. The further away he got from his car, the more alone he felt.

As he reached the edge of the canal, he stopped. He bent over, his hands on his legs, as he struggled to breathe. He'd taken the easiest route across the field, and the disused building was further along, but he felt like he'd been for a long hike.

The derelict cottage looked more ominous as he got closer. He'd driven past it countless times and never thought anything of it, but in his book Sean had written how he and Trudy used to love cruising along the canal and picnicking on the bank, fantasising about buying an old cottage and bringing it back to life. It was the postscript to the story that sealed it, because in it Sean described how progress had ruined their dream by running a motorway past it, taking away the tranquillity.

Sean's taunt during the celebratory party had come back to him, where he'd leaned in, sweat on his upper lip, and hissed, 'By the western corner, just under the surface, below the mason's mark – an itch you can't scratch.'

A mason's mark. Somewhere old. It made so much sense. He didn't know whether Dan would be able to use whatever he found, or even if he'd find anything, but his quest had become more important than that somehow. It had become about his own mental peace, as if he was the one needing redemption. He needed to know.

The ground became more uneven, and he almost tripped over a rock embedded in the ground. That forced him to go slower. He couldn't afford to injure himself and be left out in the field all night. Spring had arrived but the nights were still cold, particularly away from the warmth of the town and in the path of the winds that rolled over the hilltops. He was determined to keep going though.

He stopped when he got to the cottage and pressed his hands against the stone. It had long since fallen into disrepair and nature was slowly taking it over. The roof had gone, slate thieves wouldn't leave the tiles there for too long, along with all the pipes and guttering.

He hadn't brought a torch, and he cursed himself for that.

He glanced into the house through the shell of a window. The inside was swallowed up by darkness. It looked like it might have been a kitchen, as he could just make out the edge of a cupboard, but beyond that it was all black.

For a moment, a headlight from the motorway made the walls and doorways inside bend and move.

Pat stepped away, his heart beating fast, his chest aching.

He was scared. He should go back to his car and go home, where Eileen would pour him a whiskey and he could seek solace in the glow of the fire. He could tell Dan about his suspicions in the morning.

But it seemed stupid not to look now he was here. He couldn't just leave, not when it was the question that had haunted him ever since Sean's release party. He thought about his phone and whether he could use the screen as a light, but then he remembered that he hadn't brought it with him. It had been part of his promise to Eileen, that he wouldn't be wedded to it like he had been before, always waiting for a call from a police station. It was turned off and in his study.

He peered again at the cottage. He tried to work out which corner of the cottage was the most westerly and went to it. The moon wasn't strong enough to allow him to see properly, so he felt along the stones with his hands. But then another set of headlights swept the cottage and he saw it – scratches embedded in a cornerstone, a mason's mark, an inverted triangle on top of another triangle, making a shape like an egg-timer.

He grinned, despite the cold and the ache in his chest. This was the place, right where he was standing.

The ground was overgrown with weeds and nettles that spread right into the wall. He pulled those away first, pausing to take ragged breaths. Once he'd cleared that, he dragged his spade along the ground, feeling for a slight bump or indentation. After a few metres, he stopped and sighed. He was wasting his time; the whole area was uneven.

He was about to give in when he had another thought. If he could just remove the turf, it might reveal something.

He took a deep breath and thrust the spade into the ground, the soil soft and moist and heavy. Pat strained as he removed the first large clod and then went along the ground with his spade, marking out a straight line, the house in front of him. He started to remove turf along the line, digging methodically.

It was warm work. He took off his coat, the night air turning his sweat-soaked shirt into a cold rag.

It took him an hour to cut away a large square of turf running up to the western corner, the grass often tangled with weeds, the sound of his breaths loud. Once he finished, he got on his knees, his gloves off, and started feeling the ground again.

He stopped.

There'd been a noise. There'd been a steady hum of cars in the distance, but this seemed different. Closer, slower.

He straightened and looked across the field behind him, and cursed again his lack of a torch. All he could see was a dark and empty field. He went back to running his hand over the ground, trying to ignore the feeling that he was being watched. It was his nerves playing tricks in the dark.

He was almost by the corner of the house when he felt it. A rustle of plastic, like the top of a knotted bag but thick. He got to his feet and went for his spade, excited now.

He was about to start digging when he heard the noise again. It was closer this time. Someone moving through the long grass.

'Hello?'

His voice was timid.

There was no reply.

Thirty

'If we're concentrating on the ones who are missing,' Jayne said, 'we should look for patterns.'

'What, not just focus on the fact that they're missing?'

'No. If we want to classify these cases as abductions leading to murders where the bodies haven't been found, it means the killer is organised, every part planned and thought out, but thoughts create patterns.' She shrugged. 'I told you, I watch too much true crime, but isn't that how it is? You're either organised or disorganised. If we're using this, we've got to show that someone could go for years without being caught, which means they're organised, as disorganised people leave clues. And to get away with it for so long, you've got to hide the bodies, because there would be some forensic hit eventually.'

Dan stared at the papers and started to nod. 'Damn, you're right, and if we're going to steer the attention away from Peter, we've got to find abductions that he couldn't have been involved with.'

Jayne knelt down by the column of papers for those who had simply vanished and said, 'What about her, Charlotte Crane?' and she lifted a small bundle of clippings from the floor. 'She went missing the same night Lizzie Barnsley disappeared into the darkness of the towpath. She was at a pub further along the canal from where Lizzie was found, the Hare and Hounds, and was certainly there after midnight. If we're going to suggest that

Lizzie was an abduction that didn't go as planned, was the killer's need for blood unsated, so he had to keep on going until he found someone he could abduct and do whatever he wanted to do with her?'

'But could that person still be Peter?' Dan chewed his lip as he thought about it, until he scurried across to his court papers. He rummaged through them before holding up a statement in triumph. 'Here!'

'What's that?'

'The centre of the prosecution case, that Peter sought treatment for a wound to his head that night, except he was in the hospital by one o'clock, waiting to be stitched. That means he can't have had anything to do with both Charlotte's disappearance *and* Lizzie's murder, as he'd have to kill Lizzie, then get to where Charlotte was last seen, abduct her, take her to a place where she couldn't be found, and then get to the hospital. He wouldn't have had time.'

'So, we look at Charlotte's case to see whether we can link it with the other missing persons, and then somehow link it to Lizzie, make the killer one and the same, and show it couldn't have been Peter?'

'It's the best we can do. It's a stretch though, and we might have left it too late.'

Jayne looked at the pictures of Charlotte from the clippings. 'One minute she's celebrating the new year with friends, and the next she's nowhere to be found. It fits with an abduction.'

'But Murdoch's going to be the police witness in court, and it's so local and recent that she'll know all about the case. She might give an answer that makes the whole collection look shaky.'

'But Charlotte Crane's the right sort of victim in terms of age and location. Like with the other ones, we should be looking at the victims first. We've ruled out men, and anyone under twenty or over forty.' She ran her finger along the papers, picking up three sheets. 'Start with these, because they're the furthest back in time. Bill went back a long way.'

'Yeah, he was desperate to find a pattern.'

'Like us. Look at these. Two in Yorkshire along the same Leeds-Liverpool canal, and one here in Highford. One year between the first two, and then eighteen months before the next. Three women who went out and never came home. They're all different though. Look, the first one, Annie Yates, she had a good job and was happily married, but she went out for a walk and never returned.'

She passed Dan the clippings, along with Bill's typed summaries.

He read them and was filled with sadness. The publicity photo of Annie Yates showed how happy she'd been, hugging her husband, both wrapped in walking clothes. Just a woman forgotten by time, but to her family it would still be as raw as the day she left.

'It's so long ago – seventeen years,' he said. 'These pictures capture a moment, but no one knows what was going on in her life. It could even be her husband behind it all.'

'I thought it didn't matter whether it was true? You're defending Peter Box. We're just telling an alternative story. Isn't that how it works?'

He held up the clippings. 'Her family won't be quite so forgiving.'

'You'll be okay with this one, then, because it doesn't seem like anyone cared about her.' She thrust the clippings towards him. 'Sharon Coates. She worked as a prostitute. A bit old school, short skirt and handbag over her shoulder, hanging around the warehouses by the canals. She went missing a year after Annie, but there's hardly any newspaper coverage for her. It's as if the papers weren't as bothered about her.'

'I've met enough prostitutes through this job to know that there's usually a very sad story behind what they do.'

'What about the creeps who used her?'

'They're the guilty ones, and there isn't always a sad story there.' Dan smiled. 'There was a purge on kerb crawlers in Highford a couple of years ago. The police used the data from the number-plate recognition cameras to identify vehicles that circled the red-light area, looking for when the same vehicle cropped up on the same street a few times in the same hour. They wrote to the registered owners, advising them of the law around soliciting and how their activities might be perceived.'

'Sounds like a good idea.'

'It was, and particularly as the owner wasn't always the husband but sometimes the wife, or even the boss. You can bet that there were some interesting conversations at home.'

'Cameras didn't help with Sharon Coates, though,' and she pointed at the clippings. 'Just another prostitute forgotten by everyone.'

'And the one after that, the Highford one?'

Jayne skimmed through the clippings. 'More than fourteen years ago. A woman who set off for a night out and never came home.'

'Let me have a look.'

Jayne passed him the clippings.

'Claire Watkins. I remember her,' Dan said. 'There was a lot of press coverage. Even made the television specials. There's still the occasional update and appeal, but I've never heard that they have a suspect.'

'Her pile of clippings is the biggest. That must be why.'

Jayne continued rummaging through the papers as Dan read through the details of the three they already had, picking some out, shoving others to one side, until she had a pile she could put on the table. 'Location might be important. The first three all disappeared near the canal that runs through Highford. Bill cast his net wider, looking for the numbers. Why don't we concentrate on locality, those who can be linked to Lizzie? It sounds less scattergun.' She patted the pile. 'Here we are. All the women from twenty through to forty. Bill's son is excluded, so he won't be pleased, but this is what we've got.'

'How many?'

'Twelve. Hang on, I'll just put them in date order.' Jayne moved the papers around as Dan grabbed more wine, until she stepped back. 'There we are. All in order.'

Dan glanced over them as he passed Jayne a glass. 'Thank you. I couldn't do this without you.'

'We're a good team.'

He caught a look, a gleam in her eye, a quick widening of the pupils. Dan turned away.

They both stayed silent for a few moments before Jayne blushed and said, 'You're doing it again.'

'Doing what?'

'Making me wish I hadn't come here.'

'I haven't done anything.'

'That's what I mean. We go a few weeks without any contact, but then you have a case and we're here again, drinking wine at your place and me wanting more.'

He felt a flush creep up his cheeks.

They'd been here before, those long silences with Dan stopping himself from saying how he felt about her. They clicked. Even when they were lawyer and client, there was something between them that was hard to define. Their conversations during prison visits had turned to more than just the case, and she used to say that he was the only person who could make her laugh in there.

What he'd never told her was that he was nervous before every visit, his stomach rolling from the anticipation of seeing her but also dread at the thought of her case going wrong. He'd remained professional: he was her lawyer, nothing more. It could never be more; he'd forced himself to push different thoughts away.

But he couldn't stop the spark of excitement he felt whenever she came round, or the desire whenever she looked at him a certain way.

'Don't you think I wish things were different?'

'Those are just words, Dan Grant. You know how I feel about you, I've made it obvious enough times, but the last person I fell for ended up dead in my kitchen. I can't go there again. I'm not a murderer, you proved that for me, but I still hold myself back.'

'You were a client,' he said. 'That makes it different for me too.'

Her eyes closed momentarily, and when she opened them again, her gaze was different. More focused, her pupils like black stones. 'I'm not a client anymore.'

He held her gaze and fought the urge to lean across to kiss her, wanting to feel her lips on his, to lose himself in her.

He looked away. 'I know, but it still makes a difference.'

Jayne swirled the wine in her glass. 'Okay, I get it.' Her tone was flat. She put the glass on the table. 'I'd better get going. It's getting late, and you've got a big day in court tomorrow.'

'Don't be angry with me.'

She shook her head. 'It's not anger I'm feeling.'

'What then?'

'I don't know. Disappointment, frustration perhaps?' She grabbed her coat. 'But it's business as usual, I know that.'

'Yes, just that.'

He didn't look up as she went. There were no goodbyes. Just the slam of his door and then her footsteps on the stairs, as if she didn't want to hang around for the lift.

He took her glass and poured away her wine. Part of him wanted to go after her, but the thought of the trial prevented him. If he intended to use any of this new material, he had to be ready. It could go very badly, and he had one evening to somehow stop that happening.

*

Pat carried on digging, his gloves cast to one side and his fingers clawing at the soil around the plastic bag, the exertion forcing his breath out in sharp rasps.

The plastic had hardened after all these years underground. The dirt got under Pat's fingernails, even cracked one of them, but he wasn't going to stop.

The sweat dripped from his forehead despite the cold. One of his fingers was bleeding, but after a few minutes he'd cleared away the soil. He took a deep breath and gave a sharp tug on the bag, falling backwards as it came free.

The bag was small, just a thick shopping bag, knotted at one end. He turned the bag in his hand, resisting the urge to rip it open, knowing that he didn't want to spoil any forensic traces left on whatever was inside.

It felt like a tool, with a handle and a long thin blade, except it didn't feel sharp. It was solid enough to be made of metal, and his mind went to his own shed at home.

It was a bradawl, he was sure of it. He remembered the pathologist's report, that Rosie had been stabbed multiple times with a thin, sharp object.

He grinned in triumph, wanted to jump and shout, but he restrained himself. The murder weapon. He had it, dug up exactly where Sean Martin said he had hidden it. If Sean's DNA was on the handle and Rosie's blood was on the blade, he could face a retrial. The thought gave Pat a new surge of energy. He had a new goal now: to be in court when Sean Martin stood trial.

He pulled a bag of his own from his pocket and put one bag in the other, before letting out a long sigh. All he had to do now was get the bradawl to someone who could do the right tests on it. He could try the police, but he thought of Dan first. This could be the first step in proving Sean Martin's guilt. What he couldn't work out was how that would help Dan in Peter Box's trial.

Pat was about to stand up when there was another noise. Like before, it was the sound of movement, but closer, like someone brushing against one of the rocks embedded into the ground. A rustle of clothes, the squeak of feet on the wild grass.

'Hello?'

Still no reply.

He picked up the bag and put it inside his coat before standing up.

'Is anyone there?'

He moved away from the cottage, nervous of the deep darkness. If someone was going to rush him, he didn't want the shock of a hard landing. He might have more of a chance in the open field. His mouth was dry.

He kept the canal to his back as he moved away from the old cottage, the field in front of him. His eyes strained but everything was in shadow.

He saw it and jolted, clasping his chest. A figure, standing still, just a faint silhouette between Pat and the cottage.

Pat started to run, reaching in his pocket for his car keys. His car was a hundred metres away, but it was uneven ground, dotted by thick tufts. His lungs hurt as he ran, but he had to keep going. His legs ached sooner than he'd hoped. There were footsteps behind him, moving quicker than he could.

He tried not to panic but the gate by his car didn't seem to be getting any nearer. His heartbeat was loud in his head, along with the steady thump of his feet and the rustle of the bag in his coat.

He grimaced at the ache in his chest. He couldn't make it any further. The person behind him was getting closer.

He stumbled and went to his knees. The chasing footsteps slowed down.

He toppled forward, the grass moist and cool under his head. He sucked in air, his chest rising and falling as he gasped.

The figure got closer. Pat tried to focus but everything seemed distant. He closed his eyes for a moment and let the night sounds take over. The rustle of grass under his head. The whoosh of distant traffic. The rattle of his breaths.

The footsteps got closer and stopped.

Pat coughed, shaking his chest, a rattle in his lungs. It wasn't supposed to end like this. Cold and undignified, in a field.

He opened his eyes. There was someone holding a long-handled axe, the blade glinting in the glow of the half-moon.

There was no hesitation. No final splutter of rage from whoever was there. Instead, the axe was raised without a word being said, poised in mid-air for a second, and then there was a grunt as it swung downwards.

Pat screamed as he thought of Eileen, alone at home, wondering where he was.

The axe seemed to be moving slowly but he knew it was an illusion. He thought he saw moisture flicking from the blade as it made its downward arc, the blade getting brighter. He couldn't move, didn't want to move. He knew it was over.

He saw Eileen as the blade hit. Warm, loving, gentle. He saw her in their house, looking out of the window, looking for him, and he was with her, rushing across the countryside as the axe kept moving.

He thought he saw her crying as his head was pushed into the ground, and then the world faded to black.

Thirty-one

The morning had come too quickly for Dan. He had been up until well after two, trying to sort the bundle of notes and clippings into those he could use and those he couldn't.

He'd whittled the list down to nine victims, although he had gone off-script. He and Jayne had decided that they were going to focus on those who were missing, but Dan had decided to include Rosie in the list, just to keep alive the link with Sean Martin. He knew what he had to do when he got to court, and it would make him unpopular, but it was the only way he could think of to make it work. His eyes felt heavy and his breath sour from lack of sleep.

He'd arranged to meet Bill and Jayne in a greasy spoon in Highford's shopping district. He'd wondered whether Jayne would refuse to meet him, after the way they had ended the night before, but she'd agreed with a tired grunt. He got there first, cradling a large white mug on a chipped and scarred table, the sugar in a pouring jar and the street outside lost through the fogged-up windows. There were some builders in the cafe, wearing hi-vis vests over dusty ex-army gear, and it would fill later with those wanting a cheap and warm way to spend an hour, but Dan enjoyed it here. Unpretentious.

The bell over the door tinkled and Bill and Jayne came in, Bill holding the door open for her. Dan raised his hand to let them know he was there.

They made their way through the tables, the builders stopping their chatter to watch Jayne. One of them nodded to his friend, a wolf-whistle in his mind.

'Morning,' Dan said. 'Just coffee or are we eating?'

'I could murder a bacon sandwich,' Bill said. 'Anyone else?'

'Make that two,' Jayne said. 'And coffee.'

'And me,' Dan said.

Bill went to the counter as Jayne slid along the vinyl seat until she was opposite Dan. She looked at the table and then away.

'Everything all right?' he said.

She looked back. Her gaze was hard. 'Just keeping it professional. I need the work. You need my help. That's all that matters.'

'I'm not playing games. And it's too early for an argument.'

She tried to look nonplussed. 'No argument. Why have you called us here? Have you found something?'

'Nothing more than what we talked about last night, but I felt I owed it to Bill to tell him first.'

'Will he like it?'

'I doubt it.'

She sighed and sat back. 'I feel like we're letting him down.'

'I've got to put Peter first, not Bill.'

'Do you think Peter Box is guilty?'

'It's not a question I ask myself. I've said this to you before.'

Jayne leaned closer and whispered, 'What if Peter Box is the person killing people along the canals? It's all right for you to brush it off, but how will Bill feel if you use his research to free the man actually doing the killing? What kind of irony would that be?'

'We can be sure Peter had nothing to do with the death of Bill's son, because it's too different.'

'Well, yes, you're right. Just be gentle with him. He's desperate for an answer.'

'He already knows the answer. He just hasn't accepted it yet.'

Bill came back to the table, the mugs clattering as he put them down, and then said to Dan, 'Have you been busy with my research?'

'I was up most of the night. Bill, I'm really sorry, but if you come to court today, you'll be disappointed.'

'I don't understand.'

'There's no easy way to say this. I'm hoping to use some of your stuff, but I'm not including your son in it.'

'Why not?'

'There are patterns in your research but if I try to use your son, the judge will query its relevance. There are some similarities, like the fact that he died in a canal, but everything else is different from Lizzie – gender, for a start. No obvious sign of a struggle. And, it took place miles away from Highford. There is no chance of me using his death in this case. I'm really sorry.'

Bill looked across at Dan, and then to Jayne. 'Do you think the same? I thought you were different, from how you reacted last night.'

Jayne looked at Dan and then back to Bill, before she sighed and said, 'I'm sorry, Bill. We went through all that you gave me and decided what we could use and what we couldn't.'

He shook his head, tears welling in his eyes. 'You use my stuff and then treat me like Tom doesn't matter.'

'It isn't that,' Dan said. 'I can only use what will help my client. This case might raise awareness though, make people look a bit closer, which might help you find out what happened to

Tom. It won't help my client if the judge throws it out before I can even start.'

Bill shuffled along the vinyl seat and stood up. 'Thanks for nothing. To both of you, but you' – he jabbed his finger towards Jayne – 'I thought I saw something different in you.'

He turned and stomped through the cafe, the builders watching him yanking at the door.

The woman from behind the counter appeared next to them. 'Bacon sandwiches?'

Jayne held out her hand to Dan. 'It looks like we've got seconds.'

Lack of sleep was gnawing at Dan and he needed something more solid than the muesli he'd tackled when he first woke up.

They ate their sandwiches in silence before Jayne pushed her plate to one side and said, 'So what now?'

'I want Murdoch in the witness box today. I'll use what I can.'

'And me?'

'Keep on looking into the ones who've gone missing. I need whatever I can.'

'Are we forgetting about Sean Martin?'

'How do you mean?'

'On Sunday night, it was all about proving that Sean Martin might be involved in Peter's case. Now, it's all about a serial killer stalking the canals. If you don't mind me saying, Dan, your defence is sounding a bit chaotic.'

Dan finished his sandwich. 'I've got a client who won't talk to me. That makes it pretty hard from the start, so I've just got to run with whatever I can pick up.'

'Are we ignoring Sean Martin, then?'

'Not completely. I'm including Rosie in my list, just to keep him as an option. She's not wholly irrelevant. She died close to where Lizzie did, and we can suggest that if Sean Martin isn't her killer, he might have disturbed the real murderer.'

'How will Pat feel about that? We're almost cementing Sean's innocence, not proving his guilt.'

'He'll understand, and I have no choice, unless Peter decides to start telling me what happened and he's had long enough to do that.' He pushed the bacon sandwich left behind by Bill across the table. 'Here, enjoy this. I've got to be at court soon. Let me know how you get on.'

'I will.'

He slid out of the bench seat. 'And I'm sorry about last night.'

'Don't make it a big deal. I've dealt with worse things than being rejected by you. I'll survive.'

Dan left Jayne reaching for the brown sauce, to smother the bacon in the second sandwich. Once he got outside, his phone buzzed in his pocket. He didn't recognise the number. 'Hello, Dan Grant.'

'Sorry, Dan, it's Eileen.'

Dan's mouth went dry. Eileen had never called him before, and their contact had only ever been limited to polite chatter at parties.

'Is Pat all right?' Dan said, his nerves obvious in his tone.

'Well, that's just it,' she said, and Dan recognised the break in her voice that told him that she was trying hard to keep calm. 'I don't know where he is and I can't get hold of him.'

Thirty-two

Trudy stared at the bedroom ceiling as the daylight made slow progress. Sean was next to her but asleep. He was always last to bed and last to rise. He claimed that his work kept him up and that sometimes he would get too engrossed in some miscarriage of justice to come to bed early, but sometimes she wondered whether it was more than that.

She rolled onto her side and looked at him.

He was bigger than when they'd first met, his hair thinning and going grey at the sides, his scalp visible in the morning, before he'd had a chance to tease his hair over it. Large freckles dotted his back and hair had sprouted on his shoulders in the last couple of years.

She couldn't complain. She'd hardly kept back the steady march of time either. She couldn't sleep as well as she used to, so her eyes looked heavy most days, and her hair was kept dark by dye but it was never quite convincing enough. She'd kept her figure, and she could see the younger Trudy in the mirror if the light wasn't too harsh, but she felt her years in the aches in her back.

It shouldn't matter but it did. Ageing didn't seem to hit men in the same way.

She couldn't think like that. She'd waited for Sean. He knew how much they meant to each other.

As she looked at him, she noticed a scratch mark on his back, above his shoulder blade. She pushed down the sheet to get a better look. Had she done that? No, it couldn't be. It had been a couple of weeks now since they'd had sex and it had been unspectacular. Just an awkward quickie to satisfy a need.

It had been different when they were younger, when sex was new and exciting, with boundaries to push, but time changed everyone.

She told herself not to worry about it. He could have snagged himself tending to the boat. The ceilings were never quite high enough for Sean, and they both had to duck down to climb in.

He turned over, his arm flopping over her as he stirred. He lifted his head, one eye still closed. 'What time is it?'

'Eight o'clock.'

'So early?' He pulled the pillow over his head.

'You were out late last night.'

He yawned and stretched, reappearing from under the pillow. 'These events drag on, you know that.' He rolled over and lay on his back, his arms behind his head. 'Sold a few books, though, which is good, but there's always someone who wants to talk, or tell you about their relative who was unjustly locked up once upon a time.'

'Isn't that what you're about though, righting wrongs?'

'It doesn't mean I need to know about every wrong.'

She reached out to play with his hair, running her fingers through it. 'Anyone nice there?'

'There were a lot of nice people there.'

'You know what I mean. You're more of a celebrity now. You'll attract hangers-on.'

He moved closer. 'No one will ever do what you do. You know that.'

'It's easy to get swept along though. Your book is out and you're back in the press, and women like famous men.'

'You're being stupid.'

She put her leg over his hip, hooking her foot behind him and pulling him closer. He dangled his arm over hers.

'Prove it to me,' she said.

She closed her eyes as he rolled her on to her back. She gave a passionate moan and buried her face into his shoulder, to hide her grimace as he entered her.

It wouldn't take him long.

*

Dan's office was on the other side of the town centre from the cafe. No one else was there, and he was scouring Pat's diary for appointments when there was a knock on the front door.

It was Eileen.

'I couldn't find the office keys,' she explained as he let her in. 'Pat must have taken them, along with the car keys.'

She looked tired, not in her usual attire of upturned collars and trousers, a country look as affected as Pat's routine of being the local eccentric. Instead, her hair was pulled back into a knot and she was wearing grey jogging pants underneath a long green coat.

'Eileen, tell me what you know.'

'That's why I'm here, to find out from you.' Her voice was hoarse, and Dan noticed that her eyes were red, as if she'd spent the previous hour crying.

'I don't know what you mean.'

'Don't take me for a fool, Daniel. I know you men stick together, but spare me the lies now, when he hasn't got long to go.'

'Come into Pat's office.'

It was at the back of the building and on the ground floor, kept dim by blinds so Pat could hide from his clients. Files were in small piles on the desk, with elastic bands and papers scattered over the top.

'It smells of him,' Eileen said, looking around. 'It's hard to define. Cigars and old suits, I suppose, but it's him.'

Dan went to her and took her hands. He spoke in a soft voice. 'I'm worried too but I'm sure he'll be fine. Trust me when I say that if you think he's got another woman, he's fooled me too, because I'm not aware of anyone.'

Her chin trembled but she took a deep breath and straightened her shoulders. 'I've been married to Pat for nearly forty years. We've been through a lot together and I know he wasn't always faithful to me.' She grabbed his hands as he tried to drop them. 'I don't care about that, not anymore, the silly little ego-boosts that happened at parties. Do you think I was always an angel? But there were never any feelings towards anyone, not from me, not from him. That was the deal, Daniel. I don't know if he knows that I guessed, but I know there's never been anyone that meant anything. That was the whole point. Pat and I were meant to be together until the end. But now? I'm wondering whether he's got a few more goodbyes to make.'

Dan pulled his hands away. 'Tell me what happened.'

She moved some files from a chair and sat down. 'Last night, he went out but didn't tell me he was going. I came downstairs from having a bath and he was gone. His coat wasn't there, and neither was his car. I didn't think too much of it. I'm used to him going to the police station at all hours, and he's been telling me how caught up you are in this murder case. I presumed he was dealing with a late-night call, but I expected him back.'

She looked up at the ceiling and blinked away some tears. 'I woke up in the middle of the night and he wasn't there. Something is wrong, I can feel it, I don't know why. I tried calling him but his phone is switched off.'

'That might mean he's in a police station.'

'I called the police station and he isn't there. He's spent the night somewhere, and I don't know where.'

'Have you reported him missing?'

She shook her head.

'I've gone through his diary,' Dan said. 'There's no appointment for last night. His car isn't here. I don't know where he is either, Eileen. I'm not keeping his secrets. If he's having a fling, I'm not aware of it. If he's got a long-time lover, he's never told me.'

'That makes it worse,' she said. 'If there's nowhere else he could be, it can't be good news.'

*

Jayne threw her car keys onto the sofa.

The bottle of wine was where she'd left it on the coffee table, the cheapest one they had in the shop, next to some takeaway cartons, the room stale with congealed food. The unexpected breakfast had woken her up, but she didn't feel ready to start the day.

She opened the window and sucked in some fresh air, looking out over the town as she did, her arms resting on the frame.

Her time in Highford was done, she knew that now. After she'd left Dan's place the night before, she'd felt the need to get trashed, although she didn't really know why. It was the same the morning after as it had been the night before, and Dan wasn't the only one who kept it purely as business. Every time she thought about pulling him closer, the smell of Jimmy's blood filled her nostrils, the memory of it hot on her hand as the knife plunged into his leg.

She moved the bottle to the kitchen and stared out of the window. The view was much the same as from the living room. Just grey stone and some low clouds over a distant hill. She was twenty-five and living in a grotty flat in a small town, rubbing away another hangover.

Spare me the self-pity, she thought, as she dumped the takeaway cartons in the plastic bin under the sink. There was only one person who could change her life, and that was her. Finish this case and leave town, that's all she had to do. Go home, forget about Dan and her own failing business and go back to living a normal life. Get a job. Be near her family.

Then she remembered something.

As she'd ploughed through the wine bottle the night before, she'd researched the cases Dan wanted her to focus on. She'd called Bill and drawn out more details.

It was the case of Claire Watkins, the woman from Highford who'd left her house for a night out and never returned. Her disappearance had led Jayne to make a connection. Starting with the most local seemed to make the most sense, but whatever she'd discovered the night before was lost in the wine-fuelled haze.

She went back through the papers as the kettle boiled, throwing the sheets around, looking for that little snippet that had made sense. All she saw was a pile of scribbles that became gradually more illegible as the wine bottle emptied.

Then she found it. She had to call Dan, catch him before he went into court. She checked her phone. Typical. The battery was dead. She plugged it in and ran to take a shower.

Thirty-three

Dan was finding it hard to concentrate as he waited for Peter to be ushered into the holding cells beneath the court.

The journey along the motorway had been stop-start, an accident extending the rush-hour crawl, and all the time he'd been focused on Pat Molloy. Eileen was right. Pat's disappearance was unusual, and it was time for the police to get involved, but that wouldn't gain him any special treatment from the judge. He had to focus on the case.

That didn't stop him from worrying though. Pat was ill. He could have collapsed somewhere.

His attention was dragged back to the case by the thump of boots on the other side of the glass screen. The door opened and Peter was brought in.

When Dan first started out, lawyers used to sit in the same room as those being held for trial, but there'd been too many phones and drugs smuggled into prisons to allow that to continue. Criminal law didn't attract the talent it used to, and it was now the last resort for the chancers and failures, and those too willing to ignore the rules.

Peter sat down and leaned forward, so that his face was almost touching the glass, steaming it up immediately. 'Day two.'

'We need to talk. I've got a new strategy.'

Peter's eyes narrowed. 'I'm listening.'

Dan reached into his bag and pulled out a folder filled with paper, coloured separators dividing the different cases. 'There are eight women here, all of whom disappeared near a canal, plus Rosie Smith. These go back seventeen years. I'm going to show the jury that there might be someone else involved, another person attacking women, the canals being the link. If I'm forced into it, I can produce more, but nine is a good number. Before I do that though, I need to know that the person behind these isn't you.'

Peter looked at the folder and let out a deep breath. His eyelids flickered and some colour jumped into his cheeks.

'Peter? You okay? It will only work if there's no trace of you in these cases.'

'Go on then, tell me what you've got.'

Dan had printed pictures of the women and put them into a separate section. He pulled them out. 'This is the first one,' and he put a picture against the glass. 'Annie Yates. She went missing seventeen years ago, and then Sharon Coates a year later,' and he put her picture alongside. 'Both lived in Yorkshire. One a young mother, the other a sex worker.'

'A prostitute.' Peter's lips curled when he said it. 'Call it by its proper name.'

'It's just a word, and arguing about that isn't important right now. Look at the pictures. Do you know about them?'

He glanced at them before shaking his head.

Dan put the pictures back and picked out two more, slapping them against the glass. 'What about these? Eighteen months after Sharon, there was Claire Watkins, then Katie Boardman a year later. Claire lived here in Highford, and Katie the next town along the canal.'

Peter winced and looked away. 'Stop it, I don't know them.'

'I need to know, Peter.'

'I said, *stop it*.' His voice rose in its intensity.

'There's Rosie Smith too.' Dan waved her picture. 'You know about her case.'

'I've had enough of this.'

'I haven't even started yet. There're four more left.'

Peter sprung to his feet and banged on the door.

'I just need to know, Peter. Will your name come up in these investigations?'

Peter turned round, tears in his eyes.

'I need to know, Peter. Are you the monster who took these women, who killed Rosie?'

'I'm no monster,' he said, and as the door opened, he rushed through.

Dan was aware of his fast breathing, the race of his heart, as he collected the papers.

When he came out of the cell complex, Dan went straight to the robing room to look for Francesca McIntyre. He couldn't see her as he looked around the door and, when he asked, a barrister bumbled that she'd already gone to the courtroom.

Dan let the door slam behind him and marched after her, his footsteps echoing along the tiled floor.

The atmosphere changed as he opened the courtroom door. It slowed him down every time, with sound deadened by deference and thick carpets.

Francesca was in the well of the court, cracking a joke with the court assistant, no one else present. Francesca had learned the first rule of being a good lawyer: notice everyone. The ushers, the security guards, the cleaners, the people behind the counter in the court canteen. Treat them well and they can make your life a lot easier. Look down on them and they'll delight in making your day more difficult, and deservedly so.

'Mr Grant, good morning. More fun and games today? I hope so.'

Dan smiled, but her sarcasm irritated him. 'I'm here to entertain. There is one thing I need you to do though. Or rather, I need your witness to do it – DI Murdoch.'

'Apart from give evidence truthfully, what on earth can you mean?'

'I'm going to ask her about a number of cases where women went missing near to the Leeds-Liverpool canal.'

Her eyes narrowed for a moment. 'And she's expected to know?'

'She will if she looks them up. She was told about them some time ago, months even, so none of this is new.'

'Told about them? What do you mean?'

'An informant suggested there was a link. Murdoch wasn't interested.'

'And what should she be looking for?'

'To see whether Peter Box's name ever came up in them.'

The court assistant busied herself with paperwork, avoiding whatever argument she feared was about to start.

Francesca held out her hand. 'Show me.'

Dan opened the folder and put it on the desk. 'Help yourself, but the material stays with me.' He reached into one of the sections and pulled out a list. 'This should be enough for her to locate the right cases.'

Francesca glanced down the list. 'This is your defence now, that there is some undetected serial killer on the canals?'

'If Peter didn't kill Lizzie, someone else did.' He tapped the folder. 'That might be your answer.'

'Why didn't you write in with this stuff? It's going to delay the trial this morning, and if you want to spend the day annoying the judge, go ahead, but that's what he'll ask.'

'I was approached last night by someone who has an obsession about this. His son was killed and he's convinced someone is pushing people into the water, or attacking them. I sifted through it last night and came up with these. Criticise me all you want, but the police have known about it for longer than I have.'

'And you're going with this? It's all a little bit, you know, late-night trash TV.'

'The sort of TV watched by ordinary men and women, you mean? Like the twelve jurors? I agree, it'll go down well.'

She pursed her lips. 'What will you do if Peter Box's name does appear as a suspect? Will he accept the game is over and plead guilty?'

'He hasn't shown any willingness so far, but you know there's still a risk the jury will think there's an untold story here. If you can show that he's come up as a suspect in these other cases, I'll agree you can raise it in evidence, on one condition.'

'Which is what?'

'That I can raise his absence as a suspect if he doesn't.' He held out his hands. 'Your move now.'

She folded the sheets of paper and marched towards the door. 'I won't be long. You can explain it to the judge.'

As the door closed, the court assistant looked up. 'At least it's getting interesting now.'

Thirty-four

Jayne was able to find a parking space a street away from where she wanted to be.

She was in a grid of terraced streets, ten long lines running up the hill, the green dome of a mosque at the top. Cars occupied every space and net curtains were in every window. Some women in plain black hijabs were watching her, making her conscious of her baggy T-shirt and tight jeans, but they smiled as she passed them.

Built to house the workers employed in the mill that had long ago closed down, the mosque standing in its place, the area was typical of so many parts of Highford, an enclave for those families who'd moved there in the sixties to work the shifts the local population wouldn't, until it had grown into a small community.

It was the mosque that had made Jayne think of it when, looking out of her window the night before, she'd seen its dome.

She was looking for number 12, the house where Trudy was living when Sean married Karen. It had been a call to Karen that had got her the address. Number 12 was at the bottom of the hill, where the road started to level out before a junction, the houses continuing along the other side of a busy through road.

Jayne turned around and looked at the street diagonally opposite, one terrace along and on the other side of the junction. She was right.

The door of number 12, like all the others in the terrace, was right against the pavement. She knocked on it, and it was opened almost immediately by a young woman in her late teens, wearing tight hipster jeans and with gleaming dark hair, straight and flowing over her shoulders.

'Hi,' Jayne said. 'I'm an investigator for a local law firm.'

A voice shouted from the back in a language Jayne couldn't understand, and the woman replied in the same language before speaking to Jayne in unaccented English. 'What do you want?'

'I'm looking for anyone who has lived here a long time, more than ten years, who might remember a previous occupant, Sean Martin.'

The woman frowned. 'Is he the guy who went to prison? I can't help you. We didn't know him. We've heard about him, but we lived on a different street before moving here. Try her across the road though.' She pointed. 'She's been here for ever.'

Jayne followed her gesture to a house that was grubbier than the rest, with paint flaking on the window frames and an England flag stuck to the bottom corner of the front window.

'Is she friendly?'

The woman laughed. 'She'll be fine with you. With me, she'd slam the door in my face, but she's the one who knows all about the history of this place. She certainly rants enough about how we've ruined it all. But we look out for her, just the same as everyone else.'

Jayne thanked her and went across the road, tapping on the door. A dog barked, followed by the sound of someone trying to calm it down. The door was opened on a chain, wary eyes peering through.

Jayne introduced herself. The door slammed. She was about to knock again when it became apparent that the person inside the house was merely trying to stop the dog from bolting into the road as she wrestled with the door lock.

Jayne turned to see a woman in her sixties with pinched cheeks and grey hair cut in a bob, greasy and lank, holding on to a dog collar with nicotine-stained fingers.

'You say you're an investigator? For what? Claims? I can say I was a passenger if you want.'

'No, it's not that.'

'Why not? Some good money there. There was a man who came round all the time. Every time a bus had a bump, he'd come looking for people to say they were on it. I bought my new telly with the money he got.'

'I'm more interested in the people who used to live in the house opposite. The young woman there told me that you know all about this area.'

'Did she, now?' She glared past Jayne towards number 12. 'You'd better come in.'

Inside, the house smelled sour, like unwashed clothes and a dog that needed a bath. The sofa Jayne was instructed to sit on felt greasy and thick with cigarette tar.

'What else did she say, across the road?'

'Why, what's wrong?'

'They want me out. They all do. They want to take over the whole area, and people like me are blocking them. All my family have moved out, sick of seeing how this place has gone to the rats.'

Jayne decided not to debate the point. The street looked well cared for to her, but the house she was sitting in seemed one of the grubbiest.

The woman reached for a cigarette. 'What do you want to know?'

'About the woman who lived at number 12 before that family did – about twelve years ago. Trudy. She was going out with Sean Martin.'

'The one who went to prison?'

'It is –' Jayne paused as she opened her notebook. 'I'm sorry, I didn't ask your name.'

'It's Geraldine. Yes, I remember her, and him, of course. I wasn't surprised when I read what he'd done.'

'Why weren't you surprised?'

'Because he was arrogant. Thought he was so much better than everyone else, so damn special. I laughed when he went down.'

'I don't understand.'

'He was always carrying a book, tucked under his arm, and it was always a poncey one, like really old or highbrow, as if we were supposed to ask him about it. And they had parties there all the time. People around here now talk about him as if they knew a celebrity, but really he's just someone who got lucky, because we all know he did it.'

'Did what? Killed Rosie Smith?'

'What else?' She leaned in closer, as if sharing a secret. 'People like us don't get breaks. If we go before the courts, we get convicted. But Sean?' She waved her hand. 'He was always going to walk.'

'He went to prison first time around.'

'Yeah, but no one stopped fighting for him though, because people like Sean win every time. I didn't like him, didn't trust him, and I bet he killed that poor girl. Not even Trudy could see what he was really like.'

'What do you mean?'

'She thought the sun shone out of his proverbial. I could see it in her eyes when they were out together. His eyes? Wandering, that's what, but she must have been blind to it. Obsessed with him, she was, together all the time, like glue, drinking until late, always loud laughter and music coming from the place at all hours. I was surprised when they split up. But look at them now, living it up.'

'Do you know why they split up back then?'

'I'm not that nosey, but one day they were together and then they weren't, and he moved away. But it was bad news for that young lass, wasn't it, the one who died. Once he came into her life, she was as good as marked.' Geraldine looked confused. 'Why are you asking about him?'

'He might be relevant to a case I'm involved in, that's all.' Jayne leaned closer and spoke more quietly. 'And I want to ask you about another girl. Well, a woman.'

Geraldine's eyes widened. 'Who?'

'She lived on the other street, just over the junction. Claire Watkins.'

'What's she got to do with this?'

'You know who I'm talking about?'

'Of course. I know her parents. Don't know what happened to her, but not many people go missing round here.'

'What kind of woman was she?'

'Lovely. Bubbly and chatty and not snooty at all, and she was going places. Had a job at a doctor's surgery, on the reception, I think. One day she went to meet a friend in town, so the story went, and she never arrived.'

'What do people round here say about it?'

'They were scared for a while because there could be a kidnapper roaming the streets. Not that it stopped Sean Martin, because he carried on like it meant nothing, swanning around on his boat like he was the big man, the damn thing done up like it was from a child's story. Red and green and with flowers. Saved on the council tax, I think. He used to park it by the canal down there. Do they say park it?'

'Moor it, I think.'

'Well, whatever they call it, he had one and that's where he left it.'

'Do Claire's parents still live in the same house?'

'No, they moved away not long afterwards. It broke them, it really did. It was the constant waiting. They used to say that they wished she'd turn up dead somewhere, just so they could know when to rebuild their lives.'

'Did Sean Martin know Claire well? Were they friends?'

Geraldine stared at the ceiling as she thought back. 'I don't think so. She wasn't one of Sean's gang. Too sensible. I never saw her at his house. Go speak to her friend, Mandy Rogers. On the same street, the end house, by the canal.'

Jayne thanked her and made her exit, trying not to sniff too obviously at her clothes when she got back onto the street, aware that Geraldine would be watching her.

She cast one last glance across to the house where Sean and Trudy had spent so much time together. What secrets had it seen?

Thirty-five

Dan paced as he waited for the reply from the custody sergeant.

He'd found himself a quiet corner of the courtroom as Francesca waited for Murdoch to complete her enquiries. He'd called all the custody offices in the county. Clients travel to commit crimes, but the answer from all of them had been the same, that Pat wasn't there.

He'd known the answers all along, Pat would have let him know, but he had to do something.

The sergeant came back on. 'Sorry, Mr Grant, he's not been here. I checked the logs from last night and the only legal reps who came weren't from your firm.'

'Okay, thanks anyway,' and he clicked off.

For a moment, he was alone, and he felt the dread of knowing that Pat was in danger. Pat wasn't the sort of person to disappear, he was too fond of the grand farewell for that, so Dan prayed for a simple explanation.

Before he could think any more about it, the courtroom door opened and the calm was disturbed by a flurry of movement. He watched as Francesca strode towards him. She slapped the list onto the desk in front of him and raised an eyebrow. 'You're a lucky man, Mr Grant.'

'Peter's name hasn't come up?'

'No intelligence on him and he doesn't get mentioned anywhere. Shall we start?'

The court assistant didn't wait for Dan's response. She made a call to the cells and asked them to bring Peter Box into the dock, and then went through the door in the wooden panelling to collect the judge.

Dan stared at the desk as he waited and tried to control his breathing. He made a silent apology to Pat that he had to push him to the back of his mind for a few hours. He had to focus on the case, Pat would understand that, and it was either going to be a momentous day in a no-hoper's case, or he would spend the day fending off a judge's fury.

There was a rattle of keys and Peter Box shuffled into the dock. Dan looked round. Peter stared at him as he sat down. His usual blank look had been replaced by an expression that was harder to define.

'I might not mention it at all,' Dan said to Francesca.

Francesca's eyes flared for a moment. 'What the hell have you had me doing for the last hour?'

'It's my choice as to whether I use it or not,' Dan snapped, before holding his hand up in apology. 'I'm sorry, but there are other things going on. You use the list, if you want. Ask Murdoch about them, just so that you can take some of the sting away from my questions, but you can hardly call me desperate if you do. I'll just be responding to what you've raised.'

'My dear boy, there is no sting to your questions.'

Before Dan could respond, the court assistant entered and ordered everyone to stand, followed by the slow shuffle of the judge, his every step a performance. He gave a slow bow, everyone in the courtroom responding, before taking their seat.

Francesca leaned across and whispered, 'Whatever's going on with you, leave it behind when you enter the courtroom. All that matters is the case.'

As the usher went to fetch the jurors, the judge glared at Dan over his glasses. 'Any more delays, Mr Grant?'

He rose and glanced down at Francesca. 'I'm ready to proceed, My Lord.'

'Ms McIntyre?'

She stayed seated and nodded her assent.

Murdoch walked with confidence to the witness stand. She put her shoulders back and swore the oath in a loud voice without reading the card held in front of her by the court usher. Dan knew what she was projecting, that she was an experienced detective who'd been to court before. She was wearing a sober blue suit and a plain white blouse and nodded her greetings to the judge.

Francesca's questions took her through the murder scene, using photographs to display the horror of it, to make the jurors hate Peter before they heard anything else about him. The atmosphere in the courtroom was tense and sombre. A few of the jurors gasped as they leafed through the photographs.

Francesca made as if to look through her papers, although it was only for effect, to let the images sink in, before she asked, 'When did you first hear of Peter Box?'

'Once we'd learned that there was blood on the victim's shoe, we surmised that she had injured her attacker. When we asked around the local hospitals, we discovered that Peter Box had received treatment for a head wound from Highford Royal Infirmary. When we went to his house, we saw what appeared to be stitches to his temple.'

'What did you do?'

'I asked him how he'd got his injury. He wouldn't tell me. I asked him where he'd been on New Year's Eve. He wouldn't tell me, so I arrested him.'

'And then?'

'We took him into custody. Took DNA samples from him and interviewed him.'

'What did he say in his interview?'

'Nothing.'

Francesca faked surprise. 'At all?'

'Not a thing. He wouldn't even give his name. We went through five interviews and he didn't utter a single word.'

'Was he legally represented?'

'He was.' Murdoch pointed towards Dan. 'Mr Grant was there throughout.'

Every one of the jurors seemed to be sitting more upright than before, some of them looking at Dan. There were murmurs from the public gallery, silenced by a glance from the judge. Dan knew what they were all thinking, that he'd shielded a murderer. He'd turned into the bad guy.

Francesca paused so that her words could settle, before she said, 'Thank you,' and sat down to allow Dan to ask the questions.

Dan was slow getting to his feet. It risked making him look hesitant, but he knew it would make Murdoch nervous. He was right. Murdoch shifted her weight and put her hands on the edge of the witness box. It was subconscious, but it looked as if she was waiting to be hit.

'Until you heard about the hospital visit,' Dan said, 'Peter Box had not featured in your investigation at all, had he?'

Murdoch turned towards the jury to give her firm response in the affirmative. It was a delaying tactic. It made her look assertive, but it slowed the questions down too.

'You searched Peter Box's home. Correct?'

'Of course we did. We investigate cases like this thoroughly.'

'Please tell the jurors what evidence you found in his home, during this thorough investigation, that corroborated the fact that he was on the canal bank.'

Murdoch's lips pursed for a second, before she complied. 'His computers and phone were inconclusive.'

'Isn't the correct answer that there was no evidence?'

She clenched her jaw before replying, 'Yes.'

'Have you investigated the life of the deceased thoroughly?'

'I have. I insist on it, for the sake of the victim and her family.'

'Spare us the press conference speech, Inspector. In your thorough investigation of Lizzie Barnsley's life, does Peter Box appear anywhere?'

Murdoch glanced towards Francesca. 'No, he does not.'

'In summary, therefore, there was no prior connection between Peter Box and Lizzie Barnsley?'

'That's right, none. We treated it as a random attack.'

'What about Peter Box and the police?'

'I don't understand.'

'Has he ever come to the attention of the police before?'

'No, he hasn't.'

'Is there any evidence that he was out on the streets that night?'

'Yes, his blood was on the victim's shoe.'

Dan threw his papers on to the desk. 'Don't be facetious, Inspector. Did you check any CCTV from the town-centre pubs or on the streets, to look for him?'

'We did.'

'And the cameras close to the location of the attack?'

'We always do that.'

'And does Peter Box appear anywhere on any piece of footage?'

'No, but there's a way through the estate on the other side of the canal.'

'The answer is no, I believe. Is that right?'

'Well, yes.'

'And how many hospitals did you visit once you discovered Peter Box?'

Murdoch was about to answer but faltered.

'Inspector, you're allowed to say the word. It's none, isn't it?'

'I get where you're coming from, Mr Grant, but I lose either way. I say I stopped looking and you say that I'm blinkered. I say I carried on looking and you say that I didn't really suspect Peter Box.'

'Stick to giving the answers, Inspector, not making excuses.' Dan's tone had become angry, making the judge look up from his notes. 'You found Peter Box and didn't look any further.'

Murdoch looked to the judge and then back to Dan. 'That's correct.'

'And a man who had sought treatment for a wound had a wound?'

Murdoch nodded but added, 'And his blood was on her shoe.'

'Tell the court about Meladox.'

Murdoch's eyelids flickered.

'Inspector?'

'That's the name of the lab we use for blood analysis.'

'Still?'

Murdoch looked to Francesca but there was no help there. Francesca was looking through her notes, feigning disinterest, hoping that the jurors would think that if she wasn't concerned, neither should they be.

'I don't know who we use at the moment.'

Dan leaned forward. 'But not Meladox anymore. Is that right?'

Murdoch's cheeks flushed. 'No, not at the moment.'

'Why is that?'

'They're being investigated for irregularities, but only in relation to alcohol and drug analysis.'

Dan held up his hand. 'Your force has stopped using Meladox for alleged irregularities in their testing. Is that right, inspector?'

Murdoch pursed her lips before nodding in agreement.

Dan slammed his hand on to the desk, making everyone jump. 'Is that a yes, inspector?'

Her voice was quiet when she replied, 'You know it is.'

Dan closed his eyes for a moment. Now was the time.

He looked at the jury. Some of them had furrowed brows, tilted heads, as if looking at the case differently. He'd alleviated some of the negative effects of Peter's blood being found on Lizzie's shoe by throwing in the possibility of a mistake, but he had no way of knowing whether he'd done enough. There was Peter's injury as well, along with the biggest problem of all: his silence.

He had no option. Dan had to ask Murdoch about the other canal murders.

Thirty-six

Jayne peered over the top of the five-foot fence that separated Claire Watkins's old street from the canal. The towpath was directly below her. A high brick wall bordered the other side of the canal, with a small factory or workshop beyond it.

Jayne knocked on the door of the house next to the fence. A woman close to thirty answered the door.

'Mandy Rogers?'

She looked uncertain. 'Who's asking?'

Jayne introduced herself. 'I want to ask you about Claire Watkins, and Sean Martin.'

Mandy's eyes widened. 'Whoah! Where has this come from?'

'I know, I'm sorry that I'm digging it all up, but I was told that you were a good friend of Claire's.'

'Why do you want to know?'

'It's connected to a case I'm working on. It might help me find out what happened to Claire.'

Mandy thought for a moment and then stepped out of the house. As she let the door close, she pulled a packet of cigarettes out of her shirt pocket. She offered one to Jayne, who declined, before lighting one herself.

'Yes, I'm Mandy, and Claire was my best friend.' She took a long pull and waved her hand as if to correct herself. 'I have to hope she's still alive somewhere, but' – she shrugged – 'I'm guessing not.'

'Did Claire ever mention Sean Martin?'

'The guy who went to prison for killing his stepdaughter? Not really. Why should she? She knew who he was, we all did, but we didn't bother with him, or his girlfriend. We were different from them.'

'Different? How?'

'Just normal, if you know what I mean. We had normal jobs and liked the same stuff as everyone else: clubbing, shopping, having fun. Sean Martin? He thought he was better because he was being so "alternative".' She sneered when she said the word, making speech marks with her fingers. 'Do you know what makes me laugh? People who try to be different always end up looking just exactly the same as everybody else who tries to be different, but they still act like they're better somehow.'

'I don't understand.'

'He acted like he was some undiscovered genius. He had a guitar, would walk round with it on his back, but I never saw him in a band. The same with his writing. He was always saying how he was working on some book or other, but I never saw it in a bookshop. It was as if he lived in this bubble, and in it he was this great mind, but to ask anyone to give an opinion might pop it, so he hid away. He didn't want to be told that he wasn't good enough to be in a band, or that carrying books around with him didn't make him a writer.'

'Did he tell you all of this?'

'Of course he did, because to him we were just silly young women, even though he was only about ten years older, if that. He'd stop and talk, but only ever about himself, as if he was chatting us up, trying to impress us. He was like that even when his girlfriend was there.'

'Trudy? What was she like?'

'Quiet, I suppose. She'd just stand back and let him talk, but she was always watching, a real hard stare.' Mandy pointed to the canal. 'He left his boat here a lot, thought it made him so clever, living some way-out lifestyle, but he used it like a pleasure cruiser.'

'And you can get to Trudy's house from the canal?'

'Through that ginnel there.' She pointed to a gap that ran between the houses opposite. Mandy frowned. 'This is a lot of talk about Sean Martin and not much about Claire. Are they connected in some way?'

'That's what we're looking into.'

'Why?'

'It's for a trial this week.'

'Who is it?'

'A man called Peter Box.'

Mandy raised her eyebrows. 'Oh I know him, all right.'

Jayne felt a tremor. 'What do you mean?'

'He had the hots for Claire big-time. He thought he had a shot with her, because he used to hang round with Sean Martin. Whenever we bumped into them, Peter would stare at Claire, as if he wanted to chat her up but didn't have the nerve. A bit creepy, really.'

'Hang on,' Jayne said, incredulous. 'You're saying that Peter Box and Sean Martin knew each other?'

'There was some connection with Peter's girlfriend and Trudy. Sisters, I think.'

'What's she called, Trudy's sister?'

Mandy looked away as she thought about that, until she said, 'Emily. I see her around sometimes. Works at a clothes shop in town. The one opposite that new cafe in the middle of the market square.'

'I need to go.' Jayne pulled her phone out of her pocket.

'What is it? What have I said?'

Jayne was already halfway up the street, texting Dan. They needed to speak, urgently.

*

Murdoch shifted weight again. She knew what was coming. Dan felt hyperaware of everyone else in the courtroom.

During most cross-examinations, he didn't think of anyone else. It was Dan and the witness, no one else there, the questions following a pattern but going their own route, one answer sometimes taking the case on a different path. But he was about to take a riskier line, and there was a whole courtroom waiting for him to make a mistake.

Dan cleared his throat. 'Inspector, did you look into whether Lizzie's murder could be linked to other cases?'

Murdoch seemed to have regained her poise, her hands clasped together, turning to the jury when answering, 'If there was a forensic link, the system would have flagged it up on the database.'

'What about a non-forensic search?'

'Do you mean the cases you gave to me earlier?'

'Thank you for raising them, Inspector. Earlier this morning, I gave my learned friend a list of cases involving missing women. Let me take you through them.'

Murdoch reached down and picked up the folder she'd placed on the floor by her seat as she came into the witness box.

'I'll start with Annie Yates,' Dan said. 'Do you have the details of her case?'

Murdoch reached into the folder and pulled out some sheets of paper. 'I've got the crime report.'

Dan knew he was in dangerous territory. The first rule of the courtroom is never to ask a question to which you don't know the answer. He was about to break it, and not for the first time, because sometimes you've got to take a gamble and hope the truth swings your way.

'What does it say?'

Murdoch raised it to read from it. 'Annie was a young mother who went for a walk, heading towards a park in Gargrave with her dog.'

'For the benefit of the jury, Gargrave is a small village by the Yorkshire Dales National Park. That's right, isn't it?'

'It is.'

'And it's further along the same canal that runs through Highford? Am I right?'

'You are.'

'The same canal where Lizzie Barnsley was murdered?'

'You know it is.'

'Carry on. About Annie Yates.'

'She was going for her usual walk along the canal, and she simply disappeared.'

'Come on now, Inspector, people don't simply disappear. You mean she was either abducted or ran away of her own accord?'

'Well, yes, those are the two possibilities.'

'Or murdered and her body concealed? Another feasible reason why she hasn't been seen since?'

'Yes. Along with an accident.'

'There were no concerns that Annie might have met someone else and run away?'

Murdoch raised the piece of paper. 'I don't know enough about the case to give an in-depth analysis.'

'What about a suspect? I'm guessing you spoke to the senior detective on the case while readying yourself.'

'There were no suspects. Her husband had an alibi and there were no eyewitnesses to confirm an abduction.'

'Did the dog go missing, too?'

Murdoch frowned. 'No, it made its own way home. The senior investigating officer commented on that. It seemed unusual.'

'And Peter Box?' Dan gestured towards the dock, where Peter stared blankly ahead. 'Does he appear anywhere in the investigation?'

'No, he doesn't.'

'Not a suspect at any point?'

'No.'

Dan turned towards the jurors as he asked his next question. He had their attention. 'Annie Yates's case wasn't the only one you were asked to look into, was it?'

'No, it wasn't. You came up with all of this earlier today.' Murdoch raised the folder in the air. 'A bit of a rabbit out of a hat, you could say, Mr Grant.'

The judge intervened. 'Inspector, we could do without the argument. Just answer the questions.'

'Sharon Coates was the next one,' Dan said, ignoring the interruption. 'She disappeared a year after Annie Yates.'

Murdoch compared the two dates. 'Just over a year.'

'And what happened?'

'She went out to work and was never seen again. Her case was different though.'

'Because she wasn't a young mother?'

Murdoch looked through the paperwork she'd assembled. 'She was a young mother. She had a daughter, three years old.'

'What's the difference then?'

'She was a prostitute.'

Dan's eyes went to the jury, to see how they registered her answer, because Murdoch had made it sound as if she was worthless somehow.

'Any press appeals? Televised reconstructions?'

'Not in the notes. The disappearance wouldn't have been publicised in the same way as Annie Yates's murder.'

'Why not?'

'Because prostitutes often lead chaotic lifestyles, and a disappearance doesn't necessarily mean foul play. She might have gone to work in a different city.'

'And left her daughter behind?'

Murdoch had no answer to that.

'How far from Gargrave was the last sighting of Sharon Coates?'

'Five or six miles.'

'Along the same stretch of canal?'

Murdoch glanced at Francesca. 'Yes.'

'And did Peter Box appear anywhere in that case?'

'No, Mr Grant, he didn't.'

'Was anyone ever arrested in that case?'

'Yes.'

Dan glanced upwards quickly. He was thrown by the answer. He looked towards the judge, who had raised an eyebrow and allowed a half-smile on to his lips.

'Sorry, I'll rephrase the question.'

The judge shook his head. 'No, you won't, Mr Grant. You asked a specific question. The inspector should be allowed to answer.'

Dan didn't hide his frustration when he sought clarification from Murdoch, who answered, 'The punter who'd picked her up.'

'But he wasn't charged?'

'No, he wasn't.'

He wondered whether he dare ask the obvious question, but then realised that he had no choice. If the question was an obvious one, the jurors would think of the same one and make up their own answer. He'd started down the route of hoping for the best. He had to keep going and hope that Francesca had been honest with him.

'Does it say in your papers why he wasn't charged?'

Murdoch rummaged through until she found what she had been looking for. 'There was footage of his car leaving the area, and there was only one person in the car.'

'What did he say?'

'That they went to a deserted spot and she wouldn't do what he wanted, because he didn't want to use a condom. She got out of the car and set off walking.'

Dan stared down at his papers and swallowed. He'd almost been caught out there. He'd made some headway, but he had to be wary of asking one question too many.

'This deserted spot. Where was it?'

Murdoch's eyes narrowed. 'By the canal.'

'The same canal that runs past where Annie Yates was last seen?'

'Yes.'

'The same canal that runs past where Lizzie Barnsley was found?'

A sigh. 'Yes.'

Dan became aware of the silence in the courtroom. Usually the public gallery was full of whispers and murmurs, too quiet to disturb but part of the background noise, like the crackle of a stylus on an old vinyl record. The court was transfixed.

'Let's jump forward eighteen months and a little closer to home. 'Claire Watkins. Do you know about the case?'

'I do. I was one of the investigating officers. I wasn't the senior investigating officer, but I was involved in it.'

That jolted Dan. Murdoch would know more about the case than what she could glean from a crime report. He ploughed on regardless.

'Claire Watkins also went missing, from Highford this time, Lizzie Barnsley's home town. Is that correct?'

'It is. She went out to meet someone and she never came home.'

'Who was she meeting?'

'We never found out. She was making a lot of calls to an unregistered number. That phone was in Highford when she went missing, but the SIM card had been bought a long time before from a shop in Manchester. It wasn't registered to any-one, and the CCTV at the shop had been scrubbed.'

'What did you conclude in the end?'

'We kept an open mind. There's a strong possibility that she ran away with whoever she was meeting.'

'And where had she arranged to meet this person?'

'We don't know.'

'But she was never seen again.'

Murdoch didn't answer.

'Inspector?'

'Sorry, I thought it was a statement, not a question. Yes, no reported sightings of her.'

'Look at the next case, a year later. Katie Boardman.'

Dan stopped. There was a noise at the back of the courtroom. Peter was leaning forward, his hands on his head.

The judge peered over his glasses. 'Is your client feeling unwell, Mr Grant?'

'If Your Lordship will give me a moment.'

The judge waved his hand dismissively.

Dan stepped out from behind his desk and went to the dock at the back of the courtroom. He leaned into a gap in the glass. 'What's going on, Peter?'

He moved his hands from the top of his head. 'How long will this go on for?'

'Stick with it. Trust me.' Dan was surprised to see tears in Peter's eyes. 'You okay? Do you need a break?'

'No. Get on with it. I want it all over.'

'Just keep it together.' Dan went back to his place.

'Are you ready to carry on, Mr Grant?'

'I am. Thank you.' He turned back to Murdoch. 'Katie Boardman. What can you tell the court?'

'Similar to Claire, except she was from Turners Fold. Went for a walk along the canal and didn't come home. She was having a hard time: she was being investigated for stealing some money and there was some talk of her losing her job. There were no signs of foul play and we concluded in the end that she might have taken her own life or run away, that she went missing intentionally.'

'Or she could have been murdered and her body never recovered?'

'It's a possibility.'

'And she was from a town further along the same canal.'

'Yes.'

Dan leaned down to make a note, although it was really to let the last comment sink in and for his own nerves to settle. His mind flashed to Pat and the anguish in his eyes when he'd recounted what Sean Martin had told him.

When he straightened, he said, 'Most people will have heard of the next victim. Rosie Smith.'

There were whispers from the public gallery.

Murdoch frowned. 'I wasn't asked about Rosie this morning.'

'I didn't need to ask you about it, because I know about her murder, as do you. For the benefit of the jury, you'll agree that Rosie Smith was a fourteen-year-old girl murdered on Highford's canal towpath, and that her stepfather, Sean Martin, found her.'

'Yes, that's the one.'

'Twelve years ago now, and it was a few months before Sean Martin was charged with her murder.'

'Correct.'

'And that Sean Martin was convicted of her murder, but a few years later was retried and acquitted.'

'That's right.'

'And that at this moment, we don't know who murdered Rosie Smith.'

Murdoch swallowed, and Dan could see that she wanted to say that Sean Martin killed Rosie, but Dan knew that she wouldn't. It would rebound on her somehow.

'No, we don't.'

The judge intervened. 'How many more of these cases are there, Mr Grant?'

'I'm going to raise a further four, My Lord.'

The judge turned to Murdoch. 'And you have been given details of these?'

'This morning.'

'I'm going to give the jury a short break. It will do them good.'

Everyone stayed silent as the jurors filed out. Once they'd cleared the courtroom, the judge considered Dan for a moment before saying, 'These other four. Are they all similar?'

'More recent, and along the same canal.'

'Is that right, Detective Inspector?'

'Broadly, yes.'

'How broad?'

'I haven't had the chance to go into any detail, and it's a long canal with many towns along it. I was asked to see whether Peter Box appeared in the investigations. I've found out what I could in the time available.'

Francesca stood up, causing Dan to give way to her. 'My Lord, being aware of that, I do feel I should be allowed to ask the officer about those cases in re-examination. My friend has raised the prospect of a serial murderer, or kidnapper or whatever label he wants to apply to it, and has asked the officer to research various cases. I asked the officer to assist. What Your Lordship should not do is allow my friend to cherry-pick from them, because that is exactly what he has done.'

'You make a fair point, Ms McIntyre, and it's duly noted. Mr Grant, it is a matter for you as to whether or not you raise those in cross-examination, but I will allow the prosecution to examine in greater detail all of the cases you asked the officer to look into this morning.'

Dan stood and nodded. 'As you please, My Lord.'

'And Mr Grant. I've allowed you some leeway this morning, and I understand the geographical proximity, as well as the fact that the cases are unexplained. We are left with vague answers, however, because of the lateness of these enquiries, so I will allow the prosecution to bring forth any statistics on missing persons to put those cases in a better context. You are taking a snapshot but there is a broader view.'

Dan took a deep breath. The judge was right. At least he had more than what he'd started with the day before.

'I'm grateful, My Lord.'

'Can we resume?'

'I'm ready.'

'Ms McIntyre?'

'As always.'

The judge sat back. 'Allow the jurors ten minutes for a comfort break and then bring them back.'

Dan sat down to wait for the case to resume and let out a long breath of relief. The judge had rescued him, even though Dan suspected he hadn't seen it that way. There were inconsistencies ahead that may make his questioning look desperate.

He turned to look towards the dock. Peter had his hands on his head again, looking at the floor.

The case would feel so much more rewarding if his client would just take an interest.

Thirty-seven

Jayne walked into the shop in Highford town centre, a small chain store on the precinct, the sort with racks of clothes churned out by some sweatshop factory and with cheap bangles by the till.

It took a few seconds for her eyes to adjust as she went in. There was a woman behind the counter. Her name badge declared her name was Ann.

'Can I help you?'

'I'm looking for Emily. I've been told she works here.'

'And you are?'

'A private investigator.'

Ann raised her eyebrows, making Jayne laugh and say, 'It's not as exciting as it sounds.'

'Must beat selling clothes,' Ann said, before turning to shout through a door that led to a stairwell. 'Emily?'

Jayne tried to stay still, but she felt a small tingle of excitement as she heard Emily's footsteps on the stairs. She was uncovering a link they hadn't known was there.

Emily was small and petite, her hair bleached straw-blonde and cut short, with bold make-up that made her cheekbones jut out. 'What is it? I'm on my lunch.'

'This woman here wants to talk to you. She's a private investigator, so she says.'

Emily looked confused.

Jayne reached for a business card. 'It's about Peter Box, and Sean Martin.'

Emily's eyes flickered wide before she took a deep breath. She looked at Ann. 'Can I take her upstairs?' When Ann nodded, Emily said, 'Come up, if you don't mind me eating.'

She turned to go up the stairs. Jayne followed.

A brightly lit stairwell led to a stockroom, shoeboxes and clothes in plastic bags crammed on metal shelves, and long coats on racks. Emily turned into a small staff room, with a round table in the middle and a shelf and sink further along, a microwave and kettle the only amenities. There was a half-eaten baked potato with butter and baked beans on the table. Emily picked it up and went to a bin in the corner.

'Not hungry anymore?' Jayne said.

'No, not now.' She sighed. 'Is this about Peter's trial?'

'You know about it?'

'He's an ex-boyfriend. I'm bound to notice his name when I see it in the papers. It was a long time ago, yes, but it's still a shock that he could do that. I've got a new life now. I'm married. Got a couple of children, a boy and a girl. If you want me to give him a character reference, forget it.'

'No, it's not that. I want to ask you how it was back then. We want to understand him, that's all.'

'This is all very late in the day.'

'We didn't know about you, or anyone else who knew him well.'

She thought about that for a few seconds. 'Peter could be a little quiet and hard to get to know, but he was, well, you know, a decent guy. The way he was supposed to be: attentive, loving.'

'What changed?'

'Sean, I think.'

'Your brother-in-law.'

'Yeah, just great, isn't it? My sister married a killer. Well, a cleared killer.'

'Do you think he did it?'

'I don't know.' She pulled a face. 'No, of course not. Trudy wouldn't have married him if he had, but, you know, there's always that doubt.'

'Are you close to Trudy?'

'She's my big sister.'

'And Sean?'

'It's not my business who she marries.'

'That doesn't answer the question.'

'And I'm not in a courtroom.'

Jayne blushed. 'Yes, I know, I'm sorry. I just need your help, that's all.'

'I get why you're asking about Peter. But why do you want to talk about Sean?'

'Because we think Sean might be connected to Peter's case.'

Emily drummed her fingernails on the table as she thought about that. Jayne stayed silent as she let Emily's thoughts percolate.

Eventually, Emily said, 'Sean changed him.'

'How?'

'Peter worshipped him. I was close to Trudy, so we'd go to her house nearly every weekend. Sean was living in a canal boat back then, but he'd spend most nights at Trudy's. It was all right at first, but Sean drank too much and he was a bit mouthy. You know, sounding off all the time. Politics mainly. He had a view on everything and thought he was the authority on it all. I used to get bored and fall asleep, but Sean would ply Peter with vodka and go on and on all night. Sean likes an audience, but even Trudy would get bored. It was harmless at first, but then Peter started to think Sean was right about stuff, and a lot of it was horrible.'

'What like?'

'Sean was fixated with being in control, how life is about getting what you want, fulfilling your fantasies. That seemed to get into Peter's head. He changed. He became arrogant and started to treat me badly.'

'How do you mean?'

'It's embarrassing to talk about this. I don't want to say it in court, in public.'

'Think of it as girlie chat, just between me and you.'

'Sean was a creep. When Trudy wasn't there, he'd be all flirty, saying how awkward it is when you prefer the younger sister, stuff like that, and would drop hints that we should get it out of our system. But there was nothing to get out. It was just Sean being sleazy, and he'd grab at me, paw me. How could he? He was going out with my sister. It was wrong. But Peter? It excited him.'

'How?'

'If Trudy went to bed early, crashed out or whatever, Sean would suggest we had a bit of fun, and I knew what he meant.' Emily blushed. 'A threesome. He never said it when Trudy was around, and it was like he wanted to use Peter to have me. And then he started to behave like that even when Trudy was there: grabbing at me, molesting me in front of her, as if he had no respect for Trudy either. And then there was a night when it all got out of control.'

'What happened?'

'It was demeaning, and it's when Peter and I really fell out, because I expected him to stand up for me or object, but it almost seemed like he wanted it. Can you believe it? Peter wanted to watch me have sex with Sean, just to please Sean. I went mad, shouting and throwing stuff, and Trudy joined in, except she made it sound like it was all my fault for encouraging Sean. She grabbed me by the hair and threw me out.'

'And Peter?'

'He stayed behind. That hurt most of all, that I mattered so little to any of them, Peter included. That's when I finished with him. I'd had enough. I mean, how can you stay with someone like that? He kept in touch with Sean but that was it for me. I didn't want to have anything to do with any of them.'

'Did Sean and Peter stay close?'

'I don't think so. Sean's a user, you see. He didn't like Peter. He just liked the fact that Peter idolised him. Peter was young and stupid, that's all. He came round one night, drunk and cry-ing, really desperate to talk to me, but I closed the door on him. That was the last time I saw him, except when I bumped into him in the street, but he was a different person by then. More nervy, almost a little strange.'

'And you and Trudy?'

'We didn't speak again until she split up with Sean. One night she called to say she was sorry, that it was all Sean and that sisters should get on.'

'Did she say why they split up?'

Emily shrugged. 'They were too combustible. Too much fire for each other.'

'And now?'

'We're close again, and prison changed Sean. He wasn't quite so clever when he came out, as if he knew people thought differently of him. Prison must do that to you, knock off your edges.'

'Thank you. You've been a big help.'

'Have I? How?'

Jayne exhaled. 'Honestly? I don't know, but I feel like I understand it all a little more.'

'What happens next?'

'I report back to Peter's lawyer and he decides what to do.'

Emily smiled. 'How is Peter?'

'I haven't had much to do with him. He's got a good lawyer, though.'

'Did he do it? Did he kill her?'

'The police say he did.'

'What does he say though?'

Jayne couldn't give the truthful answer, that he hadn't said a word about the murder, so she fell back onto the two words he had said. 'He pleaded not guilty. That's good enough for us.'

*

Dan's pulse was quick as he left the courtroom, racing from the adrenaline rush of a crucial passage in the case. He didn't want to spend any time making small talk with Francesca, but instead get outside for some fresh air, so he could refocus for the afternoon ahead. It had been a draining morning. He'd been tense all night, his sleep restless, with his morning starting too early and his mind jumbled by lists of cases and facts. The rush would pass and all he'd be left with would be fatigue. He needed to stay active and he thought walking the streets might keep his focus more than sitting around in the robing room.

Then thoughts of Pat flooded him.

He checked his phone, hoping for a message about Pat. There was one from Jayne. *Need to speak. Now!*

He was about to call when he saw Bill in the court corridor, sitting on one of the seats and wringing his hands. He looked up at Dan and seemed as if he didn't know what to say, whether he was grateful to Dan for raising some of the cases he'd researched, or if he was still angry he'd ignored his son's murder.

Before Bill had a chance to say anything, Dan was distracted by the approach of a reporter, who rushed over and handed him a business card. She was young and eager. 'I heard what you said in there. Do you really believe there is a serial killer stalking the canals?' She held out a voice recorder, her eyes sharp.

'I can't discuss an ongoing case without my client's instructions.'

'But you raised it in court, in evidence.'

'Report that then, if you like, but this conversation isn't happening.'

The reporter sighed and clicked off the machine. Her eyes softened, and some of that professional ruthlessness was replaced by curiosity. 'What about off the record? It sounds like a great piece.'

'Off the record, I'd love to help, but I need to see how the case goes first.' He pointed towards Bill. 'He fed much of the information to me. And there are more cases than the ones I mentioned in court.'

'Are there?' She glanced over at Bill, who was paying a closer interest to the conversation. 'How many?'

'A complete catalogue. He'll help you. Just be gentle with him. His son was one of the victims.'

There was another flash of ruthlessness in her eyes. As Dan turned away, she was handing a business card to Bill and switching on the voice recorder.

At least Bill was going to have his say.

He called Jayne.

'Hey, Dan, about time.'

'I was in court. What was it?'

'Sean Martin and Peter know each other. Peter used to go out with Trudy's sister.'

'What? How?'

'Yeah, that's what I thought. And they both knew Claire Watkins. I spoke to one of her friends, and she reckoned that Peter had a bit of a thing for Claire, and Sean was an old flirt too.'

Dan turned away and cupped his mouth over his phone, so no one could hear what was being said. 'We need to meet. This could be big.'

'I thought so.'

'I'm back in court soon. We'll talk later.'

He clicked off and tapped his phone on his chin, wondering how the new information affected his case. It dragged Sean Martin into it but straightaway he knew it made the case worse. He'd brought up the missing women, and it turned out that Peter had a thing for one of them.

'Shit!' He stormed towards the robing room, needing to find some solitude to get his mind straight, when Murdoch appeared ahead of him. She was deep in conversation, her telephone pressed to her ear. She looked over towards Dan and pointed. *Stay there* was the message.

Dan wasn't interested in apologising or being given the 'how can you sleep' speech. He made as if to go past but Murdoch reached out with her hand to stop him, her palm in Dan's chest, her attention never shifting from her phone.

Dan was about to object, to knock away her hand, but there was something other than hostility in her eyes.

Murdoch ended her call.

'Are you sure you want to have this conversation?' Dan said. 'I was just doing my job.'

'It's not about that,' Murdoch said, and she sighed. 'It's about Pat Molloy. We've found his car.'

Thirty-eight

Dan parked close to Pat's house. What was usually a tranquil setting seemed to have got darker, with the hills around more brooding. He was there to support Eileen and to find out what she knew, but he had to steel himself first. Pat had been his mentor, his boss, his colleague. He brought colour into the office with his courtroom anecdotes and witticisms. He couldn't cope with the thought of that no longer being there.

Before she'd left, Murdoch had told him that Pat's car had been found in the car park of Greencroft railway station, a small country stop on the Highford to Langton line. The station was unstaffed, and police officers were looking through CCTV from the local trains. Dan knew that once Eileen told the police about Pat's cancer, and how he'd been making preparations for the day that would come too soon, they'd start wondering if he'd brought that day forward.

But Pat was a showman. He wouldn't go out with so little pizzazz. He wanted a send-off, an audience. And he'd told Dan that he wanted to spend whatever time he had left with Eileen. There was no way he would bring it to an end so quickly. Nor would he have jumped on a train and gone away without her.

Dan had requested an adjournment for personal reasons, which the judge had allowed, although he suspected it was mainly to allow Francesca and Murdoch more time to look into the list of cases he'd produced. Dan was grateful anyway, because he would have had trouble concentrating.

There was a police car outside Pat and Eileen's house, as well as a couple of other cars he didn't recognise. The police would be tactful, aware that Eileen was desperate with worry, but would also need to find out why Pat had gone out without telling her. They'd want to search the house and work out whether Eileen might be involved in his disappearance.

Dan wanted to go in, but he couldn't move. He needed to know what was happening but he was afraid of knowing.

If he stayed in his car, he wouldn't have to confront Pat's disappearance. He could put up his mental barrier and stay the emotional rock he tried to be. Finding out that Pat was dead could get behind that barrier, and he wasn't ready for that.

A car drew to a slow halt behind him. Dan checked his mirror, but he didn't recognise it. He went back to staring ahead and then jumped at a small tap on the passenger window.

It was Murdoch.

Dan thought about ignoring her, wanting to be alone, but his need to know more about Pat made him press the unlock button.

'Any sign of him?' Dan said, staring straight, his jaw clenched as Murdoch climbed in.

'Not yet. I need to know if I should treat his wife as a suspect.'

Dan shook his head. 'No. Not Eileen. I saw her this morning and she was worried about where he was. She told me he went out last night without telling her. She thought he'd gone to a police station, but he never came home. He was dying. He had cancer and didn't have much time left.'

Murdoch nodded to herself. 'I didn't know that. Thank you.'

'Is this your case?'

'We don't know if there is a case yet, but a missing lawyer attracts the media so we're making sure to stay on top if it.' She looked towards the house. 'One thing though, before I go down there to talk to her.'

'I'm listening.'

'Pat was a defence lawyer, just like you, and that involves knowing a lot of bad stuff about a lot of bad people. You lawyers don't like to talk about your clients, but if you tell me now, I promise no one will know it came from you. Give me a steer, are there any threats from anywhere that his wife might not know about?'

There was an uncomfortable silence as Dan wondered what to say. His own thoughts were running too fast. Eventually, he said, 'Sean Martin.'

'What about him?'

'Timing is important. It's Peter's trial this week. Pat told me to look into the Rosie Smith case, and now he's missing.'

'You mentioned that case today in court, to do with this ridiculous serial killer theory you're talking about? Come on, Dan, you're better than that.'

'Pat came to see me on Sunday. He was worried about Sean Martin. Pat helped get him released but, once he got out, Sean told him a secret.'

'What?'

Dan hoped that this was the conversation Pat had wanted him to have. 'Sean told him where the murder weapon was hidden.'

Murdoch's mouth opened, but a few seconds passed before she spoke. 'So, he was guilty?'

'Sean might have been winding him up, a sick joke.'

'Did Pat Molloy think that?'

'No, he didn't.'

'Why did he tell you?'

'He wanted to die with a clear conscience.' He could see that Murdoch was about to say something, possibly a wisecrack about lawyers having a conscience, but his glare stopped her. 'I went to see Sean Martin on Sunday.'

'What were you hoping he'd do?'

'Break cover, if he thought Pat had told me.'

'If he did, is this how you wanted him to do it?'

Dan was about to snap at her, but he realised that she had pinpointed what he'd been thinking. It accounted for the feeling of nausea, the knowledge that his own actions might have put Pat in danger. Could he live with that?

'Did Pat tell you where the weapon was hidden?'

'Sean had been too vague to be sure. He told Pat that it was by the western corner, below the mason's mark, an itch he couldn't scratch.'

'The western corner of what?'

'That's the point, he didn't know, but don't you think it's odd that within a couple of days of Pat talking about Sean Martin, he's gone missing?'

Murdoch pondered that for a few moments before reaching into her jacket pocket and handing over a business card. 'Contact me if you think of anything else.'

Dan took it and tapped it against the steering wheel as Murdoch got out.

Murdoch was just about to close the door when she leaned in and said, 'Be careful, Dan. If Pat Molloy was attacked because he went out alone, it means he was followed. And if he thinks you know, that puts you in danger too, and anyone else who might know about it.'

As she walked towards the house, his thoughts went to Jayne and he remembered that Sean Martin knew about her involvement, had *liked* her Facebook page. His nausea escalated into a cold sweat. He couldn't let anything happen to her.

He called her. When she answered, he asked, 'Are you all right? No one's following you or anything like that?'

'Dan, slow down. What's wrong?'

'Pat's gone missing.'

'Missing? What do you mean?'

'Like it sounds, and it's all too coincidental. I'm worried about you too.'

She paused before replying, 'I'm fine. I don't need a man to look after me.'

'I didn't mean it like that.'

'Good. I've got a couple more things to follow up and then I'll come to yours.'

'Just be careful.'

'As ever,' and then she hung up.

He threw the phone onto the passenger seat and closed his eyes. He couldn't deal with this.

Thirty-nine

Sean had been busy all day, scouring through documents for whatever his latest cause happened to be. Trudy didn't interfere with that, it was his hobby, his enjoyment of the spotlight keeping him there. At last, he'd found his audience.

She heard him start a video call to one of his student helpers and crept to the doorway to watch through the gap. The student was a young woman, early twenties. She giggled and fawned as Sean played at being the experienced hand, the famous one.

He wasn't wearing his glasses. That's what stood out. He wore them all the time at home, especially when going through his paperwork, either on his nose or pushed up on his head. But now they were on the table and out of reach to ensure they they didn't betray his age.

He gave a small, cutesy wave as he signed off. She moved away from the door.

She brooded in the living room as he whistled his way through the afternoon, slamming cabinet drawers and moving paper around. At one point he came in to check what she was doing, his glasses back on his head.

Before she could answer, her phone rang. It was Emily, her sister.

She didn't want to answer, not with Sean there, but she needed to end her malaise.

'Hi, Em.'

'Trudy, a woman came to my work earlier, asking about Sean and Peter.'

Trudy went cold. 'What do you mean?'

'Just that. She wanted to know about Peter because she's helping out his lawyer. It's his trial this week, I don't know if you've read about it, but she wanted to know about back then too. About Sean.'

Trudy closed her eyes for a moment. 'And what did you tell her?'

'I told her how it was. The conversation just went that way, I'm sorry.'

'Why are you calling me?'

'She might come to see you, to ask about Sean. It seemed like she was more interested in Sean than Peter, now I think back.'

'Okay, thank you.'

Trudy clicked off without saying goodbye.

She put her head back and closed her eyes. All she could hear was the gentle clunk of that damn grandfather clock, and Sean whistling in the other room, still basking in the glow of his flirty video call.

*

His father's living room had a familiar antiseptic aroma when Dan walked in. The electric wheelchair was abandoned in one corner, the battery removed and on the seat. He was watching a film, sitting in a chair that looked old and ragged, holding a glass in his good hand. He turned, straining to see who it was, and said, 'Look at me, getting popular now.'

'I just thought I'd say hello.'

'Yeah, yeah, you were just passing, same old refrain.' He pointed towards a cupboard at the back of the room. 'Could you get me a refill?'

'You should slow down. Drinking all day will kill you.'

'You're a lawyer, not a doctor. If you want to dispense medical advice, put on a white coat. And what's this sudden concern? Most times, you bring me a bagful.'

'Perhaps I'm hoping you'll stick around a bit longer.'

That silenced him. He went back to watching the film, although his focus seemed a little more detached.

Dan moved some old newspapers from a sofa and sat down. He put his head back and closed his eyes. The emotion around Pat's disappearance threatened to swamp him, but he couldn't let it. That would come later, he knew, but there was too much going on for him to lose focus.

'What's eating you, Daniel?'

Dan opened his eyes. His father's voice was softer, more concerned. 'Pat Molloy's gone missing.'

His father's eyes narrowed and he put his glass down. 'How come?'

'Just that. He went out and didn't come home. The police are looking for him, but it doesn't look good.'

He frowned. 'He's a good man, Pat Molloy. He did a lot of good for us back when we needed him, but criminal law attracts criminals. He might have upset the wrong person. You need to be careful.'

'It feels weird. I've only just found out he's very ill, and now he's just disappeared? He's always been like a ... well, a good boss.'

His father picked up his glass again and took a drink. 'A father figure.'

Dan smiled, despite himself. 'Yes, that.'

They both sat in silence for a while, before his father said, 'If you're stopping, take off your jacket. You're allowed to relax. Watch the film with me.'

'Just for a bit, I'd like that.'

And he did. The film washed over him, some nonsense about two mobsters driving a snitch to an execution, but he enjoyed the nothingness about it all. They didn't talk. He refilled his father's glass when he needed it, and they laughed at the film as they watched it.

When he left, his father didn't say much. Just raised his glass and winked, but as Dan walked back to his car, swallowing down the lump in his throat, it felt like his father had said so much.

He'd needed it.

Forty

Jayne was pleased with her day's work so far. She was certain it was of some use, but she wanted to know more before she went to Dan with it. She'd discovered a link between Peter Box and Sean Martin, so she wanted to find out more about Peter.

The news about Pat going missing had shocked her, but she didn't know him what well and it could mean anything. All she knew was that Dan was worried, which was enough to spark her own concern.

She put Pat's disappearance to the back of her mind and dug around in her papers for Peter's address, where he'd lived before he was arrested. It was only a short drive, and when she arrived there, it looked totally unremarkable.

Until his arrest, Peter Box had lived on a terraced street. It was a grade higher than the old industrial terraces that filled so many parts of Highford with long strips of grey stone right against the pavement. The small bay window of Peter's house overlooked a front garden, and a neat grass verge divided the pavement from the road.

But that was as far as the neatness extended. Someone had smeared BEAST over the front in red paint and the windows had been boarded up, no doubt to protect the building from further vandalism.

There was a shop at the end of the street, a small grocer's that sold the usual mix of newspapers and alcohol. They might know more about him.

The door tinkled as she went in.

The man behind the counter was portly and bald, rough-shaven. There was a stale smell in the shop, as if he'd stopped caring too much about the place. Jayne introduced herself, but the man's expression was impassive.

'I'm trying to find out more about Peter Box. Was he one of your customers?'

'I've told the police all I know.'

'Which is?'

'That he came in sometimes and that I've known him since he was a boy. I've been here thirty years.'

'What is he like?'

'Polite, shy. I used to ask him how he was, because I remember his parents dying and I knew he lived on his own. He gave the same answer each time. That he was fine.'

'Hard to get to know?'

He shrugged. 'Just shy. Never given me a problem, even when he was younger.'

'What do you mean?'

The first sign of a smile. 'We're all foolish when we're young. You've got a full set of balls for the first time and you think you can rule the world. You soon get over it. Like me. I got this place expecting to build an empire. Now? I'm just hoping the Co-op will come along and make me an offer I can't refuse.'

'Does Peter have any friends around here? Or interests?'

He put his head back and thought for a few moments. 'He was a customer. I don't know what his hobbies are. He was friendly with a woman a couple of streets away. Mrs Henderson. I think she knew his parents. One of those people you call auntie even though you aren't related. He used to pay her paper bill sometimes.'

'Who is she? Which street?'

'Who are you again?'

'I'm working for his lawyer.'

'Did he do it? Did he murder that woman?'

'I hope not.'

He nodded to himself and then scribbled an address on a scrap of paper. 'Don't tell her I sent you.'

The houses became a little grander as she walked away from Peter's street, set further back from the road and with driveways. The house she was looking for was the most unkempt. Moss was growing on the roof and the curtains looked faded. The other driveways were wide and neat and filled by cars, often more than one, but all Mrs Henderson had was a strip of cracked tarmac with weeds poking through. The door was old and wooden, dark in contrast to the gleaming white PVC doors everywhere else.

Jayne knocked and waited.

She thought no one was going to answer, but just as she stepped away the door opened.

The woman was old and stooped, her grey curls thinning so that the pinkness of her scalp showed through. Her cardigan was faded and threadbare, her trousers so cheap and shiny that they looked like they might make sparks when she walked.

Once Jayne introduced herself, she was shown through to a living room that was warm enough to send someone to sleep, with gas flames roaring over fake coals, even though it was warm outside. It was welcoming though, with family photographs on every wall, showing off grandchildren and family weddings.

The woman sat down and put her head back against the high back of her chair.

'Mrs Henderson, I want to talk about Peter Box.'

'Please, call me Evelyn. But why do you want to talk about Peter?'

'I work for the firm representing him in court. I just want to know more about him, some background to help his case.'

'It makes me so sad, this court case. He was such a lovely boy. So quiet, so gentle. I wrote to him, to ask if I could see him, just to understand it a bit more, but I don't even know if he got my letter. How is he?'

'All right, I think, but nervous about his trial, obviously.'

'You do a good job. Peter wouldn't do what they said he did. Not Peter.'

'It sounds like you know him well.'

'I've known him all his life. He was such a good boy for his parents, but things were difficult for him around here.'

'How do you mean?'

'Because he's different. Not sporty or loud, but quiet and thoughtful, and kids don't like that sometimes. It made him seem weak. He put up with a lot, did Peter.'

'Bullying?'

'Yes, but there'll always be bullies, and they pick on the quiet ones, the ones who won't fight back. And everyone else goes along with it because they're just glad it isn't them.' She sighed. 'It's just how it is.'

'What did the bullies do to him?'

'Mean stuff, like trapping him behind a classroom door and throwing heavy books over the top, or making him walk through a windmill of bags. Sometimes, people would hit him, like bang smack on the nose, and he'd go home like that, walk the streets with blood streaming from his nose. I saw him once. Made him come into the house to clean up.'

'What did his parents do about it?'

'It upset his mother, really broke her heart, but his father was a tough man and so unlike Peter that people wondered whether his mother had been having it away with someone else. His father used to say that it's a tough, tough world, so you've got to be tough in return, but Peter wasn't like that.'

'I heard he visited you.'

'Oh, all the time. We'd sit and chat and he was such a comfort to me.'

'Has anyone ever said that he could be violent or nasty?'

'Not Peter. Too gentle.'

'Did you ever meet his girlfriend, Emily?'

'I remember her. She was nice. I liked her.'

'Did he have many girlfriends?'

Evelyn chuckled. 'Emily was the only one I met, lovely girl, but I just don't think it was the right time for them.'

'Why do you say that?'

'He seemed so ... I don't know how to phrase it. Fragile, probably.'

'Did he say why they broke up?'

'Not to me, but why would he? He was the sort of boy who kept things to himself. But I could tell he wasn't all right even before they broke up, though, and I told him to go see a doctor. He wasn't sleeping or eating. I mentioned it to his parents too;

it was as if he didn't notice anyone. Dark circles around his eyes and haunted-looking. Do you know what I thought? Drugs. It gets a lot of them round here. Horrible stuff. His girlfriend left him in the end, and who could blame her?'

'How was he when she left him?'

'Just the same – maudlin. But I don't think it was because of her.'

'Did he ever mention anyone called Sean Martin?'

She frowned. 'I've heard that name.' She tapped her finger on the chair arm as she thought. 'Isn't he the man who went to prison for killing his stepdaughter?'

'Yes, that's him, although he got out after his appeal.'

'Ah, well, don't they all? Why do you ask?'

'Peter knew him. Did he ever mention him?'

Evelyn shook her head. 'No, sorry. I've heard the name on television and seen it in the papers, but that's all.'

Jayne thanked her and went to the door. As Evelyn followed her, she said, 'Say hello to Peter for me. If he's done what they say he's done, he should pay for it, but I don't think he would. Not Peter.'

Once she left the cloying warmth of the house, Jayne took a detour along the canal. She parked in a small retail park and cut through, just to try and get a feeling of what had happened there.

As she looked along the towpath, she couldn't see the pub where Lizzie had been drinking the night she died. It was in a converted warehouse and it crowded the water, but a road bridge leading from the town centre blocked it out, the pub recognisable in the distance only by a couple of benches and a table visible. Further on, boats were moored, smoke billowing out of one. The canal curved out of sight and disappeared between high walls. There were no ways off the towpath. Between where she was and the pub, Lizzie would have had nowhere to go, except back the way she'd come, back to where Liam was prowling.

It was between the same pub and where Jayne was standing right now that Rosie Smith was killed too.

Jayne turned the other way. The sweep was different. The part of the canal where Lizzie had been fatally assaulted was on a long and gentle curve, the towpath always visible, bordered by high fences, so that there'd be no opportunities for her to escape, a housing estate on the other side.

Jayne remembered the small marina Sean had driven to after Dan's visit. It was further along, just a couple of miles in the same direction. From the marina, it wouldn't have taken Sean long to get to where Lizzie had died, away from the traffic jams and the New Year revellers and the CCTV cameras. Just a boat chugging gently, the sound of the engine almost lost amongst the late-night din of the town centre. The taxis, the screams of drunks, the repetitive thump of loud music every time a pub door opened.

An idea was forming.

She called Dan. Before she could say anything, he barked, 'Come to my place,' and hung up.

She stared at the phone for a few seconds before she went back to her car. Whatever was behind his bad mood, she needed to let him know what she'd found out.

Forty-one

Dan didn't say anything as he let Jayne in.

'What's the urgency?' she said.

'It's spinning too fast. There's Pat going missing, and Sean following you on Facebook, and then there's the damn case.'

'Tell me about Pat,' she said. 'What did you mean when you said he's gone missing?'

He leaned back against the wall, his arms folded. 'Can it have more than one meaning? He went out last night without saying where he was going and never came home. Now his car has turned up outside the station at Greencroft.'

'Why would it be there?'

'I've no idea, but I feel like I should know, because he was more than my boss. Eileen's worried to hell, I am too, and then there's you and Sean Martin. It's all too much.'

Jayne put her hand on his forearm. 'You look like shite.'

He almost laughed. Instead, he put his head back against the wall, his voice choked unable to respond.

He felt Jayne's hand in his and he let her guide him to the sofa. When he sat, Jayne put her arms round him. She was warm, her face buried into his neck.

Her voice was muffled when she said, 'Stop playing at being the strong man. It's allowed to get on top of you.'

He pulled away. 'No, it's not. If I let it, this job could swamp me. And I don't mean this case. I mean the whole thing. I deal with the job, the cases and the clients and the late nights by keeping my focus, but this case is different. They don't always get this personal.' He stared into her eyes. 'And whatever you might say, I'm allowed to worry about you.'

She held his gaze before saying, 'I like that you do.'

Dan stood and began to pace. He could lose himself in Jayne, her warmth, their closeness, but he forced his focus back on the case. 'How have you got on?'

'Are you okay to talk about it? I know your attention is on Pat right now, rather than this case.'

'The two might be related somehow.'

'Because of Sean Martin?'

'We start asking questions about someone who Pat thinks is a killer and suddenly he goes missing. Quite a coincidence, don't you think?'

'Do you think Bill is in danger? After all, Rosie was one of the victims in his theory. Sean doesn't know about him yet, but Bill isn't a man who wants to stay quiet.'

'He was speaking to the press when I left. Whatever happens with this case, he's got an audience now. That's all he wanted.'

Jayne put her jacket on the back of the sofa. 'What do we do now?'

'I don't want to talk about it. I just feel like getting trashed.'

'You got any wine?'

'I've always got wine.' He went to the fridge. It clinked as he opened it.

As she took a glass from him, she went to the balcony window and looked out. 'Did you mention the missing women in court?'

'Yes. I had to.'

'And?'

'Who knows? I got some traction with it, but I might just look desperate to the jury.' He joined her by the window. 'I don't know what to do. This is the most serious case I've dealt with on my own and I feel like it's spinning out of control.'

She rested her head on his shoulder. He put his arm around her. It felt natural somehow, and he needed to feel close to someone.

'What are the theories about Pat?'

'Just what you'd expect. Pat has a reputation from when he was younger, and Eileen wondered if he'd gone to see a girl-friend. But Pat wouldn't have caught the train, not the small grotty service that runs through Greencroft.'

'If it's bad news, what about an old client who was unhappy with the service he got? You keep on talking about his flam-boyance but perhaps he wanted to disappear somewhere rather than have other people see him become diminished. That's his flourish, the mystery.'

'No, it's more than that. I feel it.'

'Let's do something about it then.'

Dan looked at her. 'What do you mean?'

'Let's go after Sean Martin. After all, what did Pat expect you to do when he told you about the link between Peter Box and Sean?'

'I've raised it in court already.'

'What Sean told Pat?'

'No. Just that Rosie is another unexplained death because Sean has been cleared.'

'I thought you said that it would make Peter look guilty, because if not Sean, why not Peter?'

'I had to use Sean's case somehow, and I couldn't use whatever he said to Pat. It's privileged, client to lawyer.'

'You told me.'

'I told Murdoch too, but that doesn't mean the judge would allow it to be used. Pat would have known that, but all he had burning inside him was that Peter and Sean are connected in some way and wanted this link to come out.'

Jayne thought about that for a few moments. 'Where does this leave the case then, or Bill's theory?'

'We try to link them to Sean Martin. If we can prove he killed Rosie, and leave him as a suspect for the rest, it might help Peter.'

'Is that the reason?'

His jaw clenched. 'If he's connected in any way to Pat's disappearance, I want to bring him down.'

'Remember, I've found a link. Sean Martin already owned his canal boat at the time when Rosie was killed, and had for years before he went to prison, when he and Trudy were still a young couple.'

'Yes, you said, and Sean and Peter knew each other.'

'Peter was going out with Trudy's sister, Emily.'

'Why hasn't Peter told us? Or why didn't Sean tell Pat back when he confessed? He said Peter was just "some local oddball".'

'I realised last night that one of the missing women, Claire Watkins, lived on the next street up from where Sean lived before he married Karen, Rosie's mum. It was Trudy's house really, but he stayed there all the time, except when he was out on his boat. He used to moor it nearby when he went to Trudy's house. I spoke to one of Claire's friends and she remembered Sean, and Peter.'

'What did she say?'

'It was all about Sean, really. Back then, he thought of himself as a big deal, the cool guy in the neighbourhood; he used to speak to Claire if he saw her in the street, but it was Peter who fancied Claire, even though he was with Emily, Trudy's sister. Peter spent a lot of time with Sean, and Emily said he looked up to Sean, as if he idolised him. I get the idea that Sean Martin prefers an audience to a friendship.'

'I don't remember Peter from Sean's trial. Why wasn't he there to support him?'

'Well, claiming responsibility for Rosie's murder looks like support to me. Perhaps he wanted to be Sean's saviour?'

Dan took a drink as he thought about that. 'It's a lot to expect of someone.'

'That depends on what type of hold he has.' She frowned. 'What if . . .'

'Go on.'

'What if Peter murdered Rosie with Sean?'

'An accomplice?'

'Why not? It would explain Peter's confession, and Sean's eagerness not to use it.'

'Does it fit with Rosie's murder though? Why was Sean left holding her?'

'Perhaps Peter ran away.'

Dan raised an eyebrow. 'There's an even better possibility, that he spoke to Pat about being responsible for Rosie's murder out of some misguided attempt to help Sean. We've got a link now, between Sean Martin and two of the women in Bill's research. There might be something else if we dig deep enough. Put that drink down. If we're going after Sean Martin, we need to go where the information is. My office.'

'Good idea. Let's go.'

Forty-two

The dead files were stored in the cellar. Pat kept the murder files separate from the others, because those cases never went away. The stigma, the long sentences, and the risk of another incarceration even after an early release, meant that clients always wanted to appeal murder convictions. Those files had a special place.

The cellar was cold and dusty and smelled of damp cardboard. Boxes and files were lined up on shelves, waiting for the date when they could be destroyed. The murder files were crated in one corner. Sean Martin's was easy to find, the biggest of them all, the case having gone through two appeals before the retrial was ordered.

There were five crates in all, but it was the first two Dan was most interested in. These contained the witness statements, correspondence and interview notes. He didn't need to see the photographic exhibits or the court documents and trial notes.

He carried them up two flights of stairs, staggering into his office out of breath, his arms aching. Jayne was waiting for him on the sofa, her jacket over the back.

He dumped the crates on the floor. 'This lot will keep us busy.'

Jayne lifted the lid on the first one as Dan wiped the sweat from his brow. She picked up a file marked STATEMENTS. 'Shall we start with these?'

'You read those and I'll do the letters and notes.'

'And what are we looking for?'

'It's hard to know. Just read and see what jumps out. Look for any link to Peter Box.'

Jayne started to leaf through her papers on the sofa. Dan went to his desk and began to filter the correspondence file.

Pat's records were meticulous, a hangover from the days when payment was based upon time-recording, when every six-minute unit, every letter and phone call, could be billed. Nowadays solicitors' fees in criminal work were calculated by base rates and page counts. Doing more work didn't earn more money, but old habits were hard to lose.

'It's so sad,' Jayne said. 'Rosie was just a child. If he killed her, why?'

'We'll never know but you've read the rumours, that she was going to spill some family secret.'

Dan flicked through the file notes from whenever Pat met Sean, but of course it was all sanitised. Pat had to write it up as if Sean were telling the truth, couched in terms that were persuasive. The notes would never be seen by a jury, but every lawyer wrote them as if they had an innocent man for a client – there wouldn't be a shred of paper that said otherwise.

'Why was he there?'

Dan looked up. 'Huh?'

'At the canal. What was he doing there, I mean really? I'm reading all these statements and they're all about why Rosie was there, that she'd gone to see a friend and got the bus back. The canal towpath was a shortcut, but no one knew Sean was going to be there. They couldn't get the phone messages back, and Rosie's mother made a statement that said that Sean had been out for most of the day. He did that often, apparently, but she didn't know where he went or where he'd been that day. How did he end up there, to cradle Rosie as she died?'

'The story he gave was that he'd gone to meet her from her bus and told her to take the towpath as a shortcut so that he wouldn't have to go through the one-way system to take her home. He said that he must have missed the killer by seconds.'

'Do you buy that, really? Because if he was just going out to collect Rosie, why didn't Karen know that? It means he was somewhere else first, so did Rosie contact him, or did he contact her? If he was out, why was it so much hassle to meet her at the bus stop?'

'He never came up with good answers. He said he'd gone for a drive, and then a walk, and texted her on the off-chance.'

'Pretty damn convenient.'

'Especially as it couldn't be proved either way. He said he'd deleted the text. And her phone was missing.'

'Why did he delete it?'

'He said that he did routinely, because his phone didn't have much memory and he thought it would slow it down if there were too many texts on it.'

'But what about phone records?'

'There was a text, but it was around the time that she was found. The police thought her phone might have gone into the water, but they didn't find it when they sent the divers in. The theory proposed at trial by the prosecution was that it was a fake text he'd sent to make it look like he was in contact with her, but he was caught holding her. How could he be killing her and texting her at the same time?' He smiled. 'Whatever questions we can think of now were thought of back then, by people who'd worked on the case for a long time. Including me.'

Dan carried on turning the pages, hoping to see Peter Box's name come up. His eyes were starting to glaze when something made him go back a page.

'It's here,' he said, jabbing the paper with his finger. 'A short file note,' and he read it out.

Attendance note. 24 May. Someone called Peter Box came into the office. He said that Rosie's murder was all down to him. I asked him what he meant but he wouldn't elaborate. Instead, he contradicted himself, saying that I should make sure that Sean Martin stayed in prison, but then said again that it was 'all down to me'. Box was hard to get details from. He became near frantic with panic at one point. He left the office before I could ask him anything further.

   Action: discuss with client. Consider informing police, to put it on record.

'What the hell does that mean?'

'What it sounds like,' Dan said. 'Pat was telling the truth, that Peter Box claimed responsibility for Rosie's murder.' He continued to turn the pages. 'Here we are, the note from Pat's prison visit. It sounds like it was Peter Box's confession that made Pat visit. Here listen,' Dan said, and read it out.

Attendance note. 28 May. Visited Sean Martin in prison. Discussed the development with Peter Box. Client instructed me not to bother pursuing it, said that Peter just sounded like some local weirdo. Whoever killed Rosie was ruthless and cold and wouldn't visit me to make a confession like that.

Advised client that we should inform the police, just so that it's on record that someone else was claiming responsibility. Client disagrees. States that it will look like we are trying to engineer another suspect by picking on some local oddball and getting him to make a false confession. Further, he knows what it's like to be falsely accused. His conscience won't allow someone else to suffer his fate.

On reflection, I agree. If Peter Box's confession, such as it is, turns out to have no substance, and can easily be negated, and the enquiry was initiated by us, it will make us look as if we are fabricating red herrings.

Action: ignore Peter Box. Client in agreement.

Dan put the file down. 'It's hard to see Pat's words like this because they make him come alive, and right now we don't know where he is. And how far does it take us anyway? We can't prove that Sean Martin was the real killer. All it does is prove what Pat told me, which makes Peter a serial killer, if the jury believe what he said. Knowing what Pat thought doesn't mean much. I'm caught between wanting to defend my client and wanting to prove that we all got it wrong with Sean Martin.'

'This is partly my fault.'

'What do you mean?'

'I brought Bill Maude into this and it's made it harder for you. I could have just left his house, but instead I called you and showed you what he had. Go back to doing what you were doing.'

'Yes, you're right.' He rubbed his eyes. He was weary.

'Come here,' she said.

He closed the file and went over to her. He sat on the sofa, close enough to smell the wine on her breath from before.

She took his hands. 'I know it's easy for me to say, but don't get too hung up on this. Let the police look for any connections to Pat's disappearance. Just do your job in court and let the jury decide.'

'I know, you're right.'

She pumped his hands. 'I mean it. You're trying to do too much.'

His eyes met Jayne's, and there was something in them that he needed. In that moment, he felt lost, the pressure of the trial and Pat's disappearance all swirling together. Normally, he could cope, but he felt like he was buckling under it all, no obvious way forward. For a moment, Jayne seemed distant, his mind filled with the sound of his own heartbeat, sweat on his brow like warm prickles.

His fingers tightened around hers. His earlier restraint began to slip away. He needed her closeness, a connection, his emotions sweeping over him.

She hesitated.

His breath came faster.

Her eyelids flickered before she closed them.

Her lips were soft as he kissed her. Gentle, uncertain at first, but then her urgency mixed with his and the kiss became firmer.

His hands went to her back and he pulled her against him. The air was filled with the rustle of their clothes. He started to lose himself in her.

Images of her came back to him, of Jayne in the police station, vulnerable and scared, and of her in a prison bib, awaiting her trial.

They slid down on the sofa so that she was lying on top of him.

'Can anyone see in here from across the road?' She gasped as she spoke, her cheeks pink, her eyes showing her need.

'I don't think so.'

She kissed him again and ran her hand down his body, pulling his shirt out of his waistband before moving lower and her palm enveloped his hardness.

More images came into his head. The trial. Her relief at the acquittal. His client.

He pulled away. 'Stop, stop.'

Jayne looked up, breathless. 'What is it?'

'We can't do this.'

'We're doing it.'

'No, no.'

Jayne rolled off him. '*What the hell?*'

'It's not right, we both know that.'

Tears jumped into her eyes, but they were tears of anger. 'What games are you playing? Seriously, what the *fuck*?'

'Jayne, no, calm down.'

She stood up and shouted, 'I really don't believe you,' her voice choked. 'What is this? Just keeping me dangling in case you get the urge one night? Is this how you get your kicks? I'm not some fucking ego-boost.'

'Jayne, it's not like that. I want to, but . . .'

'Forget it. Never again.'

'Jayne.'

'I've had enough. I hope you enjoyed your feel,' and she stomped out of the door, throwing it back against the wall.

Dan put his head in his hands as he listened to her running down the stairs. The front door slammed.

He didn't go after her. Instead, he let the office fall silent as he was left alone with his thoughts. The office was filled with memories of Pat, from his colourful swagger that Dan remembered from his early days as a trainee, to the old man Pat had become in recent months, much older than his years would have warranted.

He closed his eyes. How could it all go so wrong? He thought of the box of papers. He wished he'd never seen them. Wished he'd ignored Pat and stuck to what he was doing. Pat might not have gone missing. Jayne might not have run from his office. There was a chance it wouldn't feel like his whole life was unravelling.

Forty-three

All Jayne could hear was the music.

A few hours had passed since she'd run out of Dan's office, her thoughts whirling. She'd gone down the main street at first, not knowing where she was going, or why.

She was angry, and not just with Dan. She shouldn't have allowed herself to surrender like that, as if she'd spent her life waiting for him. She was stronger than that. They weren't a couple, and she'd hardly been celibate during their acquaintance.

But it had been different this time, because there'd been a look in his eyes she hadn't seen before. Desire, emotion, need, hurt. It had drawn them both in, her defences relaxed for a moment, which had made his rejection of her feel like a punch in the stomach. Even when the moment had been right, she hadn't been good enough.

It made her feel overlooked, trivial, just a bit part in his life.

The booze had gone down quickly. It had been angry drinking, and now she was swaying. She hadn't eaten. It was midweek, and the town was quiet, but she'd found a club that catered for the crowd who never wanted to go home. The dance floor was empty but there was a group of men at one end of the bar.

Jayne felt the urge to obliterate the night, have one last big hurrah in Highford and make a new future in the morning. Fuck this town. Fuck her life. And fuck you, Dan Grant.

She was swaying to the music, halfway through another vodka, just losing herself in the steady drum-drum of whatever music was blasting out of the speakers. An eighties vibe, appealing to the middle-aged men by the bar. She knew they were watching her. Good. Let them.

Someone came up behind her. One of the men, moving his hips in time with hers, whiskey breath, edging closer. She thought she heard someone cheer from the bar.

She stayed with him. This was what she deserved, dancing with some old soak in the dregs of the midweek pub-life. Her life had taken her down this path. His chubby hands went to her waist. She wanted to tell him to get off, knee him in the balls and scream at him, but she didn't. Instead, she joined in his rhythm as he swayed behind her. He smelled of stale cigarettes and sweat.

He pushed his rotund stomach against her back, the small prod of his arousal making her grit her teeth.

Perhaps she needed this. Sink right to the bottom so that her life could only get better. She closed her eyes. Could he satisfy a need? Could she use him like he wanted to use her? No, the revulsion in her stomach told her that she could never enjoy it. She let the music take over.

He kissed her ear. There was sweat on his lip. His lank hair brushed against her temple. She pushed back against him, to give him what he wanted. His hand crept up the front of her body, his fingers on her stomach, groping for her breast.

'Jayne?'

She turned around. It was Dan. His shirt was undone, his tie loose, and his eyes had the unfocused look of a man who'd hit the booze as hard as she had. He came close so that she could hear him above the music. 'I've been looking for you. Your flat. My flat. Every pub and club.'

She pushed the man away. 'Good for you. What a hero. What do you want?'

'Come home with me. Don't stay here with him.'

The man straightened and puffed out his chest. 'What's that supposed to mean?'

As Jayne took a better look at him, she saw he was twice her age, with veins on his nose and a deep flush to his skin. 'Don't fight over me, boys.'

'Don't do it, Jayne.' Dan's voice was low and soft.

'Do what?'

'Try to prove how worthless you feel by letting this ape grind against you.'

The man stepped up to Dan, looking up. 'Don't call me an ape.' His voice had got deeper. More of a growl.

Dan ignored him. 'Jayne, come with me. I'm sorry.'

'You don't own me, Dan Grant.' She jabbed his chest with her finger. 'I can go where I want, and with whoever I want. And I'm not someone you can just pick up and drop whenever you feel like it.'

The man grinned. 'That told you.'

'Please Jayne, let's talk about this.'

The man gripped Dan's forearm. 'You heard her.'

She swallowed back a tear. 'Just go, Dan. Please.'

No one spoke for a few seconds. Jayne put her back to him. Eventually, the man said, 'He's gone now,' and put his arm around her waist. He twirled her round so that she was facing him.

She looked beyond him, Dan was no longer there, so she buried her face into the man's shoulder as he swayed against her, the music playing some old George Michael song. His hands went to her behind and pressed her against him, his arousal pushing harder, her own arms slack over his shoulders.

This was her life. Just make the night end quickly.

Forty-four

The club was a small spray of neon in the drab town centre. Dan checked his watch. Nearly 1 a.m. He should go home. The booze was wearing off, a bottle of wine drunk too quickly, and he was cold, waiting in a shop doorway opposite. The trial would continue in the morning and he needed a clear head, but he couldn't leave Jayne like that.

He was angry with himself though. For how he'd pushed her away to how he'd hunted her down. He had no right to do that. That didn't change how he felt though, and in that fog of booze there was the hope that he could make it up to her. He could wait until the morning, but he didn't want to do that. He wanted to go back to how it was before he messed it up, where he enjoyed their connection, and her company.

Most of all, he didn't want to leave her to those goons, pawing her and hoping to take advantage of her own attempts to obliterate the evening.

He wished he could see past her as a former client. So many times he'd wanted to reach across to her, whenever she smiled in a certain way, or bit her lip in concentration, or when she laughed that free, bright belly laugh at something that really amused her. The sensible part of his brain acknowledged that their relationship was unequal.

But he still wanted to hear her laugh more.

The night was disturbed by the sounds of conversation, drifting from across the road over the gentle thump of music that was playing in the club. Two men emerged from the building with Jayne propped between them. They all swayed as one of the men waved at one of the cab drivers waiting in the taxi rank.

Dan walked across the road.

'Jayne?'

Everyone turned round. The man who'd been dancing with her scowled. 'What do you want, dickhead?' He wobbled on his feet as he stepped closer to Dan, letting go of Jayne, who stumbled against the club doorway.

'Jayne, don't do this.'

She grinned, in that exaggerated way drunks do. 'Dan, my knight in shining armour.' Her voice was slurred, her eyelids drooping.

'Come home with me.'

The man stepped even closer, until his stale breath washed over Dan's face. 'She's told you to piss off already. Just do one.' He snarled and bared his teeth as he said it.

Dan pushed him. He tottered backwards and fell against the wall. He made as if to go back to Dan, but Dan shook his head. 'You really don't want to do that. Even if there are two of you.'

Jayne doubled over, sucking in large breaths, as if she was trying to stop herself being sick. 'What do you want, Dan?'

'I want you to come home. Either to your place or mine, but don't go home with these guys.'

Jayne lifted her head to look at them, both standing with their fists clenched by their waists.

'You'll hate yourself tomorrow.' He looked the men up and down. 'You've never gone this low.'

The taxi pulled up against the pavement. Dan nodded to it. 'Just go, both of you.'

The two men looked at Jayne and back at Dan, and realised their night had ended. They got into the taxi without producing any more threats, although, as the car pulled away, one of the two men wound down a window and gave Dan the finger.

Dan went towards Jayne and held out his hand. 'Come home.'

She straightened and put her arm round Dan's waist, her head against his shoulder, uncertain on her feet as they both meandered down the street.

Neither of them said anything as they walked. Dan spotted another taxi, and they both stumbled into it. She wound down the window and let the cool breeze wake her up, staying silent.

She leaned against him in the lift to his apartment. He put his arm round her. 'Can we just write off tonight? And I'm sorry for hunting you down.'

'I'm glad that you did. You rescued me.' She looked up at him. 'Are we still friends?'

'Always.'

'Can I sleep here?'

'That's the idea.'

Once they were inside, Jayne went straight to the bathroom as he stripped down to his underwear and climbed into bed. Sleep started to overtake him. Jayne came into the bedroom in her T-shirt and knickers.

As she climbed in with him, she put her arm across him and rested her head against his chest. He pulled her closer.

She fell asleep before he did, soft nasal whistles letting him know.

He smiled. She felt good against him.

Forty-five

Dan woke with a start and then winced at a sharp jab of pain in his head. His mouth was dry, his eyes heavy, and there was someone was in his apartment.

Then he remembered. Jayne. He reached across to feel the indentation in the pillow. It was still warm.

He checked his watch. Just after six.

He threw back the covers and groaned. He couldn't face going to court. He could taste the booze and his vision swam. He took a few deep gulps of air before he padded through to the living room. Jayne was there, fully dressed and kneeling on the floor, her hair dishevelled, staring at the television.

'What are you doing?' His voice came out as a croak.

'I had an idea, but with all that happened I forgot to mention it.'

'This is early though. Don't you have a hangover?'

'It'll come later. I woke up and remembered and then I couldn't get back to sleep. I was going to wake you, but you looked out for the count, and you've got court, and what if I'm wrong?'

'Are you?'

'I don't know yet.'

Dan went to the kettle and clicked it on, before going back to put on some jogging pants and a T-shirt. When he returned, taking two teas with him, he sat on the sofa behind her.

He passed her a mug. 'What have you found?'

'Nothing yet.' When Dan looked confused, she said, 'The canal boat. Don't you see? I went to the canal yesterday, and it's a long, easy run from the narrowboat marina I saw him at on Sunday. When we watched the footage of New Year's Eve before, we were looking out for Sean's car. We hadn't thought of a simpler explanation, which is that he wasn't in a car at all, but on a boat. How could you ever trace where it had been? No traffic cameras. No number-plate recognition cameras. Away from CCTV. Just a boat drifting along a quiet canal.'

Dan grinned. 'Oh, you're good.'

'We should be looking for that, the boat.'

Dan leaned forward. 'And what have you found?'

'This is the disk that gives the best view of the canal.'

'How far have you got into the footage?'

'Just started it. I was trying all the different disks, and this one has a view of the canal facing towards where Sean keeps his boat.'

She pressed play.

As they watched the familiar scene, the town centre at night, Jayne pointed to a narrow silver ribbon at the top of the screen. 'That's the canal.'

The water glinted in the moonlight, different to the dirty orange of the streetlights below.

They both remained silent as they watched. They drank their teas and concentrated on the screen, on the small blurs of people in the distance and the flashes of headlight beams. Fifteen minutes passed before Jayne rose up.

'There,' she said, her voice filled with excitement, looking around to Dan.

In the far distance, a small round light moved towards the camera, just a speck, but its progress was unmistakable. Slow and steady. They were transfixed, watching it approach the camera.

Dan stood up and peered at the screen. 'Lizzie was killed around here.' He pointed to a spot obscured by the large stone buildings opposite the pub. 'Look at the time.' He tapped the digits in the top corner of the screen. 'That was when Lizzie was being assaulted in the pub car park. The boat is heading right for the place where she died.'

Another few minutes passed and there was no sound in the apartment apart from their breathing.

The boat stopped. The beam of the headlight was just strong enough to pick out the canal banks.

'He might be getting out,' Jayne said. 'Hiding on the bank.'

It stayed for a few minutes longer, before the beam was turned off.

'It's mooring,' Dan said.

'I can see why the police missed it. We can only see it because we're looking for it.'

'But we don't know whose boat it is.'

'Does that matter?'

'It's too vague to be useful in court.'

'Has Peter ever mentioned a boat?'

'He's hardly mentioned anything. Just some ramblings about the darkness, how it hid so much and made the night special.'

'He should have noticed a boat coming towards him. You could ask him. It gives us another suspect.' She smiled. 'And Sean Martin has a boat.'

'We'll go to the canal on the way to court and work out how far along the boat was. You're right – if I can diminish the DNA evidence, the presence of another suspect might help him. Particularly if it's someone the public have mixed opinions about. But I know one thing: Peter is going to have to start talking.'

Forty-six

Jayne put a finger to her lips as Dan followed her into her apartment building.

'They're not early risers in here,' she said.

'Yeah, I can smell the late nights.'

Her smile told him that she knew what he meant. The smell of cannabis was strong, drifting up from the flat below hers, grown in the tenant's bedroom under bright lights to maintain his own habit and to deal small amounts to people he knew.

'He knows the police will kick his door in one day, but he's normally too stoned to care.'

'Don't you ever fancy getting a bag from him? Might be a cheaper night in than wine.'

She shook her head. 'I prefer alcohol, but it keeps him quiet. I'd rather live above a pothead than a drunk.'

They moved quietly upstairs and then into her apartment. Jayne went into her bedroom with a shout that she was having a shower. As the water started to run, Dan went into the living room and sat down.

As he looked around, it struck him how the place still didn't feel like a home. It was as if she'd never really planned to stick around. No pictures. No personal touches. He guessed that it wasn't a conscious choice, just a desire not to settle. He knew she was in Highford because she'd run away after her own acquittal. She'd visited her hometown since and he wondered for a moment if she was thinking of going back for good. The fear of what her ex-boyfriend's family might do had eased now. She'd stuck with her changed name, but she could revert back easily enough and return to her old life.

He didn't like the thought of that. He enjoyed having her around. He may have just lost Pat. He didn't want to lose Jayne too. She brought laughs into his life, even a little bit of chaos sometimes. She brightened him.

He thought of Pat and called Eileen. It went to voicemail. He left a message. 'It's Dan. Have you heard anything? Please call me.'

The shower stopped as he hung up. He went to the window and stared out. Highford. It was his town, and he was being selfish. It wasn't her home. He could hardly blame her if she left. All he knew was he didn't want that.

There were footsteps behind him. Jayne came into the room with wet hair, tucking her shirt into her trousers, looking around for her shoes.

'Come on, it'll dry when we're out.' She found her shoes behind a chair. 'Canal first, then breakfast.'

The roads were getting busier as they stepped outside, as the early morning drifted into rush hour. They drove down the hill and stopped in a small car park by a stretch of canal, close to a cinema and a collection of American-style restaurants.

Dan was about to get out of the car when Jayne leaned across and put her hand on his. 'Thank you for last night.'

'I was out of order.'

'How do you mean?'

'I shouldn't have started what we did. And afterwards? I treated you like a possession, some precious object I had to protect, while you're one of the toughest people I know.'

'But you did it for the right reason: because you care. Sometimes, that's enough, and I didn't want to go home with those men. I was doing it to spite you, which wasn't even fair on him, even if he was a complete tool.' Her smile grew and she blushed. 'I enjoyed the kiss, if it makes you feel better.'

He wanted to hold her, feel the warmth of her body again, but he checked himself. Not here, not like this.

He reached for the door handle.

They stepped out onto concrete and cut through a gap in a wall to get to the towpath. The water was still, insects flicking at the surface. A duck glided on the water with a line of ducklings trailing behind her, and small birds swooped from nearby bushes.

'This is where I came yesterday,' Jayne said, and she pointed along the sweep of the canal. 'The boat was coming from that way.'

Dan thought back to the footage. 'The boat stopped just before it got to that footbridge.'

Jayne frowned. 'That's what? About fifty metres away? It didn't come far enough.'

'Perhaps Lizzie ran away once Sean jumped off the boat, and he chased her?'

Dan thought about that but then realised something else. 'We can't prove it was Sean's boat anyway. It was just a distant speck on the footage.'

'Can't we still use it though?'

'It depends on how far we go with it. We can ask whether the police traced the boat owner, and the answer will be no, because I bet they never looked. It'll give me something for the closing speech, which is more than I have now.'

Jayne sat down on the low wall. 'If Peter did it, because the evidence sounds like he did, does it matter whether we can't prove anything against Sean Martin? At least some justice will be done if Peter is put away for it.'

'Pat is still missing. For as long as it stays like that, it matters.'

'Don't let it blind you, Dan. Peter needs you like I needed you once. For his sake, keep your focus.'

'That's always my focus, but I swear to you, if Sean Martin had anything to do with Pat's disappearance, I'll make it my business to make him pay. Come on, let's go. I've got a court case to defend.'

Forty-seven

As the courthouse loomed ahead, Jayne said, 'How are we playing this?'

'One last crack at getting Peter to talk. It's today or never.'

'And me?'

'Stay with me. You're my investigator, and I need your input.'

'How are you feeling?'

'Tired, and smelling like an old wine barrel.'

As they got closer to the courthouse, Murdoch was outside, puffing on a cigarette, as always.

'Any updates on Pat?' Dan asked, as they got closer.

She shook her head. 'No, I'm sorry. He's not on any train CCTV boarding at Greencroft, and the car park isn't covered by cameras.' She leaned in closer. 'And Sean Martin had nothing to do with it. He's got an alibi. He was at a book signing all evening, and his car was seen on CCTV heading out of Highford and towards home minutes after he left the venue.'

'I'm not finished with him. His boat is the key.'

'His boat? Why?'

'On the footage from when Lizzie was murdered, a boat appears in the distance and then the light goes off.'

'How do you know it was Sean's?'

'I don't, yet, but if there's anywhere to search after today, start with his boat.'

He headed into the court building. As he waited at the security barrier, he saw Bill ahead. Once he was through, Bill marched over towards them.

'Any new information, Mr Grant?'

He shook his head. 'Sorry, just as it was, but stick with the case, Bill. You've been helpful. I just wish I could do more for you.'

'That's all right. At least you listened.' As Dan carried on past him, Bill shouted out, 'Good luck.'

Dan didn't respond. Lizzie's family and friends were ahead. He didn't want it to seem like a game.

Dan pushed the door that took him down the stairs and towards the court cells, Jayne following.

'Will they let me in?' she said.

'You're with me. It'll be fine.'

The stairs to the cells echoed as they walked down, Dan's stomach rolling, unsure whether it was tension or the effects of the night before. He was shown into the small booth, the guards nonplussed by Jayne's presence. She sat next to Dan, so squeezed in that their knees touched. Peter's arrival was heralded by the usual jangle of keys.

When he sat down, he looked to Jayne and then back to Dan, his eyes wide with excitement. 'I heard about your boss. Has he turned up yet?'

Dan clenched his jaw. Had Pat's disappearance become just common gossip already?

'Let's focus on your case, shall we? I've been looking into you, Peter. Do you want to know what I've discovered?'

Peter sat back, his eyes narrowed. 'What do you mean?'

'Any guesses?'

He shook his head but stayed silent.

'You should have. I've already asked you about why you told Pat Molloy you were responsible for Rosie Smith's murder. You freaked out. We carried on digging though.'

'We?'

Jayne leaned in to the glass. 'Me too, Peter.'

Dan reached into his pocket and pulled out a piece of paper. 'Pat Molloy made this note when Sean Martin was waiting for his murder trial.' He unfolded it. 'Can you guess what it says?'

'Why don't you just tell me?' His voice was quieter.

Dan read it out. 'That's Pat's note from when you went to see him. You wouldn't talk to me about why you confessed to Rosie's murder. Have you had a rethink?'

'I didn't confess. I said I was responsible. That's different.'

'How is it?'

Peter shook his head. 'I'm not talking about it.'

'You are, Peter, because today's the day. You can't keep up the silent act. Let me ask you one thing: did you kill Rosie Smith?'

'No.'

'Do you know who did?'

Peter didn't answer. He stared at Jayne and Dan, then began to shake his head. 'No, no, no, no.'

'I kept on digging, Peter, so you can imagine how surprised I was to find out that you were friends with Sean.'

Peter's eyelids flickered.

'Jayne was asking around your old neighbourhood. Tell him what you found out?'

'Almost in-laws,' she said.

Peter sat back and folded his arms. He glared at her, his lips pursed, until he said, 'I wouldn't go that far.'

Jayne met his gaze but lowered her voice and gave a sympathetic smile. 'We just want to help you, but you've got to help us too.'

'I'm not discussing it.'

'Why not? We've found out a lot already. I've spoken to Emily.'

His eyes widened and then filled with tears. 'How is she?'

'She's fine, and she wants what's best for you. She still cares.'

A pause, and then, 'Does she?'

'And do you remember Claire Watkins? I spoke to one of her friends too.'

His hand shot to his mouth. He blinked a few times and tears ran down his cheeks.

'What is it, Peter?'

He didn't respond. Dan and Jayne let the silence grow. His hand stayed over his mouth as his silent tears turned into steady sobs.

'Poor Claire,' he said, eventually.

Dan and Jayne exchanged glances.

Dan was about to speak but Jayne held up her finger to silence him. 'Tell us, Peter. Now's the time.'

There was a rattle of keys behind him. The security guard said, 'The judge is waiting for you, Mr Grant.'

Dan waved him away. 'Not yet.'

'What do I tell him?'

'You tell him not yet.' His entire focus was on Peter.

Peter dropped his hands and wiped his eyes. He took a few deep breaths and his whole body sagged. 'It started with Sean.'

'What did?' Jayne said.

Peter stared at his hands for a few seconds before answering. 'It was just daft stuff. He's older than me, and I'm . . . I'm quiet. Sean was different. He seemed clever, worldly.'

'How?'

'He was talented. He could draw, and would copy out these really great comic covers, huge canvases, and frame them. And he was knowledgeable.' Peter seemed more animated. 'About politics. About the world. That's how we'd spend our weekends, drinking and talking politics. He'd be the one talking, anyhow. I'd listen and learn. You know how it is when you meet someone who is so clever, and you just can't help being dragged along by it all. People round here thought he was too far up himself, that he thought he was better than everyone else.'

'Is that why you tried to confess? To help him out?'

Peter snorted a laugh. 'You can never understand.'

Jayne gestured towards Dan. 'Help us.'

Peter stayed silent, so Dan said, 'Remember the questions I asked yesterday, about the women who have gone missing? That's a line of defence we might have, that there's a serial killer stalking the canals, but if the jury believe me there's a risk that they'll think that person is you.' Dan leaned forward, drawing Peter in. 'I don't think you've got it in you, but is that how you want to go down, as someone who murdered lots of people? A sadistic butcher?'

'That isn't me.' Peter's eyes were wide.

'Tell me the story then.'

Peter looked down at the desk. His fingers tapped on the surface, and at first Dan thought Peter was getting angry, and braced himself for an explosion of rage or another sudden retreat, but then he noticed more tears.

'Peter?'

He gulped and wiped his eyes. 'People can't think I'm a monster. I'm no monster. Do you believe that?'

'How can I believe you when you hold so much back? Now, it's time for the truth.'

Peter nodded to himself for a few seconds and then it was as if the air was sucked out of the room when he said, 'I killed Lizzie, and I can't stand it, but you've got to know the full story.'

Forty-eight

Everyone looked round at Dan and Jayne as they emerged into the busy court corridor – Lizzie's family, her friends, Bill. Dan didn't pay them any attention. Instead, he stormed into the robing room, Jayne rushing to catch up.

Once they were inside, he kicked a chair. 'Fuck!'

'Dan, calm down.'

'Calm down? You heard him. After all his silence, he was motivated by one thing: too cowardly to admit what he'd done.'

She held her hands out as he paced, his hands in his hair, his cheeks flushed. 'Dan, you've got to hold it together. You'll be back in court soon, and whatever you've just been told will be part of the case. You've got to deal with it.'

'How? Go on, help me out here. You've suddenly turned into the genius.' He kicked the chair again, this time sending it clattering into a bookcase.

'I'm not your enemy here.' Her voice was soft, soothing.

Dan leaned back against the wall, his eyes closed, and took some deep breaths. 'What do I do?'

Jayne took his hands in hers. 'You do your job. It's what you're good at.'

The door opened. It was the usher. 'Mr Grant, the judge wants to see you.'

'Aye, I bet he does.'

As the door closed, Jayne said, 'The reason you kept me sane was because of your strength. That's what you meant to me. None of this is of your making. Peter has let you down by not being honest with you. So what if the judge bawls you out? Can he really say you were at fault?'

Dan nodded to himself, still breathing hard. 'Thank you.'

'And, of course, there is the other thing.'

'Other thing?'

'You can go after Sean Martin.'

His eyes narrowed. 'Yes, there is that. Come on, let's go into court.'

They emerged back on to the court corridor and the usher appeared ahead, holding her hands out in exasperation.

'You wait out here,' Dan said to Jayne, and headed for the courtroom.

'Why can't I come in?'

'I've had an idea.'

As Dan got to the door, with everyone else crowding behind him, he said to the usher, 'Can this be in chambers?'

The usher shouted, 'Everyone will need to stay outside,' and held the door open for Dan.

Francesca was waiting for him, her leg crossed, her arms folded. 'More fun today, Mr Grant? I thought we were never going to start.'

He wasn't sure how to respond to that because his plan was still forming loosely in his head. 'Possibly. I need some time with the judge.'

The court assistant rose from her seat. 'I heard you say that you want it to be in chambers.'

Dan nodded.

She went towards the door that would take her into the tranquil space behind the scenes.

Once she'd gone, Francesca said, 'What's going on now?'

'I've pinned down his defence.'

Francesca looked surprised. 'Halfway through his trial? That'll go down well with the judge.' Her gaze grew suspicious. 'What is it?'

'Loss of control.'

'Is this a joke?'

'A woman died. I don't joke. And I thought you'd be pleased. If it succeeds, it's manslaughter, which is still a prison sentence, and still a tick in your conviction column.'

Before Francesca could respond, the door opened and the assistant said, 'The judge will see you now.'

Dan and Francesca followed her through the door, into the hush and calm of the judges' corridor. A knock on the door, and they waited until they heard the command to enter.

The judge looked impatient, glowering at Dan as he gestured to them both to sit down.

'Mr Grant, there'd better be a good reason why you have kept the court waiting this morning. I've been told that even though you knew that I was waiting, that the court was waiting, you refused to end the conversation with your client.'

'It wasn't a conversation, it was a consultation, and he was providing me with up-to-date instructions.'

The judge leaned forward over his desk. 'There is never a good time to keep me waiting. Do you understand that?'

Every ounce of common sense was telling Dan to apologise and puff up the judge's ego, but fatigue, stress and all of his worry about Pat came flooding back in.

He met the judge's glare. 'This was more important than court etiquette. My client's liberty is at stake and that comes first.'

The judge's nostrils flared. 'Tread carefully, Mr Grant.'

'I am, because for the first time my client has told me what happened on that night. For over four months he's refused to talk to me about the case for reasons he would never say. I couldn't risk leaving him because he might clam up again. If Your Lordship wants me to apologise, I will. I'll say the words. If Your Lordship wants me to mean them, that'll be a longer wait.'

The judge said nothing for a few seconds. The tension in the room grew. Francesca was sitting back, wanting whatever was going to happen to not involve her.

The judge broke the silence. 'What's his defence?'

'Loss of control.'

'Explain.'

'I prefer to wait until Peter Box is giving evidence.'

'This is not your courtroom, Mr Grant, but mine. I will tell you what will and will not happen.'

'I have told Your Lordship the defence that is to be advanced. I have told the prosecution. Elizabeth Barnsley died at his hands, he admits that, but he was so overwhelmed by a combination of events, very grave events, that he could not control himself.'

'You're stating the law, nothing more, Mr Grant.'

'Another person has been committing murders, and Peter Box reacted to that threat; he couldn't cope with the thought of it.'

'Are you going to name this person?'

'I am, My Lord.'

He turned to the prosecutor. 'Ms McIntyre, what do you have to say?'

She was silent for a few moments. Eventually, she said, 'He can't do this. Up until now, he's been rubbishing the case, pointing to problems with the DNA. Now, he accepts he killed her, that it's his DNA on her shoe. It's a farce.'

'No, it's your closing speech,' the judge said. 'Are you objecting to this line of defence?'

'It's an attack on someone's character, whoever this person is.'

'Sean Martin,' Dan said.

Francesca whirled round at that. 'The Sean Martin?'

'One and the same.'

A smile played on the judge's lips. 'Ms McIntyre, do you object? I'd be surprised if you did. If Mr Grant wants to conduct his trial like this, I'm surprised you're concerned. The jury will see what you see, that the defendant is changing his defence mid-trial.'

'And all the time the defendant has an appeal ready, because there is no way this will be seen as adequate representation.'

Dan tutted. 'Save your barbs. You can call him as rebuttal evidence. I can hardly object.'

Francesca turned to him. 'You're reaching too high, Dan, can't you see that? You're out of your depth, plain and simple.'

The judge slammed his hand on the desk. 'Both of you, enough. And as for you,' he said pointing at Dan, 'I'll deal with your competency afterwards. I'll give the prosecution an hour to consider their position, but the case will resume then. Now get out.'

'The prosecution can close their case now,' Dan said. 'I'll agree the rest of the evidence. Let my learned friend read it all out to the jury. It all falls now on the defendant.'

'You're not in control, Mr Grant. One hour.'

They both filed out of the judge's chambers. Once in the courtroom again, Francesca threw her papers on the desk. 'What the hell are you playing at?'

'I'm playing the only hand I've got. Just call the case back on. I want this over with.'

He rushed out of the courtroom. Normally, this was where he felt he belonged, but it was all spinning too fast now. He needed air. He felt everyone's stares on him as he swept through the security barrier, but he kept on going, stopping only when he got to the street. He leaned back against the wall and closed his eyes. The case was about to get even more testing, but at least he was going to get some truth out there. Lizzie and Rosie and all the others deserved that.

Forty-nine

Dan kept his eyes closed as he leaned back against the stone wall of the courthouse. Perspiration speckled his forehead, and he knew it was the pressure of the case. He could feel his nerves showing in the flush of his cheeks. Perhaps the robing room taunts were right. Perhaps he was out of his depth.

On top of it all were his worries about Pat's disappearance, like a gnawing pain, the certainty that the outcome wasn't going to be a good one.

Footsteps came close. He opened his eyes. It was Jayne.

'I wondered where you'd gone. Any developments?'

He shook his head. 'I had to get out. The prosecutor is taking some time to think about her next move.'

'And you're going to loiter here until she does?'

'What else can I do?' He straightened back and stretched. 'I had to get out. It was smothering me.'

'What do you want me to do?'

Dan thought about that for a few seconds before he said, 'Follow Sean Martin, like before. The news will filter back somehow, and I want to know how he reacts.'

'Listen, Dan, are you sure you're doing the right thing, and for the right reason?'

'How do you mean?'

'Are you sure that you're doing this for your client, what's best for him, and not for Pat? You keep telling me how your job is to help people, no matter what they've done, but Pat's disappearance might be clouding that.'

'No, I can't be sure, but I have a client who has told me a story that makes sense, in its own way. He wants to tell it, and I can't think of a single good reason why I should stop him. If it helps to trap whoever is behind Pat's disappearance, I'm happy with that. And it might be the only way.'

'If you're sure.'

'I'm sure.'

'Good. I'll go then. I'll keep you up to date.'

Just before she went, Dan said, 'Be careful. I might already have lost someone I care about this week. Don't let me lose you as well.'

Her eyes glistened for a moment. 'You're stuck with me. Sorry about that.'

Dan leaned back against the wall again, wanting to close his eyes again, but he saw Murdoch heading towards him.

As she got in front of Dan, she folded her arms. 'What's going on?'

'Francesca not shared the news?'

'She's told me that Peter is going to admit to killing Lizzie, but if Peter killed her, why are we still having a trial?'

'Loss of control, that's the defence. He saw Lizzie and he snapped, could no longer control his anger.'

'That's the game then? Pretend he wasn't involved but as soon as you realise you can't get out of that, you come up with something new?'

There was a growl to his voice when he said, 'I'm not answerable to you, Murdoch. Not now, not ever.'

'I'm not your enemy, Dan.'

'If that's the case, do one thing for me: nail Sean Martin.'

'How? Your firm got him released, remember?'

'This case is all about Sean Martin. It always has been. I just never realised how much. Do you want to get him or not?'

Murdoch stepped closer. 'I've been wanting to get that bastard ever since he walked out of prison.'

'This is your chance. I told you what he told Pat. This all ties in.'

'How?'

'I can't tell you, not until Peter makes it public, but look for the links between those deaths I mentioned. You were looking for Peter in them before. Look again, but this time look for Sean Martin.'

'He'd have shown up before if he's connected, because his name is like a beacon to us.'

'Not back then it wasn't. He's in there somewhere, but you've got to go after him when you find it. He knew Claire Watkins. Did you realise that?'

She looked confused. 'No, I didn't.'

'There you go. At least two deaths are connected to him, if you include his stepdaughter. Look for the rest. Just promise me that you won't let it go.'

'You know me well enough now, Dan.'

'I do. That's why I'm glad it's you.'

'Is this why you're doing this, to get Sean Martin?'

Dan stayed silent for a few seconds before he began to nod slowly. 'The prosecution won't let me blame Sean Martin without giving him a chance to rebut it, because if he can answer for himself, it'll destroy any chance Peter has. Francesca won't allow

Peter's testimony to be given unopposed. He will have to come to court. Speak to him, tell him that. It'll spook him.'

'And when he comes to court—'

Dan clenched his jaw. 'I'll be waiting.'

*

Jayne headed for her car, pleased that her day had acquired more purpose than just sitting in court and watching Dan do his stuff. Bill Maude was on a bench further along, waiting for court to resume, muttering to himself. When he saw her, he stood and rushed towards her.

'What's happening? Why is there a delay?'

Jayne put her hand on his. 'I can't say but go inside and watch. Today you might get some answers.'

'What, about my Tom?'

'No, not about Tom, I'm sorry, but some of what you believed turned out to be true. Not the part you wanted, but you've done some good.'

'Don't make me wait. What is it?'

Jayne rolled her eyes. 'I can't. It's confidential. Until Peter gets in the witness box and makes it public, it has to stay private.'

'At least give me a clue.'

Jayne thought about that for a few moments before she said, 'Sean Martin is the key, and his boat.'

'His boat?'

'You said someone was roaming the canals. There's your answer. But that's all I'm saying.'

He nodded, pleased with that. 'That's what I wanted. It wasn't just about Tom.'

Jayne didn't challenge him. Instead, she went to walk towards her car.

Bill shouted after her, 'Where does he keep it?'

'The marina next to a garden centre in Highford. I've got to go, Bill. You take care now,' and she trotted towards the car park, leaving Bill and the courthouse behind.

She checked her watch. She reckoned she could get to Sean Martin's house in twenty minutes. She didn't know whether Sean realised what was about to happen in the courtroom, but she had to be in place when it did.

Something occurred to her. The day could end up being long and dull and she thought of the perfect way to occupy her mind. She made a quick detour to a bookshop and found what she was looking for. Sean Martin's autobiography.

The journey was uneventful, just a short drive along the motorway until she turned off and the countryside opened out.

She parked in the same place she did the first time she'd watched Sean, down the hill but close enough for a view of his house. Hopefully far enough away that she couldn't be seen.

As she waited, she started to read his book. Virtually everyone Jayne had interviewed about him had said that Sean Martin had a high opinion of himself. That fitted in with how he'd taunted Pat Molloy with the information about the murder weapon. Wouldn't he do the same to his readers? Were there subtle clues in the book that allowed him to laugh at the readers too?

Sean's book began with his arrest, not Rosie's death; he wrote of his surprise and shock at being accused of such a horrendous crime. The words seemed sincere, and Jayne struggled to read it, knowing the truth.

She glanced up towards the house now and then. There were no signs of anyone there, and there was only one car in the driveway.

She flicked to the plates section. Rosie was prominent in the early photos, although the pictures were only ever of her with Sean as the doting stepfather. Rosie looked happy in his company, no sign of what was to come. After that there were some pictures of the crime scene – police tape stretched across the towpath and police cars visible on the road nearby – before it moved on to images of Sean on the court steps, speaking emotionally into a sea of microphones, Pat Molloy just behind him.

The next few photographs were all about Sean and Trudy, the woman who had stood by him: on Sean's boat, the name stencilled on the side, *SOMEWHERE QUIET*, moored in the countryside near a rundown old cottage; sitting on a patch of grass, Trudy in his arms, both looking contented and carefree.

She closed the book. She couldn't stand to read it.

All she could do was watch and wait.

Fifty

Murdoch stubbed out the cigarette on her heel, careful to put the tab end into her pocket, ready to be thrown into a bin before she went into the police station. There were too many junior police staff ready to complain about her littering if they saw her chuck it on the ground. Her mind had been working hard during the journey back from the court and she realised that she was about to go against what had been pretty much the core of her whole police career: she was going to help the defence.

Everyone looked around as she strode into the incident room. DC John Richards was already taking down the pictures of Lizzie Barnsley.

'Not just yet,' she said.

'What do you mean?' Richards was one of the younger detectives on the squad, his dark hair gelled into a collection of spikes and his shirt not yet filled by a desk-bound copper's paunch. He held two photographs in one hand and had been stretching to take another down.

'The trial is nearly over, yes, and we know that Peter killed her, but he's dragging Sean Martin into it.'

'How?'

'I don't know, because he hasn't said anything yet.'

'What are we doing then?'

'We're going to get Sean Martin into court.'

'We're saving his reputation? Is that our job?'

'No. Our job is to catch killers.' She pulled a list from her pocket. 'These are the cases Dan Grant asked me to look into yesterday. We're going to go through them again and find out whether Sean Martin could have been involved in any of them.'

'When does the prosecutor want this information? It could take forever.'

Murdoch smiled. 'She doesn't. This is for Dan Grant. He reckons the prosecutor will want Sean Martin in court to rebut whatever Peter says. If Sean Martin is involved, I want that bastard. I bet we all do. Everyone in this building has been waiting for that moment for a long time. But we need to be thorough, because if we can't find something to nail him with, all we'll have are the ramblings of a madman and Sean Martin on the news, playing at being innocent again.'

'Do we arrest him if we find something?'

'Not yet. We let Dan Grant know, because I want to see what answers Sean Martin gives from the witness box. He might stay silent if we bring him in. He won't if he's in the witness box, because he'll know it will all end up in the papers if he does.'

Richards started pinning the photographs back on the wall. 'I'm confused now. Are we sticking up for Peter Box and helping his defence? It seems wrong somehow.'

'I'm more interested in catching a killer than I am in picking sides.' She clapped her hands and grinned. 'Let's catch Sean Martin.'

*

Bill drove on to the car park close to the marina and could barely suppress his smile. He was closer to getting answers. Ever since Tom's death, he'd dreamed of this moment. He felt some anger towards Dan, but he chided himself. He shouldn't have hoped for so much. Dan was a lawyer. He was only there for the courtroom showcase. It was just theatre, judged in terms of winning and losing, cold and callous.

He felt Tom was by his side and his eyes moistened as he remembered him. The most recent memories always came first, like the last time he'd seen him, or the young adult leaving home for university a few years before. Strong, happy, confident. A fine young man. It was when his mind drifted further back that pained Bill the most. The little boy who had less life ahead than he deserved.

He sat upright and took a deep breath. He had to hold it together.

The marina was unfamiliar to him. He knew the garden centre though, he'd visited it before, but had never paid any attention to what was on the other side of the high mesh fence.

He called Jayne. 'I'm at the marina.'

'Why are you there?'

'You said it was all connected to his boat. It might be a crime scene, with evidence on board, even all these years later. I can't trust Sean Martin not to destroy it. If they torched the boat, all the forensic evidence would go up in flames.'

'Anything happening?'

'No. It's quiet. What about where you are?'

'The same.'

'Will he run?'

'I hope so, because it'll be like an admission of guilt.'

'Which one is his boat?'

'Called *Somewhere Quiet*, but Bill, don't do anything stupid. Sean Martin is a dangerous man and, like you said, the boat is a crime scene.'

'Don't worry about me,' he said, and clicked off.

Bill allowed himself a smile. For the first time, he was getting somewhere.

He stared out of his windscreen for a few minutes, his fingers drumming on the steering wheel. He wanted to get into the marina. The thought of the boat being so close but locked up was unbearable. All of his research, those long nights searching the Internet, or days out visiting the places where the victims were last seen or found dead. It had cost him friends, their sympathy waning as he became obsessed with proving his theory. A man on a mission.

He needed to get in there.

He wouldn't be able to break in though. The gate securing the yard looked imposing, and even from a distance he could see an entry keypad. If Sean turned up, he could be in the yard and on the waterways before Bill could stop him.

No, he had to get closer, and he was prepared to put up a fight to stop Sean Martin getting on his boat.

The air was cool as Bill stepped out of his car. There were some people browsing the garden centre displays, but apart from them it was quiet.

As he got close to the marina fence, there wasn't much sign of activity, other than a man in paint-stained overalls touching up his boat's nameplate, bent over, focused on the lettering.

'Hey?' Bill said, making him look over.

He didn't think the man was going to move at first, but eventually he put down his paintbrush and sauntered to the gate. 'Can I help you?'

Bill pointed towards the boats. 'I'm just looking at the boats. So colourful and pretty. I've always wanted one.'

The man nodded. 'Yeah, they look fine. Take some maintenance though, but it keeps me busy.'

'Can I have a look round?'

The man looked back at the boats and then to Bill. His eyes narrowed. 'Sorry, I can't do that. These are more than just boats. They're our homes too. You look like a decent sort, but I can't let just anyone in.'

Bill thanked him and went back towards his car, trying to hide his frustration. The need to see inside was nagging him, but for now, he had to wait.

Fifty-one

Dan stayed in his seat in the courtroom as the jurors filed out and Francesca collected her papers, standing only to bow to the judge as he retired for his lunch. She'd agreed to Dan's strategy, because she knew it would make Peter's defence look ridiculous. Sean Martin's reputation came second to winning, and Dan knew that.

The prosecution case had concluded, all those statements that tidied up the evidence read out to the jury. Dan had heard them as background noise, not paying any attention. It would all be down to Peter in the afternoon.

Without the drama of live witnesses to keep their attention, the jurors had started to watch Peter Box, knowing that he would come next. All they knew was that he'd stayed silent in the police station. Dan had tried to read their gazes, and they were a mixture of disgust and curiosity. Some had already made their minds up, but enough of them wanted to hear Peter's story first before they decided.

Dan doubted whether Peter's version would sway many to a not-guilty verdict, but there was a bigger game going on now.

Francesca didn't say anything as she left the courtroom. Dan stared at his papers, hoping that some sense or logic might rise from them. Peter had told him what he could in the time he had this morning, but Dan knew he had only half the story. If Peter had given him the facts in the months leading up to the trial, he could have engaged an expert to look into Peter's background, or to give evidence about post-traumatic stress, just about anything to explain how Peter lost control when he saw Lizzie.

Dan knew the judge was never going to allow him any more time. He'd had enough. And he didn't deserve any more.

*

'I've got a mention.'

Murdoch whirled round.

She'd been staring out of the window, unable to concentrate, nervous, waiting for someone to find Sean Martin in whichever cold case they were ploughing through.

It was DC Richards again.

'What is it?'

'Claire Watkins. She went missing more than fourteen years ago, from here in Highford. Nineteen years old. Set off to meet someone but no one knew who, and she never came home.'

Murdoch went to where he was sitting, squashed into the corner of the room, his desk surrounded by files and paperwork. Most of the squad were visiting police stations in other towns, the cold case files dug out, everyone looking for a mention of Sean Martin.

'What have you got?'

'Sean Martin telling lies.' He waved a piece of paper. 'There's this, a copy of a police notebook. We were speaking to passers-by in the street, asking about suspicious people, flashing a picture of Claire. Sean Martin gave his name and said that he didn't know her. And that was it. Buried away in the file.'

He passed it to Murdoch, and everyone else in the room stopped what they were doing as Murdoch examined it.

She pumped the air. 'This is it, the start of it. A connection, a lie. Keep digging though. We need more than a police notebook. We can take our time.'

Richards smiled. 'And then there's this,' and he passed over another sheet. 'A memo, because for a moment he was a person of interest. We spoke to Claire's friends, and they were asked whether there were any people who seemed interested in Claire, sexually, whether she was being stalked in any way. Bothered by anyone.'

'And?'

'Her friend named Sean Martin, said that he creeped her out, was a bit too much when he spoke to her. It made Claire uncomfortable.'

'How was he ruled out?'

'His girlfriend, Trudy, gave him an alibi, said that they had gone cruising down the canals, and it was confirmed by the barman of the pub they were at.'

'It wasn't pursued because of Trudy?'

'That's what the file says. Remember, there wasn't even a body. Claire went missing as she walked into town.'

'Along the canal?'

'That was the quickest way.'

'But how the hell didn't we know about this? Why didn't it come up when these cases were looked at yesterday?'

'Because it was just one minor enquiry, a scrap of paper reporting a suspicion that was immediately discounted.'

'Because of Trudy.'

'And the barman.'

'People get times wrong, we all know that, and it showed he was lying about not knowing her. We should have known about the discrepancy.'

'Different officers carrying out different enquiries and not knowing what the other has found out. Each one came to nothing.' He held out his hands. 'I'm not defending it, but people slip up.'

'And people die because of it. Get your coat. We need to speak to Claire's friends. He's been a slur on this force, shoving his so-called innocence in our faces. This is our chance to get even.'

'And when we do?'

'We let Dan Grant know so he can go after Sean Martin in court. If he can expose his lies, we'll be waiting for him. But first, let's speak to Sean Martin himself.'

Fifty-two

Jayne put down Sean Martin's book. She'd tried to stick with it, but knowing so much more about the real story made it too nauseating to read, the words too hollow.

The house had been devoid of activity since she'd arrived. If news had reached Sean about Peter Box's allegations, it hadn't created any obvious panic.

Her mind drifted back to what Peter Box had said, and she wondered how much like Peter she was. He'd brought an end to someone's life, whatever reason he gave. She had too, in a different way, but that didn't stop her feeling some guilt, however much she convinced herself that she wasn't to blame. What she did to her last serious boyfriend always came back to her whenever it seemed that her own life was starting to go somewhere, as if Jimmy's final moments would forever haunt her.

Whatever Jimmy had been, he hadn't deserved to die. He should have been imprisoned, yes; alone, certainly; but not dead.

She didn't blame herself: she understood how his abuse had weakened her to the point where she couldn't see an alternative but to stay with him. She'd hurt many people who didn't deserve to be hurt, like Jimmy's parents and brothers, and his friends. They could never truly understand how she felt when she was with him, what it was like to be with Jimmy, which made it even harder for them.

She dreamed of a reset button, so she could go back to before that day – right back to the first time he abused her – and make herself leave. She wished she could stop her past self from buying into his promise to be better, from feeling bad about his tears.

She wondered how many of those thoughts plagued Peter Box. His shame was that he'd been a coward all those years ago, because if he'd had the courage to speak up a lot of women would have been saved.

She was jolted from her thoughts by the arrival of a car that parked outside Sean's house. As she saw the occupants, she smiled. Things were starting to happen.

*

DI Murdoch fought the urge for a cigarette as she stepped out of her car.

'Let me do all the talking,' she told DC Richards. She'd brought him along to distract Sean, divide his attention between them. 'If he's got any questions, leave them to me. This is my show.'

'Understood, ma'am.'

There was one car on the Martins' driveway, a Hyundai. In this location, poorly connected and far from town, she'd expected two cars.

Her knock on the door sounded loud in the quiet village. After a few seconds, Sean Martin opened the door, a flicker of uncertainty in his eyes.

Murdoch lifted her lanyard. 'We need to have a word with you.'

He looked from Murdoch to Richards, and then back again, his body blocking entry into the house. 'I don't speak to the police without a lawyer present. I went to prison for a murder I didn't commit, so forgive me if I'm too cautious.'

Murdoch tried her hardest to remain civil, although she knew her smile was thin when she said, 'I bet I can read all about it in your book, but I'm not here to arrest you or interrogate you, Mr Martin. I'm here for your benefit.'

His look of defiance faltered. 'What do you mean?'

'I'd rather talk indoors.'

He held his ground for a few more seconds before he relented and stepped aside. Murdoch made sure she neglected to wipe her feet as she went through to the living room and sat down. Richards took a seat on the sofa opposite.

'You might want to speak to your lawyer before you decide what to do,' Murdoch said. 'But you will need a different lawyer to the one you used in your appeal.'

'I don't understand.'

'You used Pat Molloy last time, but he's gone missing.' Murdoch noticed that there was no widening of the eyes, no effort at looking surprised. It was almost as if he had steeled himself to not react. 'A client of his colleague, Dan Grant, is making allegations against you in court, and we need you to defend yourself, to rebut what's being said. That's why I'm here.'

Sean did react to that, his brow furrowed, confusion in his eyes. 'I don't understand.'

'You know Peter Box?' she said. 'Yes, of course you do. He used to go out with Trudy's sister, years ago.'

Sean leaned against the doorjamb, his hands thrust into his trouser pockets, tension showing in the veins of his forearms. 'Yes, like you say, I knew him years ago. I read that he got himself into trouble. I haven't seen him since . . . well, before I was locked up.'

'Peter's in a lot of trouble, because he's accused of murder. His defence involves throwing some blame your way.'

'I don't understand. What have I got to do with whatever he did?'

'It's not that murder he's talking about. I don't have all the details because it's happening as we speak, but it's connected with some older murders. He's saying he lost control because of things you did. If you don't stand up for yourself, it'll become the new truth. It will hit you hard, what with your book coming out and all.'

'Why is he saying this?'

'Murderers say desperate things, but do you want whatever he's going to say to become what people remember?'

'Which murders?'

Murdoch detected nervousness in his voice, his query tentative, not a protest. 'A woman called Claire Watkins.' Murdoch watched him carefully. His breathing had quickened but his expression remained impassive. 'Did you know Claire Watkins?'

He faked nonchalance with a shrug, glancing at Richards before turning back to Murdoch. 'Didn't she go missing years ago? She lived on the next street to Trudy. I used to talk to her sometimes.'

Murdoch concealed her joy at the response. In her pocket was the copy of the police notebook, his lie jotted down. She thought about confronting him there and then, but she stuck to her plan. Let him give his account under oath, all of it recorded, ready for it to be thrown back in his face.

'It's crazy, I know,' she continued, 'but if you don't come to court tomorrow to contest it, Peter Box's story will be reported as the truth. You need to show that it is what it sounds like, a story to deceive the jury.' She lowered her voice. 'I know that you're all for the innocent being freed, but it's important that the guilty are convicted too. The system has got to work properly.'

'Do I have to give evidence?'

'That's up to you, but if you don't come, well . . .' She held out her hands. 'Everyone will know you had the opportunity to rebut it but didn't.'

'I have to decide by tomorrow?'

'If you need more time, let me know, but the judge wants to do it tomorrow.' A tilt of her head. 'Any reason why you can't come tomorrow?'

Sean stared straight ahead before pushing himself away from the doorframe. 'Tomorrow is fine. Thank you, Inspector.'

Murdoch got to her feet, Richards with her, and sidled past him. 'Get there for nine thirty to speak to the prosecutor. I'll take a statement from you in the morning.'

Sean stayed silent as she headed towards the door.

Once they were out in the fresh air, the cottage door safely closed behind them, Richards said, 'That was awkward.'

Murdoch allowed herself a smile. 'Exactly as I wanted.'

*

Sean Martin watched the car pull away and sat down with a slump. He looked around the room at the life he'd rebuilt. He was about to lose it all. All that he'd achieved since he'd come out of prison gone, lost in the ramblings of Peter Box.

The reminder of prison made him cover his eyes. He couldn't go back there. The hours just seemed to stretch, his life mapped out by the track of the sun across plain grey walls. He'd been on the protected wing because he'd been convicted of killing a child, the rest of the prisoners hoping to get at him if there was ever a lapse in security, someone whose life had amounted to little eager to make a name by killing him.

He couldn't go back.

He unlocked his phone, his finger poised over the list of contacts, knowing that the call he was about to make could tear them apart.

But there was no shying away from it.

He pressed the phone symbol next to Trudy's name, her profile picture filling the screen.

She answered on the second ring, the noise of the supermarket behind her. How mundane was that? Food shopping when their life together was about to crumble.

His voice had a croak when he said, 'Peter's talked.'

She fell silent for a few seconds, the air filled with the bustle of people in the food aisles. 'What's he said?'

'Everything.'

Another pause, and then, 'I know what to do.'

Fifty-three

The atmosphere in the courtroom was tense.

The judge cleared his throat. 'Mr Grant, are you ready to begin?'

Dan stood and seemed to hesitate for a moment, looking at the jurors before he said, 'My Lord, I call Peter Box.'

The jurors stared towards the dock as Peter was placed in handcuffs before being led to the witness box. Once he was there and uncuffed, a security guard nearby and one blocking the door, he puffed out his chest. The whole focus of the court was on him.

When the New Testament was passed to him, he considered it for a moment, as if he wasn't sure if he dared to hold it, before he swore the oath: he would tell the truth, the whole truth, and nothing but the truth.

Dan looked down at his notes, aware of the tension. When he looked up again, he was poised and ready. 'Mr Box, did you kill Lizzie Barnsley?'

Peter nodded and swallowed. His voice trembled when he said, 'I did, and I'm truly sorry.'

There were audible gasps from the public gallery. Someone shouted, 'bastard', before the judge held up his hand to warn everyone to stay quiet.

Once the noise died down, Peter straightened himself. 'I can't begin to describe how sorry I am, and I know that is no comfort to her family. I made Lizzie's family wait to find out what happened to her and I should have said something at the beginning, but I was scared, and confused. I kept it from you as well, Mr Grant.'

'Please tell the court the whole truth now. What did you do to Lizzie?'

He looked along the public gallery before pointing to Francesca, who was making notes. 'Like the prosecutor said, I held her under the water until she drowned.'

There were more noises from the gallery, angry chatter and the shuffle of people in their seats.

The judge raised his hand. 'I warn the people in the public gallery that this is not a theatre but a court of law. If you want to remain, stay quiet.'

Dan let it die down before he asked, 'Why?'

Peter looked down and took a few more deep breaths. 'I don't know. I meant to protect her but it all went wrong. I just lost it.'

'It?'

'Control. It was as if everything caved in on me.'

Dan allowed the words to settle before he continued. 'Mr Box, how can protecting Lizzie end up with you killing her?'

He looked up and his eyes were angry. 'Because there was something even worse waiting for her.'

'What was waiting for her?'

'Not what, but who. Sean Martin, he was waiting.'

Dan paused to allow Sean's name to fill the silence, no one was making a noise now. He tried to keep the tremble from his own voice as he held out his hands and said, 'Please explain.'

'I'd been watching him.'

'Sean Martin?'

'Yes, I'd been tracking him, because he was on his boat. It can only go slow, four miles an hour – he sticks to the speed limit on the canal – and I'd been waiting by the dock where he keeps his boat. I go there all the time, just to watch.'

Dan held up his hand. He didn't want Peter going too far ahead. 'You can explain your motives later. For now, it's about what you were doing. How long had you been watching him that New Year's Eve?'

'About three hours. I had no plans for New Year's Eve, so I decided to check up on him. I knew he was on his boat because I could see the smoke from the heater and there was a light on inside. Why would he be there if he wasn't about to go somewhere? So I waited, and I was right. The boat pulled out at around eleven thirty, and I knew I'd be able to follow him because the boat cruises so slowly. I tracked him.'

'On the towpath?'

'No. I couldn't get close or else he'd see me, but I was able to jog along the nearby streets.'

'And which way was he heading?'

'Into Highford. I had to get further ahead but I didn't want to be where poor Rosie died. I go there all the time, just to remember her, and I sit and think how it could have all been different. It's so dark at night and it feels like the past is talking to me. I sit in the shadows and wish for it to be peaceful again. For me to be at peace. It's so lovely down there, the water so calm.'

The judge intervened. 'This is about why you killed someone, not a sales talk for a canal trip. What's the relevance?'

'Because it's ruined,' Peter said, his voice rising. 'Because of what happened before. Because of what happened to Rosie. It's tranquil by the canal, but for me, in here,' he said as he slapped a hand against his chest. 'It never stops, never at peace, because of Rosie, because of Claire, and the women before and after them. And it was going to happen to Lizzie.' His fingers jabbed at the edge of the witness box. 'I ended up down there because I was following him, Sean Martin. I knew it was going to happen again and I had to stop it. That's when I heard her. Lizzie. I heard her heels, so loud, and Sean's boat was getting closer and closer.'

Peter looked up at the ceiling as he took a few more breaths and blinked away some tears.

'Sean turned off the lights on his boat. He must have heard her too. That's when I knew it was going to happen. He was going to kill her, but it wouldn't be quick. I had to stop her, to save her.'

'What did you do?' Dan said. His voice was quiet but the silent tension in the courtroom carried his words forward.

'I ran at her, to warn her, to pull her away from the towpath, because up here' – he hit the side of his head with his fist – 'up here I knew that she wouldn't listen to me if I approached her and tried to talk to her, because it was dark and she'd be frightened. She was already upset, I could hear her crying, so I thought I'd surprise her and pull her away.'

'Wouldn't that frighten her even more?'

'That didn't matter. All that counted was getting her away from the path, because if I shouted and she ran, she'd run into him. His boat was waiting further along, with the light off. If I made her run, it would be like I was pushing her towards him and who'd believe that I wasn't a part of it? And these thoughts are all going really quickly through my head, like *ping, ping*, so fast that I couldn't make sense of them. I was panicking, worried about her, trying to stop what was going to happen, but I got it wrong because I ran at her. I was going to pull her away from the towpath, get her back to the road, make her run to the street. The police might speak to me about it if they caught me, but so what? I'd have saved her life at the same time.'

'But she died, Mr Box.'

'She did, because she was stronger than I expected. I frightened her and she fought me. Her shoes came off and she hit me with one, right in the head, and it was like someone had flicked a switch in here,' and he thumped his temple again. 'I had to stop her, I couldn't let her get away, to him, to Sean Martin. I just lost it, and we fought until she ended up in the water.'

'Explain what happened next.'

'I can't!' He slammed both hands on the witness box. 'I can't explain it, because it was wrong, but all that had built up inside me about Sean Martin came bursting out. It wasn't about helping her anymore but about not letting Sean Martin have her, because whatever I did to her wouldn't be as bad as what Sean Martin would do to her.'

'What did you do?'

Peter's hands gripped the edge of the witness box. 'I held her under the water, and she struggled. I held her tighter, felt her fight for air, but I wasn't going to let go. I held her under the water until she stopped moving. And it sounds wrong and horrible, but I felt like I'd won, because I'd robbed him of her. I'd kept Lizzie Barnsley away from Sean Martin.'

Dan knew that the course the questioning was about to take would change everything. Once more, he thought of Pat. Wherever Pat was, Dan was doing it for him.

'Mr Box,' Dan said, 'why was it important to keep Lizzie away from Sean Martin?'

'Because he'd killed before. I watched him do it, and I couldn't let it happen again.'

Fifty-four

Bill had been watching for a while before he saw how to get into the marina. The man who'd been painting his boat had decided he was done for the day. As he left the marina, he pressed a large button mounted on a post and the gate swung open.

Bill waited for the man to leave in his car before going into the garden centre. He bought a hoe and then drove his car to the marina gate, using it to conceal what he was doing.

The hoe had a long handle, light and metallic, and he was able to push it through one of the gaps in the mesh fence. The button was in reach, bulbous, like an emergency button. It was hard to get the aim right, as the end of the handle swayed in the air, but after a few misses Bill was able to give the button a hard strike. The gate clicked and then swung open.

Bill took one last look around before he went in, but no one was watching him.

There were more than thirty boats secured here, all different sizes and colours. Some long and narrow, others much wider, all in rows alongside concrete jetties that stretched into the basin of the marina. Bill didn't know which boat was Sean's, but at least he had the name: *Somewhere Quiet*.

He found the boat moored further away. It was smarter than some, freshly painted, although the rubber edging on the hull was worn and faded.

He looked around, wary of being caught, but there was no one around.

The boat dipped in the water as Bill climbed aboard. The way in was through a door at one end, small and wooden, with a glass pane. He tapped on it. It wasn't double-glazed. As he peered through, he could see that it had one of those locks that could be opened from the inside without a key.

He should step away, breaking in was wrong, but he was desperate for the truth and Jayne had made it sound like the boat was key. He was entitled to see it. He'd done all that work. He'd solved this when no one else believed him.

He was still holding the hoe. Taking off his coat to muffle the sound, he wrapped it round one end and hit the glass hard. It went in with a thump, along with the shattered broken glass. He used the hoe to smash the remaining shards before reaching in and unlocking the door.

He took the two steps down into the boat and stopped. It was partly because the daylight had disappeared – thick curtains were drawn across each window – but there was also a strong smell of bleach. If Sean had cleaned the place this thoroughly, perhaps he'd already destroyed any forensic traces of whoever had been killed in here. Bill didn't know how forensics worked, or whether bleach would remove traces, but the thought made him stall. Was he ruining the scene? He'd read about these things, how CSI teams are so careful not to contaminate anything.

He closed his eyes. The need to know was stronger than any thoughts about the collection of evidence, and he'd been trying to get the police to act ever since Tom had been killed. Had they been interested in him? Had they hell.

What has happened in here? he thought, as he looked along the boat. Women had gone missing. Had they been held captive in the boat and then murdered? If they had, they would need restraining in some way. Restraints left marks. Restraints had to be kept somewhere and would have DNA embedded in them.

As he looked around, there didn't seem to be many ways to restrain someone. No iron pillars or metal rings hammered into the walls. He'd imagined something darker, more akin to a dungeon than a leisure cruiser. There was a small kitchen area and a couple of wooden chairs, the kitchen surface just a veneer top sitting on a chrome pole. There were two armchairs in front of a television further along, with the bedroom at the other end of a short narrow corridor.

He looked in the cupboards, but there was just the usual collection of pots, pans and plates. The drawers were filled with boating safety certificates, insurance documents and magazines.

There was one last drawer that looked more interesting. It contained a camcorder, one of the old-style ones that used tapes. There were also some blank hi8 tapes still in their plastic wrapping. And some that'd obviously been used already.

He opened the tall cupboard next to it, and just behind a mop and bucket there was a camera tripod.

Then he saw something else behind the tripod.

It was a roll of thick black polythene.

He pulled it out and looked at the edge. It had been used, judging by the uneven edge. He shivered as he wondered what it had been used for? To protect the furniture from whatever Sean did in here? Or to wrap up the bodies before disposal?

He had to look in the bedroom. He didn't like the way it could trap him, at the end of the boat, the route to it tight and claustrophobic, but he needed to know what he would find in there.

His heart was beating fast as he stepped into the narrow corridor.

The bedroom was mundane. A double bed occupied virtually all the space, although there were some overhead cupboards and a slim wardrobe.

He was about to check one of the cupboards when he heard a click, like a door closing.

Bill didn't move. If someone was there, he didn't want to be the first one to reveal himself. Then he remembered the broken glass. It might just be the police, alerted by a neighbour who had heard a noise.

The silence was broken only by his own quick breaths.

He crept along the corridor, trying not to give himself away, so he could turn around and hide somewhere until whoever was in there left. He might have misheard though, his nerves playing tricks on him.

The main part of the cabin slowly appeared. There was no one there.

Bill relaxed for a moment, and then yelped in shock as someone stepped in front of him. A woman.

'I'm Trudy. Are you looking for something?'

Fifty-five

The judge didn't react when the public gallery erupted, as spellbound as everyone else by Peter's evidence.

Dan let the noise subside. He glanced to the press benches and saw that the reporters were typing furiously. Just what he wanted.

He turned back to Peter. 'How did you get to know Sean Martin?'

'I was young, nearly twenty, and I was going out with a girl, Emily. She was a couple of years younger than me, and she was so sweet, so nice. Her older sister was going out with Sean.'

'That would be Trudy Martin, Sean's second wife?'

'Yes, Trudy Williams she was called then,' and the light bounce in his voice disappeared. 'She was so different from Emily, who was bubbly and outgoing. Trudy came across as quieter, but there was something deeper going on.'

'How do you mean?'

'She was headstrong, independent, wanted to live a wilder life, felt Highford was holding her back, that it was too small for her. She used to argue with her parents all the time, until the arguments became too much and she left home. That was probably why she was attracted to Sean, because he made out like he was different from everyone else. Too big for the town, if you know what I mean. He had a canal boat painted up like an old gypsy caravan. Back then, Sean lived on the water, but it was all image, the rebellious free spirit and all that, because he spent most nights at Trudy's house. Emily loved her older sister, idolised her, so we were at Trudy's house most weekends. It was fun at first, excitement, but when I look back now, Sean wasn't nice.'

'Why do you say that?'

'He drank too much, and he insulted Trudy all the time, sitting in his chair with his bottle of vodka, calling her useless or weak. He hit her too, because occasionally I saw her with a black eye. I never found out the reason.'

'Did she say why she put up with it?'

'The same reason we all put up with his abuse and temper,' Peter said. 'He was charismatic and dominating. I see now that he was a loud drunk who thought he was better than everyone else, but it was easy to get swept along. We'd talk politics late into the night. Or, rather, he did, lecturing us because he thought he knew more than anyone else and had insights no one else had. I was much younger than him, ten years or so, and he was like the big brother I never had. And it was sexy, sort of.'

'What do you mean, sexy?'

'We had nowhere else to go to be together, Emily and me, because we were both still living at home and our parents were always in. Trudy and Sean were very . . . you know, all over each other. Sometimes we got so drunk that it got out of hand.'

'Sexually?'

'Yeah. I don't mean too extreme, but Sean always wanted to take it to the next level. One night we all got so drunk that we ended up having sex in the same room. Not with the lights on, but Sean was with Trudy in the chair and I was with Emily on the sofa, and we just got carried away. That was when it started, looking back.'

'When what started?'

'When it all changed between Sean and me, and Trudy. One night Emily and I, we were, you know, getting carried away, and I looked up because I heard a laugh. We'd got carried away because Sean and Trudy had, and it seemed like it was all right, but when I looked up, I could see them, watching. Just faint shadows but I could see them staring, like we were putting on a show for them.'

'Why did that change things?'

'Because Sean tried to join in, but Trudy was having none of it, nor was Emily. He shuffled over, half-naked himself, and started to run his hands along Emily's leg.' He shook his head. 'I don't know who shouted first, me or Emily or Trudy, but it all kicked off. Emily was trying to cover herself up and Trudy was hitting her, pulling at her, Sean trying to push her back.'

'What happened after that?'

'Emily and I got dressed and left. Trudy was still shouting, Emily was crying, but Sean was sitting in his chair, rolling a joint, like he'd just enjoyed the best show ever. We didn't see each other for a while, but Emily and Trudy were sisters and close, and eventually we drifted back together. Trudy said how sorry she was, and how sorry Sean was, and that it was just one of those silly nights when booze had made it go wrong.'

'Your friendship resumed?'

'For a while, yes, but Sean couldn't help himself. It was the same all over again. Too much booze, and Sean was joking and messing about with Emily, grabbing at her, and I could tell she didn't like it, but I was too drunk to stop him.'

'How do you mean, "grabbing at her"?'

'Trying it on, his arms round her, trying to kiss the back of her neck. Emily was struggling, crying, but it just made him worse. His hands were on her breasts, like, holding them, and then he was trying to put his hand down her trousers.'

'What did you do?'

Peter swallowed. 'I encouraged him, I suppose. I laughed along, told her not to be so boring.'

'You wanted Emily to sleep with Sean Martin?'

'It wasn't as simple as that. I wanted to please Sean, which meant that I didn't worry enough about Emily.'

'You treated her like something you could give away. Like a possession, not a person.'

He nodded.

'And Trudy?'

'She went along with it at first, but she became angry when Emily became upset, because Emily was talking about going to the police, saying he'd just sexually assaulted her. I've seen Trudy get angry, and it's pretty wild, but this was different. It was more frightening, because it was, like, silent fury. She rushed at Emily and threw her out.'

'Did you go with her?'

Peter shook his head. 'I was too drunk and stupid, and I felt she'd spoiled the party because it was just Sean acting up.'

'Do you still think that?'

'No, but back then I was in his thrall. I know now that Emily was just a goal, a notch to him. He wanted her whether she consented or not.'

Dan knew he was getting to the dangerous part, because Peter had been sketchy on some parts and he hadn't had time to get all the detail he wanted. It was Peter's testimony though, and if the facts didn't help him, Dan knew he'd sleep well enough. Whatever the reason, Peter had killed an innocent woman.

He settled for the simplest question of all. 'What happened next?'

'Sean went back to his chair and drank some more, insulting Emily, telling me how I was wasting my time with her, because she had no courage. That she was a wallflower. A spectator, never a participant.'

'He was talking about Trudy's sister. How did Trudy react?'

'Like she couldn't hear Sean and was focused only on me. That's when I realised I'd read everything wrong.' He turned towards the jury. 'I thought it had all been down to Sean, but it wasn't. It was Trudy.'

Dan was confused. He tried to hide it but asked, 'What do you mean?'

'Trudy said to me, "Do you have courage?" What could I say except yes? She told me that if I promised to keep it from Emily, she would show me something that would change my life. She got close to me, her hand on my leg, and I'm ashamed to say I liked it. It was all wrong but that's just how it was.'

'And what did you say?'

'I agreed. It was the worst decision of my life.'

'Why?'

'Because of Trudy, people died, including Lizzie.'

Fifty-six

Bill stepped backwards as Trudy walked towards him

'What the *hell* are you doing in here? Who are you?'

Bill put his hand on his chest, still shocked by Trudy's sudden appearance. His mind scrambled for an explanation. 'I was walking along the canal and I heard a smash, glass breaking, and then someone running away. I was checking it out.'

There was a flicker of doubt in her eyes, until she said, 'That's not good enough. Why were you in the bedroom? You could have called the police.' She stepped closer. 'How did you get in through the gate?'

'Calm down. Please. I'm not here to burgle the place. Call the police, if you don't believe me. They can have a good look round, see that I haven't taken anything.'

Trudy flinched.

'Do you want the police?' Bill pulled his phone from his pocket. 'I can ring them now.'

'If you know who I am, and I get the feeling that you do, you'll know that I don't want you to do that. You know who I am, right?'

Bill nodded, his mouth turning dry. 'Sean's wife?'

'The one and only. Sean and I are a little biased when it comes to the police, you see, because he spent those years in prison, and we've been lied to and cheated by them. Is that why you're here? Looking for some dirt on Sean, to pass on to them?'

Bill stuck out his chest. 'I want answers, and I reckon I'll find them here.'

Trudy's eyes narrowed. 'Answers to what?'

'Questions about people who died. Women who went missing. Peter Box is in court right now, telling the world about what happened, and it all started here.'

'Perhaps Peter has come up with some lies to help his case. It doesn't make it true.'

'Why has he picked on you then? What makes you so special to him?'

'I don't need to talk to you. The way I see it, you're just some guy who's broken into my boat. It's Peter who's got to prove his stuff, right?'

'You don't have to stick up for Sean. It doesn't make you a bad person for not realising what he is.'

'You don't know anything. I know what we have, Sean and me, what we've done. I know deep down what kind of man he is.' Trudy stepped away. 'Is this why you're here, to try to find some proof, to be the hero who solves the case? You expect me to break down and confess everything?'

'Curiosity, that's all.'

'Enough to make you break in somewhere? Really?'

He held his phone in the air. 'Fine, let me call the police. I'm the criminal here. Is that how you want it? I bet they'd love to get a look in here.'

She didn't reply.

'No, I didn't think so.'

He glanced towards the door. Trudy stood in the way. She was athletic, but Bill was much heavier. He reckoned he could barge her out of the way if he wanted. He wasn't quite ready to go though. He'd waited too long for answers.

Trudy dropped her gaze and was looking at the floor, her feet tapping fast.

When she looked up, her expression had changed. Before, she had seemed wary, confrontational. That had gone and in its place was weary resignation.

'Will you leave us alone if I tell you all about it?'

'If you're honest with me, yes. That's all I want, the truth.' As Bill looked around the boat interior, he said, 'Why is it so dark?'

'We keep the curtains closed to stop people looking in. What do you want to look at?'

'Could you open the curtains?'

'No, leave it this way.'

'You must keep your boat clean. The bleach smell is really strong.'

'It's always best that way.'

'Just tell me his secrets. There must have been suspicions.'

'I can't.'

'If you won't tell me, speak to the police, please, for your sake. Those suspicions must weigh heavily. If only you knew what I'd been through, and all the others left behind. You could ease their pain.'

'Yeah, maybe. I can't do it to Sean though. We've been through so much together.'

'What about the ones you'll save in the future?' He lowered his voice, trying to calm her. 'I can help you stay away from him, keep you safe.' He went over to her. 'If you're scared of him, this is your chance. You can't stand by him anymore. Tell the truth.'

Trudy went to a drawer in the kitchen and opened it. Bill stayed with her. She closed her eyes, nodded, took a deep breath as if she were struggling to contain her emotions. Her voice was hoarse when she said, 'You're right. I knew this day would come. I've been so weak, so blind.'

Bill was suspicious, but his gaze wandered to the drawer, no longer looking at Trudy's expression.

It was enough.

He saw something moving at the edge of his peripheral vision. She'd grabbed something. There was a shout of anger, and then an explosion of pain as a heavy object crashed into the side of his head.

*

Dan stared down at his papers, his hand shaking.

Peter hadn't mentioned Trudy earlier. It had been about Sean and Rosie and how he'd felt about killing Lizzie. This was all new. He glanced at the clock. The afternoon was moving on, everyone transfixed by Peter's evidence. He told himself that it was what would happen afterwards that was important, when phone calls were made, when people started looking into Sean Martin. He was in pursuit of the truth, that's what mattered, and he wanted Peter to lead him there.

He turned back to Peter. 'Why does it all flow from what happened with Sean and Trudy?'

'Because I could have stopped it. But I was too weak to say no.'

'What did you go along with?'

Peter looked around the courtroom, as if daring to say it, before blurting out, 'Murder.'

Dan let the word settle in before he asked, 'What happened?'

'I met Trudy and Sean down at the marina. Emily had finished with me, so what did it matter if I spent the day with Sean and Trudy? We cruised down the canal and ended up just outside Highford. It was a nice trip. Trudy was being all flirty and it just seemed all so . . . I don't know what the word is – adventurous, I suppose.'

'What did you think was going to happen?'

'Honestly? I didn't know, but I thought it might end with sex, like perhaps we'd all end up in bed together. I was twenty, so it felt illicit, you know, thrilling. But then I told myself I was being stupid, that we were going hiking or whatever.'

'Why would you want to sleep with Emily's sister, and her sister's boyfriend?'

'Because it was exciting. I hadn't had many girlfriends and I was young and the idea seemed a bit wild. You only live once and all that. And Trudy was sexy. She was quiet, but there was something deep and passionate in her eyes that I hadn't really noticed before, and I liked it.'

'Was the day exciting?'

He shook his head. 'It was just horrible.'

'What happened?'

Peter's hand went to his eye and wiped away a tear. His voice trembled. 'We docked. Sean got off the boat. Trudy took me into the bedroom, and I thought, you know, this is the start of it.'

'Did you think you and Trudy were going to have sex?'

'Possibly, I don't know.'

'Did you have sex?'

'No. Trudy pulled me into the bedroom and closed the door and she changed straightaway, in an instant.' Peter clicked his fingers. 'She pulled a knife on me, with holes in the handle that she could put her fingers through and a jagged blade. She rushed at me, held it against my throat and told me to stay quiet, that I mustn't make a sound.'

'How did you feel?'

'Scared. Confused. But, well, excited too, I suppose.'

'Aroused?'

'Yes, a bit of that too. We stayed in the bedroom for around ten minutes, and it was really cramped and small, hardly anywhere to stand, and it was dark, because the curtain was closed over the small round window. Then I heard her.' Peter paused and licked his lips. His voice became thick. 'Sean was with someone. They were on the towpath together, laughing, and then they were on the boat. Trudy pressed the knife against me again and put her finger to her lips, shushing me.'

'How long did you stay in the bedroom for?'

'Another fifteen minutes. Sean had taken the rope from the mooring and we drifted further along the canal. I realised that it was to go somewhere quiet, where no one would hear us. The boat stopped, and I realised why. Sean was with the woman, and they sounded like they were kissing. They weren't saying much but there were soft murmurs and moans, and then footsteps. They were walking towards the bedroom.'

'What was Trudy doing?'

'She looked like she was going to be sick, breathing really heavily with her forearm over her mouth. I didn't understand what was happening, why we were waiting. Then the door opened, and I saw her.'

'Who was it?'

'It was Claire Watkins. I was shocked, couldn't believe it. I knew her because Sean talked to her whenever we passed her, but she never looked like she was after him. Sean was older and he had Trudy, but I realised that Claire's acting awkward whenever we bumped into her in the streets was because she felt guilty, because whatever was going on with Sean was supposed to be a secret. What happened next wasn't love, though.' Peter wiped his eyes. 'Claire cried out, like a mixture of surprise and fright. Trudy rushed at her and Sean put his hand around Claire's mouth, clamped real tight, and they took her away from the bedroom. Trudy had the knife against her throat.'

'What was Claire doing?'

'Crying and struggling. Her clothes were all loose from whatever Sean had been doing with her at the front of the boat. Claire must have thought they would go to the bedroom and have sex, but suddenly everything had changed.'

'What happened next?'

Peter took a few deep breaths. His chin trembled.

'They tied her up. Stripped her. Filmed her as she cried. They put things inside her. The handle of a screwdriver. A glass bottle. They cut her. It was, well' – he held his hands out – 'it was torture, plain and simple.'

'You said "they"?'

'Trudy was the worst, because she was getting the most pleasure out of it, as if Sean was doing it for her. She was laughing and loving it. I'd never seen her so excited, her eyes were crazy.'

'What were you doing?'

'I was curled up in a corner. I just couldn't believe what I was seeing. Trudy kept trying to get me to join in, standing behind Claire, taunting me about how I was reacting.'

'Why didn't you try to help Claire?'

'I was scared, don't you get it? Do you think it hasn't played on my mind ever since?'

The only sound was the light scratch of Francesca's pen as she made notes of what Peter was saying.

'What happened to Claire?'

'They killed her, like they were playing a game. Trudy wrapped a rope around Claire's neck and pulled it tight, but not so tight to choke her right there and then. And then Trudy and Sean . . . I couldn't believe it. They started to have sex right there, in front of her, with Sean on a chair and Trudy on top of him, straddling him, staring over his shoulder at Claire, yanking on the rope, making her watch. And the more Claire cried and tried to pull away, the more Trudy seemed to like it, until, well, you can guess what happened: Trudy pulled so hard on the rope that Claire choked to death as she watched them.'

'You could have stopped them. You could have helped her.'

'I know, I *know*, and all that is my fault, and that's why I did what I did. If I couldn't stop them then, I had to stop it happening again.' He wiped his eyes. 'Until then I'd thought it was Sean who had all these wild ideas, but it was Trudy. It seemed like she was behind it all. The planning. Making it work. Sean went along with it for the excitement, but Trudy? She hid it, as if being quiet stopped people from realising that she was the one really in control.'

NEIL WHITE | 346

'And could you stop it happening again?'

Peter shook his head. 'No. Because Rosie died.' Peter fought back a tear. 'I was a coward, but they lied to me. They killed Claire in front of me, because that's what Trudy enjoys, and I realised then what they were doing. Sean made all the noise, the overtures, but it was all for Trudy. I was meant to take part because then I'd be trapped. They wanted to prove that they could manipulate someone into being as sick as they are, except it didn't work because I couldn't do it.'

'What did they do with Claire's body?'

'I don't know. They ordered me off the boat. They threatened me, told me that if they were caught they'd say I joined in, that it was my idea. I couldn't think straight. I didn't sleep for a week, waiting for a knock on the door from the police, images of poor Claire in my head.'

'Did you tell anyone?'

'No. I told them they had to split up, Sean and Trudy. I demanded it, because it was as if they were encouraging each other. If they split up and promised never to see each other again, I'd stay quiet. That was the deal.'

'Why should they listen to what you had to say? They could have just killed you to keep you quiet.'

'But where's the thrill in that? They were excited by what they did. Killing me? Not the same. That's my guess anyway, and they did what I asked. They went their own separate ways. Sean even married someone else, Rosie's mother, but I realised after a while that was all one big pretence. Those two were addicted to each other.'

'Addicted is a strong word,' Dan said.

'That's how I saw it. I started following them. Sean would collect Trudy in his boat and off they'd go, with no record of where they went. No cameras. No traffic lights. It was as if they were invisible. I'd follow them, because I couldn't let it happen again. I told myself that if I caught them with another victim, I'd tell the police all I knew, regardless of what it meant for me, but I never did. They were too clever for that. When people went missing, I didn't know if those two were connected or not. What if I reported them and the police didn't believe me? I didn't know where the bodies were buried.' He looked down. 'It all changed when Rosie was murdered.'

'How?'

'Because he was caught, at long last.'

'What happened with Rosie?'

'I'd been following them again. Trudy and Sean were both on the boat, and it was moored in Highford. I don't know if they already had someone else in there or not, but I saw Rosie walking towards the boat. I knew who she was because I'd been watching Sean. I wanted to tell her mother, Karen, about Trudy, but what would that achieve? They'd know I hadn't reported them to the police even though they'd broken their side of the agreement. They'd know I wasn't a threat.'

'Where were you?'

'I was on a bridge further along, looking along the water. I couldn't get down to the water though, because it was just one of the road bridges going up the hill from the town centre and there were no steps down. All I could do was watch.'

'Did it look as if Rosie was going to meet him?'

'No. Just the opposite. She was walking along, headphones in, when she noticed the boat. She seemed surprised. She peered into the windows and then knocked on it. I don't know if he said something from inside, but Rosie stepped onto it and knocked on the door. Sean appeared and they both stayed there for a while, talking. I don't know what he said, but he stepped aside to let her in. Rosie went inside but she wasn't there long. The next thing I know she's running, and it was wild running, her hair streaming back, Sean chasing her along the towpath.'

'Did he catch her?'

'He dragged her to the floor. He had something in his hand, but I couldn't see what. His arm pushed down into her, up and down, violent stabs, until she wasn't moving any more. I couldn't believe it. A girl. His stepdaughter. I wanted to scream but no one else had seen it, which meant it was all down to me again. Someone came along though, a man walking a dog, on the towpath, far in the distance, so Sean cradled her, wailing and making out like he'd just found her.'

'What happened to the weapon?'

'I don't know. The boat set off and cruised past. Perhaps he threw it on to the boat because it just kept on going.'

'You could have told the police all this.'

'I know, but I was scared, and eventually there wasn't a need because he was caught. I went to see Sean's lawyer, Mr Molloy, but I got it all wrong, told him that it was all my fault, that I was responsible, and I was, but he thought I was some fruitcake.'

'Why did you speak to his lawyer though?'

'He had to know what kind of monster he was defending, but I messed it up. In the end, it didn't matter; Sean was in prison where he belonged.'

'But Sean won his appeal.'

'I know, but what could I do then? No one would believe me, and he knew it. He was back with Trudy, publicly this time, so I started to follow him again. I knew he was carrying on like before, but I just never caught him, until it all went wrong that night with Lizzie. He was cruising, just looking out for someone, and he would have snatched her, so she would have died anyway.' He shrugged. 'I suppose I took away her chance to escape. I wish I could go back and change it all. Not just to the night I killed Lizzie but all the way back, to when Trudy killed Claire.'

'And when you struggled with Lizzie?'

'All the frustration, panic, worry, fear, despair, it rushed in like a wave, as if it wasn't me anymore, and I held her, couldn't stop myself. I'm not a murderer. I killed Lizzie, but I didn't set out to do that. You've got to believe me. What I did was unforgivable, but it was because of Sean Martin and Trudy. Whatever people thought about him before he won his appeal, he's that man, and more.'

'And you know that the prosecution might call Sean Martin to give his side of the story?'

Peter spat out a bitter laugh. 'He won't come to court. He thinks he's the clever one in front of people like me, those who he thinks are below him, but coming here is different.'

'Why didn't you tell the police all this, back when you were interviewed?'

'I've kept these secrets for a long time now. How could it help me? I knew I didn't murder Claire, or Rosie, or any of the others Sean and Trudy killed, although I didn't save them. But Lizzie? That was different. That was on me. It was all the guilt and rage and frustration coming out. I wish I could change it, but I can't.'

Dan nodded and said, 'Thank you. Just remain there. My learned friend might have some questions for you.'

Francesca stared at her notes for a moment before she stood in front of Peter.

Her questions faded into the background as Dan thought about what Peter had said. Pat had been right about Sean Martin, but everyone had misread Trudy.

He had no interest in whatever Francesca asked. It was all about the next part. He wanted Sean Martin behind bars, and Trudy.

He was doing it for Pat.

Fifty-seven

The courtroom emptied as Dan remained at his bench. He needed the solitude. Unsure of his next step, it felt like he'd lost control of the case. It had stopped being about Peter and had become about Sean and Trudy. He didn't know whether that was a good thing or not.

He called Jayne. When she answered, he said, 'Any movement?'

'Murdoch arrived a while ago, with some hot young detective. They weren't there long though.'

'It will have been about going to court tomorrow. What happened when they left?'

'He waved them off and closed his door. Since then, not a peep.'

'Are both Sean and Trudy there?'

'I haven't seen Trudy. So, what now?'

He thought about that. 'I wanted their immediate reaction but, if there hasn't been one, there isn't much point in you staying there. Come back to mine. We'll think of another strategy. I need to nail Sean Martin tomorrow, but I don't know what with.'

'And if we can't?'

'I'll make the accusations on Peter's behalf. Sean will deny them. The jury will reject Peter's evidence and Sean will carry on as before.'

'What about Trudy, if I leave?'

'Unless you know where she is, what are you going to find out by staying? We need to work out what to do. Just give me time to get home.'

He clicked off and tapped his phone against his lip. Before he could work out his next move, his phone rang. As soon as he pressed the answer button, the unmistakable smoky wheeze of Murdoch filled his head.

'Dan, we need your help on this one. We have the same objective, and that's getting Sean Martin in a cell. Let's discuss.'

'What about the prosecutor? Francesca won't be happy about you bypassing her.'

'Are you going to tell her?'

'Well, no.'

'There you go then. Our little secret.'

'What did Sean Martin say when you went to see him?'

'How did you know I'd been to his house,' Murdoch said, surprise in her voice. 'Are you watching me?'

'No, I'm having *him* watched. Did he make a written statement?'

'I told him he ought to speak to his lawyer first.'

'Except his lawyer has gone missing.'

'I made that point and told him to be at court in the morning.'

'How did he react?'

'He seemed nervous, but he kept his cool, almost rehearsed, as if he'd braced himself for the conversation. That's where he got it wrong.'

'How do you mean?'

'Let's imagine he's innocent, just for a moment. Your client is making false accusations against him, and they're just like the ones that got him locked up. What would you expect?'

Dan thought about that. 'Outrage, maybe. Dismay, at least.'

'An emotion, is what you're saying. That's not what I got. It was like a barrier going up.'

'Did you mention Claire Watkins? That Peter's described her murder in court?'

'I did. He said he knew her to talk to.'

'At least he's admitting a connection. It means that something Peter said was true, which, when you think about it, is good for you. Peter has stayed silent throughout this case, which means he has never told a lie. If the jury believes him, you've got a credible witness against Sean Martin.'

'Have you spoken to anyone?'

'An old friend of Claire's.'

'Have you got a name?'

Dan shuffled through his papers until he found Jayne's notes. 'Here we are, Mandy Rogers,' and read out her address. 'Mandy and Claire used to speak to Sean when Trudy lived on the next street and Sean moored his boat nearby. Peter liked Claire. I think that's why Sean chose her, because he thought Peter wouldn't be able to resist.'

'Like some damn offering.'

'Why didn't the police speak to Mandy?'

'We did.'

'Why did you ask for her name then?'

'To check that we hadn't missed anyone.'

'What did she say?'

'That Sean Martin was creepy.'

'And he wasn't a suspect?'

Murdoch didn't answer straightaway. 'Let's focus on what we have now.'

'You said this was about sharing. Have you got anything you want to tell me that I don't know already?'

'I just wanted what you had.'

'That wasn't the deal. What about Pat?'

Murdoch's tone softened. 'Sorry, Dan, nothing so far. Have you thought of anything else?'

'No, I'm sorry, and I'm worried.'

'You've every right to be,' she said, and clicked off.

He left the courtroom. The corridor was deserted apart from a cleaner emptying the bins, the peace broken only by the rustle of a large black bag.

He headed for the stairwell that led to the cell complex. It was cool and deliciously quiet, the drama of the courtroom behind him, but thoughts of Pat continued to trouble him as he went downstairs.

He'd taken the first step towards nailing Sean Martin. He didn't know how many more he had to make, but Pat was still missing, and he was certain that Sean Martin was somehow connected.

For now, though, he had to be the lawyer and speak to his client.

His footsteps echoed in the stairwell, and by the time he was buzzed through he was ready to sag into the chair in front of the glass screen. It seemed an age before Peter appeared on the other side, although it was probably no more than two minutes.

Peter seemed brighter, almost excited.

Dan put his file on the narrow shelf in front of the glass. 'How are you feeling?'

'Better,' he said, nodding. 'It's what I wanted to do all along, but I didn't know how to do it.'

'You weren't open with me, or the police. You weren't prepared to talk about Claire Watkins, about your involvement in her death.'

'I didn't take part though.'

'You didn't stop it. Morally, that's close enough.'

He thought about that and some of his brightness faded. 'My conscience isn't clear, and it never will be, but at least I've tried to get there.' He leaned forward so that his breath misted the glass. 'Will you get them, Mr Grant?'

'I don't know, Peter, but I promise you that I'll try my best.'

He sat back as he thought about that before saying, 'That will have to do.'

Fifty-eight

Bill tried to move his head as the sounds became clearer, but a sharp jab of pain made him stop. He tried to lift his hand but couldn't.

He didn't know how long he'd been out but there were more voices now. They started as soft mumbles that came in waves, getting louder each time, as if he were walking past a busy room.

The voices were angry.

'What the hell have you done?' A male voice.

'He was snooping around the boat.' He recognised Trudy's voice. 'Why do you think he was down here?'

'People will know he's missing, and if he's told them where he's gone, the police will send a squad down. You've blown this. I can't believe it.'

'Look at him. Some sad old loner. Do you really think anyone knows where he is? But it's you who can't see what's going on. It's all coming to an end. *All* of this. *Us.* It's *over.*'

'You're overreacting.'

'*Am I?* Really? Let's ask him.'

Bill grunted in pain as he was kicked on the thigh.

'Wake up, you stupid bastard.'

Bill opened his eyes and winced. One eye felt glued together. Dried blood, he guessed.

He tried to straighten but pain flashed across his forehead. He was sitting on the floor, still in the kitchen of the boat. He pulled at his arms, but they were tied behind his back around the metal pole that supported the kitchen unit.

'What's happening?' His voice was a croak.

Someone knelt in front of him. Trudy.

'Tell him why you're here.'

Bill let his head hang down. 'It was just something I needed to know. Whether any of the victims I've discovered died here.'

'Which victims?'

'Are you going to kill me?'

'Just talk.'

'There were many victims, too many, but you know that. They go back years.'

She gripped Bill's chin and made him look up. 'What were you hoping to find?'

'I don't know. You never know until you find it.'

'Did you find anything?'

Bill sucked in air and tried to sit upright. He thought of his son and used his grief to find some inner strength. He wasn't going to bullied by them, not after what they'd done. 'Your camcorder.'

Trudy blinked. She'd tried not to react, but Bill saw it.

'Did you film your victims as you killed them?'

There was more movement in front of him, and the outline of Sean Martin came into view.

It was the first time he'd met him, and he seemed different from his media images, where he came across as warm and intelligent. His appearance now was different, his mood darker. He knelt in front of Bill and reached out for his head. He pulled away instinctively.

'Be careful,' Sean said. 'You'll bump your head again.' His voice was quiet, but through menace, not concern.

Bill sucked in some deep breaths. 'I didn't bump my head last time.'

'Why, what happened?' There was a trace of a smile.

'You know what happened. She hit me.'

As Bill looked around the boat, his focus better now, he saw a hammer on the floor. His baseball cap was next to it, knocked off when he was struck.

Sean followed his gaze and asked, 'What do you propose to do about it?'

'I don't understand.'

'If we let you go, what are you going to do?'

Bill closed his eyes for a moment. This was the moment when it would all get worse. They wouldn't believe him if he begged them to let him go and promised not to tell anyone. He had to try a different lie.

'I'll have you arrested. You know that.'

'Why should I let you go then?'

'Because whatever you do from now on will just make it worse for you. What have you done so far? Trudy has hit me with a hammer and tied me up, but she'll say that I'm a burglar and she was protecting herself. I can't dispute that, because I did break in. They won't even prosecute her for it, I reckon. They'll say I got what I deserved, and you get to be the hero.'

'Me, the hero? How does that work?'

'You get to release me and take the credit. Those out there who still doubt you might change their minds.'

Trudy paced behind them, the space tight and claustrophobic.

Sean turned around to her. 'What do you think?'

'Bullshit.' She spat the word out. 'Can you trust the police to let you walk away again? No. But no one is going to prison. Not again. Not ever.'

Sean turned back to Bill. 'You see, now we've got a whole new set of problems. Can you guess what they are?'

Bill closed his eyes as his heartbeat increased, and his chest tightened with creeping terror.

'Lost for words?' Sean said, his head tilted, a malevolent gleam in his eye. 'I'll help you out. If no one is going to prison, that's because no one is getting caught for this, which means that no one is going to hear from you.' He smiled, but it was cold, taunting. 'Can you see where I'm going with this?'

Bill opened his eyes and tried a bluff. 'What happens when the police get here? Dan Grant knows where I am.'

Sean stood up and laughed. 'Not that old cliché. Come on, whatever you're called.'

'Bill.'

'Right, Bill, this is how it works. If anyone cared about you, you wouldn't be doing it on your own, which means that no one is coming here looking for you.'

'What about my car? And the CCTV of the entrance?'

'You're a clever old man, but not as clever as you think. Can you guess your mistake?' He kicked him again, harder this time. 'Can you?'

Bill yelped in pain.

'You've just pushed us to the point of no return.' He turned to Trudy. 'Start the boat. We're going for a cruise.'

'Where to?'

He thought for a few seconds. 'Downstream. We need to get away from this place.'

'Please, just let me go.'

Sean shook his head. 'That isn't going to happen. What I know for certain is that you won't be coming back here. Not ever.'

Bill closed his eyes.

'How the hell do we do this?' Trudy said.

'Just get us away from the town.'

'At four miles per hour, for Christ's sake?'

'We don't want to attract attention. We just need to get somewhere quiet.'

'Okay, the usual place.'

The usual place? Bill didn't like the sound of that. He fought back a sob.

Sean bent down to rummage through Bill's pockets. He tried to pull away, but he couldn't.

Sean found his phone in his trouser pocket, along with his wallet. He pressed the start button on the phone and frowned. 'What's the passcode?'

Bill tried to think quickly, even though his mind was still fuzzy and unreal after the blow with the hammer. He knew Sean wanted to check his phone though: to see whether anyone knew he was there. If Sean gained access to the phone, he would know the answer: Jayne. Uncertainty was his best defence.

'I can't think. Hang on.'

'Don't mess me around.'

'I'm not, but she hit me with a hammer. I'm still dizzy.'

'What is the passcode?' he repeated slowly.

'I'm trying, but it stops being a number after a while and more like muscle memory, like your fingers know where to press.' A deep breath. 'Try one-eight-seven-three.'

Sean tapped the numbers into the phone. 'Nice try. Wrong number.'

'Wait then, try one-eight-nine-five. It's something like that.'

Sean tried one more time. Wrong number again. He knelt on the floor in front of Bill. 'We can play this nicely or we can play this horribly, but I'm going to get into this phone.'

'I've told you, I can't remember.'

'I don't believe you.' He reached around Bill to grab his bound wrists and forced them upwards, the rope sliding up the pole, his arms straining, as if they were about to pop out of their sockets, his body thrust forward.

'Stop, *please*, you're hurting me.'

'That's the point. Don't you get it?' He pulled Bill's arms up higher, until he screeched in pain. '*Say it.*'

'Two-five-eight-zero,' he croaked.

Sean pushed up on his arms once more.

'Yes, *yes*. The middle numbers on the keypad. Please *stop*.'

Sean let go and Bill slumped to one side as he sucked in air. Sean tapped in the numbers and smiled when the phone came to life.

Bill closed his eyes.

Sean skimmed through the various apps on his phone.

When he'd finished, he pulled at the back of the phone until it came off with a snap. He took out the battery and then the SIM card, bending that in half. He went to the window and threw it all out. It landed with a light plop into the water.

He turned back to Bill. 'Jayne knows you're here, but your phone won't track your location.' He laughed and said to Trudy, 'You're all ours.'

Trudy came behind him. 'What do we do?'

'What we always do.'

Bill grunted with effort as he sat up straight up again. 'Which is what?'

'Whoa, what's this?' Trudy said, laughing. 'Don't you prefer surprises?' She looked at Sean. 'His coat needs to come off. Put it on, his baseball cap too, and drive his car away.'

Sean opened Bill's wallet and grinned when he saw the driving licence. 'I know where he lives. I'll leave it on the drive. It'll stop people looking for him. He's just some old man no one will miss.'

'What if you're seen?'

'I'll make sure that doesn't happen.'

Trudy stepped closer. 'Make sure of that. I'm doing this for you, to save you.'

'And what are you going to do when I'm gone?'

Bill looked from one to the other, his stomach churning with the thought of what was about to happen.

'Bury this bastard.'

He gripped her hands. 'You know this might be the last time.'

'No, that isn't how it's going to happen. Remember what you've always said, that we're constantly one step ahead of the cockroaches.' When he didn't answer straightaway, she said, 'That's right, isn't it? To keep us apart, they've got to prove it. And to prove it, they've got to find him.'

Sean went to the knots binding Bill to the pole and tugged at them, sending pain through Bill's shoulders again.

Bill exhaled with relief as the knots loosened, the jabs of pain subsiding, and he tensed, ready to lash out and make one last bid to get away.

As the ropes slipped to the ground, Bill kicked out, catching Sean on his knee, sending him crashing to the floor. Bill tried to shuffle away, desperate to get to the door, but Trudy was too fast. She leapt forward, kneeing him in the side of the head.

The boat swirled and went out of focus as he tried to regain his feet. Someone was tugging at his coat, but he didn't have the strength to fight back. There was someone next to him, but even in the fuzz of his semi-consciousness he recognised the sharp steel of a knife blade against his neck. He felt himself being pushed against the pole again and the ropes being tied around his wrists once more.

'This thing is greasy.'

Bill opened his eyes to see Sean putting on his baseball cap.

Trudy straightened it and pulled it down. 'It's only for the cameras. You'll look just like some old man driving home. Now *go*.'

Sean glanced down at Bill one more time, and a faint smile crinkled his cheeks. 'Later,' he said, and left the boat.

Trudy knelt down. 'Don't worry, I'll look after you until he gets back. It'll all be over soon.'

He closed his eyes as she went towards the stern of the boat. He quelled a sob as the engine roared into life and he felt the boat begin to move along the water.

Fifty-nine

Dan had spent the previous hour staring at a pile of papers, as if he expected the answers to rise up from them. Since he left court he'd stalled. Faded nervous energy, and the lack of any evidence to corroborate what Peter had said, had him questioning the wisdom of letting Peter give his account.

But then, he hadn't made that decision; Peter had, because he wanted his voice to be heard.

He paced in front of his apartment window as he called Jayne.

She arrived within thirty minutes, holding two pizza boxes. As he opened the door he said, 'I knew working with you would be bad for my health.'

'We can always go somewhere classier.'

'No, let's eat.'

He opened two beer bottles and sat down to eat.

They ate in silence for a while before Jayne asked, 'What next?'

'I want Sean Martin in court. I want to bring him down. For Pat's sake, if no one else's. But,' he said as he shrugged, 'the police aren't feeding me any information so I've no weapon I can use. The best I can hope for is a no-show. Sean Martin would stay free, but Peter's evidence will be reported and his reputation will take a battering, as would his income.'

Jayne drained her beer and said, 'We haven't heard from Bill for a while.'

'He's busy doing his own thing,' Dan said, chewing. 'Don't worry about him.'

'He said he was at the marina. I thought he might have called in, just to let us know if anything was happening, that's all.'

'It'll be quiet down there. Think about it. As far as Sean is concerned, he's going to attend court tomorrow to defend some wild accusations. Trudy too, perhaps. Do you really think they'll do anything tonight? If they think the police are suspicious, that's it all a trap, they'll bluff it out until after the hearing.'

'Yeah, maybe.' She found Bill's number in her phone and pressed dial, but it went straight to voicemail. 'His phone's switched off.'

'He's an old man. He won't be glued to it.'

She pushed her pizza to one side. 'It's not right. He'd have let me know.'

They were disturbed by the ring of Dan's phone. It was Murdoch.

He lifted his phone and said, 'Coincidence,' before he answered and asked, 'Any news?'

'Dan, I'm going to send you a copy of a police notebook from when Claire Watkins went missing. It might help you tomorrow.'

His laptop pinged behind him. Dan pointed towards it, so Jayne wandered over. Wiping her fingers on a napkin, a string of cheese dangling from her lip, she opened the email and the attachment before carrying the laptop to him.

He read it. 'He lied! He said he didn't know her.'

'No one knew what he was capable of back then,' Murdoch said. 'If we'd suspected, we'd have looked a lot closer at him.'

'We know now.'

'We do, Dan, and it's a pity people at your firm were the last ones to realise.' She clicked off before Dan could respond.

Jayne's mouth was filled with pizza when she asked, 'What have you got?'

'Sean Martin trapped in a lie.'

'Will it be enough?'

'We'll find out tomorrow.'

'No, that's not good enough.'

'What do you mean?'

'We can't wait for Murdoch to do her bit. Look how long Pat has been missing, and what have they found so far? Come on, we're going out. We need to keep looking.'

'What for?'

'Bill, to begin with. But I've got an idea.'

*

Bill couldn't work out how long they'd cruised for. It seemed like hours, but he was still dazed, the boat's interior fading and shifting in front of his eyes as he drifted in and out of consciousness. They'd been moored up for a while though, and Trudy had spent that time sitting in a chair by a small Formica table, tapping the surface with a large knife she'd taken from a drawer. The blade was long and curved, its teeth jagged. There were holes in the handles where her fingers poked through. She seemed distracted and wasn't paying much attention to him.

He tried to work out which way they'd travelled. West, was his best guess, just from the direction of the turn and what seemed like the sounds of a town they'd gone through on the way. Highford, he presumed, which meant that they were somewhere rural on the other side, where the canal cut through the fields and valleys and linked all the big towns. He could hear cars in the distance, a deep hum as if there were a lot of them, travelling fast. He knew the motorway cut a straight line across the county, whereas the canal curved and changed direction as it went from town to town.

Bill shuffled so that he could sit upright. 'It doesn't have to be this way, you know.'

Trudy looked over. 'What's this? Life-coaching? Don't bother.'

The boat jolted as someone hopped on. Trudy spun round, the knife held outwards, but she relaxed when Sean came back into the boat, still wearing Bill's coat.

'Done,' he said. 'No one saw me, I'm sure. Got a taxi to a mile along the towpath so we're safe here, and no one will know he's gone.' He held his hand out to Trudy. 'Give me the knife.'

Sean went over to Bill, holding the knife outwards and twirling it around his finger. He knelt down and pushed the blade against Bill's neck, the tip just under his ear. He could feel his skin almost giving way to the blade.

'You shouldn't move,' Sean said, his voice a low hiss. 'If you do, this blade will slice you open in a moment. You'll bleed out here, and my face will be the last thing you'll ever see. Is that how you want to go?'

Sean reached behind Bill and untied one of his wrists but kept hold of the rope. He stood up and pulled on it, yanking Bill to his feet and kicking his feet apart. He re-tied his wrists behind his back and pulled on the bindings, forcing him upright, before pushing him forward.

Bill stumbled to his knees, banging his head against the wall of the boat. Sean knelt down. There was spittle on his lips.

He grabbed Bill's shirt. 'Come on, time to go. Are you going to stay quiet?'

Trudy came behind them and took the blade from Sean. She pressed it back on Bill's neck and he swallowed but stayed still. 'He can scream, if he wants, but it will be a short one.'

Sean laughed and then led Bill up the two steps and on to the hull of the boat.

Bill winced when he got outside. The blood on his shirt glued the fabric to his chest and the breeze blew cold against the cut on his temple, making it sting. He needed stitches.

Sean hopped on to the canal bank and held his hand out for him.

Bill stayed where he was at first, until he felt the unmistakable point of the knife in his back.

'*Move.*'

He stepped out. Sean grabbed his arm and pulled him onto the grass. Bill stumbled to the ground, unable to hold out his arms to steady himself, until Sean yanked him to his feet again.

They were in a field by a long curve in the canal, the nearest village far in the distance. As Bill looked round, he saw what was responsible for the steady hum of traffic. He was right, it was the motorway. There was a possibility that people would see him but, as he looked, everyone was driving past too quickly. He cast his eyes over the field and wondered whether he could get away. He could just about make out a gate on the other side of the field. If he could get to there, a passing motorist might spot him.

The terrain was uneven though, and he was too old to sprint across a pitted field with his arms tied behind his back. They'd catch him straightaway. Ahead of him was a ruined cottage, the windows hollow, just darkness inside.

Trudy pushed him towards it. 'Get in.'

The darkness swallowed him up as he followed her direction.

Bill stopped as he allowed his eyes to adjust. The house smelled damp. There was a hallway that was just compacted dirt, the stone slabs long gone. There were remnants of wallpaper peeling from the walls. There was a stairway ahead, although some of the stairs were cracked and broken bannister struts splayed outwards like bent fingers.

'Keep going,' Trudy said.

There was a room to his left, a kitchen, the cupboards hanging loose. To his right was an empty room, although the grand old fireplace against one wall told him that it was once the living room.

A push to his back propelled him along the hallway and past the stairs, to where the floor turned into creaking floorboards, dust flying up as he went.

Trudy pushed him against the wall before pulling at a door. It opened to a deeper darkness. A damp breeze blew upwards.

A cellar.

Trudy pulled on the ropes binding his wrists. She grunted with exertion as she propelled him through the threshold. He stumbled and, just as he got to the other side of the doorway, he was given the biggest push of all.

The ground didn't come when he expected. Instead, he was falling, unable to put his hands out to protect himself, his screams echoing.

He was able to turn his body, but his back hit a concrete step as he went, and he cried out again as he tumbled downwards, his legs contorted, colours dancing in his vision. The sharp edge of a step cut into his forehead as he reached the bottom, where he lay crumpled, unable to move.

Sixty

The journey to the marina didn't take long, the town-centre traffic gone. They were in Jayne's car, the rattle of her exhaust loud as they pulled into the garden centre car park. It was deserted. There was a lone floodlight over the marina.

Dan leaned forward to look through the windscreen. 'I can't see Bill's car.'

She pulled alongside the fence and they both got out to peer through. The marina was empty, apart from an old man working on a boat further away. Jayne banged on the gate to get the man's attention.

He looked up before going back to whatever he'd been doing.

'Hey! Hey!' The gate clanged as Jayne pulled on it.

The old man ignored her for a few seconds, so Jayne said, 'We haven't got time to wait,' and began to clamber up it, trying to get her foot onto the security lock so that she could hoist herself over it, despite the roll of razor wire at the top.

'Jayne, what the hell?'

'You've been buttoned up in your suit for too long.'

She was about to try to haul herself upwards when the old man shouted, 'Get down.'

'Let me in. It's urgent.'

The old man put down whatever he'd been holding and started a slow walk to the gate.

Jayne banged it again. 'Hurry up, come on.'

'Calm down. I'm slower than I used to be.'

Jayne hopped off the gate and paced.

As he reached the gate, he glared at both of them. 'What's so urgent?'

'I'm looking for a man who was watching this place earlier this evening?'

'Why would anyone be watching it?'

'He just was. Older guy, tall, thin, in a silver Fiesta.'

The man looked to the car park. 'I remember him, but I don't see a silver car. He must have left.'

Dan stepped forward. 'Have you been here all night?'

'Most of it. I had to go for some more paint, and I went home for some food, so I've been away a couple of hours.'

'Is Sean Martin's boat here?'

'Now, what kind of interest would you have in his boat?'

'I need to know, that's all. Can't you tell me? Please.'

The old man looked around the marina before shaking his head. 'Looks like it's gone out, but people like to go sailing at night. It's peaceful.'

Dan and Jayne turned away.

Jayne put her hands on her hips and shook her head. 'I'm worried. I know what you'll say but I can't help it.'

She tried Bill's number again. It went straight to voicemail.

*

Bill roared in pain as someone grabbed the rope that bound his wrists. It was Sean, he could tell from his grunts of exertion as he dragged him along the floor. His shirt rode up and loose dirt rubbed against his back.

Sean shoved him into the corner of the cellar. Bill tried to put his head against the floor, to somehow take away the pain, but Sean yanked him up by his shirt collar. He cried out, the agony blinding, as if he'd jarred and banged every part of his body on the way down the stairs.

His mouth hung open as he sucked in air. There was someone in front of him. At first, he thought it was Sean, but the breaths against his face were fresher, the grip lighter.

'Just let me go. Please.' The words came between gulps.

Before anyone could respond, the cellar was filled with light.

Bill looked away, squinting. It was a spotlight or a bright torch.

Trudy was kneeling in front of him. Sean was pacing on the other side of the beam, his footsteps loud crunches in the dirt, but Trudy was more poised. 'I hope you're not going to do anything stupid.'

'I just want you to let me go.'

Trudy turned towards where Sean had been pacing. 'What shall we do?'

Sean stepped away from the lamp. 'Kill him, of course.'

Trudy considered that for a moment, and then she shook her head. 'No, not yet.'

'Why? What purpose does he serve?'

'We've no idea what we're walking into when we go to court tomorrow.'

'There's no *we* in this.'

'What the hell do you mean by that? They'll expect me there too.'

'And they'll separate us and pick holes in our stories. If I go there on my own, there will be no inconsistencies, and if the jury believes me, you're in the clear too.'

Trudy thought about that. 'That might not stop the police. We need a bargaining chip.' She pointed to Bill. 'That's him.'

'A hostage? The police won't let us go just because he's locked up in here.'

'I'm not thinking of the police. Who's behind all of this? It isn't the police. It's Dan Grant. If we threaten Dan, it might stop him from having a go at you in court. If he pulls his punches, he'll lose his argument and we can go back to living our lives.'

'He'll know about us though, and he won't let us carry on. He'll keep coming after us.'

'Do you really think he'll say anything if it works?' Trudy said. 'The lawyer who sold his client out? The lawyer who didn't tell the police about someone being kidnapped? No, like most lawyers, he'll look at ways to weasel out of it, because it's what lawyers do, and pretending he didn't know is the easiest way.'

'If you're sure it'll work.'

'We're a bit short on options right now. We'll deal with tomorrow and then work out the next move. For now, though, he's better alive than dead.'

'We could use him as a distraction. Let the police look for him and we might be able to run.'

'Where to?'

'Does it matter? I'm not going back to prison. I don't care where we go, as long as we're together.'

'We're not Bonnie and Clyde.'

'And we're not Brady and Hindley either. We need a plan though. We've always planned. We're good together, a team, but this time you've messed up. This is too rushed.'

Trudy's voice lowered. '*I've* messed up?'

'You could have let him leave. You didn't have to hit him.'

'What's done is done. We've got to deal with tomorrow. We're not going to prison. No one will ever separate us again.'

Bill coughed and gasped. 'They'll discover you. I've got things at home, research through the years. I told people I was going to the marina. They'll start looking if you don't let me go.'

Trudy's jaw clenched as she turned to Sean. 'What did you do with his car keys?'

'I threw them. I didn't want to be caught with them.'

Trudy stood in front of Bill and slapped him across the cheek. The crack was loud in the bare space. 'What do you know about tomorrow?'

Bill let his head hang down, exhausted. 'That's up to Dan Grant, you know that.'

'But you know what Dan knows. What can Sean expect from the witness box?'

Bill took a deep breath and braced himself for another blow. 'I'm not telling you.'

Sean stepped forwards, hands on hips. 'What Peter says and what can be proved are two different things.'

'We need to know first.'

Bill grimaced. He thought about what he could say, because all that mattered was staying alive. 'He's blaming you. Don't you know that?'

Sean and Trudy exchanged glances before Sean said, 'We know that much.'

Bill tried to clear his mind. Staying alert was the key to getting through this. 'He's going to link a number of missing people to you. Claire Watkins for one. Rosie too. Whatever Peter knows, he said it in court today.'

Sean put his hands out. 'Were you there?'

Bill shook his head. 'I helped Dan though. He's got all the information I've gleaned over the years.'

'And that's it?'

He nodded.

'Why were you at the marina then, if that's all there is?'

'Because I had to know. My son was killed by the canal. This thing has eaten me up!'

'What have you found out?'

'Just a list of names. People who've been murdered near or by the canal. I had no suspects. I spoke to Dan Grant and he was interested. This was all his idea, not mine, I just want to know what happened to my son.' Tears ran down his cheeks. 'Just let me go, please. I won't say anything.'

Trudy bent down in front of Bill. 'That's why you've messed up,' she said. 'We had nothing to worry about. But now? Now we have *everything* to worry about because of you.' She swung out wildly, hitting Bill's face again with a loud smack. She turned to Sean. 'He's going to die. Just not yet. I want to know more about what he knows, and what Dan Grant thinks he can prove. Get it from him.'

Sean nodded his agreement and went past Trudy. As he looked down at Bill, he grinned.

Sixty-one

Jayne was driving too quickly as they headed to Bill's house. Dan gripped the door handle and his legs tensed, his foot slamming an imaginary brake.

As they turned into his street, Dan pointed and said, 'Look, I told you he's fine. His car's here.'

'That doesn't mean anything,' she said, as she skidded to a stop and rushed towards the front door. She banged on it but there was no reply. She went to his windows and peered through, her hands cupped around her eyes to block the glow of the nearby streetlight.

There was no one in. She could make out his sofa and the dark outline of the television. His car was there though, so he came home, at least.

She banged once more, even though she knew it was pointless. She thought about calling the police, her instinct telling her that something was amiss, but what would they do? An adult wasn't at home? Hardly enough to start a manhunt.

Dan's phone rang. It was Murdoch again.

'Anything new?' He sounded tetchy.

'Do you remember the woman who went for a walk with her dog and never came home, Annie Yates? Turns out that she knew Trudy.'

He held up his hand to attract Jayne's attention, who had gone back to looking through Bill's windows. 'Keep going.'

'They'd gone to school together, but Annie moved away when she met her husband. Trudy had looked her up not long before, which had surprised Annie's friends, because Trudy had been quiet at school, almost unnoticeable, whereas Annie had been one of the popular girls. Trudy found her on one of those Internet sites where you connect with old classmates. They met up a couple of times, but when she went missing Trudy faded into the background. And why wouldn't she? There was no reason to suspect her.'

'They must all have a connection to Sean and Trudy,' Dan said. 'These aren't random abductions. They've sought people out. Do you know anything else about Trudy?'

'If you're looking for a narrative, some story of a girl reacting against a bad upbringing, you'd be mistaken. It was ordinary. Decent parents, suburban living. If you want my take, it was about the excitement, the thrill of the forbidden, something wild. There doesn't always have to be a reason.'

'Keep on looking.'

'Don't tell me how to do my job,' she said, and hung up.

Jayne moved away from the window. 'Good news?'

'Another victim connected to Sean and Trudy. Annie Yates.'

'Do you remember when we were going through the clippings?' Jayne said, animatedly. 'We talked about Charlotte Crane, the woman who went missing the same night that Lizzie was killed. Peter said Sean was out cruising because he followed the boat. Lizzie wasn't killed by Sean, we know that now, and perhaps she was never in danger anyway. Too random. But if they select their victims, groom them almost, what if Charlotte was their target instead? We were trying to connect Charlotte's disappearance to the others to rule out Peter, but can we connect her to Sean or Trudy?'

'You're right.'

'And we don't have to leave it to Murdoch to find everything out.'

'That's her job.'

'No, that's our job. There's only one place to go.'

'Where?'

'Charlotte Crane's house.'

*

Bill huffed as the chair he was strapped to was kicked over. His knees banged on the compacted ground and the dirt scratched his cheeks.

It didn't seem real anymore. He sucked in deep breaths and tried to tell himself that he was still alive, to be strong, to get through this for Tom's sake.

It was hard though. He put his forehead to the ground. *Kill me*, he thought, almost involuntarily, *make it end and let me join Tom. No more pain*. He had no information to give them apart from some names and his own theory.

It was the pain they enjoyed, the fear, the power they had over him.

He fought against the bindings, but it was no use. He lay there, staring straight ahead, wanting it to end. *Do it*, he thought again. *Kill me*.

Trudy grabbed his hair as Sean pulled the chair upright again. They were both panting. Part-exertion, part-excitement.

'It's time for me to go,' Sean said. 'I need to rest for tomorrow. You stay with him.'

'Are you sure I shouldn't come to court?'

'No. Divide and conquer is how they would win, because we'd trip up somewhere. Me on my own, I can't do that. Just keep him alive in case Dan needs proof of it.'

'Just keep me up to date.'

'Yeah, you too. Let me know if he tells you more. I need to be prepared.'

Trudy nodded but didn't reply. Her focus was entirely on Bill.

As Sean went up the stairs and out of the cottage for another walk along the towpath and a taxi ride, Trudy stepped closer. 'Now you're going to talk.'

'How many times? I've told you everything.' Blood drooled from his mouth.

Trudy slapped him, making his cheek sting.

'Why are you doing this?'

'TELL ME WHAT YOU KNOW!'

'I've told you everything.'

'So tomorrow, Dan Grant can only throw a few names at Sean, nothing more? He can only repeat Peter's accusations?'

He nodded and let his head hang down. His lip trembled.

Trudy punched him in the ribs, making him cry out.

'Just let me go. Please.'

Trudy rolled her eyes. 'You've forgotten to say, "I won't tell anyone." And that's because we both know that it isn't true.'

Bill closed his eyes and took some deep breaths as he tried to make the pain go away, but it made it worse, his ribs sending out sharp jabs. He let out a sob. They say fight or flight, but he had nothing left for either. 'Just tell me why.'

Trudy leaned in and whispered, 'Now for the deep psychological discussion. I love this part. This is where I break down and tell you how he makes me do it. How I'm a victim too. Big bad Sean, the sicko.'

'I didn't mean that.'

'Oh, you did.' She kneed him in the side, and when Bill arched his back in pain, Trudy gritted her teeth. 'You think it's got easier because it's just me here, that I'm the soft one?' She scoffed. 'Bullshit. You want answers? I'll give you answers. I like it. No, it's more than that. I love it, because I've got the power. Little Trudy, for once I get what I want.'

'You think? He's making you do this, can't you see?'

Trudy sat back on the floor and leaned against the wall by the stairs. Bill had to squint to see her, the light still trained on him.

'You think you've got all the answers, old man, that I'm the weak one here?' She shook her head. 'You've got it so wrong. Can't you see that I brought him here, knowing how he likes the rough stuff? Yes, he's like a growling dog, but I'm holding the lead. He daren't leave me because he knows how much I know, and I know it all.'

'That makes you sound trapped.'

'No, *he's* trapped. I could leave anytime, except he doesn't realise that. I've got all the power.'

'And you like this?'

Trudy grinned, the gleam in her eyes obvious, despite the glare from the lamp. 'I love it, old man.'

'You sick bitch.'

Trudy laughed. It echoed round the cellar. 'Don't make me love it more. This is it. Don't you get it? The fun we've had, with all these people hiding away in their lives. What's the new term? Basic bitches? That's it. That's what they are. I saw them growing up, all so ordinary, wanting the job and the man and the kids and the oh-so-boring suburbia. Makes me sick. All so fucking basic.'

'I don't see that.' He spat some blood on to the floor. 'What do you have, really, that's more? Stuck here, in Highford, with your man, standing by his side. Who did you say was holding the lead? Who's the basic bitch?'

Trudy scrambled towards him and gripped him around the jaw.

He twisted out of it. 'What are you scared of?'

'Me? I'm not scared of anything, and that's what you don't understand.'

'Why am I still alive then?'

Trudy didn't respond.

'It's not about me being a hostage. Sean could make the threat to Dan whether I'm alive or dead, because it's not as if you're going to let me go if Dan does as he asks. You know I'm right. You've killed the others. Why not me? Because it's the end, and you know it. All you've got left is your legacy, whatever you think that is. You won't have each other so you want people to know what you've done. If you kill me but they still catch you, what have you got? Keep me alive and I can tell the story of how you really are. You're worried about being labelled the little woman, the victim of his manipulation. Not if I'm around to tell the story.'

Trudy gripped his jaw again. 'Or perhaps I just enjoy the torture, because when they're dead, I feel used up. I feel empty.' She laughed and pushed him away. 'Yeah, the irony of it. And do you know what's another irony? Go on, guess.'

'I'm not playing your game.'

'I'll tell you anyway. Sean has to go to court tomorrow, so he'll have an alibi, a good one. You'll die in the morning and he'll be in the clear. Do you know where he is now?'

Bill didn't answer.

'He's gone to a hotel close to the courtroom, where they'll track his credit card, and he'll buy a film too, just to give him a time stamp. And the lobby will have CCTV that will catch him when he leaves in the morning, after his hearty breakfast in front of witnesses.'

Bill tried to swallow down his fear, determined not to let it show. 'Where's the irony?'

'You came after Sean, to prop up Peter's story, but now you'll guarantee his freedom, because Dan Grant will do as he asks.'

'What about you?'

'It's Sean they want, not me. We won't let them prise our stories apart. No one knows you're here, or else the police would be all over this place. You're alive because *I* choose it, and the end will come when I choose it. Tell me, are you religious?'

'Why?'

'Just that if you are, you'll see your loved ones again pretty soon. Some solace. If you're not, well—' and she laughed. 'This is it.'

Bill closed his eyes. Some part of him wanted that to be true.

Sixty-two

Dan knocked on the door and stepped back. 'We should have called ahead.'

'What if he'd said no?' Jayne said. 'At least this way, we get to ask the questions and see his response.'

They'd found the newspaper reports from when Charlotte Crane went missing to find out which part of Highford she lived in, and a few minutes asking passing locals had got them her address. Dan had no idea what reception he'd get but Jayne was right, and it felt like they were keeping the case alive.

The house was a barn conversion, high and long, dominated by a window where the large barn doors had once been, with a view over a field with cows and bordered by drystone walls. The main door was solid wood but new, an attempt to blend with the style of the building.

Dan squinted as the door opened. There was a man in front of him, early fifties, small and squat, his grey hair swept into a side parting, his stomach protruding against a v-neck jumper.

'Michael Crane? I'm Dan Grant, and this is Jayne Brett, an investigator. I'm a lawyer defending a murder case and I think it might be connected to your wife's disappearance.'

For a moment, Dan thought the man was going to slam the door in his face. His jaw clenched and his fingers tightened on the doorframe. Then he stepped aside. 'Come in.'

Dan and Jayne exchanged glances before making their way inside.

As they stepped into the living room, Michael folded his arms and said, 'I know who you are.' Before Dan could respond, he added, 'I'm a reporter. I don't do the court stuff, but I cover local news, so your name comes up sometimes.'

Dan looked around the room. He couldn't see any pictures of Charlotte.

Michael must have guessed what he was thinking, because he said, 'There were no photographs of Charlotte on the wall before she went missing. I'm not going to turn my home into a tribute.'

Dan was surprised by his hostility. 'I'm sorry if my questions are difficult for you, but it's important.'

'I don't need the fake sympathy. You're not here to tell me how sorry you are. You want information from me but let me ask you a question first. Why do you think Charlotte's disappearance could be linked to one of your cases?'

'You've heard of Sean Martin?'

He laughed, but it was bitter. 'This is a joke, right? Your firm represented him. I know all about Sean Martin. I wrote about him when he was first convicted, and the newspaper sales were so good that the boss asked me to keep on writing about him, even after he was freed.'

'What did you write?'

'About how sick he was, a cold and calculated liar, and when he was acquitted I wrote how nothing had changed my mind. I had to stop though, because I got a letter from your firm. He threatened to sue the paper, said that we'd libelled him, but we hadn't. He's never been proved to be innocent, just not guilty, but the owner backed down and apologised. We agreed to run a story on him that was more favourable, and he was happy with that. You can guess that I wasn't.' He looked confused. 'Why are you asking about Sean Martin?'

'My client is accusing him of murder, of a few murders, in fact, and we are wondering if he might have been involved in your wife's disappearance.'

Michael didn't say anything for a few seconds, just stared at Dan and then Jayne. 'Are you serious?'

'I wouldn't come to your home and joke about this. Did Charlotte know Sean?'

He scoffed and shook his head. 'Sean Martin? Yeah, that would be about right.'

'I'm sorry, I don't understand.'

Michael's tone was angrier when he said, 'Charlotte was having an affair. I found out about it before she went missing, but I never knew who with. She was always on her phone, messaging constantly, and then she stopped coming to bed as early. One night, she was up later than normal but I couldn't hear the television going, so I went downstairs, to check whether she'd fallen asleep on the sofa, and I caught her.'

'Caught her?'

'Come on, what do you think I mean? She had her hand between her legs like some frustrated teenager, staring at her phone but too much in the moment to know I was there.'

'How long ago was this?'

'About a month before she went missing. You can guess what the police thought, that I'd killed her in a jealous rage. I can tell you I didn't, because I was out with my friends when she disappeared. And she was meant to be with *her* friends, except she slipped away. To meet whoever she was messaging, I'll bet.'

'Did you ever find out who it was?'

'No. We shouted and screamed at each other, but she wouldn't say. Told me that it was just a stupid flirtation, nothing more, and none of my business. Nearly twenty years of marriage and she reckoned it wasn't my business. She promised me she'd stop but, well, perhaps not. There might have been more than one, for all I know.'

'And the police know all this?'

'Of course they do, except they didn't know who she was messaging because her phone wasn't recovered.'

'What about billing?'

'Come on, what decade do you live in? Who uses texts these days? It's all messaging apps, everything untraceable.' His eyes narrowed. 'Are you saying she is missing because of Sean Martin? Really?'

'Did she know him?'

'Don't you think I'd have something to say if she did? But it would have been just like her to pick Sean Martin out of spite.'

'What do you mean?'

'We'd grown apart, but she felt trapped, by this,' he said, waving his hand towards the walls. 'Resented me for giving her a nice home. Can you credit it? But she knew I hate Sean Martin for the way he pontificates, the new crusader, so how sweet would her revenge be to become his mistress?' He looked to Jayne. 'That's how you women are, aren't you? Vengeful?'

Jayne wanted to say that she hoped Charlotte had just found someone better, but she ignored the comment and instead asked, 'How did she go missing?'

'She was at the Hare and Hounds, down by the canal, just outside of town. Her friends said that she disappeared just after midnight. One minute she was there, and the next she wasn't.'

Dan thanked him, Jayne too.

'Don't thank me. Just get that bastard.'

Sixty-three

Murdoch checked her watch as she rushed through the station. It said 7.30 a.m. There might not be enough time.

The message had come in the middle of the night from Dan, the buzz of her phone waking her. *Charlotte Crane and Sean Martin might be connected. Possible affair. Look for his boat. Called Somewhere Quiet.*

It had jolted her awake and ruined her sleep, her mind turning over what she knew about the case. By the time she'd set off for work, her brain was fogged through lack of sleep and she didn't know where to start looking.

The answer came to her as she drove into the station, because her route took her past the Hare and Hounds, from where Charlotte Crane had disappeared on New Year's Eve.

Was Charlotte the key and no one had realised?

The squad room was nearly empty, only DC Richards there, making a drink using the kettle in the corner, staring into a mug, as if deciding whether he needed to wash it first.

He looked up as she burst in. She pointed at him and barked, 'You're coming with me.'

She rushed out of the room, Richards trotting to keep up.

'Where are we going?'

'Looking for Sean Martin.'

'Where?'

'No, not where, but when. New Year's Eve. Do you remember all the footage we seized in Charlotte Crane's case?'

'The woman who went missing the same night as Lizzie Barnsley?'

'That's her. We didn't really go through it properly because we got swamped with Lizzie's murder, but now I think we should.'

They turned into a room further along, more like a dark cupboard with a couple of computers and a large television. She reached for a box on a shelf. 'This is all the CCTV we recovered from around the Hare and Hounds. We were looking for Charlotte.'

He looked in the box. There were discs and USB sticks, an assorted jumble of footage seized in all the different formats used by security systems. 'Yes, I remember. There were two of us looking.'

'Go through it again, except this time you're not looking for Charlotte. You're looking for Sean Martin. Or, rather, his boat.'

'What's it called?'

'*Somewhere Quiet.*'

'And if I find it?'

'Get the footage over to me. I'll be at the Crown Court in Langton.'

He peered into the box again. 'I'm on it.'

She slapped him on the shoulder. 'Good man,' she said, before heading for the exit.

If Sean Martin was going to be found out, she wanted to be there to see it.

Sixty-four

Dan was sitting on a bench, watching the media scrum outside the courthouse. The evidence from the day before had filtered out and brought the cameras. Sean Martin, villain of the tabloids but darling of the broadsheets, always made good copy.

He checked his watch. Nine thirty. There was still no news about Pat and every day that passed made the outcome more obvious: that Pat was dead. And the day was only ever going to get worse. Putting off going inside delayed the inevitable mauling from the judge and the guilty verdict for Peter. And in the meantime Pat stayed missing and Sean Martin stayed free.

He reconsidered that. He didn't care about the judge. He cared about Pat Molloy and about all that Sean Martin had done, and Trudy too. He'd sought to expose Sean Martin, for Pat's sake. If he couldn't do that, he'd be at risk himself. Pat was missing. Would he be next? Or those close to him?

Someone sat next to him on the bench. Dan didn't pay any attention at first, but whoever it was shuffled along so that he was closer and said, 'This would make an interesting photograph for the papers, us two sitting here.'

It was Sean Martin, dressed in a suit, looking groomed and poised.

Dan clenched his fists. 'What the hell are you doing?'

'Just letting you know that I've arrived. I'm guessing that was what you were hoping for: a no-show from me and crazy Peter getting his way.'

Dan swallowed back his anger. He wanted to grip him, hit him, demand to know where Pat was, call him a murdering bastard, but he couldn't. The press would love that, the defence lawyer attacking a witness before the court hearing.

Instead, he stood up and made as if to walk towards the courthouse.

Sean sat back and spread his arms along the back of the bench. 'Have you seen Bill lately?'

Dan was confused. 'What do you mean?'

'Just that. I understand that he started all this nonsense,' he said, and gave a dismissive wave of his hand.

Dan felt his pulse quicken, a flush rise in his cheeks. 'Have you harmed him?'

Sean smirked. 'Why would I do that? But I thought he'd want to be here, to see the climax of his work.'

Dan had to force himself not to react. His fingers were white with tension around the handle of his court bag. 'Why are you telling me this?'

'I'm not telling you anything. You lawyers base your work on evidence, I know that, so do you really think I would incriminate myself here? To you? But life isn't about proof. It's about suspicions and doubts and fears, and until Bill arrives here this morning, you don't know if he's in danger or not. Just your doubts eating into you.'

'What do you want?'

Sean's expression darkened. 'You're going to do as I say.' He pointed towards the courthouse. 'Once that hearing starts, you're going to duck out of asking any questions. You could tell Peter not to pursue it anymore, but he might be suspicious. No, it's better if you flounder and just do a bad job of it. No tough questions. No trying to catch me out. After all, who's going to care? Peter's a killer, after all.'

'And if I don't?'

'Bill may never get to see the end of the case.'

'Where is he, you bastard?'

'Who said I know? Proof, Mr Grant, proof. You have none, only those seeds of doubt I've just planted. I know where he isn't, and that's here. What if something happens to him? Just think how you'll feel. You could tell the police but, really, what can they do? I'm just speaking in the abstract here and you're on a vendetta. Your evidence is tainted, it wouldn't count, would be labelled as the ramblings of a lawyer pining for his boss. But in here,' he paused and patted his chest with his hand, 'you'll know, and this system you work in, all based on evidence and proof, will let you down.'

'How do I know you're telling the truth?'

Sean rolled his eyes. 'You don't. That's the point.'

Dan stormed towards the courthouse, his shoulders hunched and angry. He scoured the crowd for Bill, hoping that Sean was just trying to unsettle him, but he knew it was more than that.

Bill wasn't here.

A reporter spotted him, the one who'd accosted him in the corridor earlier in the case. She moved away from the media pack and made as if she was going for a cigarette but instead circled towards him. When she got close, he growled, 'Not now.'

'You could give me a pithy response, the first soundbite to save me bothering you afterwards.'

Dan ignored her and kept on walking.

'I've got friends in television,' she shouted after him. 'They can do one of those true crime documentaries and you could be the star, the lawyer who uncovered it all. Do one of those off-camera pieces, you in your office.'

He stopped and turned, his hand out, his jaw set, ready to take his frustration out on her, but he closed his eyes and stopped himself. He took a deep breath. 'I'm sorry. Off the record, it's just not a good time.'

She reached into her pocket and passed him a business card. 'If you change your mind, call me.'

He looked down at her card, Alison Savage, and tapped it on his knuckles. He put it into his pocket without a word.

As she went back to the media pack, he noticed Murdoch walking across the square. She looked smarter than normal. The hairspray she'd applied gleamed in the sun and the suit had that stiff look that said it was a new one. It looked like she was getting ready for a speech on the courthouse steps.

As she got closer, she nodded a greeting.

Dan looked back along the street and could see Sean watching him, his phone in his hand. She spoke first.

'Inside,' she whispered as she passed, sensing his discomfort. 'Too many cameras here. Remember, we're supposed to be on opposite sides today.'

There were some agitated shouts from the press.

'Here's the hero,' she said, and they watched as Sean Martin strode towards the courthouse, his head back, smiling for the cameras. He was confident, beaming. Dan felt nauseous.

Dan ignored her and strode towards the security barrier. Once he was through, he turned and nodded, to indicate he wanted to talk, before heading into the courtroom.

He slumped onto the seat and put his head back. The peace of the courtroom washed over him, even though he knew it would change later. Sean's threat filled his head. He didn't know where Bill was.

Then another fear occurred to him, making him sit bolt upright. Jayne was late too. She'd dropped him off at his apartment and made her way home. She should have been here by now.

Before he could make a call, the courtroom door creaked open and in walked Murdoch.

She made her way into the well of the court. 'I've put Sean in one of the interview rooms so I can take a statement from him. Can you talk?'

'Yes. Just not in front of anyone else. We're both after the same man.'

'Except I'm pretending I'm on his side, letting him defend his good name against your client's lies.' She sighed and sat down next to Dan. 'It's supposed to be a good day for me. A no-loser. Peter has admitted killing Lizzie. The worst thing that can happen is that he's found guilty of manslaughter. He's not going home today, and her family knows what happened. If Sean Martin is dragged into it as well, it's a big fat bonus.'

'But?'

'We've already got Peter. We always had him. We've always wanted Sean Martin. It will feel like a hollow victory if we don't get him.'

'But you'll keep on investigating, right?'

'Damn right. And I've got this,' and she handed him a brown envelope. 'The women you mentioned when you cross-examined me? Most of them knew Trudy. We spoke to the families last night. Either from her school or people she worked with, or girls she knew as a child. It was all Trudy. She was selecting them.'

'Claire Watkins seemed more involved with Sean than Trudy.'

'That was for Peter, to drag him in.'

'But why would she select them?'

'I don't know. Revenge? She's quiet, but there's some anger in her, you can see that. Look at Rosie. What better way to ruin Karen's life, the life of the woman who'd married her man, than to take away her child?'

'No, Rosie was different. She was just in the wrong place. She went onto his boat, expecting to find him there, and she found something else instead. Whatever she saw made her bolt, and it was enough to make Sean run after her and kill her to silence her. Keep looking. There'll be another missing woman from that day. My guess is that Rosie was murdered because of her teenage curiosity: she jumped onto her stepfather's boat and caught them at it.'

'And there's Charlotte Crane, of course.'

'Charlotte was married to one of Sean's public critics. He threatened to sue her husband. I don't know how he got to know her, but my guess is that he had an affair with her to get back at her husband. More revenge.'

'There's no sign of Trudy today.'

'Of course not,' Dan said. 'Two liars contradict each other and their lies are exposed. He's playing it safe, and it was always going to be him. He's the celebrity after all.' He raised the envelope. 'Thanks for this.'

'Just make sure you pin him down today.'

'And Trudy?'

'We'll get her. Today, it's about Sean.' With that she left the courtroom.

Alone once again, he felt trapped. He should tell Murdoch about Bill, because getting the police involved was the sensible thing to do.

But if Sean and Trudy had Bill, he couldn't stand the thought of triggering Bill's death. If Bill was still alive, that gave him something to play for.

Sixty-five

Bill wondered about the time. The morning had taken an age to arrive as he shivered through the night, the new day visible only as a faint glow at the top of the stairs.

Trudy sat opposite, curled up in her coat and a blanket from the boat, but she wasn't sleeping. She had been awake and alert all night, time marked by the slow tap of her knife on the floor.

She'd left him alone for a few minutes, and he'd pulled at the ropes, but they were too tight. His arms felt numb from being for so long in the same position.

There were footsteps on the stairs. Was it Sean coming back? No, the footsteps were too light. It was Trudy, her footsteps slow and faltering. Bill lifted his head. Trudy was carrying something heavy and it made her tentative on the stairs.

Bill tried to shrink away, but the chair stopped him from moving. As Trudy got closer, she lifted whatever she was carrying and threw it towards him.

The cold water hit him like a deluge. He gasped, his body in shock. It was dirty and rank, dredged up from the canal. Trudy threw the bucket on the floor. Bill shivered and moaned. The cuts on his chest and legs stung.

'I thought you needed a shower.'

Bill closed his eyes. He couldn't play these games anymore. 'Stop, please. I can't take it.'

Trudy knelt in front of him. 'You're desperate to get away, even die, but if I passed you a knife I bet you wouldn't kill yourself.' She reached into her waistband and took out her knife. She gripped Bill by the throat and pushed his head back, pressing the knife against the flesh just below his chin. 'I could do it now. Slice your jugular. This will be the last thing you'll see. This cellar. My face. My pleasure. Is that what you want?'

Bill didn't respond.

'I can, if you ask. Just nod, that's all you have to do.'

Bill glanced down towards Trudy's arm, the bulging vein that betrayed how firmly she was gripping the knife. The gleam in her eye told Bill that she was desperate to slit his throat, but something was preventing her.

It was fear. She was losing control of the situation. She'd lost it once before, when Sean went to prison for Rosie's murder.

At least he was still alive.

'No?' Trudy said, as she pulled the knife away. She tapped it on Bill's cheek. The sharp tip made small pricks in his skin not far from his eye, bringing small dots of blood to the surface, but he didn't flinch. He wouldn't give her that much.

As Trudy stepped away, it felt like he'd gained some ground. For as long as he was alive, he was going to beat this. He'd felt old before, not much heart for the fight left in him, but his anger was taking over, giving him energy. He couldn't let them win.

Then something else occurred to him. If this was about not letting them win, there was only one way to do it: work out how to get away.

*

Jayne checked her watch as she drove too fast on the motorway. She'd overslept, her electricity card was out of money, so her radio alarm hadn't gone off. She'd had to rush to the shop to top up the card so that she could have a shower and iron her shirt, a morning in court demanding that she wear better clothes than her usual gear of jeans and ex-army combat jacket.

Dan would already be there, dressed in his finery, and she was missing whatever was going on. She was frustrated, but angry with herself too. There were too many of these cock-ups in her life.

At least the motorway was quiet, the rush hour traffic long gone. Her gaze wandered to the views around her. It was just fields on either side. There was cattle in some, whereas others were just the long spread of the valley before the spine of heather-topped hills to the north.

Something attracted her attention, but it was gone before she could register what it was. A twinge of familiarity. Her rear-view mirror was vibrating too much to allow her a clear view.

There was a junction ahead. She turned off and followed the roundabout to go back along the motorway on the other side. It would make her even later, but she couldn't shake off the feeling that it was important.

She scoured the fields as she drove, waiting to be grabbed by the same feeling of recognition.

There it was. She banged her steering wheel and shouted, 'Yes!'

A glint of water, a gentle ribbon that ran alongside the motorway until it curved underneath, and next to it, crumbling and old, was a cottage. It was the same cottage that appeared in the photographs in Sean's book.

She turned off at the next junction and took a road that disappeared into the countryside, trying to work her way back towards the cottage, but the route she was on curved away from the canal. Hawthorne hedges lined both sides of the view as she raced towards a village in the distance and what looked like a road heading back towards the water.

The canal went out of view as she kept driving, slowing down as she reached the centre of the village. She turned in a direction that she thought would take her down a hill. She caught glints of sunlight on the water as she peered through the gaps between houses, the countryside turning into an impossible maze.

Then she saw it.

She slammed on her brakes and reversed quickly to a narrow lane that seemed to head in the right direction. As she drove down it, fast, she dreaded another car coming in the opposite direction, but the lane was clear. Looking through a break in the hedgerow and over a gate, she saw the cottage at the end of a long, rutted field.

Jayne braked hard and skidded, then backed into a small space in front of the gate, jumping out as soon as the car stopped.

The sun was shining in her face. She shielded her eyes as she peered towards the cottage.

It was definitely the same one that was in the book. She realised why the pictures had bothered her at the time. She'd seen this cottage so many times as she'd driven along the motorway but had paid it no heed. It was just another piece of a slowly decaying past. She remembered her theory about Sean and his superiority complex: that he'd wanted to taunt his readers as he'd taunted Pat. It was obvious from the pictures Sean and

Trudy had come here regularly. The cottage was important to them.

Then she saw a dark shape further along the canal, under the motorway bridge, almost hidden from view.

She remembered her camera. She went back to the glove compartment and dug it out. She zoomed in on whatever was there.

She lowered her camera. 'Shit.'

She was right. It was a boat, and judging by the colours, it was Sean's boat. She was too far away to read the lettering, but the shapes of the words, two of them, looked right.

She zoomed in further. The image in the viewfinder became shaky as she kept zooming in as much as the camera allowed her, the focus pixelating from blurred to sharp before settling down. Once it did, she saw that her suspicions were confirmed, the name on the boat was *Somewhere Quiet*.

She clambered over the gate. There was no time to waste.

Sixty-six

Francesca was staring at the witness statement given by Sean Martin to Murdoch moments before. Dan had read it through a couple of times. It was just a series of denials and bland comments about how outraged he felt.

He threw it on to the table in front of him. 'Is he definitely giving evidence?'

She looked up. 'He wants to.' She sat back and folded her arms. 'Tell me, Dan. Do you believe what your client said?'

'I do.'

'I hope this goes the right way then.'

Dan didn't reply.

'You're quiet today. I expected you to be a bit more gung-ho.'

Before Dan could say anything, the door leading to the judge's corridor opened and he entered, shuffling towards his chair. Everyone rose to their feet.

Dan looked to the back of the court as the usher went to collect the jurors. All of Lizzie's friends and relatives were in the courtroom, some of their anger dissipated, but there was also a new set of spectators. From the anguished looks on their faces, Dan guessed they were relatives of Sean's victims, desperate to hear their own truths. Murdoch was in the centre of all of them, staring ahead.

Peter was in the glass box, looking down, waiting for the hearing to start.

Dan turned away. He had no idea how the case was going to turn out, but he knew it wouldn't have a happy ending. Peter had admitted to killing Lizzie and the real story behind it had come out, so his conscience should be clear, except Bill's life was part of the picture now. He couldn't do both what Peter wanted and what Sean demanded. One of them had to be sacrificed.

There was a delay as the jurors entered, solemn and quiet. Once in place, the judge looked to Francesca and said, 'We heard the evidence yesterday of the defendant. Do you intend to call any evidence in rebuttal?'

'I do, My Lord. I call Sean Martin.'

There were murmurs around the courtroom.

As Sean strode towards the witness box, confidence oozing from him, the reporters making frantic notes, Dan's phone buzzed.

He sneaked it out of his pocket and put it on to the table in front of him. The judge was distracted by Sean's arrival, so he was able to check the message. It was from Jayne.

At a cottage by the motorway. Derelict. Sean's boat here. It appears in pictures in the book. Suspect. Going for a look.

His tickles of nerves turned into tremors of excitement. A development. He glanced towards the judge, to make sure he wasn't watching him, and texted back, *Bill might be there. Use the messaging service. Can get on the laptop. Sean Martin in the witness box. I need updates. Urgent. But be careful.*

The usher passed Sean Martin the New Testament so that he could swear the oath, but the judge interrupted him.

'Mr Martin, before we start, I must make it clear that you are under no obligation to be here. The defendant in this case, Peter Box, has made various allegations against you. I will be blunt. You are accused of engaging in very serious criminal behaviour. By coming to court today, you open the possibility of criminal proceedings being brought against you. You are not obliged to come here and potentially incriminate yourself. If you leave, it is no admission of guilt. What would you like to do?'

Sean looked around the courtroom, half a smile on his lips, catching the eye of every spectator, resting on Dan as he replied, 'My life has been ruined by one false allegation already, even though I stand exonerated of that awful crime. I feel honour-bound to speak. I owe it to all the people who campaigned on my behalf to further clear my name.'

Dan looked away, trying to keep his anger in check. He had to remain calm.

Sean swore the oath.

Francesca cleared her throat before she asked her first question, and she started with the most obvious one, the question that cleared the air. 'Sean Martin, have you ever deliberately taken another person's life?'

He looked towards the judge and spoke in a clear voice. 'I have not.'

'Do you know the defendant, Peter Box?'

Sean looked towards the dock. 'Yes, I knew him, but it was years ago. I can't remember the last time I spoke to him. He used to go out with my wife's sister. She was my girlfriend then, but we're married now.'

'Trudy?'

'Yes, that's right. She stood by me when I was in prison. Rosie's mother didn't. Rosie was the poor girl who was murdered, which caused me to go to prison wrongfully. But I don't blame Karen; she was fed the wrong information. Trudy knew what I was really like.'

'Did you spend much time with Peter?'

'Some, but he wasn't my friend. Trudy and her sister were close, so it was natural that we'd sometimes hang out as a foursome. Once they split up, I didn't see him again.'

'What did you think of Peter?'

Dan rose to his feet. 'My Lord, is the witness's opinion of the defendant relevant?'

The judge glared at him. 'Mr Grant, given the severity of the allegations made by your client, the witness's opinion of your client's character might have some weight.' He nodded at Sean as Dan sat down. 'Carry on, Mr Martin.'

Sean eyed Dan with curiosity before he said, 'I thought of him like a younger brother, because we were nearly that, brothers-in-law, but he was a strange one. One of those introverts who you feel you never really get to know. I found him a bit creepy, to be honest, but harmless enough. At least I thought he was.'

'But reliable, or truthful?'

'Not particularly.'

Francesca feigned surprise. 'Can you give the court some examples?'

'Just boasting, trying to make himself sound important. It was only natural, I suppose, because I was older, more experienced, so had more to tell. I think Peter felt he had to try to keep up. For instance, if I mentioned a festival I'd been to, he'd start talking about some great party he'd gone to and it was almost as if his had to be better, or bigger.'

'Going back to New Year's Eve, the night that culminated in the murder of Elizabeth Barnsley. Where did you spend it?'

Sean rolled his eyes making a show of it. 'It's a few months ago now.'

'Do you think you might have been out on your boat?'

'Well, it's more of a joint boat really, not mine alone.'

Dan's eyes narrowed. Sean's first mistake. He was avoiding the question.

Francesca had noticed it too, because she straightened and gripped the lapel of her gown. 'Whoever owns it, were you out on the boat that you sometimes use together?'

Sean shot a glance towards Dan. 'No, not that night. Like I told Mr Grant, when he asked me, I spent it indoors, watching television. Trudy and I shared a bottle of wine. I wouldn't have gone out that night. Too many drunks by the canals,' and he pointed towards Peter. 'And other undesirables.'

The judge held up his hand as there was a noise of someone moving along the public gallery. Dan looked back and saw it was Murdoch. She was holding up her phone and heading for the doors. She caught Dan watching as she went outside, nodding at him as the door closed.

Francesca continued, 'Referring to the other allegations made against you, did you know Claire Watkins?'

He straightened and gave an earnest nod in reply. 'Yes, I did. She lived on the next street to where Trudy lived. Peter liked her, if I remember, but she ran away or went missing. A tragedy, but young people can do strange things.'

'When you say Peter liked her, what do you mean?'

'Fancied her. Desired her.'

'But he was going out with your partner's sister?'

'He wasn't very good at concealing it. He'd get all flustered when I spoke to her, blushing and stuff.'

'Did you have any kind of a sexual relationship with Claire?'

'Definitely not.'

'Did you play any role in her disappearance?'

'Not at all.'

'And did you have any part in the murder of Rosie Smith?'

He sneered at that and shook his head. 'The last trial I had resolved that issue. I was cleared. Not guilty.'

'How do you feel about the allegations against you?'

'Angry. Bewildered. Confused. Outraged. I've rebuilt my life, with Trudy, and I don't know why Peter's saying this. Some bitterness at how my life has turned out perhaps, or disappointment with his own? All I know is that I didn't do what I'm alleged to have done, and there won't be any proof of it. That's why we're here, isn't it, in a courtroom? To find proof?'

He looked at Dan when he said it, and Dan recognised the taunt in his eyes.

Francesca bowed to the judge and sat down.

The judge raised an eyebrow. 'Mr Grant. Do you have any questions?'

Dan stood. He was nervous, confused, not knowing where to go with his questions. His laptop was open. He glanced down, to look for any kind of message from Jayne, but there was nothing.

He thought of Bill and whether what he was about to do would end up with his murder. He couldn't cope with that on his conscience.

As he looked at Sean Martin, with his arrogance and his cold sneer, the way he had acted about Bill outside, Dan decided what to do.

Sean might have underestimated him. If he had inherited one thing from his father, it was the fondness for a fight. The more he was told he couldn't have it, the more he needed it.

He was going after Sean Martin, whatever the cost.

Sixty-seven

Jayne stayed low as she crossed the field. There was no one around, an area of rural emptiness spoiled by pylons and the noise of motorway traffic.

She slowed as she got closer to the cottage, aware of the thump of her footsteps. She flattened herself against the cottage wall, her back against moss, and the uneven pattern of the stones cold against her palms. The place was crumbling from the roof down, with most of the slates missing. No one could be living here. The windows on the side of the house overlooking the field were protected by wooden boards. The ground around it was more uneven, pocked with small mounds and hollows.

She took some deep breaths before peering around the corner.

Sean's boat was fifty metres away, in the shadow of a bridge. The engine was quiet. A rope tethered it to the bank. It looked idyllic, peaceful.

She began to move towards the boat, then shrank back. The windows to the cottage on the canal side were open holes, the glass and frames gone years before. If there was anyone inside, they'd see her straightaway. The best way to the boat was along the field side of the house, where the windows were still blocked off.

She ducked down as she moved along the cottage and then took a long curve towards the boat. As she got close, she saw that the curtains were closed. There were no other boats visible. It was a perfect spot to attack someone. Isolated, but with the motorway to drown out any noises.

She pulled out her phone and took a couple of pictures of the boat and cottage before sending them to Dan, watching her screen as the upload bar crawled across. Once they were sent, she knelt down to listen at one of the windows. It was silent inside.

That wasn't enough of a reassurance.

She looked around before stepping on to the boat. Her chest fluttered with nerves as her weight made it bob on the water. She was tense, ready to run. There was no curtain over the door that led into the cabin, but as she peered in she noticed a broken glass panel. Something had happened there.

She checked the door. It was unlocked.

One last look around and then she went inside.

The interior was dimly lit, with a ramshackle feel that showed it was used for short days out rather than full-time living in. It smelled of bleach, which surprised her because it looked worn and shabby. Two chairs filled the living space, a cheap table behind, the kitchen area cramped. There was a corridor beyond that, tight and narrow that led to a room at the back.

Her instinct told her to keep on looking, that this location was somehow important. The boat was hidden away under a bridge. Sean will be at court but what about Trudy? She hadn't worked out what to do if she appeared, but Jayne was younger and fitter and fancied her odds in a foot-race across the fields. If there was nothing to see in the boat, the cottage had to be the connection.

She rushed through the boat, worried about getting trapped, her nerves shortening her breath.

Her shoes trod on something sticky. She looked down. Dark red, partly congealed, but unmistakably blood. Large splashes of it along the floor, along with a pooled area where she had stood.

Get out, she told herself and dashed for the door. The fresh air of the canal bank came like a relief.

She sprinted, to get herself out of sight of the cottage entrance. It was possible that someone saw her getting off the boat, but that didn't mean she had to make her presence obvious. The sight of the blood had turned her stomach, but it meant someone was in danger. She couldn't back away now.

She crept to the front of the cottage, staying low, listening out for the sound of someone there, ducking below the first window, and inching to the doorway. She couldn't hear anyone. She peered inside.

The cottage showed some signs of its former life, with remnants of times gone by hanging from the walls. Kitchen cupboards, old electrical cables, peeling wallpaper.

She stopped in the doorway. Further in, there was just darkness. Whoever was in there could be watching her, hidden in one of the rooms, waiting. Her common sense screamed at her to back away, but her desire for answers drove her on.

Jayne wiped her palms on her shirt and stepped inside. She wrinkled her nose. It smelled damp. There was mould at the top of the walls. Her feet crunched on the dirt.

A creature scurried nearby but still she crept forward, her mouth dry, every nerve in her body alive, the sunlight lost.

Then there was a noise.

It was hard to make it out at first. She thought it was just another animal moving but as she got further along the hallway she realised that it wasn't an animal, but people talking.

Someone was there. She had to keep going, further into the darkness.

*

Murdoch paced outside the courtroom, her gaze fixed on the external doors and the street beyond.

She'd received a message from DC Richards a few minutes earlier. He had something she needed to see. She was aware that the case was moving apace in the courtroom and if he had evidence Dan needed, it had to arrive soon.

She was cursing softly to herself when she spotted him, jogging towards the courthouse, a small rucksack clutched to his chest. There was a short delay as he was detained at the security barrier but, once through, he raised the rucksack. 'I've got it.'

'Let's find a room.'

He was out of breath as they went into one of the small interview rooms, where she'd sat with Sean Martin earlier that day to take his statement.

'What has he said about New Year's Eve?' Richards said.

'He stayed in, watching TV with a bottle of wine.'

'With Trudy?'

'So he said.'

Richards smiled and opened the bag, reaching in to pull out a laptop. Murdoch was tapping the table with impatience as it booted up. 'We've no time for drama. Make it quick.'

He pulled a small USB stick from his pocket. 'I've put it all on here.'

He inserted the stick and navigated the laptop until he found the file. A video started to play, dark grainy footage of the rear of a building, the yard lined by razor wire. The canal was beyond the wall, a gleaming dark strip.

'It's from a tool hire firm, around a hundred yards from the Hare and Hounds, where Charlotte Crane went missing from.'

Murdoch leaned forward. 'Sean would reach this place before he got to where Lizzie was found.'

'Exactly, and look at the time,' and he tapped the screen where the clock was showing. 'Twenty minutes past midnight. I called the firm. The clock on the CCTV is accurate.'

Murdoch's mouth went dry as she watched. The clock seemed to crawl forward as the screen stayed static apart from the flutter of moths caught by the glare of the security lights.

Then she saw it.

Richards pressed the *pause* button. 'There, look.'

Murdoch leaned closer to the screen and she grinned. 'You little bastard, I've got you.'

*

Dan had to remain calm. Sean Martin had his hands held in front of him, his expression serene, unconcerned.

Dan connected his laptop to the Clickshare software used by the court. It allowed him to project whatever was on his laptop on to the large television screens on the walls of the courtroom.

'Mr Martin, I'm going to play you some CCTV footage. If you'll look towards one of the screens.'

The CCTV from New Year's Eve flashed up on to the screen.

He'd put in the disk from the camera showing the pub car park where Lizzie was assaulted. The tension in the courtroom was palpable as everyone watched once more the events that led to Lizzie's murder. Lizzie and Liam arguing. His punch. Lizzie falling backwards to the floor and people intervening, pushing Liam back and keeping him away. As before, Lizzie got up and rushed from the car park, into the shadows of the buildings close to the canal.

'Can you see the time on the footage, Mr Martin?'

'Yes, I can, but I wasn't there, so what has this to do with me?'

'I ask the questions, not you,' Dan snapped. 'Twelve twenty-three and thirty seconds when Lizzie leaves the car park. Do you agree?'

'Yes, fine.'

Dan ejected the disk and put in another one, this time the disc showing the canal footage. It was mainly in darkness, apart from the jagged outlines of rooftops and the streetlights from the estate on the other side. He forwarded the footage until he got to the point he wanted.

'Can you see the time on this footage?'

Sean squinted towards the screen. 'Twelve twenty-four, it looks like.'

'In the distance, what do you think that is?'

'The small light on the water?'

'Yes.'

'I don't know, it's too hard to tell.'

'Canal boats use a solo headlight mainly, don't they, like a large torch, shining ahead just enough to show any hazards?'

'Well, yes.'

'Is that your boat?'

'How can anyone tell from that?'

Dan's cheeks flushed. Sean was hedging his bets, not knowing what else the footage would show. 'You sounded more certain about where you were a few minutes ago. You stayed in, you said, were sure of it. Now I'm showing you a boat, you're backing off.'

Sean's gaze darkened. 'Is that a question?'

Dan leaned forward, wanting to get closer to him. His teeth were bared when he said, 'It's not an ordinary night, is it? It's one of the most special nights of the year, but now you're not as sure where you were?'

'Who can be completely sure?'

'So, it's possible that you took your boat out on New Year's Eve?'

'I didn't say that.'

'You're not ruling it out though?'

Sean looked to the screen and pursed his lips, but didn't give an answer.

'Your evidence now,' Dan continued, 'if I'm getting this correctly, is that you're not sure whether you stayed in with Trudy or not, or whether you went out on your boat or not. Is that right?'

Sean faltered. 'I was at home, most likely, with Trudy.'

Dan smiled and nodded. 'Most likely,' he repeated, and pointed to the screen again. 'Twelve twenty-five. Notice how the boat has stopped?'

The judge leaned forwards. 'Save this for a closing address, Mr Grant. I get your point, as well as the fact that we have no evidence that it's the boat linked to the witness.'

Dan slammed his hand on the desk, making the jurors jolt back in their seats. 'We do have evidence, from the defendant himself, Peter Box, who'd tracked the boat from the marina. That's why he was there, waiting.'

The judge's eyes narrowed. For a moment, Dan knew he'd gone too far, but he didn't care. He wanted Sean Martin and he wasn't about to be side-tracked by the judge.

'Of course, Mr Grant,' the judge said, an angry quiver to his voice. 'I meant evidence to corroborate what he says, as you well know. Move on.'

Dan glared at the judge for a few seconds before he nodded his assent and turned back to Sean. *Control yourself*, he told himself, but he knew he was losing that struggle.

'Do you have problems with your memory, Mr Martin?'

'How do you mean?'

'You were quite certain that you knew Claire Watkins when you gave your evidence before.'

Sean left it a few seconds before answering, thinking about his answers. 'Yes, of course, it's not every day that someone who lives nearby goes missing.'

'And you spoke to her when you passed her in the street. Correct?'

'Sometimes.'

'When Peter was there.'

'That's how I knew he liked her, because he'd blush and get all nervy. Not that he'd ever have a chance with her, which must have burned away at him.'

'Your memory of her sounds vivid.'

'My memory of Peter's reaction is vivid.'

'And you knew her by name?'

'Of course.'

Dan floated a copy of the police notebook across to Francesca, whose eyebrows lifted when she read it. He passed two copies to the usher, who handed one to the judge and the other to Sean.

Dan lifted his own copy in the air. 'Please read out what it says on there, Mr Martin.'

Sean reached into his jacket pocket for his glasses, and Dan thought he detected a tremble of his fingers as he put them on to his nose. He flushed as his eyes scanned the handwritten entry.

Dan held up the piece of paper for the benefit of those in the public gallery. Even if he didn't succeed in court, he had to get the press to want to destroy Sean. 'This is from a police officer who spoke to people in the area following Claire's disappearance.'

Francesca leaned across and whispered, 'Are you calling the officer as a witness to confirm this?'

He bent down to hiss back, 'I got it from your witness, DI Murdoch, who accessed the case file. I can call her, if you insist.'

Francesca waved her hand. 'Fine.'

Dan turned back to Sean. 'Would you read it out, please, for the benefit of everyone in the courtroom?'

Sean swallowed. There was a croak to his voice. 'Sean Martin. Lives on a barge but stays frequently at number 12 Houghton Street. Does not know Claire Watkins but has seen the newspaper reports. Said that he didn't speak to many people around there and had never met her.' He looked up. 'That's it.'

He put the paper down.

'Is that what you told the officer?'

'I don't know. It was a long time ago.'

'You seem to be having trouble with your memory today, Mr Martin. I'll make it easier for you. Is what's written down there the truth?'

'It's not accurate, no.'

'I asked you about truth, not accuracy. Is it true?'

A pause, and then, 'No.'

'You told a lie to the police.'

He shrugged. 'The officer must have got it wrong.'

'An officer who has been given the job of speaking to people about Claire Watkins wrote down incorrectly what you told him about Claire Watkins?'

'I can't answer for the officer.'

Dan detected a sheen of his sweat on Sean's forehead. He was rattled but Dan knew he didn't have enough. All he'd done was give the usual collection of jabs and pokes at a witness. At best for Peter's case, Sean was inconsistent and potentially untruthful. That didn't make him a murderer.

His concentration was disturbed by the clatter of the court-room door, and then the murmurs from the gallery as someone made their way into the well of the court.

Dan was distracted. It was Murdoch, who was whispering into Francesca's ear before leaning across the desk to pass something along. A USB stick skidded along the desk.

Dan looked down at it, unsure, before turning to Murdoch, who nodded and pointed at it, her eyes wide.

'Mr Grant?'

When Dan looked up again, the judge was sitting forward, glaring at him.

'Have you any more questions, Mr Grant?'

He straightened and turned back towards Sean. All he could do was keep going.

*

Bill put his head back. 'I need some water.'

Trudy looked towards a bottle on the floor, by the lamp shining directly at him. She picked it up and went over to him. The water fizzed as she opened it. She held it over Bill's mouth, who opened like a baby bird, desperate for the fluid.

Grinning, Trudy poured it over him, bringing a gargled howl from Bill, who tried to lap at the water as it ran down his face.

Trudy threw the bottle over her shoulder. It made an empty rattle as it hit the floor.

Bill let his head hang for a few seconds, just to control his despair. When he looked up again, his resolve had strengthened. 'What if Sean is found out at court? You'll only realise when the police come down the stairs.'

'That isn't going to happen. Sean is too clever for that.'

'He might be looking after himself, selling you out.'

Trudy's eyes flared. She crossed to the other side of the cellar and retrieved the knife from where she'd put it, lying within reach on one of the stone steps. When she returned to Bill, she was angry, going straight for him.

She slashed wildly with the knife, cutting a deep gash across Bill's chest and then back across his cheek. Blood gushed down his face and spread quickly across his shirt, soaking it red.

The pain was immense, white hot, burning.

Bill put his head back and screamed.

*

Dan turned off the Clickshare software that transmitted his laptop screen to the courtroom televisions. He fumbled with the USB stick as he inserted it into his laptop.

'Mr Grant?' It was the judge, querying the pause in questions.

Dan ignored him as video footage began to play. Murdoch was engaged in a hissed conversation with Francesca before she scribbled a note on a scrap of paper and slid it across the desk to Dan.

He read. Near to where Charlotte Crane was last seen. Go to 12.20.

When he looked across, Francesca was scowling but Murdoch was nodding, imploring him to look.

He navigated to where the files on the USB stick were located and clicked *play* on the first one.

He was conscious of the jury waiting for him, curious about a possible late development, but he wasn't going to be rushed.

A grainy image filled his screen. He noted the date along the top of the screen, 1 January, along with the time. The footage started just before midnight.

He scrolled through, the image never changing except for the bugs and moths caught by the lights close to the camera, until he got to the right time.

'Mr Grant, what's the delay?' the judge insisted.

Dan allowed the video to carry on playing, visible only to him, as he turned back to Sean Martin.

'Do you know Michael Crane?'

There was a flicker of recognition, a widening of his eyes, before he settled into his practised stance. 'Yes, I do know him. One of my critics.' He shrugged. 'It happens. Despite the verdict, some people never let go.'

Dan could tell from the slight tremble to his voice that Sean's nonchalance was faked. He didn't know what was coming.

'Do you know that Michael's wife, Charlotte Crane, went missing at around the time that Lizzie Barnsley was killed?'

Sean pursed his lips and delayed his answer, trying to think ahead. 'I'd heard of a missing person named Charlotte Crane. I hadn't made a connection until I saw Michael Crane's article about the search for his wife. Quite critical of the police, I remember, but I don't know the details. Why would I?'

'Charlotte was last seen in the Hare and Hounds public house in Highford just after midnight. Were you in the area?'

'Define *area*.'

'Were you sailing along the same stretch of canal as the Hare and Hounds?'

'I've told you, I was at home.'

Dan's laptop screen distracted him. He leaned down to look. There was a boat moving slowly along the canal.

Dan jabbed at the pause button and saw it. He wanted to punch the air and had to suppress his triumphant grin, but instead he asked, 'What's the name of your boat, Mr Martin?'

'*Somewhere Quiet*. Why?'

Dan straightened. 'You abducted her, didn't you?'

He laughed. 'Nonsense.'

'You abducted her and murdered her, as an act of revenge against her husband?'

Sean looked around the courtroom, his hands out. 'How can he be allowed to say this?'

'Mr Grant, you better have some evidence for this,' the judge warned.

Dan scrolled the footage back before pressing the Clickshare button. His laptop screen filled the televisions once more.

All eyes went to the footage.

'Look at the time and date, Mr Martin,' Dan said. 'Do you see? It says the first of January, twelve twenty a.m.'

Sean glared at the television screen but said nothing.

'This is close to the Hare and Hounds, just further along the canal.'

'And?'

'Keep watching.'

The courtroom was silent as the footage played, and then there was a gasp from the public gallery as a boat cruised into view.

Dan pressed the pause button, freezing the image on the screen.

The boat was static now. Even in the graininess of the footage, the name was visible, painted on the side of the boat. *Somewhere Quiet.*

'Are you still sure you stayed in?'

Sean didn't respond.

Dan clicked off the footage. He snarled when he said, 'You abducted Charlotte Crane. That is why you were cruising the canals around midnight on New Year's Eve, to meet her, to take her and kill her, wasn't it? Admit it!'

As Sean's hand went to the edge of the witness box and gripped it tightly, Dan knew that he had him.

*

Jayne shrank back, terrified.

The scream had come from somewhere below. Stairs went to an upper floor, the bannister rails broken and jagged. Faint strains of light leaked from the bottom of a doorway under the stairs. It must lead to a cellar.

She took out her phone fumbling with it, and sent a message to Dan. *Someone here. A scream. Get help. Quick.* She dropped her phone as she tried to put it away, and it clattered along the floor.

Jayne cursed and stayed still. For a moment everything was quiet, apart from gasps of pain coming from below her. Then she heard footsteps coming upstairs.

She scrambled across the floor to retrieve her phone. She could escape, make an emergency call, just keep on running.

But she didn't know who was down there. She couldn't just run away. Someone was in agony. Running wasn't an option.

There was a room ahead to the left, at the back of the property, the light blocked off by the wooden boards she'd seen from the outside.

She bolted in there, trying to keep her footsteps silent, and found the darkest corner, on the same wall as the door but away from where the light came through in narrow beams. She crouched behind the door. She didn't want any light to catch the brightness of her shirt. At least her suit was dark.

A door opened. Footsteps sounded in the hallway. Then silence.

Jayne held her breath and closed her eyes.

The seconds dragged as she waited for someone to come into the room she was in, her ears straining for any hint that she was being approached.

The bare floorboards creaked. Jayne didn't think she could hold her breath any longer. She was about to let it out when the floorboards creaked again. Whoever it was had retreated. They didn't go back down the stairs.

She put her head back and closed her eyes, let her heartbeat slow down. She stood up and went to the doorway, flattening herself against a wall. She expected it to be a trick, that someone would surprise her.

Jayne trembled as she realised she had no choice but to look.

There was no one there. Just the sunlight outside.

She went to the door the person – Trudy? – had come from. It was old and heavy with a bolt on one side; it had been left closed but unlocked. It was from there that the scream had come. Whoever had screamed, she was sure it hadn't been Trudy.

As she opened it, she saw a strong glow coming from below.

She stepped inside and started down the stairs, closing the door softly behind her.

Somebody was sobbing down there. As she descended, she saw an old-fashioned coal cellar, undeveloped, a bare brick-walled square. The dust tickled her nostrils.

She was hesitant, aware that her legs were coming into view as she went down, but she was too far gone now to back out. There was a large lamp shining a violent light and, as her view of the cellar unfolded, she gasped, jumping down the last few steps.

It was Bill. Tied to a chair, his head hanging down, blood caked on his shirt and face.

She ran over to him, lifted his head, gave a small cry as she saw his injuries. 'Bill, it's Jayne. I'm going to get you out.' Bill gave a weak nod as Jayne went to the back of the chair. She tugged at the knots. The rope had been looped round Bill's ankles and wrists and threaded through the chair legs so that he was trussed up, unable to move any limb for fear of straining his joints too far.

'Hurry,' Bill said. His voice was hoarse, barely audible. 'Gone to wash hands, that's all, my blood on her.'

The knot was tight, but easier as the rope was thick, like a tow-rope. She found the end and tried to trace it back, pushing at it, her fingers clawing at the loops.

Footsteps above them. Trudy was coming back.

The rope slackened as she worked at the knot. Bill sighed as the strain on his muscles lessened.

The door creaked above. Bill shrugged off the rope but then shook his head. Not yet. He resumed his position on the chair, his arms pulled backwards, his feet too, his teeth gritted. Jayne realised that he was setting a trap.

Jayne pulled out her phone and took a picture of Bill, the brightness of the lamp stopping the flash from going off, before she scrambled to the space behind it, pressed against the bricks that supported the stairs, taking advantage of whatever shadows there were.

She pressed send and shoved her phone into her pocket, not wanting the glow of the screen to give her away.

Trudy's steps were slow and deliberate as she came back down the stairs.

Jayne saw her knife first. Light glinted from the blade. She tensed, getting ready for whatever Bill had planned.

Trudy walked over to Bill and stood in front of him, the knife by her side. 'One more word and I'll kill you, and you can join the rest.'

Bill nodded, weak and meek. Trudy knelt in front of him, using the butt of the knife blade to lift his forehead.

'Not so clever anymore, are you?'

Then she stopped. Her gaze moved. She'd spotted something. Jayne followed her gaze and saw what it was: the bunched-up rope on the floor.

Jayne shouted, making Trudy turn off-balance. Bill moved on the chair and swung with the rope, the bundle catching Trudy on the side of the head and knocking her to the floor, her knife tumbling from her hand.

Bill stumbled from the chair and headed for the stairs. Jayne was just behind him, but he was slow. Wincing, hobbling, his legs stiff from being tied up all night. Jayne pushed him forwards, 'Go, go', aware only of Trudy's scream of rage and the promise of daylight at the top.

*

Dan's laptop pinged with a message from Jayne. He clicked off the link that connected his screen to the televisions and stared at it.

She'd sent two pictures. Sean's boat, and a cottage. It looked familiar but he couldn't place it. He remembered her message from before and how the cottage appeared in Sean's book.

He turned back to Sean Martin. 'Where is your boat now?'

Sean's eyes widened. He stammered when he said, 'I don't know exactly.' He looked around the courtroom as if hoping he'd find the answer somewhere, but all he had were the gazes of everyone in the courtroom fixed on him.

'Is there anywhere you liked to cruise to, so you could spend time together?'

'We cruised all over the place.'

'What about a place you put in your book, in the section set aside for photographs?'

Sean didn't answer, so Dan made the picture of the cottage fill his screen and turned on the Clickshare software again, bringing the television screens to life once more.

'What about this place?'

Sean swayed as he looked at the television screen. His tongue went to his lip, nervous and edgy, and he looked to the door, as if calculating whether he could make a run for it.

'Mr Martin? Do you recognise it?'

When he still didn't answer, Dan navigated to the other picture and made it fill the screen. 'That's the boat, isn't it?'

Sean nodded.

'It's by that cottage. Have you been there before?'

He coughed. 'Yes, a few times.' His voice had developed a tremble, almost a stammer. 'It's just somewhere on the canal, somewhere secluded.'

'If I ask the police to go there now, will they find anything?'

He shook his head.

'If I ask Detective Inspector Murdoch to leave the courtroom now and send officers to that location, while you're still here, unable to use your phone and without any other way of getting a message out, will those officers find any trace of you or Trudy?'

His breathing had quickened. 'It's just a place, somewhere to go.'

The peace of the courtroom was broken by Murdoch rushing through the door, her phone in her hand. She'd got Dan's hint.

But then something else struck him. Jayne was there, and she was alone.

*

Jayne ran quickly up the stairs, past Bill, who was going too slow. She stopped and grabbed his arm, tried to pull him the rest of the way. He stumbled, groaning in pain.

Downstairs, they heard a thump as Trudy got to her feet, screeching in anger.

'*Come on, come on!*'

They tumbled through the door and into the hallway as the sound of Trudy running up the stars echoed in the cellar. Jayne turned and threw herself against the door, hoping to slam home the bolt, but Trudy pushed on the other side. Jayne screamed at Bill to help her, but he was on the floor, holding on to his leg. Before he could join her, Jayne was thrown backwards as Trudy charged through.

Trudy was enraged, her knife held outwards, growling. Bill scuttled backwards. 'Get away, get away!'

Trudy's focus was entirely on Bill, who was scrambling backwards into the room at the back of the house, where Jayne had hidden not long before.

Trudy grabbed the ruins of Bill's shirt and pulled him up off the floor. She held the knife against his throat, ready to slash. 'You bastard!'

That made Jayne move.

She ran forwards.

Trudy turned towards her, surprised, pulling the knife away from Bill's neck. Jayne grabbed the doorframe and swung, kicking out with both feet. She caught Trudy in the ribs with a satisfying crack. Trudy went to the ground, yelling in pain.

Bill crawled towards the doorway, getting ready to run, but Trudy reached out and grabbed his shirt again. She yanked him backwards before advancing towards Jayne, her knife held out.

Jayne wasn't going to leave Bill behind. She backed up against the nearest wall, her arms out.

Bill pushed himself to his feet and went to the wall opposite. Jayne moved as if she was about to rush across the room to join him, but Bill shook his head.

Jayne understood. Stay apart. Make two targets. Divide her attention.

Bill put his head back against the wall, panting hard. 'Give up, Trudy. It's the end.'

Trudy lashed out with the knife. 'I won't be separated from Sean. Not again.'

Bill dodged it and moved along the wall as Jayne spoke up, shifting Trudy's attention at the crucial moment.

'Can't you see that it's all over?' Jayne said.

'Bullshit.'

Trudy wanted to attack, Jayne could tell from the tension in her body, but didn't want to make herself a target.

'Why haven't you killed Bill?' Jayne was backing towards the door as she spoke. 'You're a killer. So why is he still alive?'

Trudy was looking more hesitant, turning all the time, the knife held outwards.

Jayne kept on backing up, making Trudy move with her, distracting her, getting her ever closer to the doorway. 'Dan Grant knows where I am. However it goes, you're finished. All you can do is get the best deal.'

Trudy was looking back towards Bill and then again at Jayne, trying to track two targets who were getting further apart.

'It was all Sean, we know that,' Jayne said. 'All you did was fail to stop him, got swept along by him.'

Trudy laughed. 'Credit me with some invention.'

Jayne had reached the stairs. She stopped when she felt the sharp jab of a wayward stair spindle in her back. Trudy was edging towards her. As Jayne moved back, the rail made a loud crack as it bent out even further.

This was the moment. She had to get it right. Trudy was focused on her, not on Bill. Jayne would engage her in a fight and give Bill the chance to get away or at least to get into open space. He was an old man, wheezing hard. He needed a head start.

Jayne twirled round and grabbed the spindle. She moved quickly, twisting it until it cracked in her hand. It snapped away from the rail and she held it like a baseball bat.

The spindle was old wood, heavy but dried out, with two twisted nails sticking from the end.

She swung it towards Trudy a couple of times, hoping to make her back up, but Trudy kept on coming.

Bill ran across the room, stumbling and limping, and through the doorway. It was enough to distract Trudy, making her turn. Jayne swung the spindle hard. She missed but Trudy stepped backwards. Jayne took another swing as Bill barged his way into the hallway. The spindle crashed against the doorframe.

Trudy swung out with the knife, slashing at Bill, but just caught air. She started after him, her eyes wild, enraged.

Jayne swung the spindle again, and heard it connect with satisfaction. Trudy dropped to the floor, screaming, one of the nails embedded in her cheek.

Jayne turned and ran after Bill, who was waiting for her in the doorway, leaning over and sucking in air.

'Come on,' Jayne shouted. 'My car.'

They both ran along the front of the cottage. They had no plan other than getting away. All they had to do was reach the car.

Footsteps behind, angry shouts.

'I can't do it,' Bill cried.

Jayne stopped, and waved her arm in encouragement. 'Come on, come on.'

'No, you go ahead.'

'Bill!'

'I'm an old man. I can't run. You go.'

Jayne went to him and grabbed his arm. 'I'm *not* leaving you.'

Bill struggled on, but as they went round the side of the house, he slid on some loose turf and thudded to the ground.

Jayne stopped, went to grab him again, but faltered as she looked down.

Bill had dislodged a strip of turf, as if it had just been dug out and re-laid, loose soil underneath. It wasn't the grass that drew her attention though, but what lay underneath.

It was skin, grey and pale, with short tufts of hair peering through the thin layer of soil. As she looked in horror, she realised that the strip of turf was around six feet long, slightly raised, as if freshly dug out. She looked around and saw that the undulating ground around her was different from how she'd first seen it, that it wasn't the natural dips of old farmland but that the bumps and hollows were all the same size.

Graves.

The photographs from the book came back to her. Sean and Trudy posing on grass by the canal, picnicking on a mound, happy and carefree. This was where they buried the bodies. The book really was a taunt.

She brushed away the soil, then put her hand over her mouth, worried that she was going to vomit. 'It's Pat Molloy.'

She didn't have time to say anything more.

Trudy appeared, running, but surprised to see Jayne and Bill still there.

Bill scrambled backwards, but Trudy was on him.

She grabbed Bill's hair and pulled it back. She held the knife against his neck.

'Don't run or I'll kill him.' Trudy was still dazed, blinking hard, blood running down her cheek.

'This is where you killed Pat. And what about the rest?' Jayne gestured to the other mounds. 'How many more will we find?' When Trudy didn't answer, she said, 'It's over. You're going away for a long time. Accept it. Don't make it worse.'

Bill shook his head, wincing as the knife dug into his skin. His body sagged, and there were tears in his eyes when he said, 'Jayne, just go.'

There was another sound. Sirens. Blue lights flashed somewhere in the distance. Trudy looked over and realised what was happening. She pulled Bill's head back, her hand trembling on the knife, her teeth bared in a snarl.

Jayne put her hands out, pleading, 'No, no, no. *Stop*. Give yourself up.'

Tears ran down Trudy's cheeks before she slashed with the knife, cutting deep into Bill's throat, blood flicking from the blade as she raised it high.

Jayne screamed. 'WHAT HAVE YOU DONE?'

Bill's eyes bulged, then he coughed. Blood spewed out of the wound.

Trudy grimaced and plunged the knife in deeper this time, just under Bill's ear.

Bill's eyes clouded and then went out of focus. His body slumped in Trudy's grip, who finally let go and stood straight.

She kicked Bill, who fell forward, blood arcing as he went, landing with a thump on Pat Molloy's partially uncovered corpse.

Jayne stood there in shock not able to believe what she'd seen. Then she lost all reason. She ran at Trudy, aiming for her ribs again, just hoping to make it hurt.

Trudy looked up, surprised, and was thrown off-balance as Jayne crashed into her. They went to the ground together, the knife knocked from Trudy's hand, Jayne on top. She punched Trudy, her fist connecting with her cheekbone, the hard smack satisfying. Two more punches as Trudy thrashed, and with the next one she groaned and stopped struggling.

Jayne rushed to Bill. 'Come on, stay alive,' but he didn't move. She looked down and saw how much blood was on the ground, and the glassiness of Bill's eyes. He was dead.

Trudy lay on the ground, curled in a foetal position and whimpered. Jayne's anger erupted. She kicked her hard, her foot crunching into Trudy's cheek.

Trudy's head snapped backwards. She went limp, only her hoarse breaths letting Jayne know that she was still alive.

The sirens got louder.

Jayne hung her head and took in gulps of air, tears streaming down her cheeks. There was the sound of heavy footsteps running over the field. She didn't look up as the police officers went to Trudy.

*

Dan leaned forward, one hand on the table, more snarl to his voice. 'That's all the cottage is to you, Mr Martin? Are you sure?'

Sean nodded but didn't respond.

A message pinged on his laptop. He turned off the Click-share software, and the televisions went blank again. He opened the message, and the courtroom swam in front of him. He clenched his fist and fought the urge to run at Sean Martin and pummel him.

Take some deep breaths, he told himself, stay calm. He closed his eyes.

When he opened them again, his vision was clear, focused.

'Do you know Bill Maude?'

Sean shook his head and tried to shrug a reply, feigning disinterest, but he looked like he knew what was coming next.

'Is that an answer?'

Sean swallowed, his eyes darting around the room until he said, 'No, I don't.'

'Would a picture help, to see if you recognise him?'

'Yeah, sure.'

Dan filled his laptop with the photograph of Bill, bloodied and scarred. He jabbed the Clickshare button and clenched his jaw as the picture filled the television screen in the courtroom.

Sean moaned and swayed in the box. There were gasps from the public gallery. Francesca muttered, 'Jesus Christ.'

'This picture has just been taken by my investigator,' Dan said, a tremble to his voice now, but it was anger, not fear. 'At the cottage where your boat is moored.'

Sean looked down and took deep breaths.

Dan banged the desk, making everyone jump. 'You killed them, Sean Martin.'

'No, no, no.'

'You killed them all. Annie Yates. Sharon Coates. Claire Watkins. Charlotte Crane. Your own stepdaughter. And there were more.'

Sean shook his head violently. 'You don't understand.'

Dan was leaning forward, his thighs jammed against the desk, trying to get as close as he could. 'You're a murderer. A fraud and a killer.'

Sean looked around the courtroom, his mouth open, and let out a moan.

Dan slammed his fist on the table. 'Did you kill my boss? Did you, dammit? Talk.'

'Mr Grant, calm down.' It was the judge.

'Where is he, Sean?'

'Mr Grant!'

'Talk!' Dan wasn't paying any attention to the judge. 'All these women. Pat Molloy. Bill Maude. Your stepdaughter, the one you've lied about to the press.' Another thump of the desk. 'Where is he? Where's Pat Molloy?'

Sean looked as if he was about to faint, but instead he bolted from the witness box, heading for the door by the public gallery. Someone screamed. The court assistant pressed a buzzer that would bring the security guards.

They weren't needed.

As Sean passed the public gallery, Lizzie Barnsley's father leaped forward and stuck his arm out, connecting with Sean's jaw and sending him crashing to the floor.

There were more shouts and screams. The doors banged as the security guards rushed through. The judge disappeared along his corridor.

Dan jumped out from behind his table and rushed to where Sean was being restrained on the floor. He gripped him by his lapel and snarled in his face, 'They'd better both be safe, or I'm coming after you.'

Someone grabbed his arm and pulled him back.

Dan shrugged it off, his anger boiling over. There were shouts from the public gallery, women screaming. Someone was banging on the glass dock.

He was pulled back again. 'Leave it, Dan. Don't make it bad for yourself.' The smell of cigarettes and the huskiness to her voice told him that it was Murdoch.

He turned to her.

'You did well, Dan. The police will be there soon. You did well.'

Dan looked down at Sean Martin, who had his face turned towards the floor, sobs escaping.

It was over.

Dan sagged onto the bench seat just in front of the dock. He put his head in his hands and sucked deep breaths in.

He looked back. Peter was smiling.

'Thank you,' he whispered. 'You got him. Thank you.'

Sixty-eight

Dan and Jayne were silent as they looked out of his car windscreen at the view ahead.

They were parked opposite the cemetery. It was two weeks after Pat's body had been discovered. The mourners were rolling into the car park, mostly high-end cars as the local legal community turned out in full for Pat Molloy.

'I'm not very good at funerals,' Dan said.

'Is anyone?'

'I'm supposed to be the strong one, the man who never shows emotion, but when I see Pat's casket, I imagine him inside, gone. How can that be so? Before the cancer, he had so much life, so much colour, and that's it. Just a shell in a box.'

'Do they know yet which one of them killed him?'

'We know it wasn't Sean because he's got an alibi, so it must have been Trudy. Pat's car was clocked on a speed camera heading towards the station where it was dumped. She must have driven it to the railway station, left it, and walked back to the cottage. It's probably an hour's walk from the station along the towpath, and of course it's quiet and dark, so it kept her out of sight.'

'And the other bodies they found?'

'That investigation will drag on for a while yet, but Murdoch knows what she's doing.'

'Does it bother you that Trudy's got a lawyer?'

'I don't understand.'

'You were close to Pat and now someone is going to try to clear Trudy and Sean, pull all the tricks you tried to pull to keep them out of prison. Does it feel different when you see this side of it?'

'A little, but that's the system. I'll keep away from the trial, except for the parts where I'm needed to give evidence. My own way of coping.'

'What drove them, do you think?'

'Each other. As simple as that. They were a volatile mix. Sean started it, I'm sure of that, but he'll have tested her willingness first. Most women would have told him no, but Trudy? She craved the excitement, and once they'd killed one person and got away with it, they realised it was such a high. That's what they were doing, chasing that high, like addicts.'

'Peter tried to do the right thing, break them up to stop the killings.'

'But, like addicts, they were trapped too. They couldn't leave each other, because they knew each other's secrets. It wasn't love. It was mistrust. Staying together kept the secrets together. Let's not make Peter out to be the hero though. He killed Lizzie. He deserves to be in prison too.' He looked at Jayne. 'One thing does hurt me though, above all.'

'Bill?'

'Of course, Bill. I feel responsible in some way, and I'm angry that they'll always be remembered while Bill will just be another of their victims. They'll have their infamy, but Bill will just be a footnote.'

Jayne clenched her jaw. 'I prefer to think of Trudy and Sean hating every day they're kept apart, locked up and always waiting for an attack. I've spent time locked up, remember, and it's the boredom that gets to you, and the lack of status. There'll be some old lag wanting the notoriety of slashing them or killing them. Let them suffer every single day, waiting for that, because I saw what they did. I saw Bill die.'

Dan nodded. 'Yeah, I think you're right.' He leaned forward to wipe away the steam made by their coffees, from the inside of the windscreen.

'I've relived every second of it since that day, over and over, always wondering if I could have saved him.' Jayne stared straight ahead as she said it.

'You can't change what was done, and you tried to do what was right. Me too. Bill was a good man.' He looked over at Jayne. 'How are you, though? You saw stuff you shouldn't have seen.'

'The shock hasn't hit me yet. It will, and I'll have to deal with it when it comes.'

'Just don't do it alone.' When Jayne looked surprised, he said, 'We need each other.'

She nodded. 'We do.' He was about to speak again but she put her finger to his lips. 'Don't say it. Answer me this instead. I'm not imagining it, am I? It's not just me thinking of you because of what you did for me as my lawyer? There's something here, right?'

He kissed her hand. 'More than you know.' He sighed. 'But, it's complicated.'

'I know. It doesn't make it any easier though. Just be gentle with me if you meet someone else.'

'That's the part I'm not very good at, meeting someone else.'

'You might do better once I'm gone.'

'You're definitely leaving then?'

'What is there for me in Highford? It's different for you, because you've got an office and a proper business, even a father. But what have I got?'

'It doesn't feel like I've got much. I'm my own boss, I suppose, but I don't know what else I could do. I've done criminal law for so long and it's what I've always wanted. Police stations and courtrooms, they're my theatre.' He turned to her. 'You don't have to go.'

Jayne sighed. 'What else can I do?'

He closed his eyes for a moment. He wanted to say that he needed her to stay, but he knew it would be unfair. She had her own life to carve out.

'Work for me,' he blurted out.

She laughed. 'I'd love to, but I can't get by on serving court papers, you know that.'

'Be my investigator full time. I need a clerk. I can't do it all on my own, and you'd be good at it. You've got the eye for a fight. And if I'm going to make a go of it on my own, I need someone with me I can trust.'

'And that's a former client who drinks too much, sleeps around, and lives in an apartment surrounded by drug users?'

'You'll bring a certain earthy quality.'

Jayne gave him a playful punch on the arm but turned to stare out of the window as she thought about it. 'It'll mean staying around here though.'

'Is it that bad?'

'It's not the town. It's me. I need to strike out on my own, and Highford is holding me back.'

'We'd make a good team.'

'I know, but I've made up my mind. I'm sorry, I'm leaving Highford.'

'When?'

'Tomorrow, perhaps. Why not? I don't have much stuff to pack.'

Dan looked out of his window as he choked up. 'I'll miss you.'

Jayne smiled, and as he turned towards her, he saw that her eyes were filled with tears. 'Yeah, me too.'

Their discussion was broken by the arrival of the hearse. Eileen and her children in the car behind it.

Dan let out a long breath. He gripped Jayne's hand. 'For today, let's remember Pat.'

She wiped her eyes, nodded and stepped out of the car.

Her arm was hooked into his as they crossed the road, until they were lost in the crowd at the cemetery gates.

Acknowledgements

The Darkness Around Her is my eleventh crime novel but that doesn't mean the process gets any easier. As always, there are late nights and long days, and those around me suffer through the long hours of solitude. For their patience, I am grateful to my wife and children.

Although it is a solitary pursuit in some respects, in many others it is a team effort, and I am grateful for the advice and assistance of my wonderful editors at Bonnier Zaffre, Katherine Armstrong and Jennie Rothwell, as well as my fabulous agent, Sonia Land from Sheil Land Associates, whose advice and support now and through the years has been invaluable.

Last, but not least, I thank you all for reading this book, and hopefully my others. Without readers, writing would be pointless, and you make it all worthwhile.

Want to read
NEW BOOKS
before anyone else?

Like getting
FREE BOOKS?

Enjoy sharing your
OPINIONS?

Discover

READERS
FIRST
Read. Love. Share.

Sign up today to win your first free book:
readersfirst.co.uk